Sea of Ruin

PAM GODWIN
NEW YORK TIMES BESTSELLING AUTHOR

Copyright © 2020 by Pam Godwin
All rights reserved.
Cover Designer: Hang Le
Interior Designer: Pam Godwin
Editor: Rebecca, Fairest Reviews Editing
Proofreader: Lesa Godwin

This is a work of fiction. Names, characters, places, and incidents are the product of the author's imagination or are used fictitiously, and any resemblance to actual persons, living or dead, events, or locales is entirely coincidental.
No part of this book may be reproduced in any form, except for the inclusion of brief quotations in a review or article, without written permission from the author.

Visit my website at pamgodwin.com

For Shea
Your beautiful soul
can be seen from space.

"Where there is ruin,
there is hope for a treasure."
Rumi

One

**September 1714
Province of Carolina**

Charleston. To anyone settling here, it was a dazzling frontier of beauty and opportunity. Its denizens comprised of wealthy planters sailing from the English colony of Barbados and the Yamasee natives fighting to destroy the white invaders.

Then there was me, the bastard daughter of noble blood, willing to do anything to escape this life.

Though I was born here fourteen years ago, I had no interest in the land or its wars. I longed for the sea, to feel the deck rocking beneath my feet, to hear the wind drumming against sailcloth, and to wear salt and spume upon my tattered sleeves.

My mother, however, didn't care a whit about what I wanted.

"Stop fidgeting." She pried my clenched fingers from the rib-crushing bodice of my gown.

Her scowl distorted the stately lines of a face that had once been the envy of high society. Her eyes, cerulean blue like mine, simmered with resentment as she scrutinized the chintz monstrosity she forced me to wear.

"Can I remove the pannier? Please, Mother?" I yanked at the cumbersome undergarment, my voice pitching to a whine. "God rot it,

I can't move!"

The hidden wire hoops sat on my hips like bread baskets on a pack animal. I pivoted left to right, taking up three times as much space as a grown man. It would be impossible to mount my horse in this stultifying contraption. Not that the countess would allow me near the barn on this day.

"Really, Benedicta, you're giving me a megrim." She stood a head taller than me, her golden hair pinned into a coiffure of ironed ringlets and ornamented with a plume of feathers. "I spent a fortnight making this gown, and by God's heart, you will wear it with dignity."

To hell with God's heart. I swore in spite of his teeth. But never in the presence of the Lady Abigail.

"I didn't ask for this." I motioned at the gown and the ornate furnishings of my bedchamber. "For any of this."

"I didn't ask for *you*. Yet here you are, an ungrateful, quarrelsome hoyden, born with both fists clenched."

It was always the same when the countess looked at me. She didn't see her only child, a daughter to love, or a girl with earnest dreams.

She only saw her shame. Her ruination. The reason she was exiled.

Shifting toward the window, I sought a brighter view outside the glass panes. The dawn-lit sea stretched eastward from the sandy shoreline, aglitter with waves I couldn't hear from my bedchamber.

I'd never ventured beyond the port of Charleston, never even stepped foot aboard a ship. But England flowed through my veins. And constricted my chest. Quite literally.

"It's too tight." I reached back, clawing at the stays that pinched my spine. "It hurts to breathe."

"Then don't."

"Don't breathe? For how long?"

"For as long as it takes to secure an offer."

An offer I didn't want.

I endeavored to live on a ship with a crew of cursing tars, not in a house with a line of biddable servants. I wanted to ride a horse with my feet in stirrups, not sidesaddle and upright. I fancied stout ale over watery tea, sword-fighting over sewing, and would rather burn my nose in the sun than sit in a stuffy parlor.

And this gown? I stifled an unladylike grunt. What I wouldn't give for a pair of trousers.

Which was why, as a girl on the cusp of a betrothed marriage, I was undesirable, uncooperative, and entirely unfit for this.

Sea of Ruin

Unfortunately, the countess didn't sympathize with my position or my improper attributes.

With a hand circling my arm, she dragged me to the dressing table and examined my appearance in the mirror.

"Well…" She tilted her head and sniffed. "I'm not a seamstress, but I daresay I've seen nothing so smart outside of London. If you remember your station and keep your mouth shut, the gown alone might win his favor."

My reflection glared back at me, clad in the flounciest, most attention-grabbing dress in Carolina. Striped in shades of pink, the skirt opened in front to reveal a white petticoat trimmed in a dozen too many frills.

The deep square-cut bosom accentuated my lack of breasts and bony shoulders. Trumpet-shaped sleeves caught up at my elbows, which naturally, would be dragged across plates of gravy and sweet cream before the day's end.

But as much as I despised the dress, I understood the necessity of pomp and ceremony and my mother's struggle to achieve it.

The upper class had clothing made for them, and the countess managed to live amongst that charmed circle, despite having no financial worth of her own.

Lady Abigail Leighton, the only child of the ninth Earl Leighton, inherited her title upon the earl's death. But nothing more. When her inglorious affair with a commoner was made evident by my illegitimate existence, she lost her dowry, her family, and her coveted status in the *beau monde*.

With no support in England, she was forced abroad—pregnant, destitute, alone—and found refuge here with distant cousins. They took her in, and fourteen years later, we remained in their opulent home, made use of their servants, and ate their lavish meals.

But none of this belonged to us. The master of the house, while ever gracious, could toss us out on our backsides without warning or reason.

We were insolvent tenants. My mother's ruined reputation ensured that was all she would ever be unless she found a way to reenter society.

I ran my hands over the gown, gilded in her meticulous efforts. She spun, wove, and fashioned our garments out of necessity. Every spool of thread was a cost she couldn't afford, every cut of cotton a labor of determination, every stitch a stab at a better future.

A better future for her. All I wanted was adventure and a pair of trousers.

She turned at the sound of a knock on the bedchamber door. "Enter."

"My lady." The parlor maid hurried in, ducking her bonnet-clad head as she offered the countess a gentleman's calling card.

Moisture trickled down my spine, and the stays grew uncomfortably tighter. I didn't need to glance at the card to know it announced the arrival of the Marquess of Grisdale.

"I'll receive him in the blue parlor," my mother said. "Prepare the tea."

"Yes, my lady." The maid bobbed a curtsy and beat a hasty exit.

I'd never met Lord Grisdale, but his letter to the countess mentioned I'd caught his eye during one of my visits to the pier.

At age forty-four, the childless widower had the wealth and influence to help Lady Abigail regain her former status. He lived in England and would return there once his business concluded in Charleston.

He was her ticket home. In exchange, she had only one thing to offer.

Me.

My worth lay in my virtue and lineage. It didn't matter that I was merely fourteen or that he was thirty years my elder. If he were the highest bidder for my hand, the countess would eagerly accept.

My breaths quickened, pulling dread down my throat and into my tumbling stomach. I'd overheard the whispered conversations amongst the scullery maids. Conversations about what men and women did together in the marriage bed.

Lord Grisdale would require me to do that with him, to breed his heirs and service his masculine needs.

The thought sickened me, but I had as much say in it as the nag horse in the barn.

"Heavens, Benedicta. Look at your hair." My mother's voice trembled, a reedy sound of disapproval and sudden nerves. "This won't do, and I don't have time to repair it."

The lady's maid had spent the past hour wrestling my wild blond coils into a presentable pile on my head. The waist-length tresses, thicker and more unruly than my mother's, were already working themselves free from the pins. Wayward spirals sprung in every direction and dangled rebelliously around my ears.

Sea of Ruin

I didn't care about my appearance, but it had a crippling effect on my mother. Her hands balled at her sides. Cords stretched in her stiff neck, and the hope that had brightened her eyes only moments before vanished behind shadows of dismay.

My throat thickened.

Oh, how I wished for her happiness. I didn't know what a smile would look like on her aristocratic face or how the sound of laughter would alter her voice. But maybe it was obtainable.

Maybe if I cooperated. Just this once.

"You mustn't keep him waiting." I leaned toward the mirror and tackled my hair. "I'll fix this."

As I added more pins, she didn't move. Her presence loomed behind me, silent and uncertain.

"Mother?" I glanced over my shoulder.

"This is important to me." Her eyes narrowed.

"I know, my lady."

Her expression softened. Until something caught her attention on my neck.

She reached for it, snatching the thin chain I'd tried to conceal beneath the lace choker. The pendant lay against my spine, hidden by the stays.

"Why are you wearing this?" She yanked on the necklace, attempting to break it.

"Don't." I caught her wrist in a bruising grip, stopping her from harming my most treasured possession.

Her eyes flared, but she surrendered her hold on the chain. "Is that the bauble you received from that savage native last year?"

That was the story I'd given her. She couldn't know the truth about how I acquired it, what it meant to me, or the pledge I'd made to never take it off.

"Yes." I closed my hand around the jade pendant, protecting it from her criticism.

"Remove it."

Never.

"Forgive me." I let my posture sag and carefully arranged my lips around a lie. "I forgot to put it away, but I'll do that—" I twisted the lace choker, pretending to work the chain free. "Blast it, it's tangled."

"We don't have time for this." Livid red rose across her cheeks as she reached for my neck.

"Go." I stepped back. "I'll put everything back in order and join you in a trice."

She glanced at the door and drew in a breath. And another. Shoulders squared, head held high, she composed herself into a portrait of social grace.

"Don't delay." She cast me a withering glare. "And if I see that disgraceful necklace again, I shall tie your wrists with it and have you flogged."

In a swish of lavender silk, she breezed into the hall and shut the door behind her.

A rush of air vacated my lungs, and I opened my hand, cradling the precious pendant in my palm.

Crowned by a filigree band of gold, the green stone was the length of my thumb and half as narrow. Serrated cuts decorated dozens of mysterious facets as if it had been painstakingly sawed from the earth.

I'd never seen anything so unrefined and magical.

As a child of English nobility, I'd been weaned on restrictive clothing, polished smiles, and the art of dissembling. But my heart belonged on a ship with the seafarer who'd given me a jade stone and loved me for who I was. Impulsive. Wild. Rebellious.

I returned the pendant to its hiding place beneath my garments and plastered my curls into a mold of proper English fashion.

It wouldn't kill me to look like a lady. But if the marquess liked what he saw, a wedding would go forth and kill my dreams.

If I sabotaged this introduction, there would be other suitors. Other offers. And a flogging, to be certain.

I could endure the flogging. It was my mother's sadness that knotted my stomach in an endless loop. I shouldn't make her work so hard to be happy. She'd pushed me into this world, and I'd been pushing back ever since. No wonder she never smiled.

With a hard shake of my head, I tested the subdued array of blond curls.

Then I heard it. The distant bark of a dog. I froze, listening with my entire being, as a second dog joined in.

My pulse careened into a gallop.

Could it be? Had I imagined it?

I darted to the window, bumping the pannier into furniture and knocking over a lamp. At the sill, I pressed my brow to the glass and studied the landscape.

Acres of woodland lay between the rear of the estate and the coast. The barking came again, and I tracked the sound to the northern edge

Sea of Ruin

of the tree line.

Two hounds raced back and forth, yelping their message, loudly and persistently, as they were trained to do.

His hounds.

His messengers.

I choked upon air.

"He returned." I stumbled away from the window, spinning awkwardly in the cage of my gown. "Oh, Lord, he's here."

If I didn't follow his hounds, I would miss him. If I missed him, more months would pass. More seasons. Another year. I couldn't bear the thought.

My heart labored. If I left, the countess would pound the pudding out of me.

I whirled back to the window and gritted my teeth. "Then a pounding it shall be."

Two

Knowing full well the consequences of what I was about to do, I should have felt the devil's claws digging around in my stomach. I should have been terrified.

But laughter swelled in me. My cheeks ached to hold it in. The prospect of seeing the only person who ever truly loved me sent my heart into a dizzying whirl.

With no time to spare, I gathered the skirts to my hips and sifted through cotton and ruffles, grunting until my fingers found the buckle at my waist.

When the pannier hit the floor, I tore off the stockings and darted to the bed. From beneath the frame, I removed a linen-wrapped package and carried it to the door.

The master of the house was visiting friends in the New York colony. Since he and his wife traveled with most of the servants, my departure might go unnoticed.

Creeping barefoot into the hall and down the stairs, I evaded detection. Good fortune followed me into the drawing-room, past the study, and through a maze of companionways. Not one person, from footman to butler to liveried maid, thwarted my getaway.

Until I reached the blue parlor and the sound of my mother's voice.

"When will you return to England, my lord?"

"Within a month," he said. "Sooner if there's a wedding to anticipate."

"You won't find a more suitable bride. And since her grandfather was an earl, she has excellent breeding."

"I look forward to making her acquaintance. She was quite stunning from my view on the pier."

Hidden around the corner, I bit down on my cheek.

What could his lordship possibly find stunning about a fourteen-year-old girl?

I hugged the package to my chest, paralyzed by the sudden image of his wrinkly old penis in an unrelaxed state.

Run, Bennett. Go!

The parlor's massive wooden door propped open, giving its occupants a direct view of my path to the main rear exit. But I'd grown up here and knew every chamber and passage.

Veering left, I ducked at the approach of the porter's limping footsteps. Another hallway brought me into the path of a housemaid, and I dashed into a closet. Then I crawled on hands and knees through the busier parts of the estate, following the aroma of plum cake baking in the kitchen.

There, I rose to my feet and peered inside.

Fire flickered beneath the spit. Syllabub glasses sparkled. Mutton stew bubbled in the kettle, and the cook maid—a young native woman—hummed a foreign tune.

Everyone knew servants weren't supposed to sing, hum, or make any noise within earshot of the master's family.

I grinned at her rebellion. With her back turned to the doorway and her pretty voice vibrating the air, she didn't catch my escape through the kitchen and out the servant door.

Morning sunlight blotted my vision, and a warm breeze tugged at my hair, loosening the curls. I squinted in the direction of the barn and listened.

And listened harder.

Damn the silence! Where were those hounds?

Don't panic.

The dogs would find me. They always did.

I bolted across the dewy lawn, tripping over the petticoat and scattering my nerves in a burst of exhilaration.

In the distant field, a tenant farmer lifted his head to watch my inelegant race to the stable. But he wouldn't stop me. No one did as I made a break for an unfamiliar horse that was already tacked outside.

Saddled in the finest leather and tied to a post, the black

thoroughbred didn't belong to the estate.

"Miss Benedicta?" The stable boy emerged from the barn and offered me a kind smile. "Do you fancy a ride today? Shall I ready a mare?"

"There's no time. Did Lord Grisdale arrive by carriage?"

"Nah, he came by horse. That one there." His freckled face scrunched as he pointed at the beast I was already mounting. "You mustn't—"

"I'll return it." I stuffed my wrapped package in the saddlebag.

"He'll have my hide!"

"Have my adventures ever earned you a lashing?" With my gaze on the surrounding copse of trees, I tucked the bulky skirts beneath my legs.

"No, but Lord Grisdale—"

"Will aim his strap at *my* behind." I adjusted my jade pendant to rest against my chest. "Hand me the reins."

He made a show out of dragging his feet, as he so often did when I involved him in my mischief. Then a curse slipped under his breath, decision made. He untied the tether and tossed it to my waiting hand.

"I'll sneak you some plum cake after my flogging tonight." My wink brought twin stains of pink to his freckled cheeks.

Snapping my hips forward, I spurred Grisdale's horse into a gallop.

Within minutes, the pins in my hair surrendered to the wind, giving flight to a tangled mane of curls. At the tree line, I shoved two fingers into my mouth and released a high-pitched whistle.

A racket of noise disturbed the undergrowth. Moments later, the hounds shot out of the woodland and bounded in my direction.

I slowed the horse, exploding with laughter, as paws and jowls scrabbled at my legs. The dogs jumped and licked with vigor, coating my fingers in strings of drool.

And mud.

It was everywhere, blackening the petticoat and streaking my sleeves. Nothing I could do about it now.

"Shear off, you rascals!" I clapped my hands, calling the hounds' attention. "Where is he? Show me!"

Just like all the times before, they took off into the trees, tails up and muzzles down, letting their noses lead them to the rendezvous point.

I gave chase, bending into the pursuit and hugging the trails. At length, I lost track of all the twists and turns and forged headlong into unknown lands.

The terrain grew savagely rugged. Twiggy branches grabbed at my skirts, ripped seams, and gouged irreparable holes in the chintz.

I'd scrounged up a lot of trouble in my life and managed to fight my way out of all of it. But stealing a nobleman's horse and destroying my mother's precious gown? There was no coming back from this.

Maybe I wouldn't have to. Maybe this time he would let me go with him.

My heart rate sped up, filling my chest with giddy anticipation.

He never ventured too close to town, so I wasn't surprised when the journey extended into the next hour. The hounds maintained a frantic northernly pace, sharing my excitement to reunite with their master.

Deep into the woods, the dirt paths grew narrower, choked with foliage and disappearing beneath unexplored wilderness. But I hadn't strayed far from the coast. The scent of brine and tang of salt lay heavily in the warm air, and the resonance of surf thundered over the clap of hooves.

A few minutes later, the trees parted to a view of oceanic blue.

The hounds sprinted toward the shore, kicking up sand in their wake. I dismounted the horse and secured him in the shade. Then I darted out of the forest and into the embrace of uninterrupted sunshine.

The narrow crescent of beach formed an inlet some sixty paces across. On the north side, waves broke in a spray of foam against the base of a cliff. Gulls circled overhead and perched on the rock face. Farther out, past the pounding surf, lay endless swells of water.

There were no ships, no signs of human life, but I felt him. He called to me in the crash of breakers upon the beach and hugged me in the clingy damp wind that whisked across the Great Western Ocean.

He was the sea. Rough. Dangerous. Dependable. No matter how far he traveled or how long he stayed away, he always returned to me.

I scanned the coastline to the south, where it curved out of view. The hounds had vanished in that direction, beyond an outcrop of trees.

Gathering my skirts, I dug my toes into the sand and took off after them. But a few steps in, something stirred in my periphery.

I spun toward the movement and shielded my eyes, squinting at the trees.

Shadows shifted in the woods near the horse. Someone was there, right where I'd been standing.

My lungs compacted as a man stepped onto the beach. A huge mast of a man, dressed head to toe in black.

His hair was red, long around the ears, and wild like the wind. He wore a flowing shirt of silk, knee-high jackboots, and a cutlass that glinted in the sun.

Despite his ignoble attire, he radiated a lord-like bearing. Commanding in stance and purpose, he stalked toward me.

My knees wobbled beneath the storm of his surly eyes.

"A lovely young lass like you should pay better attention to her surroundings." His long-legged strides devoured the distance between us. "You never know what might be lying in wait."

My throat closed, too constricted to squeeze out a sound.

When I'd dismounted the horse, I hadn't examined the perimeter or used my senses to probe for threats. In my excitement, I'd let my guard down.

The curve of his mouth descended, his face carved in stone, deeply tanned and infamously elusive.

The notorious Edric Sharp.

His visage was rendered on newspapers, edicts, and proclamations all over Charleston. They called him a pirate and offered a substantial reward for his capture.

I'd read every account of his description. Some said he was tall and mean. Others claimed he was scarred, bearded, and wore a peruke. Every word and sketched reproduction was created from the imaginations of artists who had never encountered him.

He was more handsome in person, more menacing. But I wasn't afraid.

I was awestruck.

Sand crunched beneath his boots as he paused within arm's reach. I didn't move. Didn't breathe.

A muscle bounced in his stony jaw. Then it spread to his lips, twitching at the corners. I waited for a break in his expression, and when a smile finally lit his eyes, I pounced on the seaman's massive chest.

"Father!" I embraced his wide shoulders, squeezing with all my might.

"Aw, Bennett. I missed you." He swung me up into the safety of his arms and buried his scratchy cheeks in my neck. "You must be more vigilant. Anyone could have sneaked up on you. Have I taught you nothing?"

"Forgive me. I was overcome with excitement. That's no excuse, but Father, it's been eight months. Please, don't be upset with me."

"Never, deary. Never that."

I leaned back to reacquaint myself with his hardened features. My hands went to his jutting jaw, my fingers curling around the squared edges. All blunt angles and sun-darkened skin, his face still held its youth. And it's smile.

That infectious smile widened, tickling wiry whiskers against my palms as I traced new crinkles around his wise eyes and touched the familiar gold ring in his ear.

His arms hugged me tighter, thick and muscular, and his boots spread wide beneath me as if bracing against the roll of the sea even now.

He was every inch the seafaring knave. An unrivaled buccaneer. Ruthless. And rich, if the lore could be believed.

I knew the truth about his conquests and could recall every prize he'd won and lost. His treasure was greater than anyone could imagine.

"Have you brought me more tales from the high seas?" I tugged at the collar of his shirt, searching in fear of finding fresh scars.

"Indeed. I have much to tell you, my beautiful girl."

I lowered my feet toward the ground, wriggling in his arms. Before my toes touched the sand, I spotted a dark presence over his shoulder, approaching from the beach.

The man appeared out of nowhere, sneaking toward us on silent feet. With a bandoleer of guns slung across his chest, he stared at me with eyes too jaded for a face that was nigh twenty years.

My hackles went up, and my stomach bottomed out.

But Edric Sharp hadn't taught me to tremble in the face of danger. No, he'd taught me how to fight with my fists and wit, a flintlock and blunderbuss, and my personal favorite, his cutlass. I could feel it now—the grip of the hilt in my palm, the clang of metal against metal in heated clicks, and its reliability in battle. A blade never misfired.

Without a quiver of hesitation, I grabbed the cutlass from my father's sash, swept behind him, and thrust the sharp point at the enemy. Then I charged.

The man halted, his wicked eyes growing wide at the sight of me. I must have been a fright in tattered chintz and disheveled hair whipping around my ferocious expression.

His alarm was his folly, and I used it to cleave through the sash of his bandoleer and relieve him of his weapons.

"Stand down!" I swung again, slashing a hole in the sleeve of his

Sea of Ruin

shirt.

"Damnation, girl!" He held up his hands and hissed at the rip on his arm. "What are you doing?"

"Deciding which part of you I shall cut next." I jabbed the cutlass toward his nether regions.

His huge hand landed on top of my head, holding me away as he parried the stroke of my blade.

"Unhand me, sir." I thrashed, trying to dislodge his immovable grasp. "Do it now, or I'll lop off the dull, inanimate fellow between your legs."

"Captain," he said in a bored tone. "Call off your hell-born blowsabella before she hurts herself."

"Bennett, lower the blade." My father chuckled, his eyes gleaming with amusement. "That's my new quartermaster."

"What?" I withdrew the cutlass and jerked away from the man's grip. "How? Where's Kirby?"

"He lost his legs to chain-shot. And most of his internal organs, I'm afraid."

"Oh."

My insides clenched as I pictured an explosion of smoke and cinder, thousands of pounds of red-hot iron, and blood-soaked decks littered in dismembered limbs. I'd never experienced such brutality, but I'd lived every gruesome detail through my father's stories.

Most days, I believed Edric Sharp was invincible. But sometimes, when I stared at the sea from my bedchamber, I feared the next fallen buccaneer would be him.

"Where are those dogs?" He strode away and whistled for the hounds.

"So *you* are the reason the captain shortened sail and hove to?" The new quartermaster collected his guns, eying me sidelong. "Can't convince him to drop anchor in Nassau for a night of drink, but he'll put two-hundred leagues beneath her keel to see his brazen little she-devil."

I sucked in a breath and stood taller. "You don't know me."

"You're all he talks about."

"Then I'm at a disadvantage because I don't even know your name."

"Now you fancy an introduction?" He clicked his tongue. "Have you no contrition for attacking me?"

"No." I met him stare for stare, despite the height he held over me.

"You don't mince words, do you?"

I rested the cutlass on my shoulder. "I save the mincing for tangible things."

"Quite so. Point established." A rakish smile stole across his lips. "The name's Charles Vane."

Three

My father jogged toward the beach to chase his hounds, leaving me in an incommodious stare down with his new quartermaster.

I fought the urge to cross my arms over the revealing bosom of my gown. Charles didn't rest his gaze there, but he was looking at me, scrutinizing and assessing my unsightly appearance.

"Did you come from a party?" He canted his head, and a lock of black hair fell from the defined *V* of his widow's peak.

"No." I stabbed the cutlass into the sand and leaned on the hilt.

"Did you roll in every mud puddle you could find on the way here?"

"I'm certain I missed one."

He glanced between his ripped sleeve and the soiled rags of my dress. "Are you in the habit of ruining fine garments?"

"Are you in the habit of filling perfectly good silence with tedious questions?"

"Not usually." He scratched his whiskered face. "You're nothing like the well-bred ladies I've…" He cleared his throat. "Spent time with."

"I should hope not." My cheeks heated at his meaning. "I'm not a strumpet."

His gaze dipped to his boots, and the corner of his mouth lifted. "God save the man who sets his sights on you."

"Speak plainly, Mr. Vane." I anchored my fists on my hips. "What are you saying?"

"You're Captain Sharp's daughter."

"Yes, she is."

I jumped at the growl in my father's voice and found him standing a few paces away, watching me.

The hounds bounced around his legs and nipped at his fingers, but he paid them no heed. Prowling toward me, he searched my eyes, and what he saw there made his expression grow dark, overcast, heavy like rain clouds.

I knew that look, and it hurt my heart. "Don't say it."

"It's uncanny how much you resemble her."

"Please, don't—"

"It's true, lass."

I released a sigh. The truest truth was that he still loved the countess. It was an eternal love, as deep and ungovernable as the ocean.

But she wouldn't have him. Not when she was carrying his child. Not after fourteen years of letters, in which he offered her marriage, wealth, and undying devotion.

"Do you still write to her?" I curled my fingers around his callused hand.

"Aye." His gaze slipped to Charles and shuttered before returning to me. "Naught has changed."

"Maybe she's not getting your missives?"

"She's getting them. My courier waits as she reads them, shreds them, and hands back the pieces without response." Pain flashed in his eyes. "Has she still not given you my identity?"

I shook my head.

She never mentioned his name. Not once. Whenever I asked who fathered me, she punished me with her silence. If she knew about our visits… God's blood, would she have him marched to the gallows and hanged? I didn't know and couldn't risk it.

So I never begged him to stay. Instead, I voiced my usual demand. "Take me with you."

His expression blanked, and he released my hand. "No."

"Please? I can't go back. Not after what I've done!"

"Listen, Bennett. Stealing a horse is one thing. In time, Abigail will forgive you. But pillaging the king's ships is something else entirely. There's no forgiveness in my business, and the sea is no place for a child."

"I'm fourteen!"

Sea of Ruin

"She needs you." He brushed a springy curl from my face. "I would not steal you from her."

"Steal me? She's trying to get rid of me."

He went eerily still. "You say?"

"She's arranging a betrothal. If she succeeds, you'll be visiting me in England. And that's if I can sneak away from Lord Grisdale."

His nostrils pulsed with a furious snap of breath. "Who?"

"A marquess of the realm. Deep in the pockets. Gray under the wig. I stole the old lobcock's horse and—"

"Slow down." His hands flexed, and the vein in his forehead looked ready to pop. "Did you say *gray?*"

"Well, I haven't confirmed that detail because I missed our introduction. But the rest is true! He's a whole decade older than *you*!"

In a blink, his eyes lost their humanity, the depths sinking into an abyss of malice and ice.

A shiver rippled down my spine as his entire demeanor took on that coldness. Rigid shoulders, white-knuckled fists, uncompromising scowl—he no longer stood before me as my father, but rather as the infamous captain of an eighteen-gun warship.

His blade-sharp eyes cut to the tree line behind me. "That's his horse?"

"Yes."

"You stole it?"

"I was in a hurry."

He glanced at Charles, and a hint of pride softened the edge of his anger. "Already pirating, this one."

"And thrusting blades at devilishly good-looking rogues." Charles arched a brow at me.

I winged up mine in return. "Careful, Mr. Vane. One might think you enjoyed it."

"She makes a point, Charles." My father's voice grew quiet. A deep, bone-chilling kind of quiet. "Around my daughter, your eyes are for decoration only. If you use them on her, I'll carve them out and feed them to the gulls."

Charles looked away with a grimace. "I'll head back to the ship and give you some privacy."

"Good plan. Return for me at dusk."

The bothersome yet curiously droll quartermaster ambled toward the south side of the inlet. When he vanished beyond the outcrop, presumably where the jolly boat waited, I turned back to my father.

He stared out at the sea, his eyes a turbulent aqua green. The line of his jaw was so unyielding I could've sharpened a blade on it.

"You're angry with the countess," I said.

"Rightfully so." He scraped a hand through the thick tousle of his red hair. "She's stubbornly ambitious, stubbornly independent, stubbornly beautiful…" He blew out a breath. "Just flat-out stubborn."

"If I stay here, her stubbornness will send me to England."

"Don't concern yourself with that."

"What does that mean?"

"I'll deal with her." He paced toward the woods and picked up a fallen branch from the ground. "Your skill with the cutlass needs work."

He tested the weight of the stick and tossed it away to grab another.

With my thoughts still whirling around his plan with the countess, I wasn't prepared for his attack.

He lunged, wielding the stick like a sword, and swept my feet out from under me. I landed on my backside and rolled, all flailing limbs, tangled skirts, and curse words. He swung again, and I dodged, flinging myself toward the cutlass.

With the hilt in my grip, I rose into a strike. He blocked. I slashed, and for the next hour, his training distracted me from stolen horses and betrothed marriages.

As the fire-orange sun hauled itself across the sky, sweat pooled beneath my stays, and the wind blew knots of curls across my face. I clawed the wild tresses out of my eyes until my tangles had tangles.

My father went through multiple sticks, each one hacked away by the blade of the cutlass.

"You've been practicing." He dropped another broken branch and wiped the sweat from his brow.

"Only with wood." I gestured at the chopped twigs around his boots. "If I had my own cutlass…"

"I would give you my finest blade, lass." He tapped my nose. "But Abigail would discover it."

"How are you going to deal with her?"

A strange expression creased his face, and he looked away. "What I have planned for her isn't proper for your ears."

"I don't understand."

"Would you like to hear about my latest prize?"

"Yes!" I bounced on my toes and dropped the cutlass. "Was there a battle?"

Sea of Ruin

"Many battles." He laced his fingers through mine and led me to the shade of the woods.

Lowering to the ground, he gathered me on his lap and told me every heart-pounding detail of his attacks on the king's warship, a French brigantine, and numerous merchantiers.

"Then, two months ago, I encountered a Spanish treasure fleet. Twelve ships in total." His eyes lost focus. "We were outgunned and would've never attempted something so dangerous, but there was a deadly storm on the horizon. We waited in safe waters for the tempest to take its toll. Then we moved in, attacking the battered ships and claiming their salvage."

"They fought back?"

"The storm did. I thought it had passed, but a surge unlike any I've seen followed in its wake. I lost my ship." At my gasp, he pinched my chin and smiled. "I seized a new ship that night."

"You did?"

"Aye. A Spanish galleon. She was neither broken nor sinking like the others in the surge." His expression glowed with veneration. "She was spitting fire and laughing at the storm."

He explained how he rallied his surviving crew and boarded the fifty-gun galleon, even as his own ship was swallowed by the king tide.

I committed the particulars of his ambush to memory, hoping one day I might have a need for such knowledge and become half the wise, courageous captain that he was.

"What did you name her?" I asked.

"*Jade.*" His gaze lowered to my necklace. "She's a beauty, she is. When I saw her, I knew I had to take her. For *you*."

"For me?"

"She's yours, Bennett. I'll captain her until you're old enough to decide."

"Oh, Father!" My heart burst from my chest and soared with savage joy. "There's nothing to decide. I want to be a buccaneer like you."

"You're too young to know what you want."

"I'm old enough."

"But not too old to sit on your father's lap, are you now?"

"Just so." I wrapped my arms around his shoulders and burrowed into his hard chest.

"Someday you might wish to travel to England in your own right and follow your mother's dream." He chuckled. "God knows, you would make a meal out of the *beau monde.*"

"No, thank you. I wish to follow *you*."

"I'm honored, lass, and should you choose the sea, you have a ship. But I fear that path might end with your neck bent on the gibbet."

My breath stilled, and a metallic flavor rose beneath my tongue. "What about *your* neck? You could be captured or killed in battle. I can't lose you."

His gaze sank into mine. "Such big grown-up worries in your child's eyes." He ran a thumb across my cheekbone. "I'm careful. Which is why I cannot visit as often as I'd like."

I didn't remember the first time he came to me, but there wasn't a day I didn't know him. He'd always been a part of my life. My very own secret to cherish and protect.

When I was younger, he visited more frequently and stayed longer. Sometimes months. But as his reputation grew, so did the risks. Now I was lucky to steal a few hours with him each year.

"I have something for you." I jumped up, retrieved the linen-wrapped package from the horse's saddle, and proffered it to him.

Nervous energy flapped beneath my breast as he unfolded the cloth and removed the gift.

"The natives wear these on their feet." Crouching beside him, I traced the deerskin coverings. "The women scrape and smoke the skin to make it feel soft like this."

The shoes were gathered at the toe and sewn above and behind with a raised flap on either side. Colorfully dyed porcupine quills and white glass beads decorated the folded edges in artistic designs.

"Exquisite." He removed his jackboots and slipped the shoes onto his bare feet. "A comfortable fit. I shall wear them every night and think of you."

My heart turned over so hard I felt it in my throat.

"How did you acquire such a thoughtful gift?" He guided me back onto his lap and stroked my hair.

"The servants make them. The cook maid is always kind to me, and she traded them for a spool of ribbon. I was discreet."

"You did good."

I snuggled into the warmth of his embrace, perfectly content and blissfully happy. I loved him so deeply and so completely. It went against logic that my mother could not.

"I've been stowing my prizes in a safe place over the years." He kissed my forehead. "Enough riches for you, your children, and your grandchildren."

Sea of Ruin

"I don't care about that."

"You will. I want you to have this." He removed the compass that hung from a chain on his belt. "It's a map. When you're ready, you will follow it and claim what's rightfully yours."

"A map?" I cupped the gold casing and lifted the lid to reveal the navigational needle within. "I don't see a chart."

"It's there if you know how to unlock it."

I turned it over in my hands, rubbing the polished surface. "Is there a key?"

"You already have it. Start and end north. When you're ready, you'll know what to do."

"I don't know how to decipher riddles." I handed it back to him. "You could just take me there now. Kidnap the countess. You love her. We could be a real family and live off your treasure."

"A child's fairytale. Life isn't so simple."

"It could be."

"Not for us." He threaded the chain of the compass around the sash on my gown, securing the instrument to my waist. "When Abigail was exiled from English society, it destroyed something inside her. We're from different worlds, she and I. Imagine her living with a criminal, always on the run and in fear of capture. It would suck the life out of her." He wet his lips. "If I could, I would give up the sea and stand beside her in society. But I'm neither a nobleman nor a law-abiding man. That path was never an option."

"But she was with you once."

"In secret." He grunted. "When she was young and blinded by love."

Blinded by love.

The sound of that made me feel warm all over, and I smiled against his shoulder. "If I ever marry, he will be a man of your fortitude and spirit. A man who loves me above all else. Only me. And we shall be blinded by our love for life and beyond the ends of the sea."

"Accept nothing less, Bennett." He lifted my chin with a knuckle. "Promise me."

"I promise."

His eyes glittered with approval, his voice a deep well of affection. "That's my girl."

A few paces away, the hounds lounged in the shade. Seagulls cawed overhead, and late afternoon sunlight sparkled on white-crested waves.

He would be leaving soon, and his impending absence built a

burning ache behind my eyes. Anguish coursed through me, so internal, so deep, it embedded itself before rising to the surface.

After a lifetime of goodbyes, I'd learned how to cope. To smother the hurt. Crying never took the pain away.

"Tell me another story about her." I lay my cheek on his chest, relishing his scent of leather and salt. "Like the day you met."

"You've heard that one many times."

"I wish to hear it many more."

"Very well." He settled into a sprawl with a tree at his back and his arms holding me tight. "I spotted her from the ship deck I was scrubbing. The sun was so bright that day, high in the sky and heavy with heat. But it wasn't worthy in the light of her radiance. She stood on the dock, glowing in ivory silk, so fair and arresting I couldn't feel my legs."

I devoured every word as he told me how he approached the noble maiden, whisked her away from her chaperon, and fell hopelessly in love with the Lady Abigail Leighton.

A poor Irish seaman and a beautiful English countess. It was my favorite fairytale.

He always ended the story on their first kiss, but this time, his tone was different. Harder. More determined. "I couldn't let her get away."

"You couldn't?" I leaned back and searched his flinty expression.

"She's had fourteen years to move on, and she hasn't." He lifted me from his lap and stood.

A question wasn't voiced, but it was there, flickering in his eyes.

"No, she's not happy." My heart skipped a beat. "It's not me that she needs, Father. She needs *you*."

"Aye." He paced along the tree line in his deerskin shoes, each step growing faster and more resolute. "I want you to return to the estate." His gaze turned to the sea, where the horizon darkened with the approach of dusk. "I'll come for you tonight. For both of you."

Exhilaration and confusion tangled through me. "I thought living with a criminal would suck the life out of her?"

"Is she living? Does she smile? I will put life back into her!" He bared his teeth. "By God and the devil, I will spend every last tarnal breath in my body making her happy."

An overpowering sense of hope welled up in my chest. "I believe you."

"I love you." He pulled me against him and lowered his mouth to the top of my head. "I've committed a lifetime of crimes and paid

Sea of Ruin

dearly for them. Fourteen years without my girls. There is no greater punishment."

"It ends tonight?"

He released me with a wolfish grin. "Yes, it—"

A deep, threatening growl erupted behind me.

I spun toward the hounds and found them standing, noses pointed toward the shore and hackles up. My father went still, his hand locked tightly around my arm.

The dogs exploded into snapping snarls and took off toward the southern end of the beach. They sprinted around the copse of trees and out of view as their barking rose in volume.

My scalp tingled. I'd never heard such ferocious sounds. "Has Mr. Vane returned?"

"That's not Charles." He hauled me toward the horse and lifted me onto the saddle, his voice low and urgent. "Return to the house at once."

"Father, what is it?"

He untied the reins and removed a sheathed dagger from his belt. "No matter what happens, keep going." With a grip on my wrist, he wedged the sheath into the sleeve of my gown, concealing it beneath the fabric on my upper arm. "Do *not* turn back."

In the distance, the barking grew feral, high-pitched, and terrifying. My belly twisted into knots, and my lungs couldn't take in enough air beneath the vise of my stays.

"Go!" He slammed a hand onto the horse's flank, sending me into the woods.

I grabbed the reins and adjusted my balance before twisting to look over my shoulder.

He was gone.

My hands trembled, and a fiery pang stabbed beneath my ribs. I tried to ignore it and focused on controlling the horse.

Until startling, pained cries rent the air.

The cries of a dying dog.

My heart stopped as a second agonized yelp echoed through the forest before fracturing into whimpers. Then silence.

The hounds. Mercy God, what happened to them?

What would happen to my father?

Panic surged, freezing muscles and locking joints. Only my pulse hammered wildly as the horse raced onward, hurdling fallen trees and putting more distance between me and my entire world.

I couldn't leave him.

No matter what happens, keep going.

I trusted him implicitly and had never disobeyed him. *Never.*

My jaw clenched. He'd told me once to trust my instinct, and right now it was screaming at me to go back.

I pulled on the reins, and with a savage howl, I turned the horse about.

How many minutes had passed? How many kilometers? Too damned many, and I experienced every one of them in breathless agony as I galloped back to my father.

Nearing the beach, I approached slowly. The sound of the crashing surf reached my ears, bringing with it the din of voices. Stern, commanding voices.

Dozens of them.

My heart thundered toward hysteria as I nudged the horse closer, quietly picking along the brushwood and squinting through the trees.

When the sea came into view, I slapped a hand over my mouth.

Redcoats.

They swarmed the shore, their distinctive regimental facings gleaming white against the darkening sky. Armed with rifles, some mounted horses. Others invaded on foot as they overtook my father with fists and guns and sheer numbers.

There were too many to count, and he went down fighting and spitting blood.

Sticky nausea filled in my belly, clotting with fear and helplessness. My lungs ached to contain the wheeze of my breaths, and my fingers and toes shook uncontrollably. Why the rest of me refused to move, I couldn't fathom. I was paralyzed.

When his body fell limp beneath their strikes, they grabbed his arms and lugged him toward a waiting cart. His head lolled between his shoulders. The deerskin coverings on his feet dragged through the sand, and something inside me broke.

His jackboots lay just beyond the tree line, and a few paces from there was his cutlass, the blade sharp, lethal, *beckoning.*

With visions of rescue and bloodshed in my head, I inched the horse toward my father's weapon.

Until a twig snapped behind me.

"Benedicta." The familiar masculine voice sent a chill through my veins.

No, no, no! God damn me and the devil, too!

Sea of Ruin

How would I explain my presence here, sitting astride a stolen mount, while planning an attack on the king's soldiers? I would be arrested alongside my father, unable to save him.

I swallowed, caught up my breath, and schooled my features into that of a well-bred maiden who would have no association or attachment to Edric Sharp.

Then I turned in the saddle and met the ratlike eyes of the Marquess of Grisdale.

Four

"Lord Grisdale." My pulse thrashed in my ears as I bowed my head in feigned respect.

"Delighted, Benedicta. And perplexed." He nudged his steed alongside the one I'd stolen. "I sent the king's men to search for a horse thief and look what I've found."

I followed his gaze to the uniformed men who were shackling my father's unconscious body in the cart.

Everything inside me burned to shout, scream, leap for the cutlass, and run it through every soldier who put their hands on him. But I pushed down the rage, the bone-deep terror, and relaxed the muscles in my face.

The brigade marched off the beach with my father in tow, leaving me powerless to stop it. But there would be a trial. I had a day, maybe two, to signal *Jade*. My father's loyal crew would assist me in his rescue.

"What have you found, my lord?" My gaze clung to the retreating cart.

"Why, that's the infamous Edric Sharp." Bony fingers curled around my upper arm. "And this is my stolen horse."

"You're quite right." I watched the last soldier leave the beach and turned my attention to the marquess.

He was a twiggy stick of a man with a face like day-old death hanging loosely from sharp bones. If his beady brown eyes sat any closer together, they would've crossed at the bridge.

He tucked his weak chin into the cravat at his neck as if attempting to hide that hideous feature. A cane dangled by a loop from one of the buttons on his justacorps. No traces of lint flecked the red brocade. Not a mote of dirt on the white stockings over his breeches. Not even a smudge on his buckled shoes.

But his lordship was sweating. Beads glistened upon his wrinkled brow and dripped from his high-parted periwig.

Not even the Marquess of Grisdale could escape Carolina's heat. His blood gave him power and privilege, but he was still a mere mortal like the rest of us. He sweated. He pissed. And he bled.

"You confess to stealing my horse?" His hand tightened around my arm.

"Yes, my lord. I was anxious about meeting you and went for a ride to calm my nerves."

"Virtuous girls bred to proper living don't take rides into the wild alone. Imagine what would've happened had I not tracked you. I daresay you might have been ravaged by a pirate!"

Realization cleaved through my chest. By stealing his horse, I'd unknowingly led the soldiers right to my father. If it weren't for me, he would be safe on his ship, free from the clutches of a town that salivated to see a buccaneer hanged.

The bitter taste of regret hit my throat, and my eyes burned with tears. The flood of guilt blurred my vision, and I couldn't stop the wetness from searing my cheeks. The devastation was too powerful, the pain too big to hold.

"I was foolish." I wiped my face on the sleeve of my gown, and more tears shook free.

"How touching." He stroked his thumb along my upper arm. "My betrothed sits upon a stolen horse, crying with remorse for the poor choices she made."

"Betrothed?" I choked on a sob.

"Indeed. I made an offer just this morning."

He could shove his offer up the hole upon which he sat.

"I shall return home at once and accept my punishment." I tried to pull from his grip, a useless effort. "Remove your hand from my person, if you please."

"I'll accompany you."

"Not without a chaperon, my lord. It's not allowed."

"Do you see a chaperon in the vicinity?" He gestured at the surrounding woodland and scowled at my appearance. "You look like you were attacked by a pack of ruffians."

"I just lost my way is all."

"I'll see to your safe return."

I flexed my hands around the reins.

Above the canopy of trees, dusk deepened into ribbons of purple. Every second I spent with this grabby, cross-eyed addle pate was another moment my father sat in the gaol, awaiting a fate I wouldn't accept.

"You're a busy man, Lord Grisdale." With a hard yank, I freed my arm from his grasp. "I must refuse and insist that you return to where you are most needed."

"No one refuses me." His eyes narrowed with a thousand blade-sharpened threats, all of which promised unspeakable pain. "Insolent little bitch."

I saw his arm assail too late. The back of his hand slammed into my cheekbone with excruciating force, and the impact knocked me from the saddle.

The ground crashed into my back, jarring me so viciously I couldn't move. Spots dotted my sight, then nothing at all as unconsciousness swallowed my senses.

I woke in a haze of pain. The scent of earth tickled my nose. Dead leaves crunched under my twitching body. I was still in the forest, lying on my back with hard dirt beneath my head. But my hands…

I twisted my wrists, yanking on the rope that restrained my arms above my head.

Blinking rapidly, I cleared fresh tears from my vision and stared up into chilling eyes.

"Do you know how I bring naughty little girls in line?" The marquess stood over me, tapping his cane against his leg. "A decent beating is most effective."

"The countess will see to my punishment." My voice scratched like sand in my throat. "You needn't trouble yourself with—"

"Silence!" His roar shook the sagging skin on his cheeks. Then he straightened, drew in a regal breath, and composed his smile and his voice into polite refinement. "As it was *my* horse you stole, it will be *my* welts upon your fair flesh."

As Lady Abigail's disobedient daughter, I was accustomed to discipline. For propriety's sake, my punishments were always dispensed in the presence of a lady's chaperon. And usually delivered with a strap. Never a cane.

If I were found alone with the marquess, it would ruin my reputation. I didn't care about that, but as his gaze made a sluggish, skin-crawling voyage over my person, this felt alarmingly, decisively wrong.

"Roll over." Bending down, he whacked the cane against the soles of my bare feet.

Biting pain bowed my back and hurled me into a fog of righteous fury.

"God damn your blood!" I wheezed, thrashing against the restraints on my arms. "Untie me! It's getting dark, and the countess will be worried."

"The countess answers to me." He lowered to his knees and shoved my skirts up my legs, baring skin that had never been seen by sun or man.

"What are you doing?" I kicked and screamed, helpless to stop him.

He exposed my body all the way to my waist, and I could only stare in horror, the humiliation more than I could bear. The way he leered at my womanhood struck fear so deep in my heart I no longer felt it beating.

"Your beauty confounds me." He caught my upper thighs in a bruising grip and forced my legs apart. "Untamed and untried, snarling and writhing like an unlicked cub."

"A pox on your eyes." My pulse exploded, shooting feverish chills across my flesh. "God's wounds, cover me!"

"It's not consistent with reason that a lady invokes God by vain and careless swearing."

"By God's feet, his tongue, and all his unmentionables, may he refuse you and condemn your soul to hell."

His forearm landed across my hips and pinned me to the ground.

"You *will* roll over." He pressed the tip of the cane against the private place between my legs. "Or you'll bleed in ways you're only beginning to fathom."

The shivering started in my belly and spread to my limbs. By the time I wriggled onto my stomach, I was trembling so violently I had no control of my tongue. It flopped between my chattering teeth and filled my mouth with blood.

With my backside exposed to the air, I clenched every muscle, bracing for the strike. But when it came, I wasn't prepared. Without the buffer of clothing, the blow crashed into me like fire, penetrating deep into muscle and bone and robbing my ability to scream.

Sea of Ruin

The agony throbbed through the next hit, and the next. The crack of the cane landed hard and fast, with no breaks in between and no sign of stopping.

"No! Please, stop!" I dug in my toes and scrambled away on elbows. "I beg you. Stop!"

He stayed with me, smiting my backside with unleashed brutality.

"You're stronger than my other wives." He pressed a shoe onto my back, holding me immobile. "They swooned upon the first cut."

"Wives?" My voice broke on a guttural sob. "But you're a widower!"

"Indeed, I am. Three times over." His hand gripped my behind, squeezing abused flesh. "Perhaps, you'll be the one I keep."

My stomach heaved. Saliva pooled around my gums. My chest convulsed, and everything came up in a spray of vomit. It saturated the dirt and clung to my hair and chin in strings of slime.

His touch vanished, and the cane swung again, harder and more intense than before.

The blinding agony didn't spare a single nerve in my body. It devoured all thought and stunned me into a sobbing pool of snot and tears.

Pain was all that existed.

It lasted longer than I thought I could survive. "No more. I beg you to stop. I'll do anything. Anything! Please!"

I needed the torture to end. I needed my father. I needed mercy, and I pleaded for it, screamed for it, willing my soul unto any god who would have me in exchange for a moment of relief.

Nightfall wrapped the forest in shadows, and my cries lost strength. Blood soaked my broken fingernails, and dirt coated my cracked lips.

When the cane finally dropped to the ground, I couldn't move, couldn't think past the dense, trembling misery.

Until he touched me there.

Inside my center.

Then I was screaming, kicking at the legs that crawled between mine.

He grabbed my waist and pulled my hips to his naked groin.

"No! Don't do this!" I twisted and slid through the dirt, dragging my chest through vomit. All the rolling and wriggling moved my body toward my bound hands until they were caught beneath me.

That was when I felt it. The hilt of the dagger in my sleeve.

A spark of hope.

As he wrestled my lower body into position against his, I pulled the blade free. But with my arms tied at the wrists, I couldn't cut through the rope.

"Not like this." I adjusted my fingers around the hilt. "Turn me over. Please, my lord?"

He rubbed invasive fingers between my legs and groaned a vile sound. "As you wish."

The trumpet-shaped sleeves of my gown concealed my hands. I pinched the folds of fabric around the blade and pointed it outward as he rolled me.

The instant my back hit the ground, he dove between my legs.

And landed directly onto the dagger.

My heart pounded as I thrust with all my strength, piercing the soft meat of his abdomen.

He stared down at me, eyes wide. His jaw opened in a soundless scream, and ropes of red-tinged drool stretched from his gaping mouth and plopped onto my cheek.

I pushed harder on the blade with both hands, my fingers slipping through wetness as I carved a line toward his chest.

A choking sound gurgled from his throat. His body spasmed, sinking onto the dagger before collapsing on top of me.

I strained to hear his breath, but my heart beat too loud, banging in my ears. And the trembling… By the grace of almighty God, I couldn't stop shaking.

But he didn't move.

His stillness avowed his departure from this world. I'd plunged a blade into his belly and sent his soul to hell. I couldn't bring it back. Nor did I want to.

Relief rode in on waves of exhaustion and horror. My mind lagged, struggling to process, as my stomach retched in great dry heaves.

By sheer will, I managed to push the body off me. It landed in a lifeless heap of limbs, breeches unbuttoned at the waist. The protrusion of male flesh flopped to the side like limp seaweed.

The periwig hung off-center, revealing the skull beneath. Bald, not gray.

With a shudder, I went to work on the rope around my wrists. Endless minutes flogged me as I twisted one hand free, ripping skin in the process. The bounds unraveled, and I shoved knots of crusty hair from my face, scouring the trees for the horses.

My eyes refused to adjust in the dark, and the forest blurred around me. My insides didn't feel right. It was the coldness, the shivering, the constant twitching.

My shoulders jerked in tight convulsions. Spasms attacked my eyelids, throbbing swollen skin. My fingers didn't work, the joints kinked from prolonged clenching.

An attempt to stand sent me spinning, stumbling, and plummeting to my knees. I rose again and forced my numb feet over the ground, propelled by a single imperative.

Save my father.

If I reached a horse, I could guide it back to the beach and find Charles Vane.

Every step shifted the gown against my backside, blazing agony across my skin. I cried out and reached blindly for something to grab onto. My hands grappled air, and I turned my ankle on a rock. The startling pain sent me wheeling back to the ground.

I sobbed in frustration and sprung back to my feet, pushing my body beyond its abilities. Everything hurt, and the uncontrollable trembling threatened to suck the last of my strength.

I twitched forward, centering my mind on each dragging step.

Twitch. Step. Twitch. Step.

Every branch in my path was a test of coordination, every uneven bump beneath my feet a challenge to overcome. My balance wavered, teetering on the edge between awareness and oblivion.

At last, my legs gave up, but I didn't feel the ground hit me. I might have blacked out.

Sprawled on my side, I rubbed dirt from my sightless eyes and crawled on my belly. My thoughts tried to abandon me, but I held on, kept moving, determined to reach my father.

Until I couldn't move at all.

The abyss pulled me into its yawning void, and as I fell, part of me hoped I would never wake again.

Five

Of course, I woke. Life was too cruel to grant me a permanent reprieve from the pain. I lay face-down, my body a single pulsing ache wrapped in the welts of my mistakes.

I'd failed, and my shame took on a horrifying new meaning in the silver light of dawn.

With my cheek pressed to the leaf-littered ground, I blinked the grit from my eyes, disoriented by the view before me.

A pair of dirt-coated slippers peeked out from a hem of lavender silk. I twisted my neck, following the wrinkled skirt of a gown, up, up, up to the glaring visage of the countess.

She stared down at me, hands on her hips, scrutinizing the remains of a dress she'd worked so hard to make.

Guilt crushed my chest.

"Mother…" My voice burned in my throat, raw from screaming and parched from dehydration.

"Don't." She simmered in her stillness, her jaw quivering in unholy rage. "I don't know what I did to invite such vile disrespect and hatred, but I will *not* hear your excuses. Not this time."

"I don't hate you."

"Not another word!"

A brown mare whinnied behind her, and the sight of it confused me. That horse didn't belong to the marquess.

Had my mother ridden it here? This deep into the woods before dawn? Alone?

I returned my attention to her face, her complexion drained of color in the frame of fallen, untamed hair. She looked so disheveled and tired, nothing like herself. And she was still wearing the gown I'd last seen her in yesterday morning.

"You came for me?" I rolled to my back and regretted it instantly.

A violent burst of pain blazed through my body, plaguing every muscle and joint. Dizziness mottled my vision, and I gasped through the torment, squinting at her ghost-white expression.

"Whose blood is that?" She pointed a trembling finger at my chest.

"Not mine." I sat up sluggishly and scanned the thick grove for the Marquess of Grisdale.

How much could I tell her? Had news already traveled to the house about the arrest of Edric Sharp? I'd never so much as mentioned his name in her presence. If I told her everything now, would she stop me from rescuing him?

She stepped over me in a rustle of silk and made a beeline through the shadows of the trees, ducking under branches and yanking her skirts free from thorns.

A few paces away, she stopped with a gasp. Her hand fell to the bodice at her stomach, and she bent at the waist, heaving for breath.

I pushed to my feet, swaying through a bout of wooziness, but I didn't follow her. I could see the body well enough from here.

With the dagger protruding from the torso and the breeches unbuttoned at the waist, no words were needed. Comprehension glowed in her clever eyes.

But understanding didn't beget compassion. I'd ruined her chance at returning to English society and stood before her as a murderer, covered in the blood of my crime.

Locking my knees, I braced for her condemnation.

"I would've done the same." She lifted her chin and turned away from the body.

"Truly?" Shock stuttered my breath.

"Any man who meets with a prudent woman and offers to meddle with her, without her consent, shall suffer present death."

"Even at her own hand?" My pulse raced.

"Even so. No matter the laws of man." Her expression turned to stone. "Tis *our* law. Yours and mine."

I stared at her, thunderstruck. Never had I felt a connection to another woman as I did to my mother in that moment. She met my eyes with more confidence and conviction than any titled lord. Her stubbornness was the bane of my existence, but I realized now that same ferocity would be used to protect me.

For the first time in my life, I saw what my father saw. A woman who was brave enough to cross the Great Western Ocean alone and pregnant. She was beauty and strength in her own right, a force to reckon with. If anyone could help me rescue him, she could.

I tamped down my rioting nerves and treaded carefully. "Has there been word of an arrest?"

"No one has discovered the body." Returning to my side, she gripped my arm and guided me toward the horse. "I'll send someone I trust to collect the remains. This will be our secret. One we'll take to our graves."

"No, I mean…" I stepped back from her grip, stumbling on shaky legs. "Someone else was arrested."

"I've been searching for you all night. I haven't been home to hear of any…" The blood drained from her face. "*Who* was arrested, Benedicta?"

"A seafarer." I swallowed, and my eyes burned with tears. "A buccaneer."

She went still, and her voice trembled to a whisper. "What have you done?"

"He's…" I shook my head, faltering over the confession. "My father…"

"No." She staggered backward and tripped on a branch. "No, no, no. He promised me." With an ungraceful spin, she flung herself toward the horse. "He promised he would never get caught when he visited you."

"What?" A fist clamped around my heart. "You knew?"

"Of course, I knew." She fumbled in her urgency to mount the horse, her skirts tangling around her legs. "He always sent two hounds. When one passed, the other showed the replacement how to find us. They were his couriers."

"That's how he sent you his letters?" My eyes bulged. "Why didn't you tell me?"

"I needed you to fiercely guard that secret. As long as you hid it from me, I trusted you could hide it from those who would harm him." Her slipper caught in the stirrup, and she swung up onto the saddle, her features distorted with an emotion I'd never seen there before.

Fear.

"When was he arrested?" She turned the horse about, facing the opposite direction.

"Before dusk." I floundered after her, my pulse tripping in my veins. "There will be a trial."

"Not for a pirate, you foolish girl. And certainly not for Edric Sharp. Don't you get it, Benedicta? We made him weak."

"No, he loves us!"

"And I gave him up because I… I couldn't be the reason for his demise." She turned away and signaled the horse to move. "Go home and burn that gown."

"Mother, wait!" I grabbed the bridle, halting her. "If there's any love for him left inside you, you will save him!"

She bent down and slapped my hand away, her lips pulling back in a sneer. "I love him so viciously I would die for him."

Her declaration slammed into me, knocking the wind from my lungs. She lunged the horse forward and dashed into the gloom of shadows.

I staggered after her, but she was already gone.

My father would be in the town gaol, so that was where I needed to go. But not drenched in blood. And not without a horse.

Stripping out of the gown, I found only a few stains on the petticoat and bodice of my stays.

I stuffed the dress inside the hollow of a dead tree, retied my father's compass to my waist, and turned in the direction where the sky was the lightest. East. The beach. Once I reached the sea, I could follow it south to the port of Charleston.

As I walked, I pushed through the pangs in my body and listened for the neigh of a horse.

Thirst was the most gnawing ache. And hunger. The throbbing in my face, backside, and feet dulled in comparison. But when I spotted a horse through the trees, all physical pain gave way to exhilaration.

It took me several minutes to mount Grisdale's horse, and several more to race to the beach. When I emerged from the woods, the sun was already cresting the horizon.

My father's boots and cutlass still lay in the sand, but I didn't stop to collect them. I galloped south, eyes on the water, searching for his ship as I followed the shore to town.

If I had a spyglass and climbed one of the tallest trees, perhaps I would spot *Jade*.

I sped onward, spurred by images of a noose around his neck.

Sea of Ruin

Would they hang him at dawn? Or force him to attend Sunday service, preach to him about his sins, and hang him after?

Tears stung my eyes, and my entire body shook in the saddle.

My mother would stop them. She loved my father. How had I ever thought she didn't? She would save him, and we would sail away.

We would be a family.

The thought was so comforting I let it play out in my head—my father standing at the bow of his ship with his hands on the railing and the wind in his hair, the countess and me flanking his sides and sharing joyous smiles. He would sing off-tune, and we would laugh and join in. The destination wouldn't matter because we would already be home, together at sea, as we were meant to be.

I choked on tearful laughter and propelled the horse faster. Chest tight and fingers clinched around the reins, I abandoned the fringe of forest on my right and approached the edge of town.

Piers stretched like fingers out to sea, and buildings scattered along the walkways that lined the beach. The sun sat just above the water, and a few townsfolk meandered from one place to the next.

The gaol wasn't visible from the beach, and I questioned the wisdom in entering the town half-dressed and guilty of murder.

In the distance, a bell tolled, signaling the start of Sunday service. Most of the residents would be gathering there.

With a shaky breath, I searched the buildings for a sign of the countess or her horse. My gaze darted over pathways, faces, shadowed alcoves, and... An ominous structure. One that didn't belong on the beach.

I urged the horse closer, squinting at the wooden platform that appeared to have been moved from the center of town.

Two uprights towered over it, and something hung from the crosspiece.

Not some*thing*.

Someone.

A cold sweat swept over me, and sickening dread muted everything around me.

My mind fractured, and I didn't recall dismounting the horse. One moment I was in the saddle. The next I was standing at the foot of the gallows, staring up at a dead man.

A tide of tears warped my inspection of his face, so I focused on the feet that dangled at eye level above the platform.

Feet that were covered in deerskin shoes, decorated with porcupine quills and glass beads. And splotches of blood.

Numbness spread across my skin.

The shoes weren't real.

Not real. Not real. Not real.

None of this was real.

I pressed the heels of my hands to my eyes, rubbing away the blur of a nightmare. Then I forced my gaze back up.

Broad shoulders. Wide mouth. Sun-bronzed skin. Gold earring. Red hair.

No. It wasn't possible. Captain Edric Sharp was invincible.

"Father?" My arms reached for him, and I willed him to lift his chin, to open his eyes, to give me a smile. "Father, please!"

Sunlight cast his body in stripes of gold and shadow. The rope creaked, but the wind seemed not to stir.

Nothing stirred. Not his arms in the restraints. Not the lashes fanning his cheekbones. Not a twitch on his lips.

He floated above me, suspended, unreachable, unmoving.

Dead.

Gone.

He was gone.

My mouth hung open, but no sound came out. No scream. No breath.

He would never hug me again.

He died alone.

I gripped the back of my head and curled around the anguish in my chest, rocking, shaking, unable to stem the onslaught of pain. It gathered in my throat, throbbed along my teeth, and broke the air in a wailing, guttural howl.

I didn't know how long I lay bent over the platform, sobbing in a pool of loss and heartbreak. I didn't lift my head until voices sounded in the distance.

Cupping cold fingers over my mouth, I captured the cries that tumbled out.

My legs turned to water, and I collapsed beside the gallows, unable to mute the sounds behind my hand.

In the back of my mind, I knew I couldn't stay here. Not without being questioned about my inappropriate attire, the stains on my undergarments, and the disappearance of the Marquess of Grisdale.

I thought of my mother. She'd ridden off in this direction and would've found him, same as me.

Sea of Ruin

She needed me as I needed her.

I needed her strength, her wisdom, her arms folded tightly around me. I just…

I desperately needed my mother.

Moving through a fuzzy, grief-leaden trance, I peered over the platform and spotted a group of redcoats gathered on the road that led through town.

My only escape was back the way I'd come.

As I rose to my feet, something caught the men's attention. They turned away to greet the approach of a loose horse.

The horse I'd stolen from the marquess.

My chest tightened. I'd lost my ride.

I lost my father.

With the soldiers distracted, I stared up into his face and choked, "I love you with everything I am, and I don't want to leave you. But I think…" I stole a glance at the redcoats. "I think you would be angry if I didn't run now."

Drawing in a tear-soaked breath, I forced myself to turn away. Then I ran.

My feet pounded the warm sand, and my arms pumped with the motion. I didn't look back, didn't slow, no matter how shaky my legs became.

Seashells and rocks sliced the soles of my feet. Labored breaths scorched my dry and thirsty throat. The pain pushed me harder, faster, and when I reached a stretch of barren shore, I screamed.

Tears streaked my face, and I kept running. Crushing sorrow strangled my insides, and I quickened my pace. Muscles tore in protest, and I cried louder, sobbing brokenly from a bottomless well of pain.

Every kilometer was a just punishment, the abuse on my body a price for my failures. No one deserved a beating more than me, and I absorbed that pain until my bones buckled upon the beach.

The sun's heat burned my back, and I lifted my pounding head, squinting through tangles of hair.

A towering cliff rose before me, and the shore curved inward, forming a crescent that spanned sixty paces.

The beach where my father was arrested.

I crawled to the shade of the nearby outcropping of trees, and my ears perked to the sound of buzzing.

Swarms of flies hovered over the brush, and as I drew closer, I saw the blood-soaked fur.

My father's dead hounds.

With a nauseated cry, I pushed to my feet and staggered along the inlet in the direction of his cutlass and boots. I summoned just enough energy to gather his belongings before crashing to the sand.

My heart pulled toward my mother, and my desperation to find her seemed to conjure her out of the sky.

Lying on my back, I gazed up at the cliff, and there she was, floating on the edge of the precipice.

Golden hair whipped around her head, her arms stretched out to the sea. She was an apparition of unearthly beauty, screeching fiercely into the wind.

"Edddddric!" A loud shrill cry shattered her voice as she chanted his name over and over.

She didn't look down at me, didn't move her attention from the sea.

How was she in the sky? Soaring over me like an angel? I must have been dreaming her.

Because I needed her.

But something didn't feel right.

I curled my hands in the sand, testing the scratchy grains against my skin. Would I be able to feel that in a dream?

Why was she on the cliff? Had she floated there? Or climbed?

Panic stitched through my chest, and I fumbled to my feet, clinging to my father's possessions.

Seagulls swooped and cawed around her, and she mimicked their form.

"Edric, my love!" Arms open like a bird, she stepped off the cliff and took flight. "Edric!"

Her gown rippled around her, and the bellow of her cry broke with the tide. But instead of gliding out to sea, she plunged to the rubble of boulders below.

My entire body jerked as she hit the rocks.

I would die for him.

Numb paralysis spread through me.

Not real.

My feet carried me forward, but there was no feeling. No breath.

Muscles failed, and I used the cutlass for support, stabbing it into the sand and stumbling closer. Closer. Until her broken form filled my view.

I didn't feel the surf batter me into the cliff as I climbed the moss-slick boulders. The ocean would've been frigid this time of year, but I couldn't feel the water as it soaked into my clothing.

With fingers locked around the boots and cutlass, I made it to my mother's side.

She lay on a rock twice her size, her neck twisted at an unnatural angle. I curled up against her chest and touched the red skin around her open eyes, collecting the tears there.

"I loved him, too, Mother." Agony unfurled in my breast. "Why did you leave me? I needed you."

Blue eyes of glass stared back.

She doesn't see me.

I tucked the boots and cutlass between us and pulled her arm around me. A trickle of blood fell from her mouth. I wiped it away and burrowed closer, burying my face in her neck.

The soft silk of her hair fluttered against my lips as I sobbed. Her delicate frame lay like twisted driftwood against me. I pulled her closer, straightening her skirts, arranging her limbs, and clinging to her embrace.

There was only so much suffering a person could endure before they broke. Sometimes, broken things couldn't be put back together.

My body wasn't broken like my mother's, but I was empty all the same. And tired. So very tired.

Closing my eyes wasn't hard. They pulled shut on their own.

When I opened them, I was greeted by nightfall.

Moonlight sparkled over my mother's skin, giving her an ethereal glow. Eventually, someone would find us and take her away from me. Or maybe the crabs would take her. I leaned up to flick one from her hair, and a pair of jackboots stepped into my view.

Craning my neck, I looked up to find Charles Vane standing over me.

I licked cracked lips and rasped, "My father…"

"I tried to rescue him." He crouched beside me, his expression unreadable in the moonlight. "They hanged him at dawn. Moved the gallows to the beach and did it right there to send a message to us. His crew."

"You were there?"

He nodded stiffly. "So was she." He glanced at the countess. "Your mother?"

"Yes."

"She arrived as it happened and…" His brows furrowed as he gazed up at the peak of the cliff. "She went mad."

I followed his gaze. "Did it take her pain?"

"I suppose it did."

"This day took everything from me. Everything I loved. Everything I had." I studied the rocky face of the cliff, wondering if I had the strength to climb it.

"Not everything." He bent over me and scooped up my mother's body from the rock. "I couldn't save Captain Sharp, but I can save you."

As he strode away with her, I pondered his words with a sluggish mind. Did I want to be saved? What was left to salvage?

Moments later, he returned and lifted me into his arms. I'd never felt so weak and lifeless. I didn't even have the will to struggle as he carried me into the sea.

Muscles flexed beneath me as he lowered me into a jolly boat. My father's boots and cutlass joined me.

And I wasn't alone.

Two dead bodies lay at my feet, and the sight of them together breathed life into my heart.

"How?" I crawled toward my parents and gripped their cold hands, lacing their fingers together in the squeeze of mine.

"I stole his body from the gallows." He climbed into the boat behind me. "Captain Sharp deserves a burial at sea."

"Thank you." I lay down beside them and wrapped my arms around my father's chest. "What will happen to me?"

"That's up to you." He stabbed the oars into the black water and pushed out to sea. "*Jade* is yours. The captain was very clear on that point the night he took her."

"I'm only fourteen."

"I'll captain her until you earn the crew's trust." He tipped his head, studying me. "I was younger than you, orphaned like you, when I chose this life. I have no regrets."

"I'm a girl." *A broken, empty girl.* I tightened my hand around my parents' entwined fingers. "The crew won't accept me without my father."

"Don't give them a choice." His gaze flitted over me, and a smirk touched the corner of his mouth. "I saw a fearless fire burning inside you yesterday. Get that back, Bennett, and naught will stand in your way."

I felt it. A spark of something beneath the cold, heavy weight of pain.

Sea of Ruin

Something to live for.
My hand fell to the compass that hung from my waist.
When you're ready, you will follow it and claim what's rightfully yours.
I closed my eyes and cried.

Six

March 1721
Port Royal, Kingston Harbor Jamaica

Seven years had passed since I lost my parents. I still felt it, the deep gnawing pain in the torments of my soul. I tried to shake it loose, tried like hell to pretend the damage wasn't there. But it clung.

Especially tonight.

The mantle of twilight shrouded me in desolation as I stood before another corpse hanging from a noose.

Another buccaneer.

Another great man ripped from my life.

One day I might find the hempen halter around my own neck. Pirates never died in their beds. But today wasn't my day.

A reminder that I shouldn't be here.

I'd been on the run since I was fourteen, constantly looking over my shoulder. Even now I subtly tilted my head, probing the empty alleyways around me, my senses on alert for the one thing I couldn't outrun forever.

Death.

My would-be reapers came in many forms. Pirate hunters sought the bounty my capture would award them. Navy officers desired the accolades from bringing down the pirate daughter of Captain Edric

Sharp. Enemy buccaneers and fellow criminals wanted to eliminate me as the competition. And there were others, one in particular, who hunted me with single-minded focus, determined to reclaim what he'd lost.

He was the most dangerous of them all.

My presence in Jamaica was a risk. But I had to come, even as I knew I would arrive too late.

When I'd learned of Charles Vane's capture, I was a week's journey away.

I arrived three days after he hanged.

And he was still hanging.

I covered my nose against the stench and ordered myself not to cry. I hadn't exposed that kind of weakness in a very long time.

Charles had seen me at my lowest point. One of them, anyway. The night he collected my parents' bodies and carried me away from Carolina, we began a friendship that survived battles and sickness, victories and losses, time and distance.

And now death.

I owed him my life. A debt I would never be able to repay.

My trembling hand went to the jade stone that hung on the leather choker around my neck, one of the few things I retained from childhood. I'd lost so much in the past seven years and smiled so little.

Just like my mother.

But unlike her, my dream had always been to live on a ship. I'd obtained that and fought every day to keep it. *Jade* belonged to me, and I'd wrangled her under my command with a ferocity that would've made my father proud. I loved the life I'd chosen, craved the rocking beneath my feet even now, but it wasn't easy.

I'd made a lot of mistakes, one of which left a terrible hole in my heart.

Shadows stirred in my periphery, and a well-built pirate approached my side. We didn't make eye contact as he paused to view the body with a respectable amount of space between us.

He towered several heads taller than me, all lean muscle and vibrating intimidation. His brown hair was sheared up the sides, leaving a stripe of tousled length from the peak of his forehead to the base of his skull. Rings of gold lined his ear, and a square jaw underscored his hard mouth.

As wickedly attractive as he was ruthless, he could probably eat me in one bite.

Sea of Ruin

I trusted him with my life.

Reynolds wasn't just my quartermaster and second in command. He was one of my closest friends.

"We should go, Captain," he said under his breath. "A lady of your station wouldn't linger at Gallows Point after dusk."

"I never claimed to be a lady." I ran a hand over the bodice of my disguise.

Since I couldn't enter busy ports dressed as a woman pirate, I had to exchange my trousers and weaponry for an appearance that was more readily overlooked.

I'd spent my teenage years clad in boy's clothing with my hair chopped to my ears. Then my hips rounded, and my chest expanded, leaving me little choice but to don the stifling torture devices women favored.

It had been a long while since I'd pinned up my wild mane and wore the alias of a respectable lady. I'd forgotten how much I hated it.

"I look like a sunbaked pear stuffed in shrunk satin." I tugged at the bosom of the gray gown, feeling trapped and miserable. "Wouldn't you agree?"

He didn't spare me a glance. "I'd rather not say."

"Why not? You're never one to hold your tongue."

"You're in a simmering mood." His brown eyes darted over the perimeter. "Causing a scene isn't my aim presently."

"You fret like a lady's maid."

"Rot in hell."

"Someday I shall. But—"

"Today isn't your day," he said, finishing my favorite motto.

Voices drifted from a nearby alley, followed by the tread of footsteps.

Reynolds faded into the shadows as a smartly dressed couple ambled by, making a wide berth around the decaying corpse.

When they vanished beyond the corner, Reynolds returned to my side. "Pay your respects to Captain Vane so we can gather the crew. The faster we weigh anchor, the better."

He retreated again, blending into the darkness.

With his ever-vigilante gaze on my back, I blew out a breath and stepped toward the wooden platform.

Another wave of pedestrians passed, and I bowed my head, hiding my face until they strolled away, seemingly unmoved by the dead pirate hanging above them.

My heart ached.

Slipping a hand into the discreet slit in the gown, I accessed the hidden dimity pocket and stroked the polished surface of my father's compass. *A map*, he'd called it. One I'd yet to unlock.

Charles and I had spent a couple of years trying to open the instrument. He eventually gave up on it, and we parted ways. But we always managed to find each other. Whether it was at sea or in a tavern, we would trade stories and reconnect over pewter tankards. He never missed an opportunity to tease me about my father's unattainable treasure.

"I'm still searching for the key," I whispered too low for Reynold's ears. "I bet you're laughing at me from your throne in hell, you droll, mean-spirited scrub."

I waited for Charles' witty retort, but it would never come.

Lifting my eyes, I flexed my hands against the onset of crippling emotion.

Dark, blood-soaked hair fell from his widow's peak to his chest, his face bloated and clinging to what had once been a devilishly handsome bone structure. Tattered clothing hung from rotting skin, which served as a feeding ground for flies and maggots.

Tears gathered in my throat, and I swallowed them down, transforming my grief into the temperament that had kept me alive all these years.

"Damn you, Charles." My cheeks burned, and my nails gouged my palms. "You look like the pustular aft of a diseased dog. Is this what you wanted? To hang on display like a damned pirate martyr?" I slammed a fist onto the platform, unleashing the rage in my voice. "I should have kept you in my bed. If it was death you wanted, I would've sent you there myself, stiff and hard, with a smile upon your face!"

"That's enough." Reynolds hooked an arm around my waist and dragged me into a dark alcove. "What, pray tell, was that all about?"

"We never exchange goodbyes." I pushed him away and composed myself. "We exchange insults."

He leaned around me, scrutinized the quiet road through Gallows Point, and turned back. "You and Charles Vane were lovers?"

"Not *lovers*. I gave him my maidenhood. He was a gentleman about it. Waited until I was sixteen before he stripped me from stem to stern and made me bleed."

His eyes hardened, and a muscle ticked in his jaw.

"Don't be offended on my account." I patted his rigid arm. "I enjoyed it far too much, and we remained dear friends after."

"Friends, you say?" He cleared his throat. "Even when you seized *Jade* from him?"

"She's my ship, Reynolds. When my father died, I was only fourteen and needed Charles to command her. But even then, she was my ship. Until the day she sinks. No matter who captains her."

"We should return to her now."

With a nod, I exited the alcove and made my way toward the tavern at the edge of Port Royal. My faithful crew of miscreants would be stirring up mischief with their bellies swimming with ale.

Reynolds trailed at a distance as to not draw attention to me. This wasn't Boston or St. Augustine, where the streets overflowed with English soldiers. But the governor of Jamaica was known for his terror against my kind. His men hunted and hanged pirates with ruthless enthusiasm.

Up ahead, light spilled from an open doorway, illuminating the dirt road between the buildings. Boisterous laughter and the off-tune clanging of a piano announced the merriment of hard-drinking patrons.

I stuck to the deepest shadows and slipped behind a wagon that sat across the road from the tavern. Peering around bags of grain, I had a direct view of the activity within.

The structure was a story and a half high with bedrooms on the upper floor. The ground level connected to the buildings on either side and served as an inn, trading post, courtroom, and post office.

But tonight, its only purpose was entertainment.

Customers shouted, and tavern wenches heckled back, sloshing quarts of ale and trading coins. The tables overflowed with all manner of freeborn life, from lords and navy sailors to scoundrels and doxies.

I marked the familiar faces of my crew. Most of them bewhiskered and unkempt, they clustered around the bar and pawed at the courtesans like a legion of grinning, belching, rough-talking demons.

A smile pulled at the corner of my mouth. I'd kept them at sea too long. Six months on this last stretch. They needed this. They'd *earned* it.

So had I.

From my hiding spot across the street, several strangers caught my eye. Roguish, virile young men, who would eagerly spend a few sweaty hours with a flamboyantly dressed woman.

I glanced down at the round flesh that threatened to spill over my bodice. Perhaps I was pretty enough, but I knew naught how to flirt or seduce. It had been two years since I'd tried.

Two years since I'd been kissed, touched, or brought to the acme of pleasure by a skilled hand.

The last time I'd succumbed to the spell of a man's charm, it ended in devastating agony. A tragedy I should have avoided but now credited as a necessary life lesson. The next time I fall into someone's bed—no matter how clever, potent, or irresistibly handsome he might be—I would not involve my heart. Never again.

A blond sailor stepped into my line of sight, lingering just inside the tavern. His eyes glimmered in the overhead candlelight as he watched the crowd and sipped his drink. There was an innocence about him, a harmless curiosity in his expression. Perhaps it would be easy to fuck him with no recoil or attachment after.

Footsteps advanced, and Reynolds appeared at my side, ducking his tall frame behind the wagon.

"Your crewmates are enjoying themselves." I kept my gaze on the blond man, imagining the feel of his lean body moving against mine. "We should stay a few more hours. I could use a drink." *And a dark corner with an attractive sailor.*

"There's a flush upon your neck, Captain."

I cupped my hand there and ground my teeth.

"I know what beckons you, and it isn't ale." His voice lowered, hesitant yet assertive. "I would help you with that. We could return to the ship, set her a-sail, and I would come to your cabin and provide what you need. It's safer than what you're considering here, with a stranger."

"I appreciate your concern—"

"You're not the only one who goes without. It's been too long since I indulged in a woman's favors."

Because he never left my side.

Overprotective idiot.

Exceptional quartermaster.

"Go indulge, then." I gestured toward the tavern. "I'm not stopping you."

"I won't leave you out here unguarded."

I expelled a sigh. "What do you need? Five minutes? Ten? If it's been as long as you say—"

"With you, I would take my time and tease it out. Every lick." His eyes remained fixed on the perimeter, even as his voice turned to gravel. "Every bite. Every stroke. I would make it last long after eight bells of the mid watch."

Sea of Ruin

Heat rolled through me, arousing a quiver in my thighs. It was potent enough to silence the objection on my lips, to make me pause and actually consider his offer.

Meddling with a quartermaster wasn't the worst idea. I was Charles Vane's first mate when he bedded me. I could give Reynolds the same thing I gave Charles. A few blissful hours. Nothing more.

But my quartermaster wasn't cut from the same cloth as Charles. Intimacy would make him possessive and even more attached than he already was. I couldn't abide that, and not just because I was emotionally incapable of reciprocating. Our friendship was complicated for reasons neither of us was willing to discuss.

"The answer is no, and you know why." I nodded at the tavern. "There are some dashing ladies in there waiting to be corrupted by a seductive blackguard. While you're doing that, I'm going to find a quiet place to sit inside. The crew will keep an eye out."

I didn't wait for a response as I breezed around the wagon and strode into the tavern.

The aroma of ale and tobacco teased my nose, and the cacophony of drunken voices smothered my thoughts. The crowd packed in around me, shoulder to shoulder, and my shorter-than-average stature made it easy to slip between the bodies unnoticed.

With a peek over my shoulder, I located Reynolds. He stood taller than the tallest man, the unruly stripe of hair on his head identifiable over the masses as he made his way toward the bar.

I moved in the opposite direction, keeping my chin down and senses sharp. Garments were the best indicators of trouble. I avoided clusters of uniforms and gravitated toward gowns similar to mine, blending in with the wives of thirsty gentlemen.

At length, I worked my way through the tavern and felt reasonably confident no one recognized me. Standing amid a herd of well-dressed patrons, I listened to dull conversations about English politics and the woes of sea voyage.

Just as I began to relax, an ominous sensation moved through me. My shoulder blades twitched. A feverish chill bathed my back, and the hairs on my arms stood straight up.

"Found you." The dark purr rasped against my nape and reached into the blackest part of my soul.

That growly, toe-curling Welsh accent had haunted my dreams for two years.

Ice-cold fear shivered down my spine, and I spun, bumping into the occupied chairs at a nearby table.

"Forgive me," I muttered and turned away from the glares, searching the throngs for the owner of that voice.

My pulse slammed through my veins as I examined every face, pushing through the crowds, listening for him, and losing my mind.

I must have conjured him out of paranoia. He couldn't have found me. How would he even know I was in Jamaica?

A gust of realization stole from my lungs.

Every pirate alive would've learned about Charles Vane's capture, and the pirate I hated most knew exactly what Charles meant to me.

Nausea like I'd never felt at sea surged through my body. Urgency moved my legs. I flattened a hand against my stomach and shoved my way toward the exit.

Then I saw him.

In the dark corner of the tavern sprawled the king of libertines. His face angled away, but I knew that forked tongue. It had stroked every inch of my skin under a veil of lies, breathing promises that had coiled around my heart and crushed me bit by broken bit.

Priest Farrell.

Notoriously known as the *Feral Priest,* his moniker was whispered with more fear and reverence than of those who'd ruled the high seas with my father.

I couldn't see his expression, but that profile was etched permanently in memory. Straight nose, strong jaw, and a dark sweep of lashes over captivating gray eyes that could drill into the deepest, most private places of a woman's being.

He wore a shadow of stubble on his face and the sides of his head. Strings of beads, thin braids, and long twisted locks wove through the silken mane of brown hair on top, all of which scraped back into a handsome queue.

His given name, Priest, wasn't what it implied. Surrounded by lewdly dressed women, he was as ungodly and rakish as the doxies who draped their breasts about his shoulders.

With a single look, he could make a proper, God-fearing lady wet between her thighs. His unchristian temper was negligible once a woman set her gaze upon him. There was no man alive who could compete with the well-thewed musculature of his physique or the perfectly sculpted masculinity that shaped his features. He radiated godlike beauty, and he knew it.

When I'd fallen for him, it had happened hard and fast. I'd been as

Sea of Ruin

weak then as I was now. It physically hurt to be this close to him.

With my breath stuck in my throat, I backed into the crowd until the press of bodies engulfed my view. Fear ruled my heart rate, and self-preservation kept me moving.

Countless men sought to capture me, but Priest's pursuit was personal.

He'd been hunting me for two years.

My pulse raced as I hurried toward the exit. A few paces from the door, I caught sight of my master gunner, Chops, who was named after the full sideburns that swallowed his narrow face.

I swept past him, pausing long enough to whisper, "We're weighing anchor. Gather the others, or I'll leave without them. Where's Reynolds?"

"Outside." He rose from the chair without question, responding to my urgent command just as he would on the ship.

I dashed out the door and found Reynolds leaning against the building with his lips fastened to the neck of a pretty blond girl.

Damn me to hell, my timing was horrible.

He lifted his gaze, sensing me instantly.

"He's here," I mouthed and took off.

I didn't need to elaborate. The pounding of his footsteps caught up and stayed with me through the town, past the tents on the beach, and down the long stretch of the pier.

"Did he see you?" He gripped my arm, halting me at the first jolly boat.

Found you.

"Yes." With a shiver, I peered out at the dark sea, wishing I could see *Jade* on the black horizon. "He's toying with me."

He released my arm and turned toward the moonlit shore. "I'll kill him."

"No." My chest tightened. "My edict on that hasn't changed."

No matter how much I detested Priest, I wouldn't survive his death.

"Very well." He untied the boat tethers. "Get in. We're not waiting for the crew. They can cram into the second jolly boat when they catch up."

My hands trembled as I patted my hidden dimity pockets. My fingers found the hilt of my dagger, but my other pocket was empty.

Empty. Empty. Empty.

A gasp strangled in my chest. "My compass. It's missing."

"God's blood, Bennett. How?"

He knew it had belonged to my father and that I treasured it above all else. But he didn't know it was the only map in existence that led to Edric Sharp's infamous treasure. I'd only ever told two people. Charles was dead, and that left…

"Priest." My stomach sank. "In the tavern, he sneaked up on me from behind. He must have taken it then."

"We're leaving without it." Reynolds grasped my waist and moved to lift me into the boat.

"No!" I pushed back and planted my feet onto the pier. "Release me at once!"

He jerked his hands back with a growl. "I overstepped."

"Yes, you—"

Footsteps sounded behind me, the tread of a single pair of boots approaching from the shore.

Beads of sweat trickled between my breasts and gathered beneath the stays. I knew that lazy, arrogant gait. I feared it.

So did Reynolds.

"Get in the boat." He removed the cutlass from the sash at his hips. "Please, Captain."

Fastened on the shore, his eyes confirmed who was coming, and a war waged across his savage expression.

"I'm not leaving without my compass." Pushing back my shoulders, I girded my spine and turned to face my biggest mistake.

A few paces away, the pirate leaned against a wooden post. His thumb hooked casually in the straps of leather that wound around his trim hips. His other hand hung at his side, dangling my compass by the chain.

Rancor battled longing. Scorn collided with sadness, and my outrage bowed beneath the helpless, banal attraction I'd always felt for him.

His brown breeches fit him like a glove, the threads molding around powerful thighs and the sizable bulge of his groin. His loose shirt tucked into multiple belts at his waist and laced up his chest to open at the neck. A strong neck, covered in scruff and sinew.

I swallowed thickly, my entire body pulsing with an unwanted ache as my gaze rose to his.

Eyes glinting like polished steel glared down at me. Moonlight cast his prominent features in stark relief—stern forehead, defined cheekbones, perfect nose, full lips—leaving the rest of his face in shadow. The severe straight line of his mouth amplified the intensity in his expression.

Sea of Ruin

He was furious. Seething with two years' worth of blistering, unresolved ire.

My heart died a thousand deaths before I found my voice. "Priest."

"Bennett, my love." He spilled the endearment into the air, each syllable a vicious growl of torment. "How I've missed my beautiful, infuriating wife."

Seven

Three years ago, a confident, sexually charged, uncommonly handsome pirate strolled onto my ship. Little did I know, his sinful gray eyes and traitorous mouth would twist my entire world wrong-side-out.

Priest had joined my crew with Reynolds, who was looking for work. But Priest had a different agenda.

He was on the prowl for his next conquest.

Within a fortnight, I found myself pinned beneath his thrusts in my cabin, screaming, writhing, delirious in the throes of the most profound, erotic, and emotionally penetrating coupling of my life.

The raw, uninhibited magic I'd felt with him hadn't been one-sided. Entangled in sweaty limbs, stripped to the skin, and deeper still—deep enough to expose our hearts—we were buried so far inside each other there would be no unraveling.

What began as an unstoppable explosion of passion forged into something pivotal, essential, and *more*.

We'd become addicted to each other. Insatiable. Inseparable. We couldn't keep our clothes on, our hands to ourselves, or our hearts closed off. It had happened so suddenly it knocked us off our feet and fundamentally changed us.

How quickly I'd trusted him with my secrets and my future. Even more shocking was the intoxicating intensity in which the hedonistic king of libertines had returned my love. It was widely known that his cock had been under more skirts than a dressmaker's needle.

But not once did I try to trap him or tie him down with marriage. He was the one who demanded commitment and monogamy while swearing off his profligate lifestyle.

I just want you, he'd said. *Only you.*

I'd believed him, joyously and blindly.

A year after we met, we'd made it official and exchanged matrimonial vows aboard *Jade*.

Since my love for him was my greatest liability, we kept our marriage hidden. Outside of Reynolds and a few other loyal members of my crew, no one knew.

In Charleston, I was Benedicta Leighton, granddaughter of the ninth Earl Leighton.

Everywhere else, I was Bennett Sharp, daughter of the notorious Pirate Edric Sharp.

The only living person who knew Benedicta and Bennett were one and the same was my husband.

He knew everything about me.

Every.

Vulnerable.

Weakness.

Exposing our relationship would've made both of us susceptible. Then *and* now. Didn't matter that I no longer looked at Priest through the lens of blind love. If he were captured by an enemy and tortured as a means to control me, I would surrender to any demand.

Pathetic, wasn't it? He'd hurt me in the worst way possible, and I would still exchange my life for his.

Even more pathetic, I'd gone as far as amending the Articles drawn up by my crew on board *Jade* to include: *If any man shall harm Priest Farrell, whether in aggression or defense, that man shall be marroon'd or shot.*

I stood by that code today. If he died, it wouldn't be on my watch. I would protect him at all costs.

There was a time when I was certain he would die for me, too. But that was before.

Before he betrayed me.

"Have you broken our agreement?" A hot prick of resentment smarted at the base of my throat. "How many know we're married?"

"I told no one. But I would've announced it to the world if it had aided my search for you." He set the compass into a lazy spin on the chain, taunting me with it. "Turns out, I only had to wait for Charles Vane to hang."

Sea of Ruin

My chest tightened. "Go to hell."

"Been there since the day you left me in Nassau." His expression contorted with fury as he stretched out his arms. "I have nothing left, my love. You must know I've exhausted every resource at my disposal, coin in my purse, and tarnal breath in my body pursuing you."

Irrational guilt tried to surface, but I shoved it down. "What about the breaths you dribbled upon the bosoms of tavern wenches? Were those for me, too?"

"Yes."

"You're a despicable liar. The biggest scoundrel of them all."

"You're angry." His silver eyes flared in the moonlight. "You're not alone in that."

Reynolds remained quiet and vigilant at my side. He would guard me with his life, but he couldn't protect me from Priest. The damage my husband inflicted on me was never delivered with steel or gunpowder.

"End this marriage." I straightened my spine. "Let me go, and you can have the compass."

I didn't mean it. Relinquishing my father's gift would've been worse than losing a limb. I wouldn't give it up without a fight.

"I already have the compass." He twirled the instrument beside his leg. "As for you, I'm incapable of letting go."

The instant I'd heard his Welsh lilt in the tavern, I knew it would come to this. He wanted me for reasons I couldn't fathom, but none of those reasons mattered. Not after what he'd done to me.

Evading him for two years had been sheer luck, and now my luck had run out. The only way to escape him was to kill him.

Might as well run a sword through my own heart.

I couldn't do it.

His gaze stayed on mine, and somewhere in that cruel scowl, he knew.

He knew I still loved him.

But if he thought we could pick up where we left off, he was out of his mind. Did he think that after the lies and infidelity, I would graciously forgive him? That I would welcome him back into my bed?

As if he gave a damn what I wanted. Priest Farrell took, plundered, and raided for his own enjoyment. He was a cold-blooded pirate who acted without moral restraint or conscience, especially when it came to his primitive desires.

"Where's your ship?" I glanced at the shore behind him,

unsurprised to find him alone. "No crew?"

"I released them this morning when I located you. Gave them the ship as a parting gift."

Cold, silent dread filled my stomach, solidifying what I'd already surmised.

He had every intention of coming with me. And why not? His loyalties lay with no one and nothing. He was a lone sea wolf, bouncing from ship to stolen ship, seizing and discarding without attachment to the crews or the vessels he captured.

He meant to treat me with the same callousness.

Again.

"Return the compass." I held out my hand, knowing damn well he wouldn't surrender his only insurance.

"Not until we're aboard *Jade*." His mouth curved up at the corner, and his tongue caught the crease with a teasing lick, as his gaze descended to the bodice of my gown. "Once I remove that garish travesty from your body with my teeth, I'll reacquaint myself with what *lawfully* belongs to me. Then I'll return your precious compass."

My nipples hardened in memory of his fastidious touch, and my pulse fluttered angrily in my throat. "The devil fetch you, you rotten, unfaithful bastard."

"Your temper still makes me hard." The velvet darkness of his voice curled beneath my rage. "Not an inch of your satiny skin will go unmarked before I'm hilt-deep inside you again."

Reynolds leaped in front of me and thrust out his cutlass. "You lost the privilege to touch her."

"Watch yourself, Reynolds." Priest slipped a dagger from his belt and picked his fingernail with it. "I'd hate to kill you. You're like a brother to me."

"I *am* your brother, you bleeding cunt."

"By half. God knows I have enough of those to fill a galleon."

"Because your mother was a whore with the sores of syphilis dangling about her stretched lips."

Priest closed his eyes and went preternaturally still. The air cracked on the next breath, and they lunged at the same time. But I was braced for it, already jumping between them with my arms outstretched.

"Enough." With a hand on each marble-hard chest, I shoved them apart. "By my account, both of your mothers were whores, and your father was no better, seeing as he tried to kill his only sons."

"Just so." Reynolds stepped away from my touch. "We *were* pirating his ship."

Stealing from their own father. It had been Priest's idea, and Reynolds and I had gone along with it. I almost lost them both that day, but in the end, the battle had turned in our favor. It had been my sword on which their father fell.

"I saved both your backsides, remember?" I shoved them farther apart, keeping an eye on Priest, as my hand tangled in the laces of his shirt.

I should have pulled away, but it had been too long. Two years too long. I felt that separation in the pads of my fingers as they slid across familiar ridges of hot muscle, basking in his masculine strength. Fearing it.

His nostrils widened, and he leaned in, pushing against my palm, testing my courage.

In the blackness of night, my senses sought the tempo of his heart, which pounded as furiously as my own. "Don't come any closer."

One touch would be my undoing. I could barely breathe in his presence.

His jaw set, and the lonely gap between us swelled with years of contempt and distrust. If I allowed him aboard my ship, in my cabin, I courted a harrowing outcome. He would seize the last of my determination, my dignity, until there was nothing left worth salvaging.

Unless I turned the tables and gave him a dose of his own deception.

I relaxed my fingers in his shirt and let him press into my space. He didn't hesitate to crowd in, dipping his head and placing his words against my throat.

"We need to go." He bit my neck, his teeth sinking fast and deep, making me whimper. "We have company."

I jerked back, slapping a hand over the hurt as I searched the pier behind him.

Sure enough, silhouettes emerged from the shadows on the shore and strode in our direction. Moonlight illuminated their uniforms, and my pulse took flight.

Priest and I were wanted for murder and piracy and would be hanged if those men recognized us. Priest wasn't even wearing a disguise, but his face didn't show a trace of concern. On the contrary, the abyss in his eyes pledged to slay anyone who tried to interfere with his plans for me.

I spun toward the jolly boat while keeping the compass in my periphery. Staying alive was more important than a sentimental trinket, but I desperately needed both.

As Priest moved to leap into the boat, I swiped at the compass. He caught my wrist, yanked me against his solid frame, and pulled me down with him.

We landed against the stern, and my descent lacked all the grace of his. I stumbled back, stubbornly blocking his attempt to catch me. My backside hit the middle seat, and my feet went up, giving him an indecent view beneath my skirts.

Damnation!

Frantically putting myself back in order, I waited for a licentious comment. Thankfully, he spared me that, but there was no escape from his smoldering gaze.

Those hooded gunmetal eyes knew how to seduce a woman without words, pleasure her without touch, and make her feel like she was the center of his entire universe. He did all of that now. With a millisecond look.

My blood pounded, and my insides quivered as hunger spiraled through me, making it impossible to focus, to plan, to reason, only to crave the ecstasy I knew he could give me.

But I wasn't his one and only.

How many women had he fucked over the past two years? How many times had he panted *I love you* into someone else's ear?

God damn him, it hurt. The pain was never-ending, festering inside me and wringing my emotions into something ugly, vile, and unrecognizable.

I could never be with him again. Never trust him again. Hell, if I were even half the fierce pirate captain the stories claimed, I would torture him to the point of death, heal his wounds, and torture him again.

Another thing I could never do. But I did have a plan for him and would see it through before the night's end.

Footsteps sounded on the pier near the shore, announcing the approach of the governor's men.

I held my breath and gripped the side of the rocking boat as Reynolds jumped in behind me. I didn't have to look at my quartermaster's face to glean his thoughts about our unwanted passenger. His silence roared against my back, making me shiver.

Without a word, Reynolds stabbed the oars into the water and shoved us out to sea.

Sea of Ruin

To *Jade*.

My home and refuge.

I knew every cable, spar, and inch of canvas she carried. Every day I toiled as hard as her hardest-working crew member, proving I deserved to be her captain. After commanding her through years of cruises, with prizes and booty to show for it, I'd more than earned my position among the crew and thereby their respect.

Priest's return to *Jade* jeopardized everything. He cared more about satisfying the urges between his legs than the common good of my ship and her mates.

The one-hundred-and-twenty-man crew was always spoiling for a fight. That worked to my advantage as long as the fight wasn't against me. But if Priest undermined, manhandled, or challenged me in front of them, I would appear weak.

A weak captain fell in disfavor, and a democratic crew wouldn't hesitate to rid themselves of the weakness and vote in a new leader.

Rallying that kind of mutiny was my husband's specialty.

Through cunning, charisma, and clever language, he knew how to talk his way onto a ship, inspire the crew into throwing their captain overboard, and coerce them into voting himself in as the ultimate authority. Once he grew bored with his conquest, he moved on to the next one.

Three years ago, he boarded *Jade* intending to do exactly that.

Then he met me.

Somewhere between his shameless flirting beneath the ratlines and my orgasmic gasps to God against my cabin door, he decided he was more interested in my body. And my heart. Both of which he consumed, betrayed, and irretrievably lost.

Now he was back to reclaim and repeat.

I would let him believe he won, let him get physically close enough to lower his guard. Then I would clap him in irons and throw him in the hold.

As Reynolds rowed us into the shrouded safety of the sea, Priest's steady gaze never strayed. He watched me with the focus of a hunter, heating my blood and affecting its flow through my veins.

"I'm sorry about Charles Vane." Deep, predatory, and unapologetically lustful, his voice purred across my skin.

That voice, by Christ. It caressed me in places I gave no license to touch, and that enraged me beyond reason.

"You're not sorry." I flexed my hands, my breaths seething. "You knew I would come out of hiding for Charles and jumped at the chance to use my grief for your own gain."

"I'm resourceful." He wet his lips. "And truly, I regret the way Charles died. I would've preferred to execute him myself."

He'd always despised my relationship with Charles, specifically the part where I gave Charles my virginity.

Priest's jealousy had no restraint or shortage of skill with a cutlass. As several maimed men had discovered, anyone who touched me without Priest's consent lost their hands, their tongues, and the flesh between their legs.

There was a time when I found comfort in his savage overprotectiveness. But now I saw it for what it was.

Mad hypocrisy.

While Priest didn't allow anyone near me, he didn't apply that rule to himself and the random doxies who stirred his lust. He loved women. He loved to fuck, and I was under no illusion about what he'd been doing the past two years. Imagining it prickled heat behind my eyes and spread poison through my gut.

"I hate you." My broken whisper exposed too much. Too much pain. I gave him too much power to hurt me.

"I'll rectify that." He sprawled on the seat across from me and stretched out his legs, flanking mine. "When I kiss you, undress you, and lick you…here…" He hooked his boot between my legs and pressed the toe against the juncture of my thighs. "I'll remind you why you married me."

"Your cock isn't the reason I married you. It's the reason I left you. Because you liked to put it inside other people." I shoved his boot away, but my fingers clung to the worn leather.

Familiar leather. Black and soft and creased with heavy use, it wasn't just any pair of jackboots. Seven years ago, they were left on a beach by a pirate who died wearing deerskin moccasins.

"It sickens me that I gave you these." A clamp squeezed around my heart, and I closed my eyes against the anguish. "You're not at all the man I thought you were."

"Perhaps not. But no man will ever live up to the ideal you hold for Edric Sharp." He slowly pulled his foot from my grip and softened his voice. "I treasure these boots. For two years, they were all I had of you. For that, I don't regret keeping them."

His words hit their mark, burrowing beneath my ribs. Would the pain ever stop? It wasn't supposed to end this way. *He* had done this to us.

I breathed carefully through my nose, trying to silence the agony he so expertly ran through me.

But Reynolds had heard enough, given the threatening growl in his voice. "If you loved her, you'd leave her be."

"That weak mentality is precisely why you're still alone." Priest wedged my compass into the waistband of his breeches and scrutinized his brother. "Still pining after my wife, I see. You've had two years to stake your claim. How many times did you attempt to warm her bed in my absence?"

The oar smacked the water behind me, and Reynolds surged to his feet, jostling the boat.

"Don't answer that." I gripped Reynold's arm, holding him back until he sat and resumed rowing.

"He doesn't have to answer." Intelligence glinted in Priest's bladed eyes. "Had he claimed you, he would've killed me before I stepped onto this boat, your rules be damned." He slanted forward, resting an arm on his knee. "Had he claimed you, I would've—"

"Mutilated and castrated him. I haven't forgotten your threats." I bent in, leaving a sliver of space between us. "Give me the names of everyone you bedded since we married. It's time I follow your practices and collect some body parts of my own. It's only fair."

His mouth flattened into a severe line, and he leaned back. Effectively silenced. And there he remained until we reached *Jade*.

With my compass fastened to the leather straps around his waist and secured beneath his breeches, I had no choice but to follow him up the ladder and onto the deck with Reynolds at my heels.

The majority of the crew had gone ashore to debauch in the town for a few hours. But my most loyal men remained on board to defend *Jade* against anyone who might attack her. These seamen didn't just know my husband. They had attended our nuptials and been his closest friends.

Priest rested a possessive hand on my lower back and escorted me past the boatswain, pilot, surgeon, carpenter, and a dozen other concerned faces. They all knew he'd betrayed me. They knew I'd been running from him ever since. I would only need to give them a signal, and they would charge him with weapons raised. He would fight back. Some of them would die. He would be injured, possibly killed, as well.

There was a better way to deal with this.

Judgment and distrust wafted from them as we walked by. Priest's presence wasn't just horribly belittling. It was openly belittling as he marched me across my own ship with nothing more than a hand on my back.

I pushed him away and squared my shoulders.

No captain could ever be certain of her command or crew. If I didn't prove to them by the morrow that I had this under control, I would lose their allegiance. And possibly my ship.

Without a nod, glance, or so much as a twitch in their direction, Priest led me toward the companionway that descended toward my cabin. I focused on keeping distance between us and many steps ahead, as if I were the one steering this madness.

Trailing behind, Reynolds barked orders to set sail the moment the remaining crew boarded.

At the threshold to my quarters, I glanced back, casting Reynolds a warning look. One that demanded he not interrupt until I called for him.

"Run along," Priest said to his brother. "Unless you prefer to watch."

I shook my head at Reynolds as he bared his teeth and released a menacing sound.

Undeterred, Priest shoved me into the cabin and kicked the door shut behind him with a rattling bang.

Eight

"Two years." Priest prowled toward me, unleashing the force of his temper with a soul-shivering roar. "You are my wife!"

I flinched at the violence in his voice and swept around the desk in my private chamber, putting the heavy furniture between us.

Rather than chase me, he listed over dishware and maps on the scarred surface, using the long reach of his fist to ensnare the neckline of my bodice.

"So help me God." He hauled me right up to his icy gray eyes. "I'm going to bloody your arse for the hell you put me through."

"The hell *I* put you through?" My hackles rippled. "*You* betrayed *me*!"

A lantern glowed beside him, casting his expression in terrifying relief. He was all menace, vibrating rage, and man.

Predator.

His grip tightened on my bodice as his fingers tunneled into the valley of my breasts. My feet scrambled backward, but my body held fast, restrained by that large, callused, invasive hand.

The heat of it made my breath hobble, injecting an edge of thrill into the fear. The scent seeping off him was every bit the sun and sea, hot and male, leather and sin, everything I remembered and more, scrambling my senses. Disarming me.

And those unremitting iridescent eyes... Never in my life had anyone looked at me with such ardent concentration. It unnerved me.

It aroused me. I lowered my gaze, evading the dark, dangerous, masculine beauty that caved in my lungs.

"Two years without you." He pounded his free hand on the desk, nearly toppling the lantern. "You punished me for two unbearable years." Yanking me closer, he gave me a hard shake. "Dammit. Look at me!"

Livid heat radiated off layers of muscle and seething brawn, dissolving my strength of will.

I lifted my gaze to his.

"I love you." His brittle whisper barely penetrated the sound of blood beating in my head.

Outrage thrashed through me. Outrage and pain. All I could see was him clinging to another woman the same way he held me, whispering the same three words with the same arresting passion.

It put my life in perspective. A life that must continue without him, no matter how badly it hurt.

With a calm resolve that made me proud, I opened the desk drawer at my hip and removed a worn, heavily creased vellum letter.

"Do you love me as much as you love her?" I set the paper on the desk between us, turning it so he could read the bold, elegant scrawl.

He stared at it, refusing to answer, as his expression twisted with recognition and grief. His eyes darted over the words, and his hand fell from my gown to trace the handwriting.

"My dearest Priest…" I lowered into the desk chair and recited the opening from memory. "Last night, I didn't just welcome you into my body. I let you into my heart. Again."

My voice quivered, and I closed my eyes against the anguished look on his face.

To hell with his anguish.

A week after we became husband and wife, he sneaked out of our bed and left the room we'd rented in Nassau. Early the next morning, he returned, saying he hadn't been able to sleep. Given his pallid, disheveled appearance, I thought he was ill.

Until I found the letter in his discarded trousers.

I'd memorized every painful word over the past two years.

His gaze remained fixed on his lover's words, his demeanor darkening, as he read in silence what I recited in my head.

My dearest Priest,
Last night, I didn't just welcome you into my body. I let you into my heart.

Sea of Ruin

Again. I won't call it a mistake. Never that. But it was desperate. A wildly pleasurable, terribly desperate moment of weakness.

I should have waited until you woke to say this in person. But we both know I cannot deny you. Not face to face when you look at me the way you do, with a love so intense I think you might die from it.

So I shall pen this clearly and with a coward's heart.

We cannot see each other again.

No more stolen nights. No more sneaking around. No more risking our lives to be together. My family, my obligations, my very existence put you in danger, just as yours threatens everything I've accomplished.

I cherish every trice we had over the years. Not just the orgasms, but the friendship we shared. The familiarity. The laughter. The sorrow.

The passion.

My love for you will endure, even though last night shall be our last.

It is my most devout hope that this ache will dull on both sides with time. Even so, in these final moments before I must leave, I realize I will be less happy, less honest, and less human without you.

I know I must let you go, and someday I will. But for now...

For now, respect my wishes.

Stay away. Move on. Find love.

Forgive me.

I must leave now before I give into the temptation to join you once again in bed. As I stare at you from across the room, I'll never forget this view of your flawlessly nude body sprawled across the tangled counterpane. Sated. Peaceful. Magnificent. I'll remember it well, knowing I put that tranquil expression on your handsome face if only for one more night.

May God watch over you and keep you safe, my heart.

No signature. No name to put with the words that so effectively destroyed my marriage.

When I'd confronted Priest about the letter that morning, he hadn't made excuses or denied the adultery. He'd been too distraught to form words. More distraught, it seemed, about his paramour leaving him than about his wife discovering the affair.

Upon that realization, I'd lost my ever-loving mind, screaming, throwing dishes, and demanding answers. But he'd only sat there, dazed and speechless, drowning himself in a bottle of rum. He drank so much, in fact, he didn't notice I'd left the room, boarded *Jade,* and fled Nassau without him. By the time he sobered, I was long gone.

To this day, the identity of his lover remained a mystery.

I suspected she was a titled lady of breeding, someone like my mother, who couldn't live beyond her dowry, her role in high society, and her obligation to marry a lord.

As a wanted criminal and son of a prostitute, Priest Farrell didn't stand a chance with a woman like that. He was lucky she'd given him her virtue. If that had even been the case. Maybe she was a widow.

"Who wrote the letter, Priest?" I reclined in the chair, draping a leg over the armrest in feigned indifference.

"I can't give you that." His fist curled, wadding the letter beneath it. "Don't ask me again."

He was still protecting her.

My molars ground together. "Does she know you had a wife?"

"Following our agreement, I've told no one about our marriage."

"If you followed our agreement, you wouldn't have rutted between every pair of legs in a skirt!"

"One person." His gaze shot to mine, igniting with the same ire that roughened his Welsh accent. "Since the moment I met you three years ago, there's only been you and one other."

That couldn't be true. Not that it mattered.

If I knew his lover's identity, maybe I wouldn't kill her. Perhaps I would just ruin her the same way my grandfather had ruined my mother.

Did that make *me* the villain?

Whomever this woman was, she loved Priest. Her letter said as much. And she'd met him before I had, which meant *I* was the other woman. A woman she didn't know existed.

He didn't just fuck her while he was married to me. He *loved* her, deeply and completely. That was the greatest, most destructive source of my torment.

I'd watched the devastation of his love bleed out around him the day she left him. He'd loved her long before he knew me and would've given her his life. But he wasn't good enough for her.

So he married me.

His second choice.

A consolation prize.

"If it was aristocratic breeding you wanted in your bed…" I met his eyes. "My lineage isn't lacking. My grandfather was an earl and—"

"Don't flatter yourself, madam." His disgusted tone scalded the air between us. "I don't give a damn about your noble blood."

Of course not. Priest Farrell wasn't motivated by power or money.

Sea of Ruin

His pursuits were carnal, drawn from the irrational, volatile, dark well of lust beneath his skin.

To be a recipient of such an all-consuming desire was every woman's dream. I'd lived that fantasy for a year, ignorantly, unknowingly sharing him with another.

I would've welcomed the thrust of a blade in my chest over the insufferable pain that crushed me from the inside out. If I could only let this go.

But I *had* let it go. At least, I'd been working on it quite successfully before tonight.

"Are you still together?" I shouldn't have cared. Caring prevented me from moving on.

"No." He glared at the crumpled letter in his fist. "That night in Nassau was the last time we made contact."

He was telling the truth, the agony in his voice undeniable.

I wanted to delight in his suffering and mock him with cruel laughter. But I felt his pain too deeply. I empathized with every bitter breath, self-destructive thought, and excruciatingly lonely night he'd endured.

Because I loved him. If I didn't, I wouldn't feel so scared and hurt. I wouldn't feel so compelled to lace my hand with his, pull him to me, and comfort him in his sadness.

Gripping the edge of the chair, I stopped myself from reaching out.

"It was a mistake." He stepped to the wall of windows behind me and stared out at the black sea. "The affair we had behind your back, the terrible pain I caused you... I regret it deeply."

"Your regret doesn't begin to compare to how I feel about our marriage."

His jaw flexed, and he shoved open a pane of glass, letting in the warm breeze.

"There's no one else, Bennett." He ripped up the letter and flung the pieces out the window. "I haven't been with anyone since I woke in an empty bed beside this cowardly note."

"You expect me to believe that *you*—a shameless rakehell much given to wenching, consorting with widows, and bilking maidens of their virtues—have been celibate for two years?" I gaped at him. "Because your lover left you?"

"I've been celibate for two years because my *wife* left me."

"Now I know you're lying."

"I don't give a damn if you believe me or not."

His responses confused me, which was probably his intent. What had I been thinking, bringing this woman-eating shark aboard my ship?

There were so many things I wanted to scream at him. Why did he marry me if he loved someone else? How long did he intend to carry on a clandestine relationship behind my back? Why was I not enough for him? Was I not pretty enough? Delicate enough? Demure enough? Did I not make him happy? What could I have done differently?

I swallowed every unhealthy, self-deprecating thought and focused on recovering my compass, which was hidden inside his snug breeches.

Those needed to come off.

One thing I knew about Priest… The quickest way to get him out of his clothes was to remove my own.

"Why are you here?" I stood and crossed the chamber to the built-in armoire, reaching behind me to loosen the ties on my bodice.

"You know why." His voice deepened, and his footsteps trailed after me, as expected.

"You want to fuck me."

"That's a given, but not nearly the heart of it."

"What, pray tell, could be the *heart* of your intentions, if not to wet your cock?"

"It's really quite simple. I want to take care of you."

"Oh, please." I yanked at the ties. "I've been doing that well enough on my own since I was fourteen."

"Here. Allow me." He rested a warm hand over mine against my spine.

Lowering my arms, I drew in a deep breath and let my plan play out.

A tug here, a gentle pull there, he knew his way around a woman's garments. But rather than freeing me from mine, he abandoned the task to caress my nape beneath the fallen wisps of my hair.

At that unexpected touch, a quiver hurried through me, and my heart shook, skipping over beats and rushing blood to my face.

My attraction to him terrified me, but if I kept my wits sharp, I could rid myself of this problem, once and for all.

The fingers on my neck made tight circles, pressing deeper into skin, rubbing sore muscles, and massaging out knots at the base of my skull. The strength in his hands was diabolical, the sensuality hypnotic. Only a demon could be so potent.

My mind numbed. My blood thickened, and my body grew heavy with warm languor. Masculine heat blanketed my back, and I breathed through it, maintaining a calm outward composure. Until he plucked a pin from the coiffure of curls on my head.

I closed my eyes in bliss as he slowly removed the remaining pins. The weight of sun-bleached tresses tumbled down, lock by lock, the descent of each spiral controlled by his hands, his indomitable will.

I ached for more affection, more comfort, and sighed as he teased me with it. Hands slid beneath the weight of my hair. Fingertips lingered in the dip between my shoulder blades. Knuckles glided along the curve of my neck. Palms ghosted over my trembling shoulders.

Lord have mercy, he excelled at torturing me.

"I wanted to do this the moment I saw you in the tavern." He ran his fingers through my waist-length hair, scraping trim nails across my scalp and coaxing a moan from my throat.

The torment continued in rhythmic strokes as he combed from roots to ends, taming my annoying spirals with more patience than any maid had ever shown me. He seemed content to do it, to just stand behind me, petting, untangling, and *smelling* my hair. His nose slid down my nape, over my shoulder, and across my back, scenting every inch within reach.

I failed to contain my raspy breaths, too far lost in the sublime pleasure of being touched by this man. My entire being reached toward him in anticipation of the next caress, and he gave it to me with startling tenderness.

When the last tangle pulled free, he gathered the weighty mass and rested it over my shoulder, out of the way. Cool air kissed my bare neck. Then the seductive, shivery heat of his breath.

"One of the many things I've missed," he said, feathering warm lips across my nape, "is falling asleep with your silken curls splayed across my chest. With your cheek against my heart. With your arms, your legs, every inch of your magnificent body hugging mine."

I missed that, too. Tremendously. And I despised myself for it.

His mouth trailed across my back, tracing the lines of my shoulders and spine. He took his time, doting upon every hollow and arch, kissing prickled skin, and fingering the top edge of the stays.

Continuing downward, he yanked at the laces, released a few more, and journeyed ever lower. Brazen fingers molded to the flare of my hips, clenching tight to curves that no man had touched since I'd met the Feral Priest.

Then, as promised, his teeth sank into the back of my gown and began an erotic assault on the satin, pulling at hooks, ripping through ribbon, and freeing me from the air-depriving restraints.

His breathing accelerated, and his hands dug into my waist, holding me immobile and recklessly affected. I was so distracted by the wreckage of his teeth and the sounds of his hunger I didn't notice he'd finished with the gown until it landed around my booted feet in a puddle of shredded fabric.

A thin ankle-length shift and matching ivory corset of quilted linen covered what remained of my modesty. The undergarments failed to confine everything, and as he turned me to face him, my chest spilled out, right into his greedy hands.

"Look at you." With a groan, he scooped up a breast in his huge palm, lifting it toward his mouth. "As stunning as I remembered. Irrationally beautiful."

His thumb flicked the nipple, and his lips covered the swell of pale flesh. I felt it everywhere. Hot breath. Velvet tongue. Torture.

Exactly as planned.

I would let him believe I was his again. Then I would strike.

He suckled my breast, nipping my nipple, licking, biting, and kissing with increasing aggression. I arched against his irresistible mouth, caught in the trap of his glinting silver stare. It seared my skin and zapped the air, leveling my insides like a hurricane.

I couldn't stop him from looking. Couldn't stop my body from throbbing in female delight. Couldn't stop myself from wanting him with every sinful thought in my head.

My hands went to his hair, gliding over the exotic adornments of beads and braids amid the thick brown strands that swept off his brow and caught in the back with a knot of leather.

With his mouth on my breast, I ran my nose along his temple, breathing in the masculine scent of his skin, the clean earthly fragrance of his scalp, and the dark distinctive essence of the only man who knew how to knock my knees out from under me.

"Priest." My body thrummed, grinding shamelessly against his.

"Bennett." He raised his head and bit my neck, my jaw, my face, my lips, scraping his teeth across my skin and devouring me without restraint.

With a hand on my nape, his other clutched my bottom, flexing and kneading with bold fingers, before sliding to the back of my thigh to hook my leg around his waist. Then he pulled me tight against him and kicked his hips, reintroducing me to the hardest part of him.

My brain frantically composed objections, but I could only vocalize a ragged moan. His touch transformed me into a willing victim. His kisses reduced me to a writhing creature in heat, desperate to reunite with her mate.

Nothing could deter me from indulging in the taut well-honed shape of his physique. I touched him through the shirt, tracing firm pectorals, trim hips, and slopes of bulging shoulders, biceps, and forearms. He was just as I remembered—built with dense power, carved from solid stone, and smoothed to godlike perfection.

When my hand caught the belts at his hip, he released me to remove the straps, sashes, and shirt, leaving his body bare from the waist up.

Lean muscle rippled across the inverted triangle of his torso. Lantern light glinted off smooth tawny skin, accentuating thick shoulders, defined arms, and deeply cut abs.

Christ almighty, he was gorgeous. Too immaculately designed. Too much man for one woman. I'd known that when I met him. I'd acknowledged the promise of heartbreak all over that divine face.

I'd mistakenly believed my heart was immune to it.

His grip returned to my jaw, angling it upward to expose the curve of my throat to his plundering mouth.

My breath fled as I flattened my palms on his chest, shuddering at the hard heat of him. His body was an effigy of chiseled art, an omnipotent sculpture to be coveted and revered. By the eternal God, I wanted to rub up against him, climb him like an animal, and ride him until I reached nirvana.

My plan didn't require me to fuck him. But dammit, what would be the harm? Would it be so bad to escape the loneliness for a little while? Just an hour or two of mindless bliss? I could still have him chained in the bilge by morning.

My body decided for me, rushing heat between my legs and spasming inner muscles. My hand moved on its own, slipping between us and gripping his swollen length through the thin breeches.

"God's blood." He groaned against my throat, and his teeth sank in, laying siege to delicate skin and nerve endings.

I curled my fingers around his girth and explored the thick shape of him, thrilling in the way he jerked and throbbed in my fist. "You feel positively feral, Mr. Farrell."

He choked on his next breath and lifted his head. "It's been two years, Mrs. Farrell."

Our eyes met, and it hurt to look at him. Hurt to feel him this hard and coiled with arousal. He was so insanely, potently attractive. His neck muscles tensed with need. Sculpted cheekbones sharpened with intensity, and full lips parted on a famished breath.

"I will not lose you again." He grabbed my throat and dove in for the kiss.

Nine

My pulse went wild as Priest slanted his mouth over mine, possessing me with ravenous audacity. The fury he'd carried aboard my ship disintegrated beneath his desire, and I melted with him, surrendering to the fire that burned so fiercely between us.

Sweet heaven, the way he dragged the flat of his tongue against mine, licking me, panting, and vibrating guttural noises across my lips… His loss of control was an aphrodisiac, driving my own heedless plunge from hatred to lust.

His hands wandered, and his kiss hungered, feeding on me with voracious, impatient strokes as if I embodied what he needed to survive. I wanted to give him what he sought. I ached to give him everything.

"Bennett." He growled and bit down on my bottom lip, sucking hard and humming deep in his chest.

Maybe I imagined the devotion in the fingers that caressed my back, but I didn't care if it wasn't real. He was holding me, kissing me, taking pleasure in being with me. His love and fidelity were all I'd ever wanted from him.

He fisted my shift, gathering it up my legs. Crisp air hit my wetness, and competent fingers slid up my bare thigh. Fingers that promised wicked pleasure. And pain. Years of it. Because they belonged to a cold-hearted philanderer.

An adulterous knave.

A cheater who would cheat again.

My mouth stopped moving against his, and my breathing fell into simmering stillness.

I was dancing with the devil, a master manipulator. He was so adept at reading people, reaping their weaknesses, and furtively using them to his own advantage that I wouldn't know what he was taking from me until it was gone.

Like the compass.

And my undivided focus on recovering it.

He leaned back and narrowed his eyes, marking the hard anger in mine.

I thought I could deceive him at his own game, but here I was, falling under his spell again, letting myself get swept away by the mysterious alchemy that bound us together. I wanted this man to the point of madness. His body. His love. I craved him with a recklessness that would cost me everything.

Oh, how I wished I could indulge in a night of bedplay, just once more, then toss him away after. He deserved no better. But my heart wasn't strong enough for copulation. Not with Priest.

I looked away and focused all thought on the goal. Without warning or so much as a glance in his direction, I made a swipe for the compass in his breeches.

He caught my hand and made a scolding sound. "Once I have you as my wife, in every way, you'll have the compass."

Of course, I knew it wouldn't be easy.

"No." With a hard push against his chest, I broke his hold and staggered backward.

The muscles in his jaw flexed, tensing with frustration. Then a determined gleam rose in his eyes, flickering like silver stars in the dangerous dark of night.

He would never force himself on me. He wouldn't have to. The look on his face glowed with chilling self-assurance. Because he knew.

He knew how easily he could seduce me, knew exactly how I liked to be touched, and the moment I slipped, he knew how to do things to my body that would splinter my mind and make me forget my own name.

"Don't touch me." I retreated until my backside bumped the desk. Meanwhile, my insides heated and tightened, silently screaming for him to finish what he started.

An ordinary predator would've prowled after me, rubbed up against my space, and unleashed an arsenal of seductive weapons to shatter my resolve. But Priest wasn't ordinary.

He hooked a thumb in his waistband and reclined against the wall at his back, lounging like a great cat as he managed, quite successfully, to touch every part of me without touching me at all.

I shivered. "What are you doing?"

"You're within eye-shot, which naturally requires that I do what any man would do in my position. I'm *looking*." His leonine gaze took a timeless stroll along my transparent undergarments, pausing on my throat, stroking my breasts and abdomen, and darkening on the apex of my thighs. "Although, most certainly, I'm not just any man. As your husband, it's my privilege to explore you with more than my eyes." He pulled in a long breath, flaring finely chiseled nostrils. "You're the most strikingly beautiful woman I've ever seen."

He was a rake. God only knew how many beautiful women he'd explored with more than just his eyes. I meant nothing to him.

"You disgrace the one person you vowed to love and call yourself a husband? A man?" I gave him a scathing look up and down. "I'm twice the man you are."

"You won't feel like a man in a moment when this distance between us starts to bore me."

I gripped the edge of the desk, needing more than three meters of separation. "I feel naught for you."

"The devil you don't. I know you're wet. That infernal ache between your thighs must be growing increasingly uncomfortable. I don't see why we can't commence with the part where I assuage that ache."

A gentleman wouldn't dare speak to a lady like that. But Priest had never censored his ill-bred language around me. Nor had he ever treated me like a craven fragile flower. The fact that he considered me his equal was one of the things I loved about him.

But it wasn't enough.

"You'll assuage nothing." My body—lustful thing that it was—trembled in disagreement. "You're a soulless bastard who keeps a wife on retainer while you chase something better. Two years later, you return to your backup plan, your second choice, and kiss her as if she's the only one you ever wanted. But you kiss them all like that, don't you? It's no wonder you want to hurry this along. What, with women waiting for you in every port, all those opportunities are beckoning. If you fuck your wife tonight, you could be inside another wet, warm body by the morrow."

"Wrong as usual." His gray eyes iced over, his beautiful voice a steel blade. "You're the only one. Second to none."

"Hmm. Where have I heard that? Oh! I know. Right here in this cabin. The night you asked me to wed you."

With all the hindsight of a woman scorned, I wanted to reach back through time and strangle the lovesick twat who said *I do* to the king of libertines. Had my mother been alive, she would've stopped me from making such a disgraceful mistake. Hell, my father wouldn't have even allowed a man with Priest's reputation anywhere near his daughter.

And there it was, the deep, sucking hole inside me, trying to drag me into its misery. I missed my parents with soul-bleeding agony. If only they were here now. I needed their counsel, their strength, their love.

"I made a promise to my father." I blinked back the tears before they formed and raised my chin. "If I ever married—"

"You promised him I would be a man of his fortitude and spirit. A man who loves you above all else. Only you. And we shall be blinded by our love for life and beyond the ends of the sea."

I snapped my mouth shut and stared at him in shock.

He remembered? How? It'd been so long since I'd whispered that promise into the warmth of our post-coital cuddle.

"You said those words the night Murphy finished your bed." He directed his gaze across the cabin, studying the ornate box bed that had been built into the wall.

Under Priest's orders, the carpenter, Murphy, spent weeks constructing and engraving a bed large enough to sleep a pirate captain and her lover.

The ubiquitous structure stood like a separate chamber in the wall, with its fanciful wood carvings, lavish trim, and rich, heavy curtains that fell over the opening, enclosing the massive bed on all sides. Woven straps supported a mattress that was generously stuffed with down and topped by linen sheets and wool blankets.

I would've never commissioned such a haughty luxury for myself. Murphy had better things to do than chisel decorative frippery. But it had been a gift from Priest, one he'd worked on right alongside the carpenter.

It had been our first night in the new bed. We had thoroughly broken in the mattress and fallen into a happy, sated embrace when I voiced the promise I'd made to my father.

The man who had held me so sweetly that night—the notoriously mercurial, hot-tempered Feral Priest—now watched me through a cloud of stormy thoughts. I knew an accusation was coming before his eyes narrowed into a condemning stare, causing my heart to catch.

"How many men have you taken to that bed?" The promise of brutality roughened his voice and altered his breathing.

I debated the best response, and my silence made it worse, further enraging him. Reddening his face. Whitening his knuckles. Visibly shaking him.

He was scared, if such a thing were possible.

As much as I wanted to crush him with claims of orgies and passionate affairs, I couldn't lie to him. It wouldn't get my compass back, and I refused to sink to that level of vindictiveness.

But the truth made me feel small and beaten.

My loneliness was only part of it. I'd been holding onto the residue of hope that he hadn't cheated, that it had all been a misunderstanding, which nursed my twisted need to remain faithful to him. Not to mention this sickening depth of love that hadn't faded after two years without him.

It all rose up in a wall of self-loathing, putting pressure on my chest and closing my throat. I could do nothing but gulp back the lump that tried to escape as a sob.

He didn't need to hear my answer. Comprehension softened his mean mouth. His shoulders fell with a shuddering exhale, and his gaze moved over me, not with its usual predatory gleam but in the assessing way of a concerned husband.

"If my heart was half as cold as yours," I said, holding his unblinking stare, "I would've sought comfort in the arms of another man."

"I wouldn't have blamed you if you had." He stepped toward me, his gait graceful and deadly. "Make no mistake. I would've hunted down every bastard who touched you and torn him limb from limb. But I'm…" His gaze warmed, and his fingers twitched at his sides. "I'm overwhelmingly, undeservedly relieved. You humble me."

There was nothing humble about him. His intimidating shadow fell over me, dwarfing everything in the room. Then his body closed in. Shirtless. Sculpted. Devastatingly handsome. Devastatingly dangerous. Just…devastating.

He was a feared man, a ruthless criminal, his very stance pulsing with power. But it wasn't his physical strength that made me want to run.

I forced myself to hold still, pinned between him and the desk and the thickly charged air around us.

He took forever to make his next move, and when he did, it was with his hands on my face, cupping my jaw, tilting my head back. He regarded me with long-lashed, languid, molten-metal eyes that glowed in the shadows.

"I'm sorry." His Welsh cadence was gloriously uneven as if the apology affected him more than me.

He wasn't one to hide his emotions. He wore them like a badge. Even now guilt furrowed his forehead. Regret sank into the down-turned corners of his lips. And there was something else. Something that made him look at me like he never had before.

"Don't you dare pity me." I turned my head, pulling away. "I'm not your victim."

"Pity? By God, Bennett, I *admire* you. I respect you, without reservation or design. I hold you on a damn gilded pedestal."

Words.

Lies.

Everything out of his mouth was a blasphemous ululation.

"If I wanted to fill my ears with shit, I'd dunk my head in the chamber pot." Clapping my gaze to his, I gave him my stoniest glare.

He glared back.

Unbending. Deadlocked. He wanted to entangle our future. I wanted to undo our past.

We stood at an impasse, a strait with no outlet that stretched heart beats. Fathoms. Leagues.

Timbers creaked around us. Footsteps groaned overhead. The rumbling of male laughter muffled the soft skittering of a nearby rat. And amid it all, the deep notes of Reynold's voice commanded the crew to set sail.

A moment later, the thunder of the anchor's great cable clanked through the hawseholes, and *Jade* heaved into motion.

Priest's shapely mouth curved up at one edge.

I went for the compass.

The instant my fingers pushed past his waistband, I felt brass. He jerked back, but I held on, yanking the instrument free as he broke away.

With a triumphant shout, I tucked the treasure safely behind my back and darted around the desk, watching him as carefully as he watched me.

He didn't chase. Didn't so much as flinch in anger or grimace in

Sea of Ruin

defeat.

His inaction might have put me at ease if the guilt hadn't remained in his expression. Remorse, apology, and again with the pity—it was all there in his luminous eyes.

Why was he looking at me like—?

Realization dumped ice water into my veins, and I swung the compass into view.

The instrument in my hand was the same size and shape as the one I cherished.

But this one wasn't mine.

Ten

"No." I shook my head and frantically scanned Priest's rigid stance, even as I knew the compass wasn't on him. "No, no, no—"

"Shhh." He held up his hands and took a cautious step forward. "Bennett, listen…"

"Where is it?" A roaring started in my ears, and my heart cracked in my chest. "Tell me!"

"It took me two years to find you, and right now that compass is the only thing stopping you from putting more years between us. I can't let you do that. You've given me no choice."

Fear and rage burst from my lungs in an earsplitting scream. "What have you done?"

"I'm doing this for *us*."

"You're a dead man!" I hurled the brass impostor at his despicable head.

"Calm down." He ducked, easily dodging it.

"Spineless dog!" I threw a porcelain platter, and it shattered on the wall behind him. "Heartless fiend!"

"Bennett…" He sidestepped another projectile plate, his reflexes like that of a serpent. Slippery. Venomous. Straight out of hell.

"Tell me where it is!" Blinding hysterics tunneled my vision, ravaging me from all corners and painting the room red. "Right now!"

"Can't do that, my love."

I grabbed a bottle of rum from the desk, preparing to fling it next.

But as my fingers closed around the glass neck, I remembered my plan.

My breathing tightened with determination. My muscles hardened with focused fury. Where I had compassion for him before, now there was none. I needed him to hurt.

"You know what that compass means to me." I lifted the rum, swilling it with a calm I didn't feel. "You wouldn't have left it in Jamaica."

"No."

"You didn't toss it into the sea."

"Never."

Breaking my heart was one thing, but he wouldn't destroy that gift from my father. He wouldn't be so cruel. I had to believe that.

Everything inside me relaxed. The compass was on the ship.

But where?

As my mind raced for answers, I straightened my corset, trying miserably to cover my breasts from his humiliating stare.

He knew this vessel from bow to stern. Every alcove and nook. Every shadow and hiding spot. No doubt he'd determined the best location for the compass the moment he'd swiped it in the tavern.

With sleight and quick-wittedness, he probably secreted it away on the upper deck when I wasn't looking. Or slipped it into a wall on his way down here. Or… I glanced around, deflating at the stockpiles of weapons, cocked hats, rolls of sea charts, maps, and random treasures that cluttered the cabin.

It could be anywhere.

Once I locked him in irons, I would launch an exhaustive search. I would rip up every plank. Empty every chest. Topple over every barrel. If it failed to turn up, I would resort to torture. The psychological kind.

I knew exactly how to break the iniquitous Feral Priest.

"So your plan was to hold my compass hostage. Well done." I tossed back another swallow of rum, choking on my own bitterness. "What happens next?"

"You're clouded by anger, far more than I am at the moment. Understandably so." He ambled to the bookcase, selected the smallest of my three hourglasses, and held it up. "This one measures fifteen minutes?"

"Ten minutes." I squinted at him, burning to punch his perfectly composed face.

"Good enough." He carried it to the bed and sat on the edge, testing the flow of sand between the glass globes. "We cannot have a

Sea of Ruin

fruitful conversation until we work out this tension between us."

"I will not—"

"Quiet!" The explosion of fury in his voice stopped my heart. Just as frightening was his ability to return to a placid tone. "Since you seem unwilling to abandon the discomfort beneath your skirt, I'll remedy that particular reluctance by offering an agreement."

I tightened my hand around the rum bottle—the weapon I would use to best him. "Go on."

"I'll give you pleasure, a worthwhile release, without the benefit of my own." His gaze softened. "I owe you that much."

A sting pricked my throat. Oh, how I loved and hated him. I focused on the latter. "I'll have no part of that indiscriminate member between your legs—"

"I'll use only this finger." He held up a long, thick digit. "If I fail to bring you over the edge before the sand runs out, I'll give you the location of the compass and debark at the first opportunity. You'll never see me again."

I didn't trust him. Not for a minute. "If you succeed?"

"If you come on my finger within the allotted time, I'll have your forgiveness."

"Really, Priest." I made a scoffing sound. "Never in the history of faithless husbands does a woman offer forgiveness at the crook of his finger."

"Very well. If I succeed, I'll have my position reinstated as the master gunner on this ship. I'll resume my role as your husband and *earn* your forgiveness."

"Chops is the master gunner."

"Chops can report to me. Or I can feed his innards to the gulls. I'm indifferent either way."

He set the sand clock on the mattress and folded his hands on his lap, regarding me with an expectant look. It wasn't hopeful expectancy. He *calculated* on me agreeing to this.

We both knew I would. And we both knew he would win.

Which was why I had no intention of playing by the rules.

I took another swill of rum and carried it with me to the bed. Stepping into the *V* of his spread knees, I planted my boots against the insides of his and steeled my nerves.

"So, my stunning, unmanageable, ever-vexing wife," he murmured, tiptoeing his gaze up my body to meet my eyes. "Shall we get on with it, then?"

I gave a deliberate pause, pretending indecision. "Do I have another option?"

"Hmm." He lifted my hand and kissed my fingers, his voice folding around me like nightshade—beautiful, exotic, deadly poisonous. "Perhaps I'll bend you over my knee like a bad little girl and leave us *both* aching for release."

"You owe me more than that."

"Quite so." His insidious stare taunted me over the fingers he held captive, his breath dipping into the valleys between each knuckle, teasing sensitive skin.

A shudder raked my body, puckering my nipples and unleashing hell on my focus. I ached for his touch, and my senses thickened with that need, sharpening and dulling in waves as I sought to control my reaction to him.

I knew what I needed to do. Anger would guide me. Ruthlessness would protect me. But the woman I'd once been—the wife, the lover, the sensual creature who craved affection—desperately wanted to postpone his pain.

And mine.

This was the last time I would be with my husband. I endeavored to savor it.

Hooking an arm around his broad shoulders, I held the bottle of rum against his back and straddled his lap. Then I pulled my fingers from his grip and allowed myself to touch him.

First, the soft brown hair that swept back from his forehead. Then the tender skin around silver eyes that watched me with unnerving patience. Then the blade-sharp cheekbones. The chiseled mouth that had caused me so much heartache. The wiry stubble that covered his jaw. A man's jaw. Square. Rough. Warm skin over bones forged from iron. He was majestic. Beastly. Regal. Peerless. Unreasonably handsome.

No one—not man or woman—could look at him without stealing another look, and another, until those glimpses carved themselves into memory and established the benchmark by which all beauty was measured.

"I hate that you're so good-looking." I roamed my free hand down his bare chest, marveling at the stone wall of muscle. "Your beauty was our ultimate detriment, you realize."

His gaze flickered to mine, open and distant at once. "Explain that."

"Would your lover have given you a second glance, let alone a lengthy affair, if your face looked like uncured leather? If your ribs pressed against skin or your smile bore rotten teeth?"

"I don't know." His expression blanked.

"How did you meet her?"

His eyes hardened, warning me not to mention her again. "What about you, Bennett? If I were ugly as a wart, would you have married me?"

"Yes." I traced the sculpted bow of his upper lip. "Your pretty face has its appeal. But it was the intelligence in your conversations and the intensity of your devotion that ensnared me. When I realized that devotion wasn't real, your looks held no significance."

He didn't need to know how many times tonight I'd acknowledged the effect his physical perfection had on me. It didn't matter. At the end of this, it would be the vivacious soul of the man that I would mourn the most.

His mouth flattened beneath my finger.

"Don't look so offended." I patted his cheek. "I only wonder what might have become of us had you been an average-looking fellow. Would you have been so easily lured from me?"

"I wasn't easily lured away, and though *you* are painfully gorgeous to the eye, that wasn't what enthralled me, either."

"Is that so?" I asked dryly.

"The first time I saw you, you were standing at the helm of this fifty-gun galleon, tearing into a man three times your size. He took his punishment with nothing but respect in his eyes." He smiled a reluctant smile. "I've watched great men rule great ships, and they don't hold a fraction of the esteem that you do. You, this tiny ferocious woman, commanding a crew of one-hundred-and-twenty unruly, quarrelsome, lusty-minded men, and none of them so much as touch you. They wouldn't dare."

"One of them dared." I leaned in, hovering a breath away.

"Yes, well, I've spent a lifetime taking risks." He brushed his lips against mine. "But none so satisfying as the one I took with you."

Then he took again, with his hand in my hair and his tongue in my mouth. That hot stolen kiss, from the man who broke my heart, did exactly what it meant to do.

The tension in my limbs loosened. The ice in my veins thawed, and the shreds of my reason disintegrated as I sank into his splendor. His addictive taste, his confident touch, his throaty sounds, his salt-water scent—all of it would forever reside among my best and worst memories.

I could've spent an eternity feeding on his lush lips. The seconds in which we fell into effortless passion would've required weeks with anyone else. Our bodies came together in a mutual grind. Hearts finding the same beat. Tongues sliding in sync. Breaths melding as one.

He broke the kiss.

I followed his glance to the side, watching as he flipped over the hourglass, initiated the trickle of sand, and slid a hand beneath the skirt of my shift.

With a single finger, he traced my thigh from knee to hip before sinking between my legs and tunneling directly into my soaked heat.

I ceased breathing, and my pulse ran away from me as erotic tingles swept through every inch of my body.

He slowly eased out and drew an unhurried circle around my entrance, once, twice, igniting spasms along my grasping, greedy muscles. Then he plunged that finger again, groaning when he felt how hot and tight and wet and needy I was. I might as well have been a virgin, given the way I responded to his intrusion. It'd been so damn long since I'd been touched.

This was dangerous. Insane. Unsound. And so very right.

I had years of regrets, but denying myself one last ride on his experienced hand would not be one of them.

And so it began. In and out, around and around, he fingered me with a skill of a libertine. I liquefied around every curling pull and moaned with every leaden thrust, sagging against the pillar of his torso as shivering bursts of pleasure wound me tighter, hotter.

I was slippery and unashamed, and he was the intoxicant, spinning me and drowning me with his mastery of my body. Relief was so close I could feel the shimmering, taunting edge of it.

At the centrum of the sensations was his mouth—his hot, treacherous mouth moving against mine in a languorous slide of damp flesh and heated breaths. He tasted like the ocean, deep and turbulent, liberating and comforting, familiar and sacred. There was a time when he'd represented all those things.

Sinuous pressure coursed through me, gathering around the stroke of his finger. But a peek at the sandglass filled me with dread. Such an insignificant amount of grains had passed through.

"By my estimate, that's one minute down." He crooked his finger inside me and dragged my lips back to his, panting hungrily. "Nine more to go."

Sea of Ruin

He didn't need ten minutes to give me a release. He could do it in two. But outlasting the clock wasn't my aim.

With his breaths crashing against my mouth and the impossibly long, swollen length of him pressing against my inner thigh, it was time. He was mindless enough, his guard effectively compromised as he closed his eyes and drove his finger deep into the drenched folds of my flesh.

My throat constricted as I put my lips at his ear and whispered, "Let this be a lesson in betrayal."

"Wha—?"

I shoved his chest with all the strength in my arm and smashed the bottle of rum against the side of his head. Through a spray of liquor and glass, the world stood still as he stared at me in disbelief.

Then he slumped like a sack of grain. His back hit the mattress. His body went limp between my legs, and blood spurted from the jagged wound near his temple.

He was unconscious.

The rancid taste of grief flooded my mouth. My sinuses burned, and fire scorched the backs of my eyes. What kind of woman hurt the man she loved?

"I'm so sorry." I lay my cheek on his chest and released a choking cry of relief and agony.

I cried for the marriage I'd bungled so miserably. For the man whose faithlessness had taught me a hard lesson in trust. And for the love I was letting go after so many years of holding on.

It was time to move past this. Time to find the compass, lock my demon in the bilge, and hold him captive until he was as finished with me as I was with him.

Wiping away tears, I stretched toward his face and kissed his slack lips. It hurt to do so.

It hurt to climb to my feet and not kiss him again.

It hurt to turn away and straighten my undergarments. But I did it.

I put him behind me, pulled in a deep breath, and shouted for my quartermaster.

Eleven

"Strip him." I cleared the nervous jitter from my voice and gave Reynolds my back, leaving him to deal with Priest's unconscious body. "I want him naked and defenseless when we lock him in the hold."

Where did I put my favorite shirt? Ah! There. I snatched it from the floor and pulled it on over my linen corset.

"Naked?" Reynolds asked behind me. "You sure, Captain?"

"Yes."

Was I? Seeing Priest without his breeches wouldn't exactly help me let go and move on. But I wanted his humility. I *needed* it.

"Nudity doesn't affect my brother like normal folks." He shifted, creaking the boards with the sway of the ship. "If anything, it gives him more confidence. Especially around you."

"He hid my compass, Reynolds, and you're going to search every crease and crevice, starting with the ones on his person."

"He did *what?*"

As I updated him on Priest's latest treachery, I exchanged my slip for a pair of trousers and laced on my knee-high boots.

Fully dressed, I turned to find Reynolds bent over the nude, unmoving form on my bed. "Tell me you found it."

"Not the compass. But Captain… He was hiding something else."

The caution in his tone drew me closer. When I reached his side, my mouth dried. My eyes grew hot, and I shook my head, unable to make sense of the ravaged body before me.

From hip to ankle, Priest's flesh rippled and warped like melted leather. Dear God, his entire leg was unnaturally bubbled, hairless, scarred.

Burned.

He'd been burned so horrifically and completely on his left side it made my leg throb in sympathy.

"How?" I clutched my throat, recalling the flawless lines of his physique from two years ago. "When?"

"Not recently." He rolled Priest onto his unmarred side and leaned down for a better look. "He's fully healed."

It was a wonder he'd survived the trauma. The burns all but swallowed his leg. He'd clearly lived through it, but at what cost? Had he endured the agonizing recovery alone?

I should have been there for him, taken care of him, for no rational reason I could name. He didn't deserve my help or my sympathy.

"Put his breeches back on and tie his hands." I couldn't look at his ruined skin. Not because it made him less beautiful. But because his suffering made me feel like a failure, like a worthless, absent wife. "I'll interrogate him once he's secured in the bilge."

Reynolds followed my order, restraining and heaving thirteen stones of listless muscle and menace over his shoulder.

I led him out the door and grabbed the first crew member I spotted—a rangy, malodorous, unwashed cabin boy.

"D'Arcy, assist Reynolds down to the hold." I gave the stinky boy a shove, hurrying him along. "And call for the surgeon. I want Mr. Farrell's head wound examined before the last bell of the dog watch." My next order came with all the bark of my mother's condescending voice. "Then you will find some clean clothes and a bucket to wash yourself."

"Yes, Captain!" D'Arcy jumped, eager to please.

Reynolds lumbered after the boy, adjusting Priest's body high on his shoulder. When they slipped around the corner, I returned to the cabin and leaned against the closed door.

At least, I had my father's boots back. Now to recover the compass.

The hunt stretched late into the night. Anything not bolted down in my cabin was upended, pulled apart, and turned inside out. Even with Reynold's help, the search was onerous. Frustration fused with exhaustion, and sometime after the last bell, I stood amid the debris and admitted defeat.

"It's not here." I collapsed into the desk chair.

Sea of Ruin

"Shall I help you clean up?" Reynolds rehung a Caribbee chart tapestry on the wall and rubbed his forehead. "Or continue the search topside?"

"It can wait until sunrise. All of it. Get some sleep."

"Will you?" He opened the door and glanced back at me.

Would I sleep? With my husband shackled just a few levels beneath me?

I gave a wan smile. "I'll try."

Sleep, as it turned out, proved as challenging as staying away. Priest was the flame to my moth-addled head. Every thought, every emotion, fluttered toward him, incessant. Restless. Destined to die a disgraceful death.

I waited five eternal hours before I emerged from my cabin.

In the faint light of dawn, I ordered a ship-wide search for the compass. As *Jade* sailed farther away from Jamaica, the crew scrambled to locate the prize, motivated by the extra ration of food I promised to the man who found it.

Leaving them to it, I descended below, beneath the galley, crew's quarters, lower deck, and deeper still, through the hatch of the bilge.

At the bottom of the ladder, his voice—deep, self-assured, elongating the vowels of his Welsh accent—greeted me from the shadows. "I've been expecting you."

I lit the lantern on the wall, squared my shoulders, and turned to face him. "Tell me about the scars."

His head tilted, his expression momentarily unguarded and decisively mean. Just as quickly, his features blanked. A blatant refusal to talk.

The iron shackle at his ankle connected to the wall by a heavy chain. He didn't bother rising from his sprawl in the corner, knowing I wouldn't step within his reach.

"Were you tortured by someone?" I pulled an empty cask from the stores of water and used it as a stool to sit. "Or were you caught in a battle? A fire at sea?"

His jaw flexed, and he looked away, presenting a distinguished, angular profile the likes of a man born to the upper class. But an aristocrat he was not.

He ate with the same knife he killed with. Kissed noble ladies with the same mouth that spat on their respectability. And conquered his enemies with a brutality that would never be found among echelons of the British government. He was proud to be a commoner and wielded it well, like my father.

Except my father hadn't been a lying, cheating husband.

The wound on Priest's head looked clean. No bandages or stitches needed. Perhaps I should have hit him harder.

His eyes shifted back to mine, and his mouth twisted, sensually, cruelly, provoking memories of its ruthlessness. I had an unnerving suspicion he was aware of the barest lift of my breasts, the slightest shift in my shoulders, every minuscule twitch I made to compensate muscle fatigue and discomfort.

Yet he spoke with cold, unflappable indifference. "You're still angry."

"You're still an arsehole."

"You didn't sleep a wink last night."

"I certainly—"

"We both know my proximity prevented a moment of rest. But you've always had trouble sleeping. It's the nightmares. Do you still cry out for your mother?" He gentled his voice. "Beg her not to jump?"

Yes.

My throat constricted. "You haven't seen me in two years. You don't know me."

"I know you better than anyone."

I laughed, a forced sound of disbelief.

"I know you loathe dresses and frivolous accoutrement. You wear a boy's shirt and trousers because it's practical. But it also satisfies an innate need to resist your noble blood." He inspected my clothing with a smirk. "You always wear a hat when the sun's at its highest, claiming it's to shade your eyes. But really, it's to protect your skin. Because you were bred to favor a fair complexion."

"Lucky guess," I grumbled. "All based on information I should have never given you."

"I know that pirating inspires a thrill in you like naught else. When too much time passes between raids, you chew your nails down to the quicks." He glanced at the grown-out tips on my fingers. "You've been busy. Coming off a long successful stretch at sea, I wager."

Damn his perceptiveness. I balled my hands, hiding the evidence.

"When silent and at ease, you're the picture of a demure patrician beauty, and those eyes… Christ, they're so blue and huge, like an innocent, wide-eyed child. They're beguiling. Misleading." He fingered the cut on his head and frowned. "The moment someone challenges you, the world is reminded that Edric Sharp sired a vicious force to be reckoned with."

I hadn't thought of myself that way, but the observation pleased me.

He gave me the full attention of his gaze, one that seemed intent on settling the debate of our intimacy. "I'm the only one who knows your upbringing."

"Charles Vane knew."

"He died four days ago. On your father's birthday."

I choked on an ambivalent mass of emotions, resenting his knowledge yet grateful he remembered. "That's enough."

"If you hear the words *roll over* during the heat of passion, you become violently ill. You don't just relive the Marquess of Grisdale's assault—shall he rot in hell for eternity." He flexed his hands. "You also relive the deaths of your parents."

"Stop." My voice broke, trapped against a sob. I tried to push it down, pull myself free, but it was like trying to outrun a tidal wave.

Tears began to leak. Rampant and hot, they coursed down my cheeks and gathered at the hand I held against my mouth.

"I know how badly you need the key to your father's compass." He blinked, a slow fall of lashes. "Not for the riches it would bring. You desperately hope it will lead you to a letter, words of love or affirmation, something personal he might have left for you before he died."

Mercy God, how did he know that? I never told anyone any of this. Yet every word was painfully, brutally accurate.

"Where is it?" I slammed a fist against the barrel beneath me.

He didn't flinch, didn't give me the satisfaction of wavering in the least.

What did I expect? That he would cough up the compass? Agree to a divorce? Promise to leave me in peace?

I met his stare. "How were you burned?"

Silence. A glaring, cold, stone wall of silence.

I shouldn't have come down here.

The man was locked in irons, stripped of weapons, and still managed to overpower me.

I hugged my waist and closed my eyes, wishing with all my heart I could feel my father's arms around me again. I missed him terribly. My mother, too.

What was the point of anything if I didn't have someone to fight for and fight with, to love and hate, to miss and be missed?

The only person still alive to miss me was my husband. And despite his unforgivable betrayal, he was the one I missed the most.

I missed the feel of him, the vibration of his voice against my cheek, the comforting, euphoric sensations only he could stir in me. I missed our conversations, his thought-provoking words in my ear while he held me tight against muscle that was molded and buffed like shining armor.

The truth was I hadn't come down here for the compass. What I sought had been missing for two years.

I wasn't usually this needy. From the moment I heard about Charles Vane's capture, I'd been off-balance. Then came his death, Priest's sudden appearance, the missing compass—all of it was clouding my judgment.

"Bennett." Silver-gray eyes commanded my attention, glinting like blades, sharp enough to shorten my breaths. They weren't the eyes of a captive in shackles, for they showed no fear. "I'm calling a cease-fire. A temporary truce."

"Your games wear thin."

"No games. No deceit. No seduction. We're going to yield. Just for a little while."

"Priest Farrell surrender? That'll be the day."

"No. We're simply going to set aside our disputes. The fighting, name-calling, resenting—it will all be waiting once you're rested and ready to pick up where we left off. In the meantime, you're going to walk over here, get some sleep, and I'm going to hold you while you do."

What he offered was too good to be true. There was a catch, a trick up his sleeve. Only there were no sleeves. No shirt on that delectable body.

That was the trap. Half-naked Priest held the advantage, and when he looked at me, he saw my weaknesses. My vulnerabilities. He knew precisely how to hurt me.

"Stop over-thinking it." He stretched out his legs and opened his arms. "Be a good girl and come here. Right now."

I didn't trust him. Not at all. I was the one in charge. The captain of this ship.

But he'd always been my captain. The one I could depend on while one-hundred-and-twenty men depended on me.

I saw myself slipping off the cask, my tired legs carrying me toward his waiting arms. I saw him guiding me onto his lap. Tucking my head into the warm, solid juncture of his bare shoulder and neck. Rocking me into a peaceful lull. Murmuring in his dulcet Welsh baritone. Stroking my hair, my arm, my face. I saw us sinking into the intimacy of our bodies, breathing into it, into that space where our heat gathered, where our scents mingled and fused, where there was no physical contact yet a full-body awareness of its existence.

It was unreal, just imagining it. Remembering it. I craved the feeling. Yearned to collect it, bottle it, and carry it with me always. Maybe if I indulged one more time…

No, no, I needed to stop. My heart was too broken, my head too crowded with conflict.

Priest had fooled me once, but I couldn't regret that failure. How else would I learn, if not from my own mistakes?

I blinked, drew in a breath, and forced myself to see what was really in front of me. No matter how hard we tried or how much we changed, the shattered remains of yesterday would never fit into today. Too many broken pieces.

He gazed at me with unblinking focus, assessing my body language, studying my expressions, tracking my every breath.

I couldn't stand it. "You can drop that silent stare. I'm not that interesting."

"I disagree." He patted his lap. "Come."

"Ask me." I leaned forward and hardened my eyes. "Beg."

He made a fierce face, complete with a bestial snarl, flared nostrils, and bared teeth. Just when I thought he would explode, he reined it all in.

"Will you sit with me?" His jaw worked through grinding resistance before he bit out the rest. "Please, sit with me?"

"No."

"Dammit, woman!" He flew to his feet, rattling the chain and flexing his arms. "Let me hold you for one godforsaken minute!"

"Forget it, Priest. Or better yet…" I rose from the barrel, fighting exhaustion. "Forget *me*."

"Never."

"Why?"

"You know why."

"Remind me."

"Free me, and I'll show—"

"Now, now, my unfaithful knave. I cannot trust you aboard my ship unless I carry you as a prisoner, for we both know you'll be caballing with my men, clapping me in those irons, and running away with my ship a-pirating."

"Unshackle me, and I'll spend the rest of my life showing you—"

"What will you show me?" My voice rose through several octaves. "Love?"

"Yes."

"Love doesn't betray." That familiar pain announced itself in the cracks of my voice. "Why did you do it?"

"Believe me…" He dropped his head back on his shoulders and breathed out through his nose. "It wasn't on purpose."

"Oh? It was an accident, then? How does that work? Did you fall out of my bed and accidentally land in someone else's vagina?"

"You think I wanted this?" He leveled his gaze on mine. "I never wanted to hurt you. Hell, I didn't even know I was capable of falling in love. God knows I never meant for it to happen twice and certainly not at the *same damn time*."

I gnashed my teeth. "A person can't be in love with two people."

"Wish that were true. It's caused me nothing but misery and loneliness."

"Give me her name."

His eyes drifted shut, a deliberate gesture of reluctance.

"She rejected you." My chest hurt. I didn't deserve this. "Why are you protecting her?"

"I protect what I love." His gaze returned to mine, unflinching in its cruel honesty. "Simple as that."

"I see." Everything inside me collapsed and burned as I moved toward the ladder. "Last chance to surrender the compass."

"Can't do that, Bennett."

With a boot on the bottom rung, I stared up at the hatch, composing my thoughts.

"If I overlooked your philandering… If I could be the sort of woman who shared her husband with his paramours, all our disputes would go away. You would return my compass. I would welcome you back into my bed. You would have your lovers on the side. And I would have mine."

I paused, letting him absorb that last part before glancing back at him.

Fists clenched at his sides, bare feet spread in a warrior stance, mouth a hard slash, complexion red with ire—he glared in shock.

Oh, yes. He'd heard every word.

"Don't look at me like that, darling." I cocked my head. "You set the guidelines for our marriage. I'm simply following your lead."

"No. Hell no. By the Virgin Mother's blood, I'm warning you." His breathing accelerated, and his voice strained with barely controlled violence as a long menacing finger thrust in my direction. "I will *not* share you with another."

"Know this, Priest Farrell. If you don't return my compass, *sharing* is exactly what you'll do."

"Bennett!" His roar chased me up the ladder and through the hatchway.

As I strode along the dark passages, climbed up a level, and walked aft to the next scuttle, I could still hear him bellowing my name.

My threat had shaken him, just as I'd hoped. Whether I could follow through on it was another story. Right now I was determined enough to lead a crew member down to the bilge and fuck him in front of Priest. I fisted my hands, angry enough to do all manner of horrible things.

"Captain!" Reynolds stopped me on the lower deck. "How did it go?"

"As expected." I held up a hand and listened. Either Priest had quieted, or the din from the nearby crew's quarters consumed his shouting. "Did you find the compass?"

"No." He wiped sweat from his brow and grimaced. "Searched the jolly boat. Stripped the upper deck and every wall and barrel he passed last night to your cabin."

"It's here." I pushed by him, heading topside. "Keep looking."

"Jobah spotted sails off the larboard bow." He waited until I turned around, his voice hushed. "A British slave ship."

My heart rate spiked. "Sailing from St. Christopher?"

"We believe so."

"Can we take it?"

"Aye." He flashed a barracuda smile bristling with large, sharp teeth.

I grinned with him, teetering on the verge of sudden laughter.

With the cultivation of sugar cane on St. Christopher came the need for laborers. A gluttonous demand for strong, hard-working bodies. Hence the rampant importation of African slaves.

My family owned slaves in Carolina. Native women had cooked my meals, prepared my baths, and styled my hair. I was ignorant of what that meant until four years ago when I met Jobah.

The day I decided to attack his slave ship—a year before I met Priest and Reynolds—it hadn't been out of heroism or benevolence. I had no idea what was crammed, starved, and shackled together in the cargo hold.

That horrific discovery had earned me a sword through the belly.

My hand fell to the scar that cut across my abdomen. Jobah had saved me that day. Not only had he escaped his chains and killed the guard who stabbed me, but he carried me off that ship and to my surgeon before I bled to death.

Afterward, he could've returned to his homeland with the rest of his people. Instead, he chose to stay with me.

Over the years, I taught him English and how to navigate a fifty-gun galleon. And he taught me the value of freedom. His firsthand accounts of his months aboard a slave ship still haunted me. He would always wear the scars of a slave, but he was no longer that man. In fact, he was the best damn pilot on the high seas.

"Prepare the larboard batteries." I ascended the final ladder and rose from the dark belly of *Jade,* shouting into the sunlight, "Jobah! Gather your charts and meet me at the helm!"

"Your hat, Captain." D'Arcy hopped into my path, holding out the black one I preferred that was cocked on three sides.

"Thanks, lad." I jammed it onto my head as excitement washed over my heart.

Too bad Priest wouldn't be up here to enjoy this. But he'd made his choice, and that choice wasn't me.

Shoving away thoughts of my failed marriage and missing compass, I stared up at the mighty double-spoked wheel, which stretched almost as tall as the formidable African man standing behind it.

Jobah's dark eyes blazed down at me, igniting a fire in my soul.

I hurried up the ladder to his side to prepare our attack and rid the sea of men more evil than me.

Twelve

I balanced my boots on the jib-boom, a spyglass to my eye, and a hand clenched around the tack for support. The smoke of cannon fire lingered, the raw scent of it clinging to the back of my throat. With it came the bitter taste of disappointment.

The cargo ship had surrendered upon the first shot we lobbed across her bow. Had they been anything other than slave traders, I might have let them live.

Evidence of their evil lay in the hull, which had been divided into holds with little headroom and endless chains swaying from beams and snaking across the decks. All meant to restrain hundreds of captives. And all of it empty.

The slave ship had already delivered her cargo to St. Christopher island.

I lowered the glass and found Jobah standing beside Reynolds near the helm. Together, they watched the sea swallow what was left of the burning ship off the larboard beam.

We'd killed every man on board, save two.

Two badly beaten, malnourished slaves.

They were now on my ship, under Ipswich's care. It wasn't the first time my surgeon had nursed outsiders back to life. He grumbled and griped, claiming he didn't have to obey a woman's orders. But the cantankerous old fool secretly enjoyed it. He wouldn't have stayed with me all these years otherwise.

When the last spar of the slave ship sank beneath the tide with a bubbling burp, I pulled in a deep breath and shouted, "Weigh anchor! All hands prepare to make sail!"

I jumped down to the forecastle and crossed to the rail that overlooked the expanse of *Jade's* stunning upper deck. With her topsails clewed up from battle and her stalwart stem poised to smash through wind and water, I tilted my head back and let the splendor roll through me.

Sunshine heated my face. The breeze whipped my hair, testing the grip of my hat. Sea spray misted my clothes, and I soaked it all in.

My father had once stood in this very spot, commanding a different crew and earning their loyalty, battle after battle. How fortunate was I to follow in his footsteps.

I would never forget that. Never take it for granted.

Seamen clamored fore and aft, bare feet pounding across the deck. The windlass groaned, and the kelp-slimed anchor cable snapped taut, swinging out of the sea.

"Get those jibs up." I descended to the main deck. "When we clear the wreckage, raise the mainsail."

Shouts rang out in acknowledgment, followed by the cheerful song of working men. Their chanting tune narrated each maritime task, setting the rhythm as they hauled lines and swung yards.

"Destination?" Reynolds stopped me at the companionway, his gold earrings glinting in the sunlight.

I lifted my face, estimating the angle of the wind. "Put her on a beam reach. Due east."

"That's not what I'm asking."

No, he wanted to know the *long-term* course. While we cruised the West Indies, plundering Spanish treasure ships and terrorizing the British navy, where were we ultimately headed? What did we want at the end of this? That was always the question, wasn't it?

The answer resided in my father's encrypted compass. I needed to find it, solve the puzzle, and follow the map.

"Locate the compass," I said. "I'll deal with Priest. Then we'll go from there."

But first, I needed to see how our new passengers were faring in the hands of surly old Ipswich.

Reynolds strode away, relaying my orders to the crew. A moment later, canvas rose, and the deck slanted as *Jade* heeled to leeward, luffing into the teeth of the wind.

Sea of Ruin

I descended to the lower level and made my way to the infirmary.

Ipswich had his back to the door when I slipped in, his hunched sexagenarian frame bent over an occupied bed. I moved to the other bunk and rested my hand on the limp arm of a man who glared at me with glassy brown eyes. He jerked away from my touch and winced in pain.

Bones protruded beneath layers of old bruises and fresh cuts. Blood matted black hair, his face too young to grow a beard. Too young to be in a foreign place without family. My chest squeezed.

I had an idea of what he'd suffered, but I didn't pretend to understand what he was feeling. Fear? Hatred? Hopelessness? Rage? Whatever it was that hardened his eyes, I couldn't take it away. Couldn't make it better.

"Get out!" A gnarled hand whacked my shoulder. "Always in my way, nosing around and— Don't touch that!" Ipswich smacked me again, knocking my hand from the table of surgeon's tools.

Undaunted, I pushed around him to check on the other man, whose skin glistened beneath the cold sweat of a fever. "I want an update on your patients."

"Once you remove your puny carcass from my infirmary, I'll have them convalescing successfully."

"Shear off, you miserable shabbaroon, or I'll be retaliating successfully." I anchored my hands on my hips and stared at him with a threatening set to my chin. "Let's hope you're conducting yourself in a more…*gracious* way with these men. If I learn otherwise, you shall receive forty stripes lacking one across the bare back. Do I make myself clear?"

"You wouldn't." He grunted through a nest of wiry silver hair.

Meeting my eyes, he saw the unflinching promise in them. I didn't care how old he was, if he didn't improve his attitude, he would be punished.

"Yes, Captain." He bowed his bald head. "Will there be anything else?"

"No, Doctor. I believe that will be all."

I gave the bed-ridden men a parting glance and stepped into the passageway, closing the door behind me. A few yards away, Jobah stood with a shoulder leaning against the wall, his hands clasped behind his back, and the whites of his eyes glowing in the dark.

"Doctor is not…" He rolled his lips together. "Pleasant."

"He's the worst. I should run a sword through him."

"But he helps many people."

"He follows orders." I approached him and mirrored his pose, staring up at him. "I'm sorry we were too late to save the ones who weren't on that ship." *Too late, too often,* I thought, sick at heart.

"We saved two." He smiled softly, his gaze drifting to the door behind me.

It wasn't enough. Then again, I never claimed to be a savior or a hero of any sort.

When a slave ship crossed my path, I sank it. But I wouldn't risk *Jade* or her crew in an attack against an entire island like St. Christopher. Jobah knew my purpose when he joined me, and he never tried to persuade me to change course.

I squeezed his strong shoulder, stretching my arm way up to reach it. His quiet, towering presence intimidated me sometimes. I respected that. It meant he intimidated our enemies, too.

"What about the other one in irons?" He crossed his arms.

"What other one?" I dropped my hand.

"Your mate in the bilge." He winged up a brow. "When will you save *him*?"

My breath stilled.

Jobah had been with me throughout my courtship, marriage, and fallout with the king of libertines. Along the way, he and Priest had formed a staunch friendship.

"He doesn't need saving." My tone turned icy. "If you intend to free him—"

"I will not interfere. But I'll tell you this." He leaned in. "Hear him. *Listen*."

"I do, Jobah. He speaks in lies and manipulations."

"Listen to what he's *not* saying."

I narrowed my eyes. "What do you know? Did he tell you—?"

"I visited him this morning." He held up his hands. "But if I knew his secrets, you would, too. You have my loyalty, Captain."

I nodded, trusting him implicitly.

"Whatever you have planned for him, be gentle." Jobah straightened, his expression somber. "Hurting you has already caused him the greatest pain."

Thirteen

Every surface of *Jade* was lifted, scoured, and replaced until my hands and nerves were chafed raw. Planks, doors, walls, ladders, sails, clothing… Even bodies. Every man on board was subjected to a thorough inspection by myself or Reynolds.

The compass remained hidden.

Days bled into a week, and I lost myself in the search, so I might forget the real reason my boots carried me down to the bilge every morning.

My longing for Priest refused to abate.

I tried to heed Jobah's advice and listen to what Priest *didn't* say with words. But every visit yielded the same as the first. He glared in brooding silence. I analyzed every twitch. He demanded my fidelity. I repeated my threats. We argued. He roared, and I left.

I refrained from torture or fornication—with him or anyone else. I tried *gentle*.

"Gentle doesn't work with Priest." I stood alone in my cabin, naked and resolved. "He leaves me no choice."

I grabbed a peeled orange from the desk, held it to my chest, and squeezed. The juices sluiced down my breasts, and I caught the sticky rivers, rubbing nectar into my skin from shoulders to waist.

With my torso bathed in the fruit, I donned Priest's shirt. The white one with leather laces he'd left in my cabin a week ago. It hung to my knees and still smelled like him—dark, musky, sinful. But not for long.

From a small sea chest, I removed a bottle of odoriferous water I'd bought from an apothecary some months ago. Removing the cork, I doused my hands and ran them over the shirt. The aroma of clove oil, rosemary, and cinnamon reached my nose, subtle yet strong enough to dilute the scent of orange.

That done, I scrubbed my hands until every trace of pulp was removed from my fingers and nails. Then I made my way to Priest.

At the hatchway to the bilge, I paused, breathed deeply, and gathered my strength.

Yesterday I left him seething with the uncertainty of whether I would return or *who* I might return with. If my visit today didn't produce the compass, I would have no choice but to come back with a crewmate and make good on my pledge to fuck another. Probably Reynolds.

But I couldn't think about that right now. Couldn't let myself get dragged into the anguish of doing something so shitten.

I needed this to work. If I angered Priest badly enough, he would surrender what I needed and be finished with me.

I can do this.

Cold, hard purpose soaked into my muscles, immersing the panic as I opened the hatch and descended. At the bottom of the ladder, I stood tall and turned slowly.

His silvery gaze grabbed me from across the dim space, arrowing in on his shirt. I wore nothing beneath the white linen, and though it wasn't transparent, it didn't hide the shape of my nipples or the curves of my form. His gaze feasted on every dip, lowered to where the fabric brushed my knees, and rose to my eyes.

My heart thundered uncomfortably as we stared at each other.

I felt it then, had prepared myself for it—the mysterious, knee-weakening alchemy that simmered in the air between us.

His beautiful face beckoned, the cast of his hard jaw and chiseled mouth exquisite in the flickering shadows. His bare chest flexed with slabs of muscle, his arms straining with enough power to steady two heavy matchlock guns. Or the weight of my body as he pounded me against the wall.

Yes, I was undeniably attracted to him. But the connection went so much deeper. When he exhaled, my lungs gulped. When he swallowed, my mouth dried. When he blinked, my entire body stilled. And it wasn't just me.

Everything I did—every breath, heart beat, and word—resulted in

Sea of Ruin

consequences and obligations for him. If I ran, he would follow. If I died, he would grieve. If I kissed him, he would harden, lengthen, and groan.

It had been a series of mutual actions that bound us together, and it would take a single concerted blow to permanently tear us apart.

Without breaking eye contact, I put one foot before the other and began an unhurried approach.

Surprise flashed in his gaze, his body stiff with suspicion. He'd expected me to torture him with infidelity, not return to him alone, wearing only his shirt, and stepping within arm's reach.

He sat with his back against the wall and legs stretched out before him, frozen. His mouth opened, possibly to ask what I was doing. But it snapped shut as he regarded me, seemingly finding the answer in my expression.

Desire flushed my skin, and I parted my lips. Tiny spasms overwhelmed the juncture of my legs, his shirt pulling across my breasts with my quickening breaths. I let him see every reaction he roused in me—my hunger, my vulnerability, the endless ache to mate with no one but my husband.

My body would give me the leverage I needed with him. If not today, then with another man in front of him. I counted on that. And dreaded it.

A water bucket for washing sat near his foot. I kicked it, sending it skidding and sloshing out of the reach of his chain. Then I stepped over him and planted my bare feet on either side of his hips.

His hands instantly went to my ankles, sparking a delicious fever across my skin as they slid upward, caressing the backs of my calves, behind my knees, and beneath the hem of the shirt.

Heat rolled off him in waves, his gaze never leaving mine. A lump constricted my airway, and my strength abandoned me.

I sank onto his lap, straddling him, and God help me, he felt like home.

He gripped the laces of the shirt and hauled me into him, angling for my lips. I turned my head, and his mouth caught the corner of mine, lingering, panting soundlessly.

Neither of us moved, stunned by the excruciating touch. Or perhaps fearful the slightest shift would sever it.

Heart pulsations beat by. His exhales soaked my lips. My hands locked on his shoulders. Rock-hard thighs supported my bottom, and his shirtless torso pressed in, making me warm all over.

He rested his brow against mine, and our noses slid together, side by side, affectionately nudging.

Fingers touched my face. Four points of contact curving around my cheek. Assertive warmth searing my skin. I wanted nothing more than to melt into him.

So much of my life had been submerged in sadness. Loneliness in my childhood, grief over losing my parents, Priest's devastating perfidy—all of it lay waste to my emotions and shaped my darkest dreams.

I ached for every minuscule portion of affection my husband was willing to dole out. *Pathetic.*

My thoughts swam in a nebulous jumble as the impulse to devour him battled the instinct to bash his head against the wall. But the moment his lips kissed a languid path across mine, I was ensnared.

He plunged deep into my mouth, hunting my tongue and humming a voracious groan. Pleasure coiled. Madness threatened, and my inner muscles clenched in a shuddering frenzy.

His hand collared my neck, and the other palmed my backside, yanking me against the grind of his pelvis. The feverish sensation coaxed a moan from my throat, and the sensual roll of his hips dragged my focus to the source of all our misery—his heavy, swollen cock.

Awareness that he was my husband flooded my logic. My nose knew his scent. My tongue knew his taste. My hands recognized the soft texture of his hair, and my body sang in invitation, heating and growing slick with need.

He broke the kiss to put his mouth at my ear. "You're so hungry, my beautiful girl. So responsive."

The roughened texture of his accent shoved me to the brink of orgasm. God's wounds, how I missed his heated words, the whisper of them across my flesh in the throes of passion.

His hands moved, roving beneath the shirt and unerringly finding the deep scar on my belly. His fingers shook as they traced the jagged, puckered skin before sailing up my abdomen, molding around my breasts, and closing painfully on my nipples.

With that, the plan was set. Now that he'd touched my chest, it would only take a few minutes to soak in.

Already, with his hands on my damp skin, confusion creased his forehead. Why was I sticky? Why did I let him touch me in the first place? He should have been voicing those questions and pushing me away. But evidently, he wanted me too much to listen to the warnings.

Sea of Ruin

His lips returned to mine, his tongue a wicked conqueror, pillaging the recesses of my mouth and demanding participation. His arousal stabbed my bottom, and I opened to him—my lips, my arms, my legs—drawing him tighter against me, locking my thighs around his hips, and bearing down on his hard length in my fierce need to get closer to him.

His breath stirred the hair that had fallen across my cheek as he rocked into me, savagely miming the movements of lovemaking. Every jab of his hips fed my hunger for him, driving me into blistering madness.

"Bennett." His palms chased the lines of my body beneath the shirt, stroking and kneading my breasts. "Just touching you makes my hands burn."

It wasn't me causing that reaction, and in another minute, he would figure that out.

Time to pull away.

Leaning back, I didn't move as if I were putting a stop to this. I shifted my weight, adjusting my legs to stand. But I did it seductively, slipping a hand between my thighs and stroking my soaked flesh as I slowly rose to my feet.

The motion of my fingers seized his attention. He gripped my knees, not to prevent me from standing but to spread me wider for his smoldering, gluttonous gaze.

I made a scandalous show of it, fondling and fingering myself only a breath away from his mouth. Close enough to taunt him with the scent of my desire.

Sweat formed on his temples. His breathing hastened. Every visible muscle hardened, and his pupils swallowed the gray of his eyes, giving him the appearance of a feral, mindless predator.

In a blink, his shoulders thrust forward, his face coming for my cunt. But I was ready for it, my feet already moving in an agile dance to evade him.

He missed me by a hairsbreadth. I kept backing up, dodging the swipe of his hand. With a roar of frustration, he rose to his full height and lunged.

The chain snapped taut, halting his advance and yanking his leg out from under him. He landed just short of reaching me, on his knees, with his fists grinding against the wooden planks. When he lifted his eyes, his savage glare—consumed by fire, fury, and hunger—glowed from beneath a thick shadow of lashes.

"Come here, Bennett." His voice scraped like the coarse sand of a seashore. He went for his breeches, his fingers blindly fumbling with the laces. "I need inside you."

"Yes, I know. You need a lover like I need the sea. I suppose you could say we both long for the dark wet depths of a demanding mistress." I retreated until my bottom hit the barrel. I perched there, legs spread, with my hand between my thighs. "But you can't have me. Not anymore."

He sat back on his heels, cast a fleeting glance at his palm, and dismissed the bubbling redness so that he could turn that vicious scowl back on me.

"You're intent on continuing with this plan?" His jaw clenched around every word. "You wish to torture me."

"Is it torture watching me like this?"

I hadn't stopped touching myself, my fingers stirring the slick juices around my opening. It felt nice, as it should have. I'd done this often enough over the past two years, alone in my chamber, wishing for companionship while thinking only of my husband.

But this time, I didn't have to fashion him in my mind. The sheer scope of muscle laid bare before me made my hand stroke faster, harder, squelching damp, turgid flesh and infusing the space with the sounds of my wetness.

He remained on his knees, his perfect arse resting on his heels as he strained forward, nostrils widening as if scenting the air.

Powerfully built in a way that could only be considered desirable, he was a beast in his prime. His shoulders had deep indentations where sturdy bones met thick tendons. His hands made lethal fists on his thighs, his chest rising and falling, arms tensing, every inch of him smooth and hard-surfaced.

Beneath the thinly woven fabric of his breeches, he was long and contoured, fully aroused and well-endowed, larger than any man I had ever felt between my legs.

A wash of memories rushed through me, funneling heat from my chest to my belly and lower, where fat slicks of moisture gathered and leaked out. It had been a long time since I'd been this aroused, the evidence streaking my fingers and thighs and holding his rapt attention.

So much so, he didn't seem to notice how he was rubbing his hands on his breeches, scratching his itchy palms. A sure sign he was suffering from more than just a neglected erection.

I paused my stroking and drew a salty finger into my mouth.

Sea of Ruin

He froze, tracking the movement as if carried away in an ecstatic trance. The muscles in his jaw locked, his eyes glowing like cauldrons of molten ore.

Then he blinked. His fingers flew to the ties on his breeches, one hand stroking his bulge through the fabric, as he attempted to free it.

"I wouldn't do that." I lowered my arm.

"You want to stop me from touching myself? Shackle my hands, you heartless minx. I dare you."

"No shackles needed. You see, there are two kinds of people in the world. Those who can eat oranges." I pulled off my shirt and stood before him, naked. "And those who can't touch them."

His palms were already blistering like the sores of syphilis. Except his ailment wasn't contagious. It was *strange*.

Honestly, I didn't know anyone who could break out in a rash of itchy red spots just from touching nectar. Although, I had a man on my gun crew once who fell violently ill when he ate tree nuts.

Priest looked at the sticky residue on my chest and back at his hands, his complexion paling as he made the connection.

"You bathed yourself in oranges." He glanced down, running his gaze over his bare chest, searching for invisible traces of the toxic pulp. Then his eyes widened in horror, and he raised his fingers toward his face.

"Don't touch your mouth." My pulse kicked up. "You haven't ingested it. *Yet*."

If he swallowed even a whiff of the fruit, those blisters would swell in his throat, close his airway, and kill him. At least, that was Ipswich's conclusion when we told him about the peculiar affliction three years ago. I never wanted to test the theory.

"Only your hands came in contact with the juice. I spread it here." I gestured at my nude torso. "Just...don't touch your face. Or anything else."

I directed my eyes at his groin.

If he put his contaminated hands in his breeches and tried to stroke himself, it would inflame so severely he would lose his arousal. That was the reason I went to all this trouble.

No masturbation. No orgasms. Not until I allowed him to scrub his hands.

Physical and mental torture.

"Give me the water." He glowered at the wash bucket, knowing relief was well out of his reach.

"Give me the compass."

Fourteen

Determination fortified my spine as I eased back onto the barrel, spread my legs, and resumed my erotic self-stimulation. "Tell me where you hid the compass, Mr. Farrell, and I'll wash every inch of your body myself."

Priest balled his blistered hands on his thighs and set his jaw.

"It's easy, darling." Naked from end to end, I let my head fall on my shoulders, arched my back, and worked my fingers between my legs. "Just tell me where it is, and I'll give you relief."

"If I give you the compass, I'll lose you." His voice grated, thick with agony and dangerous hunger. "You'll put me ashore on the next desolate beach, and I can't… I will *not* spend another day without you."

"You already lost me." I twisted my hand, sliding it through my slickness. "If you don't give me the compass, I'll finish myself off. Then I'll call your brother down here and let him fill me over and over until I finish again."

His low menacing growl brought my head up.

He captured my eyes. "It doesn't matter how far we fall, how much pain we inflict, or how dark it becomes in the ruin. I'm going to be with you, waiting for you, loving you, *forgiving* you. I'm never letting go, Bennett. *Never.*"

My fingers faltered with the hitch of my breath.

When he said things like that, I wanted so badly to believe him. But no words—no matter how achingly profound—could change the past.

"You hurt me." My voice splintered. "Unforgivably."

His chin descended to his chest, magnifying the slopes of his proud shoulders as he regarded me from beneath the intensity of his brow.

I was losing my nerve, my arousal, the desire to torture him.

My thoughts had never been so contorted, my tongue so knotted. Dear lord, it was a good thing none of my crew bore witness to my lapse in cruelty. They wouldn't understand.

"Give me her name." Needles stung the backs of my eyes.

"No."

My heart galloped fiercely, but I would *not* cry.

When it came to secrets, Priest was an impenetrable steel cage. He'd kept his mouth shut about our marriage, and despite my threats, he continued to protect his anonymous lover. He would never break his silence.

"Tell me about the burn scars on your leg," I said.

"No. Don't ask again."

Another secret.

I closed my eyes and curled my fingers, cupping the heat in the valley of my thighs, teetering on the verge of giving up. Sitting here, completely exposed with my legs open... I felt sick.

This wasn't me. I tortured evil men. Killed monsters without hesitation or regret. But I'd never been a tease. When I offered myself, I followed through on that promise. Anything less was weak.

"Bennett." His Welsh cadence caressed my bare skin, making me shiver. "Look at me."

My lashes felt too heavy to lift, but I opened my eyes, not surprised to find the churning storm in his.

How foolish was I to underestimate him? There were no answers in his intractable gaze, no hint of surrender beyond the next thought. There was only this moment and an offer of punishment and pleasure.

"Hurt me." His eyes gleamed with the command. "Touch yourself. Do it knowing I would die to be your hands, to slide through all that wetness, to experience the heat of your orgasm, to feel it gripping and sucking for more." He wet his lips. "To hold me at arm's length and deny me your love... It's the worst torture."

"Worse than watching me with another man?"

"Same thing." He let his gaze drift downward, absorbing every curve and indentation of my body, lingering so long in places I could have sworn my skin caught fire. "Whether you're alone or with another, the result is the same. You're not with me."

Sea of Ruin

Silence fell around us, shutting out the world and suspending us in a volatile cocoon.

He remained on his knees, head down, watching me through his lashes. His fists squeezed on his thighs, the inflammation turning his fingers dark red and swollen.

"Go on," he breathed into the hush. "Punish me. Finger that beautiful cunt. Show me what you think I lost."

It wasn't his words that stirred my hand into motion. It was the turbulent look in his eyes. The challenge. Did I have it in me to touch myself without touching him? Could he sit there and watch without losing control?

I went for it. Spreading my legs, my fingers digging into my flesh, I drove my strokes up inside, using him—the glorious view of his body, the memory of our lovemaking, the pained look on his face. I used him for my own pleasure. He was the muse that inspired the languorous burning in my veins, the uncontrollable trembling in my thighs, and the moans singing past my lips.

Sinews tensed in his neck. Muscles bounced in his jaw. His mouth opened on the surge of his breaths, but otherwise, he remained still. *Behaving himself.*

His self-restraint only further aroused me, and when I finally reached that peak of venereal excitement, I cried out, twitching from head to toe and squirting all over my hand.

I caught myself before I toppled off the cask and sucked in great gulps of air.

His breaths continued to hiss past gnashed teeth, his hands white-knuckled on his lap, and his full attention locked on my dripping swollen cunt.

As the tingling remnants of orgasm faded, the crushing need to feel him inside me didn't abate. Nothing would ever compare to what I'd once had with Priest Farrell.

My legs wobbled as I stepped to the water bucket and washed my hands and thighs. He didn't speak, but I felt his gaze caressing the lines of my back.

Snatching the shirt from the floor, I pulled it over my head and started toward the ladder.

"What if the compass isn't the map?" His gravelly voice brought me to a halt.

He never cared about the treasure. Never once expressed an interest in being wealthy. He had the dominating disposition to command his own ship, and he did that now and then. But he never kept the vessels he seized. He just…gave them away.

Priest was a slave to his carnal desires, a worshiper of the standing prick between his legs. He would follow *it* before anything else.

"Why do you care?" I turned to face him.

"Because you do. What if the map is *inside* the instrument?"

"You think I haven't considered that? There's no keyhole. No openings." My head pounded as irritation threaded through my tone. "It doesn't open."

"I located the inventor who crafted it."

"You say?" My face numbed, and a ringing sound erupted in my ears.

"During my exhaustive search for you, I found some old acquaintances of Edric Sharp. One fellow knew another fellow and so on. I followed the trail. The man who designed your compass died years ago, but I had an interesting conversation with his son. The lad didn't take up his father's skill, but he remembered some of the unusual techniques."

My heart hammered so hard I thought it might burst from my chest. "Did you tell him about my compass?"

"No, I would never risk that. But he mentioned that all his father's instruments required two things. One, a physical key." His gaze shifted to my throat.

My hand leaped to the jade stone I wore there, my fingers tracing the serrated cuts on the surface. Shaped like a thumb and half as narrow, it resembled a key. I always thought it could be *the* key, but it didn't fit anywhere on the compass.

"No keyhole, remember?" I dropped my hand, taking my hopes with it.

"The notch will reveal itself if given the correct combination of movements. That's the second requirement. Every instrument was built with a key and a list of verbal instructions. *Something to hide on your body and something to hide in your mind.* The lad's words."

When my father had given me the instrument, he'd said, *Start and end north.*

The devil knew how many times I tried that combination of movements over the years, rotating the compass over and over. Nothing had happened.

"Did he teach you any songs?" Priest asked.

Yes. A lot of songs. Most of them chants that narrated the maritime

Sea of Ruin

tasks of sailors. I couldn't possibly remember them all. If the answer was in one of those, how could my father have expected me to know which verse held a secret meaning?

He wouldn't have.

What if this was just another of Priest's manipulations? With my body buzzing from orgasm and the flavor of his lips upon my tongue, what better way to distract me from torture than to tease me with hope about my compass?

I'd come down here to learn the truth, and he didn't want me to leave. Leaving meant I would return with another man.

He was smart enough to steal my compass and earn passage aboard my ship. Cunning enough to hold it hostage as a guaranteed ticket to remain on board. Persuasive enough to send me out of here less satisfied, less certain, every damn time.

He was always ten steps ahead of me.

I couldn't dismiss the information he'd shared about the compass, but there was naught I could do about it until I held it in my possession again.

"I'll be back with Reynolds." I didn't spare him or his blistered hands another glance as I climbed the ladder and pushed open the hatch.

The moment it lifted, an outstretched arm greeted me. Long fingers, black skin, white scars… What the devil was Jobah doing down here?

He grabbed my arm and lifted me out too quickly for this to be a social call.

My rising panic exploded when I glimpsed the turmoil on his face. "What happened?"

He kicked the hatch closed and started dragging stores of food and water over the top of it. "Sails on our aft, stealing our wind and closing in fast."

I stood motionless, momentarily stunned, as he hauled and shuffled casks. There was only one reason he would conceal the entrance to the bilge.

He was preparing for boarders.

That meant the ship on our aft was fast enough, heavy enough, *armed* enough to overtake us and search our holds.

"Royal Navy?" My voice quivered.

"I'm afraid so, Captain."

Priest and I were two of the most wanted pirates on this side of the world.

It was possible our British pursuers didn't have an accurate description of my identity. I always went ashore incognito, making it difficult for my enemies to recognize me. But Priest never tried to hide who he was or what he looked like. His face was sketched in newspapers all over the West Indies.

If the king's men found him, they would hang him.

I jumped in to help Jobah, my hands shaking as I shoved the heavy containers. "How many guns?"

"More than we carry. You should hide in the hold with your husband."

I flung him a glare that would've shriveled the testicles on a lesser man.

"Yes, I know. You'd rather hang." He sighed. "It's your neck."

It would be every neck on my crew if I lost command of this ship.

"What are we dealing with?" I heaved another barrel.

"We believe she's a one-hundred-gun ship of the line."

"A warship? What the—?"

"That's confirmed!" Reynolds scrambled down the companionway behind me. "Captain! Topside, now!"

"I'll finish here." Jobah gave me a push. "Go."

My heart rate blew up as I chased Reynolds to the top, scaling ladders, sprinting through passageways, and shouting, "All hands on deck and man the guns!"

Fifteen

"Thirty-two-pounders. I count twenty-eight of them." Reynolds stood beside me on the upper deck, his knuckles blanching as he passed me the spyglass.

I raised it to my eye and swallowed a gasp. The salt-smeared telescope brought the full-rigged warship into focus. The finest ever built at Woolwich Dockyard, if I were a day old. And she prowled just forty yards to starboard, maneuvering to fire from her broadside.

"Fifty-six demi-cannons and culverins split between the middle and upper gundecks." My stomach buckled as I continued to scan the armament. "Twelve six-pounders on the quarterdeck."

"Four more on the forecastle." A heavy sigh. "We're outgunned, Captain."

One hundred guns made to sink galleons in the war against Spain. Hell, the demi-cannons alone boasted enough firepower to blow every vessel west of England out of the water. Including mine.

As I glared through the glass, the warship hummed with organized activity. Lines of uniformed officers gestured and shouted. Seamen ran along the gangways and swarmed the shrouds. Soldiers stood at the stern near a swaying jolly boat, ready to cross at the captain's command.

They can try.

My gunners were prepared to fire the moment that jolly hit the water with rowers. As long as I breathed, the king's navy would *not* board my ship.

But the flutter of fear I'd carried from the bilge was careening into a tumult. Whatever happened in the next few minutes could end my life and the lives of my men. If we fled, the warship would open fire. If we fired first, we would be blown to hell.

Our fate rested in the hands of one man.

High above the belly of His Majesty's Ship, the navy captain stood at the rail with his lieutenants, watching me through his spyglass as I watched him.

He was easy to identify in his dark blue frock coat and pristine white breeches and hose. Gold embroidery banded the wide cuffs and standing collar and edged the jeweled buttons that glinted down the front closure—all meant to signify wealth and status.

"Who is he and what is he doing in the West Indies?" Heart racing, I lowered the glass and glanced at Reynolds. "That ship was designed for naval tactic. Why isn't he in the Mediterranean fighting Spain over territories?"

"The war must have ended. If that's true, he's here on another mission."

"Pirate hunter." I gnashed my teeth and returned to the spyglass.

Fringed with white feathers, the captain's three-cornered hat matched the blue of his coat. I wished the wind would rip it off his head, so I could analyze his facial features. Was he young? Inexperienced? Just another spoiled, listless aristocrat looking for adventure?

I would love to show him a good time. With a firepot of broken wine bottles, saltpeter, resin, and rotten fish hurled at his rigging. The stink alone would cause the contents of his stomach to empty all over his gold-trimmed finery.

But in my seven years of pirating, I'd never fired upon a British warship. Because I didn't have a wish for death.

The captain shifted away, ambling to the quarterdeck rail and peering down into the waist of the warship. Hundreds of sailors stopped what they were doing on gangways and shrouds, and every head turned toward him as if awaiting his command.

Gripping the rail with all the power his rank awarded him, he spoke words I couldn't hear. Long minutes passed. Then all at once, the seamen resumed their tasks.

"I loathe them and everything they represent." Reynolds glared at the warship. "All those pompous guns, the uniformed soldiers, the elaborate figurehead with a gaping maw of teeth… Like we're supposed to tremble in fear of the king's almighty will."

"Don't you?"

"Tremble?" He shrugged. "That depends on you. What's your plan?"

With a final look at the navy captain, I handed off the glass. "I'm going to make his arsehole clench."

"It's about time." Reynolds tossed me a speaking trumpet.

I jumped up onto the gunwale, balancing on the narrow ledge, and raised the funnel-like instrument to my mouth.

"What business do you have in my waters, Captain?" I shouted across the restive waves.

He strode to the stern and gripped the tafferel. His lieutenants scrambled around him, and a moment later, a trumpet appeared in his hand. He raised it to his mouth.

"I'm Lord Ashley Cutler." His voice vaulted the distance, strong and deep. "The commodore of HMS *Blitz*."

Commodore? Above captain and below admiral. What a smug little lord.

"Good for you." I propped my elbow on a rigging cable, leaning casually as I shouted, "How many pissers did you suck to rise to that rank?"

"Strike your colors, pirate! You're under arrest."

"Pirate?" I laughed mockingly. "Clean your glass, you preening little cockatoo. I am but only a maiden. Pure and virtuous and *very* afraid of men."

"Bennett Sharp, daughter of the convicted pirate Edric Sharp, you shall be taken into custody along with your men and the stolen galleon you call *Jade*."

My blood turned to ice, and I almost dropped the trumpet.

He recognized me. How? I exchanged a look with Reynolds.

His eyes widened, fraught with disbelief. "He didn't *accidentally* stumble upon you. It's not possible."

"No." I shoved my wind-blown hair from my face. "He must have been tracking me. Probably picked up our trail in Jamaica."

"Stand down your guns and prepare to receive boarders," Lord Cutler called. "If you resist, I will show no quarter."

My heart rate went off like a cannon.

Heavier and faster than *Jade*, HMS *Blitz* carried twice as many guns and four times as many mariners. I would not win this fight with strength or firepower.

My mind whirled through every stratagem and artifice I'd used in previous battles, picking apart tricks that had worked for me and those that hadn't. If I had more time, maybe I could think up a ruse to escape this without casualties.

Movement rippled through Lord Cutler's men. The forty-yard distance made their features indiscernible, but I could make out two lieutenants walking toward the boat that swung from the stern of HMS *Blitz*.

Lord Cutler motioned to more soldiers, and they vanished down the gangway ladder, dispatched for some other ominous task.

Dread trickled down my spine.

"Bennett Sharp," he called through the speaking trumpet. "Prepare to receive my lieutenants, and I must insist that you cover yourself before they arrive."

I glanced down at Priest's white linen shirt, the hem tangling around my knees. In my hurry to the upper deck, I'd foregone trousers, boots, weapons, my hat… The only thing I wore was the jade stone and thin shirt.

Oh, I bet that inspired some horrified blushes and gasps on His Majesty's Ship. Proper Englishmen upheld modesty in a degree I considered ridiculously excessive. Not to mention, they never allowed a woman aboard a navy vessel.

And here I was, standing half-naked on the gunwale of a fifty-gun galleon, laughing into the trumpet with wicked delight. "Do I offend your sensibilities, my lord?"

He lowered his trumpet, holding it behind his back, refusing to answer. Even at this distance, I felt the heat of his glare. The tenacity in it. The man seemed impossible to ruffle.

"I must insist that you invite me to dinner, Commodore." My amplified voice crashed into the wind. "A woman likes to be courted and wooed before she gets fucked. Just ask James here…" I gestured at the scrawny, gray-bearded tar behind me. "He thoroughly woos your mother with his tongue in her unmentionables before he fucks her."

The commodore snapped out his arm, the only warning I got before the whistling hiss of incoming mortar rent the air.

My lungs crashed together as the shot punched through the tafferel of *Jade's* stern, taking out the stately panels and railings in an explosion of splintered wood. I tumbled off the gunwale, the deck shaking beneath my bare feet as the boom dissipated in every direction.

Sea of Ruin

I waved the billowing smoke from my face and glared at the jagged, smoldering hole in my ship. Thank God, Priest was held far beneath the broken timbers. No chance of injuries.

Only surface damage.

It was a slap in the face. He could've demolished the rigging, toppled the mizzenmast, and blasted away anything that would've prevented us from sailing. The fact that he didn't showed what little confidence he had in our ability to flee.

All eyes fixed on me. Under the bulwarks with daggers, in the shrouds with muskets, behind the long-range eighteen-pounders with lit matches—every man soundlessly asked me the same question.

What now, Captain?

As the pungent gray smog cleared, tension swelled, rolling through the ship. My blood buzzed. My hands flexed and shook.

I knew what I had to do.

Reynolds wouldn't like it. Priest would positively combust in a murderous rage. But it was our only option. And I needed Jade in one piece for it to work.

Dragging in a breath, I aimed the trumpet in the direction of my gundeck. "Hold your fire!"

Reynolds flashed me a questioning look. "Shall I prepare to repel boarders?"

"No." I filled my lungs and shouted, "Raise the white!"

A stunned inhale rippled through the ship and thinned the air. Then footsteps erupted into action.

I spun toward the foremast, my heart cracking into pieces as *Jade* hoisted a white flag for the first time under my command.

"What the devil are you doing?" Reynolds snarled at my ear. "If we surrender, they'll hang us."

"Stop talking." I grabbed the spyglass and trained it on Lord Cutler, positioning my hands to hide the movement of my lips. "He's watching."

Reynolds stiffened on my stern. Jobah appeared at my fore, flanking me. Brilliant. I needed them both to hear this.

"In a few minutes, I'm going to jump up on this gunwale. When I do…" I glanced at Reynolds. "You will push me overboard. Don't argue."

He worked his jaw, eyebrows pinning together, and hands opening and closing at his sides.

"Dead or alive," I said, "I'm worth more to Lord Cutler than all of

Jade and her crew."

My husband's head was as valuable as mine, but our marriage wasn't known. Lord Cutler had no reason to connect me to Priest and therefore, no reason to search my ship for him.

The only way to save my crew was to prevent the Royal Navy from boarding. I needed to keep Priest's presence a secret and remove myself from this vessel.

"After you push me over, take command of *Jade*," I said to Reynolds. "Set a course to Harbour Island and wait for me there. Your job is to hide and protect my ship and her crew. Swear to God, if you disobey me, I will keelhaul you until naught a flap of flesh hangs from your bones."

His eyes hardened, unblinking, and his lips pressed into a line. Whatever he wanted to say bobbed in his throat, but he knew better than to question.

I turned my attention to Jobah. "The instant I hit the water, head up two points and begin your run. Full and by."

"Captain…"

"Run until *Jade* is out of range of their guns and too far gone to catch up. If they believe you have no interest in rescuing me, they'll let you go and focus on pulling me from the water. I'm the one they want."

Capturing Edric Sharp's daughter, one of the most wanted pirates in the world, was a monumental boon for a pirate hunter's career. The noose around my bent neck would likely raise Lord Ashley Cutler to the coveted flag rank of admiral.

My shoulders hunched, reflexively protecting my vulnerable throat.

I'm not giving up. Not even close.

Across the water, the jolly boat began to lower toward the water. It was almost time.

Reynolds rubbed a hand over his mouth, concealing his words. "Once they have you, you won't be able to escape."

"That's why you're going to release your brother from the bilge."

His features sharpened and pinched through a squall of resisting emotions before settling into comprehension. He couldn't argue the glaring truth.

As long as Priest lived, he would hunt me with the ferocity of my greatest enemy.

Once *Jade* made her escape to safer waters, Reynolds would help Priest lay siege to another ship—a merchantier, a faster, stealthier

Sea of Ruin

sloop, anything he could use to pursue me—knowing I didn't want *Jade* anywhere near HMS *Blitz*.

As Reynolds came to this conclusion, reluctant acceptance softened his mouth, and he released a heavy breath.

"Notify the crew," I said without moving the telescope from my face.

He squeezed my hip, the gesture hidden beneath the gunwale. Then he ambled across the ship, delivering quiet, resolute orders to the men.

Forty yards to starboard, Lord Cutler watched every move through his glass. Perhaps he would reflect on this moment later and decide that this was the point when Reynolds rallied my crew into mutiny behind my back.

"Jobah." I stared straight ahead, mirroring his pose. "If this doesn't work..." *If I die...*

"I'll make sure nothing happens to him."

Him. The husband I loathed to love. The libertine who would risk his life to find me.

"Man the helm," I replied in my captain's voice.

"I already miss you, Captain."

"Likewise." My heart pinched as I glanced at him sidelong, letting him see the gratitude in my eyes. "Godspeed, my friend."

Without a show of emotion, he retreated, leaving me alone with my rioting nerves.

Jumping into the sea from the rail of a galleon was a risk in and of itself. I could die on impact or lose consciousness and drown before the enemy boat reached me. Nevertheless, I had faith in my ability to swim.

If I kept my head above the swells long enough, Lord Cutler's soldiers would pull me out.

If I survived the jump, I would become a captive aboard His Majesty's Ship. Whether I could endure that hell and evade the hempen halter at the end depended on my will to live and the indomitable, possessive fury of Priest Farrell.

Without turning around, I sensed Jobah at the helm, awaiting my signal. Behind me, seamen carried on as if nothing were amiss.

For their mutiny to appear authentic, I needed the participation of the entire ship. So I waited a few more minutes, giving Reynolds enough time to quietly pass along orders, preparing the men for the subterfuge.

Then I exchanged the spyglass for the speaking trumpet and jumped up onto the gunwale.

Near the stern of HMS *Blitz*, rowers and lieutenants began to descend the ladder to the jolly boat.

"Advance no further, impotent Puritans!" I yelled at them across the waves. "Or your livers will bleed on the end of my cutlass!"

The men filed into the jolly, ignoring my hollow threats. I continued shouting at them, solidifying the ruse that my only defense was to attack them with words.

I was so lost in my dire declarations to cause harm that I didn't sense Reynolds behind me until his arm chopped the backs of my knees.

Loss of balance sent me tumbling. The trumpet flew backward. My body toppled forward, and Reynolds shoved my legs, sealing my fate.

I fell.

It was a long, horrifying drop. Long enough for a thousand doubts to flood in and swallow me in panic.

At the last moment, I gathered my senses, arrowed my body, feet first, and pressed my arms to my sides. When I hit the surface of the water, it felt like I collided with hard earth. My teeth sliced my tongue. Air ripped from my lungs, and every bone jarred with the impact.

Then I sank. And sank. As I plunged deeper into the sea, my thoughts obsessed over what was transpiring above the surface.

Jobah would be executing my orders to flee. The crew would be hauling lines, turning canvas, and hooting in mutinous cheer, leading Lord Cutler to believe they had just sacrificed their wanted captain to save their own lives.

If Lord Cutler opened fire to stop their escape, I wouldn't just die down here. He would lose my carcass amid the wreckage and debris.

Right now I suspected he was weighing the value of my drowning body against that of my captured crew. And he would settle on the same conclusion I had.

My head was worth more, whether or not it was attached to the rest of me. He wouldn't chase *Jade* at the risk of losing his prize to the sea.

Every second was an eternity as I descended through blue water, lungs burning, legs frantically kicking, heart flailing, vision fading. I'd understood the danger of falling overboard but wasn't prepared for the sudden, petrifying attack of hysterics.

My throat spasmed, fighting the reflex to gulp. Undercurrents of water slammed into me like invisible fists, thrashing me around and jumbling my sense of direction. I searched for the surface, unable to see sunlight through the increasing black spots.

I'd hoped to avoid unconsciousness, but it was inevitable now as my strength abandoned me, giving way to violent, involuntary contractions in my muscles. The need to breathe was so vicious I didn't think I could suffer another second without gasping.

The last thing I saw was *Jade's* mighty hull overhead. She dispersed waves of water as she turned, making her utmost speed with sails that must have been full and close-hauled. With the warship still moored, *Jade* would be safely out of firing range within minutes.

I clapped a hand over my nose and mouth, stifling the agonizing ache to gulp as her wake shoved a tonnage of bone-breaking seawater over my head.

Undercurrents grabbed my useless legs and pulled me down, down, down into the yawning darkness.

Sixteen

I came to awareness, choking, convulsing, and vomiting seawater. Callused hands turned me side to side, pounding my back, and pushing on my abdomen between agonizing intervals of wet coughs and tremors.

Minutes lasted hours as every muscle and organ worked to expel the burning water. When my airway finally cleared, I lay bone-tired and grateful to be alive with a wooden deck canting lazily beneath me.

The warship.

Blinking ocean tears from my eyes, I stared up at the rank and file of uniforms on the upper deck, where I sprawled like a starfish.

Gold buttons, hats cocked on three sides, navy-issued dragoon pistols, boots of the finest leather, stoic expressions… The soldiers stood as one, symbolizing England's power.

I couldn't see *Jade's* mighty masts off the starboard bow. Couldn't hear her sheets hissing in the wind. Couldn't detect the stench of blood or the gunpowder smoke of battle. The navy sailors were all here, seemingly awaiting orders without urgency. Which meant they weren't engaged with my ship.

They'd let her go.

By the teeth of almighty God, my ruse had worked.

Jade escaped!

Quiet jubilation startled into my throat and tumbled past my lips, rolling into hacking fits of laughter.

Two men stood over me, bowing their cocked hats together. Lieutenants, given their buckled shoes and powdered periwigs.

"Why is she laughing?" one asked. "Does she not realize her crew threw her overboard to save their own hides?"

"She's mad as a March hare," the second lieutenant said.

"Oh, my foolish lads." Grinning maniacally, I pushed to a sitting position and straightened the shirt to cover my nudity. "You have no idea what you just invited onto your ship."

They glowered down their bladed noses with all the haughtiness of English nobility. I yawned, losing interest.

Meanwhile, every muscle in my body continued to shake, reminding me I almost drowned. Or maybe I did? Which one of these pretty boys brought me back to life? Why was no one addressing me or slapping me in irons?

Perhaps I was the first woman to ever step onto this first-rate ship of the line. But every seaman in the vicinity stared as if I were a mystical, fire-breathing sea dragon they'd mistakenly hauled from the sea.

They'd caught a lady pirate and seemed uncertain about what to do next.

"Don't put a ball through my heart." I thrust my hands in the air. "I'm just going to stand."

No one moved as I wobbled ungracefully to my feet and made a quick scan of the horizon. The silhouette of distant sails sent a flutter of relief through my chest. Beyond the range of the warship's guns, *Jade* was already vanishing beneath the horizon.

Keep them safe, Reynolds.

Centering my bare feet on the rolling deck, I took a quick inventory of my body. Dripping wet, Priest's shirt hung to my knees. The jade stone still sat against my throat. And that was the extent of what I carried with me.

I staggered toward the uniformed men. Numerous fingers twitched against pistol belts, but not a gun was drawn.

My fate didn't reside in the hands of low-ranked soldiers.

I searched the sea of blue frocks, looking for the one with jeweled buttons and elaborate embroidery of gold curlicues.

There. Lord Ashley Cutler, the commodore of HMS *Blitz*, stood just aft from a short raised deck, his hat tucked under an elbow, and a big hand curled around the top rail, confident, patient, cool as rain in the warm sea air under the bluest of blue skies.

Sea of Ruin

Stunning bright blue like his eyes.

How unexpectedly…*gorgeous*.

The shocking intensity of his gaze pushed against me, rudely, blatantly glaring, so distractingly at odds with the sweetness of his face. Mercy God, he had such an innocent-looking face. All marble-smooth skin, full rosy lips, thick heavy lashes, with the wind ruffling the black as ink strands of his short hair.

That sweet look, however, didn't disparage the unsettling aura of his presence. He regarded me as if he didn't care a whit if I lived or died or sprouted wings and clucked like a chicken. Apathy formed an impenetrable shield around him, and perhaps that explained why his face gave the impression of youthsome innocence.

With ordinary people, exhaustion sagged the eyes. Anger carved between the brows. Triumph etched around the mouth. But Lord Cutler showed none of that. No emotions. No wrinkles or lines. No expressions. He bore the straightest, smoothest, most polished mien of indifference I'd ever seen.

I wanted a closer inspection.

Soldiers quivered and stiffened down the line, but no one stopped me as I ambled aft, arrowing toward their commodore.

His passionless blue eyes didn't waver from mine. *Unnerving*.

Stacks of corded, well-honed brawn composed his tall frame. *Intimidating*.

Sinews neither flexed nor bounced. Not the muscles in his jaw. Not the tendons in his thick neck. Not even when I stood toe to toe with him, half-dressed, nipples protruding, with my finger poking at one of his jeweled buttons. *Unnatural*.

Was he even human?

I feigned a toothy grin. His mouth didn't move. I wriggled my fingers in a taunting wave. He didn't flinch. Not a tarnal twitch.

No sense of humor, this one. Not that *I* was feeling amorous or droll by any means. In fact, dread was rising faster than I could push it down.

As a titled nobleman, he'd been bred to hide his true feelings and intentions beneath an air of pomp and pageantry. But this level of impassibility couldn't have been learned. He was heartlessly detached by nature.

I had no evidence to back up my conclusion. It was a gut feeling. But my instincts rarely steered me wrong. Case in point… Priest Farrell. When I'd met the king of libertines, my gut had known he would ruin me. My heart just hadn't cared.

Other than Priest, I'd outmaneuvered most of my adversaries because I was a woman and considered the weaker sex by default. On a ship, at a tavern, astride a horse, in a bed, it didn't matter. Men always misjudged me and paid for that mistake.

Lord Cutler, however, didn't fit the molds of my foes. Nothing shone in his demeanor, features, or stature that betrayed his thoughts. I positively couldn't read him.

For the first time since waking on HMS *Blitz*, I felt real fear. It scraped icy fingers up my spine and flapped leathery wings in my stomach. But I didn't let it surface as I met the commodore stare for stare.

He was, quite unfortunately, a handsome son of a bitch. Inarguably handsome, but in a rigid, chillingly regal manner. His hair was trimmed close to his scalp on the sides, leaving a short length of inky etiquette on top. His blunt jawline, with all its right angles, was so porcelain-like and hairless I wondered if he could even grow whiskers on that rock-hard face.

But the longer I gazed into those menacing blue eyes, the more I realized his youthful features were deceiving. He held himself with the confident, hardened stance of a man who had more experience than me on the sea. If I had to guess, he was in his early thirties. At least ten years my senior.

He reminded me of my father with that jaded look in his stare. The one that confessed he could inflict suffering without being affected by it. Only my father hadn't been able to retain that vicious air around me.

I wondered if anything or anyone could rattle Lord Cutler's insensibility.

My blood thrilled at the challenge.

Tense silence measured the passing seconds until I realized his reticence was a weapon he used to terrorize his enemies. I wished I could apply the same tactic, but his stillness made my skin itch.

I raised my chin and held his gaze. "If saving drowning women is your way of soliciting female companionship for dinner, you're trying too hard."

"Bennett Sharp, you've been taken into custody for piracy and murder. I shall transport you to England, a month's journey thereabouts, where you will stand trial for your crimes."

His deep aristocratic voice pronounced every syllable with perfect English inflection. But his arrogance made him complacent. He hadn't considered the possibility that I'd arranged *Jade's* escape, set up my own rescue, and had a backup plan or two in the event that Priest failed.

By the time I ran this warship off course, the commodore wouldn't know what hit him.

I studied him a moment, trying to glean his true self beneath the polished veneer.

Who are you, Ashley Cutler?

I recognized the surname but couldn't place it. "Your father resides among the Peerage of England?"

"Lord John Cutler is the first Viscount Warshire and serves as the Secretary of State for the Northern Department."

A lower rank than my grandfather but a prominent peer of the realm, nonetheless. Yet, at the mention of his father, there'd been no pride in his tone. No attachment. He'd sounded as if he were reading the title off a visiting card.

Oh, how I longed to know what inspired this man. Was he deeper than his career aspirations? Weaker or mentally slower than he appeared? Was he married or betrothed? Loved by some or despised by all?

Everyone had a vulnerability. I just needed to find his.

His strong jaw, sharp cheekbones, and noble nose supplied a blank canvas for the brilliant blue of his eyes. But I found myself focusing instead on his shapely chiseled mouth. The pinkish lips added an alluring contrast to his impeccable English complexion.

And when those lips moved, every man on the ship stopped breathing to listen.

"Put the pirate in the hold." He flicked a finger against the front of his coat, giving an invisible speck more attention than he gave his captive.

Multiple hands fell upon me, restraining my arms behind my back. No sense in fighting. I was outnumbered four-hundred men to one. Besides, when I'd designed this plan, I expected to spend weeks, if not months, in irons.

As Lord Cutler strode toward the gangway ladder, the lieutenants pulled me along behind him. With my arms shackled by immovable fists, my attention narrowed on the snug coat that draped the commodore's impressive shoulders and hinted at a hard, tight arse. Long legs flexed in tailored white breeches. Defined calves stretched the wool of his pristine stockings.

The man was immaculately dressed, accentuating all his best assets.

But he had dreadful taste in footwear. The buckles on his square-toed shoes were made of pure gold with embedded jewels. I didn't care how fashionable they were. If he did any sort of work on this ship, they wouldn't last a day.

I focused on those ridiculous shoes because the rest of him was just too compelling. His physical beauty defied the laws of nature, and I wanted nothing to do with that. My opinion of him needed to ferment in the back of my throat until all I tasted was repulsion.

Down the companionway and along the windowless passages, he stopped at the door to his private quarters. The lieutenants kept moving, shoving me onward to the ladder beyond.

"What do I call you?" I twisted my neck, finding his ice-blue eyes over my shoulder. "Commodore Prick? Lord Sweet Lips? My favorite arsehole?"

His expression remained empty, his carriage rigid.

"You're clenching it, aren't you?" I glanced at the vicinity of his arse and cocked a brow.

He didn't respond.

Stoic to a fault.

Nerves of steel.

I pursed my lips and blew him a kiss. "I'll see you soon, darling."

He'd just captured the notorious daughter of Edric Sharp. Curiosity and arrogance would bring him slithering into my lap before nightfall.

Just so, he didn't acknowledge any of this as he vanished into his cabin.

Several hatchways later, my escorts dragged me through the lowest level of the warship. Weaving around coils of cables, live chickens and geese, and water stores, we had to stoop beneath the low rafters. Near the center of the ship, the crawlspace opened into a large area with more headroom.

As we turned the corner, the dank air perspired with the stench of too many unwashed bodies crammed together in close quarters.

Then I saw them.

Confined in one large hold behind an iron gate, sweaty men stood shoulder to shoulder, coughing, stinking, and spreading disease. I took in the shadowed landscape of unkempt beards, gold earrings, jackboots, distrusting glares…

Captured pirates.

Lord Cutler was a pirate hunter. Of course, I wasn't his only prize. But twenty…thirty…forty of my kind? It was horrifying.

Sea of Ruin

Worse, he meant to imprison me with the animals. I was one of them, after all, driven by the thrill of raiding, killing, and raising hell on the high seas.

With one distinct difference.

Dozens of eyes slid in my direction. Hungry, predatory eyes that saw only a female, a body to rut, and nothing more. I wouldn't survive a night in that cage.

The lieutenants shoved me toward the gate.

Seventeen

My heart slammed in my throat. "How long have they been in there?"

"Some of them a month or longer." One of the officers jabbed a key into the lock.

The clicking sound drove my pulse too hard, too fast, terrorizing my veins. Memories flooded, transporting me back into the body of a fourteen-year-old girl fighting for her virtue beneath the brutality of the Marquess of Grisdale.

My skin shuddered, tightening and pulling away from my bones. I refused to be violated like that again. Not by a marquess. Not by forty pirates. Not by any man.

But what if I didn't have a choice?

A scream wavered on the end of my tongue, urging me to call for the commodore and beg him for mercy. But he'd ordered me down here, knowing exactly what awaited. He would grant no quarter, and my useless demands for special treatment would only reveal my crippling fear.

One thing I could *not* do was enter that enclosure showing weakness. The pirates would scent it, feed on it, and become rabid.

As the lieutenants shoved me forward, I fought fearlessly, furiously, thrashing, spitting, and doing what any man would do in my position. Instinct took over until all that existed was the savage impetuosity to protect myself.

But in the end, I was too small, unarmed, outnumbered, and quickly subdued.

My knees scraped along the planks as the lieutenants shoved and kicked me into the hold. I landed on my backside, and the sound of the gate locking surged bile through my chest.

I was a pirate captain, dammit. I'd maimed, tortured, and slaughtered some decisively evil and scary men. I didn't possess Priest's magnetic ability to win over a crowd, but I could command them with my eyes closed. I just needed them to see beyond my femaleness.

A pair of trousers would have been splendid right now.

Breathing deeply, I slowed the heave of my lungs, rose to my full height, and steeled my spine. Then I turned and faced forty ravenous rogues.

"Point me to your captain." I searched the overcrowded space, taking an inventory of scars, long greasy braids, suspicious skin sores, and creatures crawling in beards.

If I'd kept Priest in the bilge for a month without a wash bucket, would he have reached this level of pungency? I didn't think so, but I was rather inclined to favor his appearance, no matter everything else that was wrong with him.

The pack of thieves leered with wild eyes. Some sniffed the air in front of me. Others grunted throaty noises.

None pointed out the captain.

My teeth sawed the insides of my cheeks. It didn't matter if they all came from the same crew or met one another in this hold. Pirates were a democratic breed, and they always had a leader.

"Were you hit on your heads?" I balled my hands at my sides, concealing the nervous shaking. "Or do you not speak the king's English?"

"The king doesn't speak English, lassie." The low, rough Scottish accent came from somewhere in the back.

It was true that King George—who hailed from Germany to England—refused to speak in the tongue of his inherited realm. But that was neither here nor there.

What concerned me was the owner of that Scottish brogue. He was the leader, and if he knew things about the English king, he wasn't without intellect. That didn't bode well for me. Neither did the rising agitation rippling through his men.

I faced the direction of the voice. "Show yourself, Highlander."

The stench of body odor shifted around me before ruthless fingers captured my wrists. Innumerable hands. There were so many attackers all at once it only took seconds to restrain my limbs and shove me deep into the sticky horde of bodies.

When I hit the back wall, I could no longer see the gate. Half a dozen men held my arms and legs, stretching me like an X with my spine against the wooden rib of the warship's hull.

Full-body tremors pummeled through me. It couldn't be helped. My arms twisted in sweaty clutches, my hands slipping uselessly, unable to find a gripping place. The more I struggled, the stronger and heavier my attackers became, multiplying in numbers and moving like a tidal wave until they formed a single unpreventable force that crashed against me, bruised my skin, and bellowed vile promises.

"Back off!" I screamed and gnashed my teeth. "Release me! I can help you!"

Everything stopped. The pirates who restrained me didn't let go, but the others fell back. The swarm divided, leaving a narrow path for one man to approach.

The captain.

Long red hair tangled around a matching beard that hung to his chest. Luminous green eyes shone out of a narrow face that might have been attractive, if not for the foreboding sneer that slashed across it.

He prowled toward me, tall, lean, and shirtless. The scars on his freckled torso and arms painted a gruesome constellation. Frayed trousers sagged low on trim hips. No boots. No jewelry. Nothing to indicate who he was.

But there was only one known redheaded pirate captain from Scotland, and his noxious reputation preceded him.

"Madwulf MacNally." I jutted my chin, my nostrils pulsing with the rush of my breaths. "I'm Bennett Sharp."

My name flickered recognition in his eyes before they hardened into cold green jewels. "I dinna care if you're the Countess of Nithsdale. Right now all you are is caged, just like the rest of us."

My stomach clenched, but I made my mouth smile. "I can help you escape."

"You?" His chuckle spread a chill across my skin. "The only release you can provide is the one I'll be taking between your bonny thighs."

My pulse quickened, but I didn't fight the hands that held me. I forced myself to remain calm and unruffled.

If I told him the notorious Priest Farrell was going to stop this warship from reaching England's shore, he wouldn't believe me. Or maybe he would, but it wouldn't dissuade him from his cruel intentions.

No, I couldn't mention Priest. Not without risking the commodore hearing my rescue plan.

"How about I save my bonny thighs to trap Lord Cutler?" I grinned despite my surgent nausea. "I'll obtain a private meeting with him, put him in a scandalous position, and—"

"If his lordship was interested in you, you wouldn't be here. *With us.*"

Hard to argue.

My stomach sank.

"I dinna mind his cast-offs if they all look like you." He crowded in and traced an overgrown fingernail along my jawline, making me gag. "Prettiest thing I've ever seen on the high seas. Right, lads?"

The men cheered and whistled in agreement.

"Momentarily, I'll be using your wee cunt quite thoroughly against this wall." Madwulf pawed between my legs, beneath the shirt, skin against skin. "You're going to cry, but dinna fash yourself about that. I *want* your tears, daughter of Edric."

"No." A hot ember formed in my throat, and I squirmed helplessly. "Not this. I'll give you something else. Anything. Name it."

"This is all you have to give, lassie." He dug a thick finger into my dry flesh and thrust.

My entire body cringed and bucked, but there was nowhere to go. Too many hands held me in place. Too many mouths panting against my face. The reek of rotten teeth made my gut turn.

"But I'm nae a selfish man." He stabbed deeper, scraping broken fingernails along my insides. "I always leave a wee bit of something to share with my laddies, and they prefer it to still be a-kickin'."

"I don't need her kicking, Captain, or breathing," a voice shouted from the crowd. "Just so long as I get me some relief in one of them holes."

Laughter erupted as the knaves shoved one another in excitement.

My joints locked to the point of pain, and tears rose, burning the back of my throat. But I kept it at bay and held Madwulf's gaze, my eyes dry and stony.

His cock was out, the bulbous head of it ramming against my naked thigh and drooling thick beads of slime. The thought of having that thing inside me dropped a hot, jagged rock in my stomach.

There was no stopping this. Even if I possessed the intelligence to talk my way out of it, Madwulf wasn't a person who could be reasoned with. All I had left was my anger, and I let it burn me up from the inside out.

"What a strong, fearsome man you are." I chewed each word and spat it between my teeth. "Forcing your lust upon a woman while she's held down by forty scoundrels. Praise be to God for big, tough Madwulf MacNally. Your kin must be proud."

With his chest so close to my mouth, I jerked forward and bit down on a hunk of sweat-slick flesh. Hard enough to make him bleed.

His hand swung, colliding with my cheekbone, as he roared with laughter.

I tasted blood, from the bite, from the strike of his fist. Instead of swallowing it, I worked it around with my saliva and spat the whole mouthful at his face.

It landed on the corner of his lips, clinging to the wiry hairs of his red beard. A depraved smile contorted his expression, and his tongue snaked out, licking the blood-tinged spittle.

Then he returned to my bone-dry flesh and the finger that he was jamming harder and faster inside me.

I fought tears and gulped down the impulse to scream. For every sob that burned through my nose, I swallowed three more. I would *not* cry.

He kicked my legs apart.

There were no atheists in the hangman's noose. As I faced the first of forty men to take a turn with my body, I found I wasn't godless, either.

Lips clamped, eyes closed, I prayed to whatever divine being that listened. I didn't make excuses for my life. Didn't beg forgiveness for the unchristian things I'd done. Didn't make solemn promises to be a chaste, obedient woman.

I just asked for strength. Courage. And *breath*. I needed to keep breathing, no matter how badly it hurt. If I held still and endured, I would get through it. I had to.

Keeping my eyes squeezed shut, I focused on praying and tuned out the vulgar shouting around me. I couldn't turn off the physical agony, but I didn't need to watch it or hear it.

Lost in my head, I let my body sag against the grips of brutal men as Madwulf jabbed his erection, searching for my opening. Tears gathered behind my closed eyes, silent and trapped.

Don't cry. Keep breathing.

Everything inside me wanted to die.

"Open your eyes." Madwulf grabbed my throat. "Or I'll peel them—"

A deafening explosion rang through the cage. Dust fell from the rafters. Pirates collapsed to their knees, and a pained scream erupted beside me, bringing my gaze to the man now writhing at my feet.

Blood bloomed from a hole in his thigh and spread a red puddle beneath him.

A gunshot.

Who the devil sneaked a pistol in here?

Madwulf released me, staggering backward. But he didn't go far. A large blade appeared beneath his chin. Another caught him under the withering sag of flesh between his legs.

Lord Cutler stood behind him, holding both daggers. His eyes, like twin flames of violent blue, roared at me over Madwulf's shoulder, seizing my breath.

"Which one do you want to keep?" He put those shapely pink lips at Madwulf's ear. "The beard? Or the beard-splitter?"

"The beard-splitter!" Madwulf strained his eyes downward, trying to see the lethal blade against his penis. "You hear me? Keep my cock!"

"Wasn't asking you." Lord Cutler regarded me, his gaze enigmatic.

He wanted *me* to choose?

His lieutenants flanked him, aiming dragoon pistols. Not one pirate attempted to touch the commodore. They were too frozen in fear.

The starch hadn't left his expression. But something new flashed across his flawless features, an unnamed emotion, for it was there and gone before I could identify it.

As the wounded man bled out on the deck, his mates continued to restrain me against the wall. No one moved. No one spoke as they stared at the blades that held their captain hostage, waiting for my answer.

Which one did I want Madwulf to keep?

I should choose the beard and let Lord Cutler sever the scoundrel's manhood, so it could never threaten me again. But when the time came for Priest and me to take command of this ship, we would need a pirate crew to overrun the soldiers and keep them in line.

As much as I hated it, I couldn't afford to make enemies with these ruffians.

I met Lord Cutler's incisive eyes and shrugged. "He can keep the pisser."

With a flick of his wrist, he sliced through the hair at Madwulf's chin and caught the wiry red nest before it fell.

Then he sheathed his blades. No expression. No fear.

Madwulf growled like an animal and swung away, straightening his trousers. When he turned back, he glowered at me as if this were my fault.

"Honest to God, Madwulf, you look better beardless. Really brings out your long dainty neck. I daresay castration wouldn't have had the same effect." I yanked against the hands that held me and hardened my voice. "Now call off your men."

A muscle flexed in his jaw.

"I want her alive when I deliver her to the gallows." Lord Cutler clasped his hands behind his back. "But the rest of you? I really don't give a damn. Release her or…" He glanced at his armed lieutenants. "Don't."

The prisoners tensed, looking to Madwulf. He ground his teeth, and a moment later, gave them a nod.

One by one, sweaty fingers sprang open and slipped off my body, leaving me to stand on my own, unfettered, and mostly covered by Priest's shirt.

"You." Lord Cutler slapped the severed beard into my hand. "Come with me."

He pivoted on his gold-buckled shoes and strode out, expecting me to obey.

For better or for worse, I tossed the beard to Madwulf and followed.

Eighteen

By the time we arrived at Lord Cutler's quarters, my nauseating terror of forty men had trickled into the uncertain fear of one.

Cutler was only a single threat. But he was the strongest, most powerful of them all, and I didn't have an inkling what he meant to do with me.

At the cabin door, a blue-coated soldier stood rigidly at attention. Armed to the teeth with pistols and blades, he was assigned to guard the life of the most valuable man on the ship.

"Sergeant Smithley." Cutler gripped my elbow and yanked me against his side. "This prisoner will be staying in my quarters. She's under *my* protection, and at no time will you thwart her actions or engage with her in any way. Do I make myself clear?"

Tingling jolts hit my circulation. From the heat of his hand on my arm? Or was it the unexpected order he gave his sergeant? Surely, he didn't expect me to behave just because he'd rescued me from Madwulf?

Staring straight ahead, the guard didn't shift his gaze. Didn't choke in surprise. Didn't move anything except his lips. "Yes, my lord."

None of this made sense.

"What if I attack him? Would he not defend himself?" I jerked my arm from Cutler's grip.

He released me. "If you harm a single hair on any of my men, you'll return to the hold with your friends."

"Yes. Right. Let's discuss that. Your timing down there was—"

Cutler entered his quarters, leaving me standing there talking to myself.

Outrageous.

I charged after him and staggered into a huge, moonlit dining cabin. Already dusk?

An adjoining day cabin and sleeping chamber lay just aft. I craned my neck, taking in the three spaces that made up the commodore's private domain, which took over the entire stern of HMS *Blitz's* upper deck.

I knew royal quarters like this existed but had never seen one. I tried not to be impressed.

He lit a lantern, then several more, illuminating charts and maps and papers stacked neatly on the table. The room said so much about him. And nothing interesting.

He liked maps. He liked to read. He lived to work. Did his dullness never cease?

I didn't see bottles of rum, tobacco, whips and chains, or trunks filled with showy, impractical finery. Though he must have an elaborate wardrobe somewhere in here with large doors and drawers to store his embroidered coats and buckled footwear.

"As I was saying…" I ambled around the table, absently picking through the papers. "Your timing in the hold was impeccable. Deliberate. You waited until the very last moment to…"

He put toe to heel and slipped off his shoes, kicking them aside.

I blinked in confusion. "Were you watching the cage from around the corner? Waiting for that animal to put something other than his fingers inside me?"

His blue frock and white shirt came off next. He draped both over a nearby chair.

Muscles? Yes, he had bricks of them. He wasn't as thickly built as Priest, but sharp outlines and flat hairless surfaces fashioned his masculine form as if hewn with a chisel.

I ate him up with my eyes, heating with female appreciation, clenching my hands, and losing my train of thought.

"You're staring." He removed his weapons—two blades he used on Madwulf—and set them on the table.

"Why did you put me in the hold with them if you knew what would happen?"

"I wanted *you* to know what would happen. Let it serve as a warning. Next time, I won't intervene."

Next time.

My pulse accelerated. There was no mistaking his meaning.

I was on probation. If I made him angry, he would throw me back in the hold with forty hot-blooded pirates who now blamed me for their captain's embarrassment.

Good thing I chose the beard.

Cutler's eyes—darker and deeper blue than mine—roamed over me, cutting, calculating. "You're tougher than you look."

Seeing him shirtless and shoeless in all his godlike beauty, a woman could misconstrue that statement.

But he wasn't Priest. He wasn't vulgar in mind. Wasn't trying to charm his way between my legs. I guessed he wasn't even thinking about fornication.

"What are you saying?" I crossed my arms.

"I've never met a siren, but you must be of the same ilk or nature. Unchristian, mysterious, dangerously enticing… If you think to lure me with those eyes and enchant me to shipwreck, you have the wrong sailor."

My eyes? I blinked them slowly, stunned speechless. Perhaps I didn't know his mind after all.

Sirens were carnal, sensual, beautiful beings. How could he possibly compare me to…? Wait. Sirens weren't even real.

I glanced at his snug-fitting breeches, the only thing he still wore. My stomach flipped. "Why did you remove your clothes?"

"I know things. I know them before anyone else. What I don't know, I figure out."

What an evasive, baffling response. And what did he know exactly?

Did he know about Priest? Or my plan to escape? Or my father's compass? No, he didn't know the important things.

My gaze snagged on the bowl of apples on the table, prompting my stomach to growl. I should have eaten the orange I'd rubbed on my chest this morning.

Mother of God, that seemed like so long ago. Even longer since I'd had a meal.

"So…" I leaned against the wall behind me, attempting a casual pose. "What do you know, Cutler?"

"You were born in the colonies, but England is in your blood."

My breath hitched. "Lots of people are English."

"Perhaps. But the blood that flows in your veins is *beau monde*. It's in your speech, your bone structure, the regal beauty you try so hard to conceal beneath sun-freckled skin and a wild mane of uncombed hair." He bent over the opposite side of the table, hands braced on the surface, head cocked, studying me too closely. "Nobility has been trained into your bearing, the way you hold your shoulders, your spine…" His gaze centered on my mouth before dipping just beneath it. "The lift of your chin."

I forced my expression to remain as blank as his, despite the panic pounding beneath my skin.

"As a twenty-year-old lady of breeding," he said, "you understand the importance of addressing me by my military rank and ennobled title."

"I'm twenty and one." I squinted at him. "And I'll call your thirty-year-old arse whatever I damn well please."

"I'm four years past thirty." He regarded the large fit of Priest's shirt on my body. "You have a husband."

Ice hit my veins. He guessed this by what I wore? Or had someone exposed my secret?

"Wrong." My throat constricted and relaxed.

"A lover, then."

"I have many."

"Whore." He spat the word while somehow maintaining his stoic mien.

"Don't shame me for being liberated. I'm a sexually transgressive woman, doing just as a man does. It's *my* prerogative to do it with whomever I like as often as I like."

That used to be my habit. Then I met Priest. After two lonely dry years, it was about time I started enjoying life again. But not here, and not with Lord Prude.

"Where I come from," he said, "you're a ruined woman."

"Are you married?"

"No."

"Have you ever sheathed yourself inside a woman?"

His eyes screwed down to slits, and from across the table, I felt the heat of them on my lips. Veins throbbed in his temples and throat. Not in outrage. His body language remained calm. But he was positively trying to shield a reaction. While thinking about sheathing himself in a woman? Who? Certainly not me.

"Yes." He licked his lips. "I've shared my bed."

"Whore." I gasped in mock displeasure. "I mean, if you were a woman, of course. You would be an embarrassment to your family. Scandalized. Exiled. *Ruined*."

"If you have a point, make it."

I released an exasperated breath. "You seem like an intelligent fellow, Ashley. Surely, you see the hypocrisy in your social traditions."

"I don't make the rules."

"You just follow them. Marvelous. Because I have some rules of my own." I rounded the table, stopped beside him, and leaned a hip against the edge. "My enjoyment in carnal relations doesn't mean I welcome it with everyone. Would you like to know what happened to the first lord who greeted me with his unwelcome prick?"

"Enlighten me."

"In hindsight, I should have castrated him before I gutted him. But I was only fourteen. Such a shy maiden, that poor girl."

"I doubt you were ever shy."

"Just so. I hadn't yet learned the art in creative, prolonged torture. Did you know a man can still maintain an erection when the skin is flayed from his genitals?"

"You're a vile creature."

"Thank you." I smiled sweetly.

It was true that I'd skinned a man who had made a habit of violating women. Only once, though. I didn't have the stomach to attempt it again.

"A woman…" His gaze slid to my lips. "Commanding a fifty-gun galleon. When did the gates of hell break open?"

"I think I liked you better when you didn't speak." I snapped my fingers in front of his unblinking eyes. "Stop looking at my mouth."

"I can't seem to make sense of you."

"It's easy, Commodore. Just think of the smartest man you know, remove all the hauteur and bigotry, and add a larger pair of testicles."

"Disturbing."

"The world is disturbing."

I swore I saw the shadow of a smile on his starched face. But in the next breath, I was certain I hadn't. The gunmetal jaw that was level with the top of my head went rigid, and his entire body hardened as if preparing for battle.

"Since your father was a known savage," he said, "it can be reasoned by deduction that your mother is a peer of the realm. Or was? Where is she now? No longer among the *beau monde*. They would've banished her the moment she became round with her bastard daughter."

Red-hot anger spiked as I tilted my chin up to meet him squarely in the eye. "You don't know what you're talking about."

"Edric Sharp destroyed your mother, didn't he? The selfish, uneducated brute deserved to hang. I wish I would've been there to witness it."

My arm moved on its own, swinging swiftly, furiously, careening knuckles across his nose with a wet, blood-spewing *crack*.

He blinked, and I found myself looking up into a face that was too relaxed to be bleeding. But his hot blue eyes told a different story, one I didn't register until his fist crashed into my jaw.

The strike hit hard enough to send me flying backward. My arms and legs whirled to remain vertical as hair tumbled into my face. Gasping, choking for air, I crumpled over my knees. By the time I righted again, the throb in my cheek had spread into my entire skull.

Outrage, exhilaration, and pure, unadulterated joy rushed through me. Nothing made my blood sing like a man who wasn't afraid to fight a woman.

With a high-pitched shrill, I charged. He met me mid-air, our fists crashing into flesh. We hit and kicked with the force of lightning, losing our footing, and wrestling each other to the floor.

The pain wouldn't surface until later. For now, all that existed was the ferocity to hurt him until he understood that no man used my father as an insult.

His muscled forearm connected with my throat. I threw a leg, an elbow, spluttering for air, and cursing him through each strike.

There was a lot more movement and effort on my end. Meanwhile, he seemed to be deflecting, redirecting, and flowing punches like a trained fighter with the veins in the backs of his hands and arms standing out like blue rivers.

He wasn't going easy on me. He just didn't have to try as hard, for he had the advantage of weight and brawn. But he couldn't match my determination.

If he needed proof of that, it came in the form of my foot in his groin. I kicked him with all the strength I could gather and waited for his roar.

But I was only met with silence. I wasn't sure he was breathing. Then he did.

In a breath that arrived in a blur, he slammed me onto my back and collared my neck with steel fingers.

Sea of Ruin

"Oh, darling." He ran the tip of his nose along my throbbing jaw and whispered in my ear, "You're going to regret that."

His other hand wrapped around my tangled curls, and he dragged me across the floor by my hair. I kicked and spat and thrashed into the legs of passing furniture as he hauled me aft through the length of his private quarters.

"What are you doing?" I clawed at the fist in my hair, my eyes watering from the agony of the strands ripping from my scalp. "Let me go!"

He dumped me onto an outdoor balcony that overlooked the endless black ocean. Before I could scramble away, his knee came down onto my throat. The other landed across my thighs, effectively pinning me to the planks.

A thick length of rope appeared in his hands, the end of which he efficiently tied around my wrists. I fought him, demanding answers, and cursing him to hell and back.

He didn't give me his gaze until he'd perfected the knot around my arms. Then he lifted his head.

Blue eyes blazed down at me, and God help me, those gorgeous, hypnotizing features... He had not one feeling among them. He didn't blink. Didn't scowl. Didn't smile.

I'd been captured by an inhuman, unfeeling non-smiler.

Tailwind blew off the warship's wake, rustling his black hair and crusting my wheezing inhales with salt.

He lifted me in his arms and stepped to the balcony rail. "Do you know what happens right before the world starts spinning?"

My pulse went wild.

"No." With my wrists tied and the waves crashing beyond the rail, I definitely did *not* want to know.

"You fall."

"No!" My heart stopped as I grappled him with bound hands. But it was no use.

He raised me over the edge and hurled me into the sea.

Nineteen

The rope caught, cutting off my scream and yanking the wind from my lungs.

As I continued to spiral toward the moonlit sea, the tension in the line wrenched my arms over my head and thankfully, blessedly, slowed my descent.

Too bad my heart didn't slow. The panicked thing galloped dangerously, shaking in my chest and making me dizzy.

The fall seemed to last as long as the one I'd taken earlier from the gunwale of *Jade*. But this time, darkness shrouded the waves below.

No sane person went willingly into the ocean at night. Not with the deadly undercurrents, venomous creatures with soft bodies and stinging tentacles, giant nocturnal eels that hunted in packs, and man-eating sharks with an unrivaled bite force—all unseen and soundless, lurking, waiting in the dark.

If and when I hit that water, there would be no rescue boat this time. I would become part of the food chain.

All of this flashed through my mind as I plunged with agonizing slowness. I fixated on the cable, tracing the length where it connected from my wrists to the ominous end that led up, up, up… Where did it go? Was Ashley holding it? Was it tied to something on the balcony? Whatever secured my lifeline was letting it out inch by inch, easing my fall but not stopping it.

My hands clawed at the knot that bound them, my fingers clamping around the rope. I couldn't see through the blackness to the balcony, didn't know why Ashley had tethered me before throwing me over. But somewhere overhead, the cable snapped tautly.

I bounced to a halt, my wrists snapping in the restraint as my weight jerked and swung in the tailwind.

Dangling just above the crashing wake behind HMS *Blitz*, I swayed close enough to taste salt water. The warship groaned as her hull carved a deep black swath in the sea, spraying my legs in a warm mist and saturating Priest's shirt.

Priest…

I wildly scanned the nebulous landscape, straining to see the horizon. *Are you out there?*

Now would be a good time for my feral huntsman to do something terrifying. But it was too soon. It would take him weeks to thieve a sloop, woo the new crew, and hunt down this ship. I was on my own.

The rope quavered. And the winds. The tides. The world narrowed to the drum and the whoosh and the dark, the dark, the dark… My heart cried.

"Ashley Cutlerrrrrrrr!" Waves spat at my legs in coughing fits, spinning me round and round. "You miserable little cock! Pull me in, damn you!"

I tried kicking, building momentum to launch myself upward to climb. But with my hands so tightly bound, there was no way to grip. I would've had better success if I were armless.

"Cutler! A pox on your blood! A pox on your king! A pox on your whole damn navy!" I screamed again and again until my voice bled and broke.

There was nothing to do but wait. And wait. I waited so long I knew he'd left me here to die.

Why would he do that? At any moment, a giant shark could leap out of the water and swallow me whole. Then he would have no lady pirate parts to deliver to England.

Why hadn't he just left me in the hold? At least then, he would still have my head.

Needles prickled my hands until they grew cold. Numb. Wet hair stuck to my face and coiled around my throat. Wuthering gusts of briny air carried away my tears and turned my mouth into a desert. Eventually, exhaustion set in, shoving me past the point of weeping.

I kept my eyes on the water as it blurred away in sparkling moonlit billows. Staying awake seemed crucial for some reason, but it proved

Sea of Ruin

more difficult with each passing minute. The wind and the strain of hanging flogged the energy from my body, and my eyelids began to sag.

As I started to drift, I felt a vibration. Movement quivered down the line. Seconds pulsed by before I realized the distance between my feet and the water was stretching, lengthening. The rope was being pulled in.

My chest surged with the tumult of my breaths, waking my bones with violent tremors. Higher and higher I rose until the balcony came into view, and just beyond it, the cold sapphire eyes of my captor.

He knotted the rope around the rail, leaving me swinging just out of reach.

"Ashley…" I followed the length of the cable up and around an overhead beam, which supported a jutting roof. "Pull me in."

With nothing but air and sea beneath my feet, I squirmed in limbo, uncertain and stricken with panic.

Why wasn't he bringing me over the rail? I tried to extend a leg toward it, but I could only brush my toe against the balustrade.

Just out of reach, he reclined a shoulder against the open door to the cabin, wearing his white shirt and breeches and holding a knife at his side. He watched me impassively, as if hanging a half-naked woman outside his balcony was a nightly ritual.

Perhaps it was.

I wanted to kill him. The impulse to scream vivid details of how he would die clawed at my tongue. But I trapped the rant behind pinched lips.

The man had just plunged me toward the ocean like bait on a hook and suspended me there for nearly an hour. Now he casually held a knife too close to the cable that might very well drop me for the last time.

My heart told me I wouldn't die tonight. Ashley Cutler had a role yet to play in my life. For good or for evil. Whichever way that went, enraging him wouldn't keep me alive.

"Are you frightened now?" He tapped the blade against his thigh.

"I was frightened before."

"Not nearly enough." He grabbed an apple from the table behind him and set the knife to it, slicing off a bite-size piece. "I'd rather not return you to the hold. You might not be tender or fragile, but a month in a cage with forty beasts feeding upon you…" He popped the wedge of apple into his mouth and chewed. "I don't wish that on any woman."

Brutal, uncontrollable shaking wracked my body. The weight of my wet hair hung in my face, my neck too weak to hold up my head. I couldn't even muster the strength to beg or complain about the agony in my hands.

His gaze swept over me, taking in my ragged, shivering appearance. "You're sufficiently exhausted."

Was that what he called this? I was living a nightmare. My muscles had long ago given out. My stomach knotted with hunger pangs, and my shoulders felt as though they'd pulled from the sockets.

He balanced the apple on the rail off to the side. Then he put the knife between his teeth, the serrated edge angled outward, and stepped toward me.

I tensed as he let out more rope, lowering me until I hung at chest level with the rail. With a hand on my bound wrists, he hauled me in, hooking an arm beneath the backs of my thighs.

Lacking the energy to move, I let him lift me up and drape my legs over the balcony. The position seated me on the rail with my arms stretched overhead and his hips between my knees.

The warmth of his proximity breathed against me, his face hovering just inches from mine as he straightened Priest's shirt over my thighs.

The knife between his lips served as a lethal barrier. One forward thrust of his head and the sharp edge would do some gruesome damage to my face.

I waited for him to cut the rope, but he didn't. He straightened, reached for the apple, and removed the steel from his teeth to carve another wedge.

The tension in the cable pulled my upper body backward, requiring me to focus all my strength on my knees, where they hooked over the balcony rail. I could only sit there, clinging at an awkward angle, vulnerable, drained, and entirely at his mercy.

"Now…" He stabbed a piece of apple with the blade and held the juicy fruit to my mouth. "What shall we talk about?"

Twenty

My stomach caved in.

Ashley wanted to talk instead of untying me? *The devil fetch him!*

With his eyes locked on mine, he waited, his head tilting deliberately as if to distract me from whatever emotion he guarded. He seemed to believe he was untouchable, impenetrable, especially holding that knife. But if he meant to cut me, he would've done so by now.

I'd punched him earlier. Hell, I'd landed a few good hits across that pretty face. Yet there wasn't a trace of blood on his person.

"Your shirt." I parted my lips and bit the wedge of apple off his blade, chewing lazily.

"Go on." His disinterested tone grated as he carved another piece.

"You removed it, the frock, and those ridiculous shoes before we fought." I opened my mouth and accepted the next slice while considering my bloody shirt. "You knew I would attack you and didn't want your precious clothing to get ruined like mine. Since you're wearing the shirt again, you must believe there will be no more bloodshed between us."

Something lit in his eyes. Appreciation. I hadn't missed it that time. He liked that I had a brain and knew how to use it.

Well, it wasn't difficult to guess that he prided himself on his appearance. He reeked of vanity.

"What you said about my father…" I pressed my lips together, refusing the next cut of apple. "You were purposefully baiting my temper."

"And you fell for it. *Literally*."

He pivoted, leaving me suspended on the rail to amble through his sleeping quarters. The apple core and knife went on a small table. From an armoire, he removed another dark blue frock and shrugged it on. Black leather boots came next. He took his time lacing them over his wool stockings before returning to me. On his way, he passed a sea chest, where he grabbed a large glass bottle.

Uncorking it, he brought the drink to my lips. The syrupy, toasted sugar flavor of rum burst across my tongue. I gulped it down, taking long, greedy swills until my chest burned.

I coughed, wanting more, my eyes locked on the bottle. Instead of taking it away, he drifted closer, *all of him*, with his nose at my throat, inhaling.

"Stop smelling me." My insides cringed.

I tried to close my legs, but his hips prevented the attempt.

"I've never met a female like you." He dragged his nose through the wind-blown curls of my hair and returned to my neck. "You smell like the sea."

Masculine heat pressed into the juncture of my thighs, which was a great degree less deceptive than the implication in his soft voice or the lazy indifference in his half-mast eyes.

"Look at you." His gaze roved from my legs to my face, lingering on my mouth. "How can something so small rouse such widespread fear in the king's navy?"

"I'm a magical witch." I squirmed and bucked, trying to dislodge him.

He patronized me with the click of his tongue and set aside the rum. Then he pushed closer, making me horrifyingly aware that my futile wriggling had hardened the flesh in his tight breeches, extending that swollen girth down his thigh.

"It seems, my lord, that you're unable to hide *every* reaction." I attempted to kick free of the iron grip on my knees. "Untie me at once."

He made a scoffing sound. "You're a snarling, immodest, uncouth creature. I knew better than to tie you up. When an animal is rabid, you don't put a leash on it. You put it out of its misery."

"Call me whatever you please. It doesn't change the bulging *want* between your legs."

"You have no idea what I want." He caught my throat in a bruising fist, immobilizing me. "If you did, you would curl into yourself and tremble for mercy."

I wanted to tell him I didn't curl up or tremble for anyone. But I was doing both now, hunching and shaking and gasping for breath in the painful collar of his hand.

Bending over me, he pressed every inch of his body against every inch of mine. His impressive height and latitude of shoulders consumed my field of view and suffocated my senses. And his scent... Dear lord, he smelled clean. The soap he used to bathe, the aromatic mint on his lips, the cedar oil on his skin—the concoction was an aphrodisiac flooding what little air trickled in through my nose.

The sight of his powerful physique before without a shirt had struck me with sizzling awareness of his beauty. And now, with the blue coat stretching across the solid expanse of his chest, his nearness had the same effect.

I bit down on my tongue, but I couldn't quell my shaking.

How many times had I faced down a cruel, attractive man and came out on top? I was more brazen than any titled lady, physically stronger than the average woman. Priest was the only person who'd managed to knock my knees out from under me. Because I'd let him. And I'd learned.

But I was no match for a man who dangled me over the bellowing sea without a hint of pity or slack. As tightly as he was squeezing my airway, his face should have been on fire with fury. Yet he maintained his usual phlegmatic expression. Chillingly calm. Self-possessed.

"Ashley..." My lips moved without sound or breath. *Please, release me.*

He shifted, trapping one of my knees between the rail and his hips. Maintaining his hold on my neck, he lifted my other leg and tossed it off the balcony.

Panic surged, and I flailed, trying to adjust my weight to straddle the balustrade. But the rope didn't reach, and he allowed me no space to move. The position suspended me in the air with one leg hooked over the rail and the other kicking into the darkness.

Fighting gravity and fatigue, I couldn't close my thighs. I twisted uselessly, spread wide open with the warm wind smiting my feminine flesh. "Ashley, stop! What are you—?"

He slammed his palm between my legs with unholy force.

Pain exploded, and I cried out soundlessly, gulping and flinching through a stunned spasm. He loosened his grip on my throat as if he wanted to hear me scream. Then he struck my cunt again, forcefully, brutally, with his open hand, unleashing hell on my tender nub of nerves.

The shirt blocked his view of my nudity, but his strokes aimed true. He hit me over and over, bending into each blow and targeting my clitoris.

His breathing shortened into bursts of grunts, and his pelvis smashed against my trapped leg, grinding his erection as he swung.

My screams came unbidden as I rotated my bound hands, desperate to be freed, buzzing from the agonizing sensory stimulation. And something else.

The fiery heat of his hand made me throb. His touch never lingered, but every time it landed, I anticipated the next strike, the stinging burn, and the deep pulsations that I refused to accept.

Priest used to torment me so beautifully this way. His spanking, choking, biting proclivities had a wicked effect on my desire for him. But that had been in a willing, loving environment. This was not *that*.

This was wrong.

I didn't have to battle my body's reaction to the sensual pain. My brain took over, shutting down pleasure centers, stiffening my joints, and tensing the muscles between my legs.

As if Ashley detected my mental retreat, he pulled back, his hand hovering in the air. Blue eyes smoldered beneath feathery black lashes, sparking as he took my measure.

"You can fight it." He straightened and cleared the rasp in his voice. "But your body is still a whore."

"So is yours." I directed my gaze at the sizable bulge in his skin-tight breeches.

The corner of his mouth rose. The tiniest twist.

"Why?" Goddammit, I hurt. Everything pulsed and scorched as if doused in liquid fire. "Why hit me *there*?"

"Because I can." He drew in a lung-filling breath and shouted, "Sergeant Smithley!"

My eyes widened, and my pulse raged. "Don't send me back down there. I can be reasonable."

"You're incapable of being reasonable or civilized. But while you're on my ship, you *will* meet the minimum standards of courtesy."

He stepped back, capturing my swinging leg and hooking it over the rail. Once again, I sat on the balustrade at a backward angle. I immediately squeezed my thighs together.

Sea of Ruin

At the sound of the exterior door opening, he folded his hands behind him and tipped his head, his eyes trained on mine.

Two chambers away, beyond his broad frame, a silhouette appeared in the dining cabin. The movement inched into the day cabin, and a shaft of moonlight illuminated Sergeant Smithley's blank face.

He paused there as if he weren't allowed to enter the sleeping chamber. "Yes, my lord?"

"Should something happen to me..." Ashley kept his back to the soldier and his gaze pinned on mine. "If I fall ill, become injured, or perish, what have you been ordered to do with Miss Sharp?"

"Return her to the hold, my lord. She shall be transported to England with or without you."

"Very good, Sergeant. That will be all."

The soldier slipped out of view without a glance in my direction. When the click of the door sounded his departure, Ashley picked up the knife.

My heart rate spun as I tried to piece together what was happening. If he meant to kill me, he wouldn't have called in his sergeant to prove a point.

Dangling me in front of Madwulf MacNally, baiting me into a fistfight, hanging me over the sea, and summoning his sergeant—every action had been calculated.

He was establishing boundaries.

Stepping into me, he pushed his hips against my clenched knees and positioned the knife at the knot on my wrists. "Open your legs."

In one tingling swoop, the command heated me with arousal and chilled me with dread. I couldn't fight him on this. If he intended to sever the rope and not my hands, he needed a closer angle.

I spread my legs.

"Good girl." He straightened the shirt over my knees without looking and stretched over my inclined body. "Grab hold of me."

He cut the knot.

As it unraveled from my arms, he didn't touch me or try to prevent me from falling. He gripped the rail on either side of my hips, forcing me to reach for him. And reach I did. Clinging with arms and legs, I wrapped myself around the formidable pillar of his rock-hard frame.

"Remember this, Bennett." He turned his head, feathering his lips against my ear. "I am the only thing standing between you and Madwulf. Turn a weapon on me, and your time on this ship will be spent on your back beneath the hunger of forty unwashed men."

The wind grabbed my hair and tried to wrench me out to the sea. I dug my fingers into his muscled back and pressed my face against his chest, absorbing his words and cleaving to his strength.

He didn't need to keep me in restraints. Didn't need to guard his weapons. Didn't need his soldiers to thwart my actions. He imprisoned me with a solid, genuine threat.

"You can wander freely." His mouth moved against my cheek. "I've been very clear about what will happen if you attack me or any man on this ship."

My stomach hardened.

He gripped my arm and pulled me down from the rail. My legs wobbled as I stepped into his sleeping chamber, looking for a place to sit.

A privacy screen concealed the washbasin and chamber pot. A chair sat beside the armoire. Within the wall across from that was a vaulted chamber made to enclose the overstuffed mattress on three sides.

The air smelled like mint and cedar and cleanliness. Every breath I took was too intimate, too masculine, too *him*. Where did he expect me to sleep?

My gaze flitted to the bed and jerked away.

As much as I needed to collapse, I chose to stand. "How did you recognize me?"

"I didn't." He set the knife on the small table beside me.

I sagged beneath the throbbing accumulation of the day's injuries with no desire to look at the knife and even less desire to use it.

"If you set that there to test my intelligence, I'm offended." I gave the hilt a hard flick and left it spinning like a wheel on the table as I strolled away. "On a good day I can wield a blade against armies of men twice my size. You should also know I'm a dead shot with a pistol. But today's not a good day."

His face, too smooth and polished to require a barber's razor, gave no reaction.

"Can I be frank with you, Ashley?" I wandered through his private space, touching everything from blankets and clothing to furniture and trinkets just to annoy him.

"I expect nothing less."

"After being thrown off a ship *twice* in one day, only to end the night with a ruthless spanking on my lady parts—"

"The night isn't over."

I flung a glare at him. "I cannot simply forget these things occurred.

Sea of Ruin

You can trust that when I fall asleep, I'll dream of my hands throttling your throat until your lips turn blue, and your eyes pop from your face like corks. But…" I held up a finger without looking at him. "I'm not foolish enough to retaliate. When I make mistakes, I learn from them."

I turned and pointed at my swollen jaw, just one of the many aches he'd inflicted in the past few hours.

"I'm pleased to hear that you understand my expectations." He braced his boots in a noble stance and raised his squared jaw, staring down his nose at me.

"God's teeth, Commodore." I squinted up at him. "Do you ever grow tired of maintaining that stiff upper lip?"

"Do you ever grow tired of mocking the great and the good?"

"No. Positively never."

He stood like a statue for a minute or twenty. At length, he dragged a palm down his face, over his mouth, and let his shoulder drop against the wall.

Better? His cocked eyebrow asked.

The stiff lip was impossibly stiffer.

I shook my head. "Lord Ashley Cutler. All suited and booted and looking polished enough to hold the king's cock while he pisses."

"Your mouth is appalling." His gaze slid to the object of his gall.

"Is that your appalled expression? It looks the same as all your others, so I can't be sure. But honestly, Ashley, if my mouth disturbs you, why do you stare at it so?"

His eyes returned to mine. Deep blue gemstone eyes, thickly lashed and sensually hooded. Oh, how they must grow weary of watching females swoon in his path.

Flickering lantern light gilded his sculpted features and cast shadows over his perfectly combed, inky black hair. So shiny and lush, that hair. It was hard to believe it had ever been exposed to sun or salty air.

He was magnificent to behold, a distinguished officer in his prime who had just won a war and sailed across an ocean to capture Madwulf MacNally and the daughter of Edric Sharp. He would be the envy of his peers upon his return.

How long had he been at sea? Was he in a hurry to sail home? I was wildly curious to know what he was thinking as he answered my shameless appraisement with a calmer, more detached reserve.

"Do you have a lady in England you're anxious to reunite with?" I crossed my arms, standing a foot away.

"No."

No surprise there. When it came to women, he put more effort into spanking a clitoris than wooing a heart.

As I understood the situation, I would have a month to scrape information from his brain. Right now I had only so much energy left before my face planted itself onto the floor. The remainder of my questions would have to wait. Except one.

"How did you find me?"

"I was hunting another pirate, and he led me to you."

Priest? It wasn't possible. No one outside our circle of trust knew our connection.

My head pounded with panic and fatigue, but I kept my voice neutral. "Who?"

"Charles Vane."

"Ah." Grief collided with relief. I showed neither on my face. "Convenient for you."

"Abundantly. With Vane dead, you were my next target. But, by the time I learned of your arrival in Jamaica, you already weighed anchor and set sail. Rather suddenly, wasn't it?"

"You're not the only one hunting me."

"But I'm the only one who apprehended you."

Arrogant fool. If he only knew that Priest Farrell had nabbed me first. Oh, how I wanted to tell him he could've captured Edric Sharp's daughter *and* the Feral Priest if he hadn't fallen for my ruse.

But my marriage was my most guarded secret and greatest hope for escape.

"If you didn't recognize me," I said, "how did you find me?"

"No one could accurately describe your image. You did well keeping that unknown. Until now. But I didn't need to know what you looked like. I studied your behavior, your track worn in the sea, and lore that follows you. Your affiliation with Charles Vane. The galleon you commanded, which boasts no flags, figureheads, or markings. And your penchant for freeing slaves."

I closed my eyes, released a slow breath, and glared at him. "You found the sunken slave ship."

"I received word of it when dead seamen and burned timber washed ashore west St. Christopher. The attack had your stamp of ownership all over it. 'Twas easy to track you from there."

My hands clenched, but I couldn't regret that raid. We'd saved two young African men that day. Besides, with Ashley on my trail since Jamaica, he would've caught me eventually. Just like Priest had.

Sea of Ruin

He straightened from the wall and breezed past me, headed to the armoire. From a drawer within, he removed a blue three-cornered hat trimmed in feathers and jammed it on his head. From another drawer, he pulled out a long swath of linsey-woolsey and splayed it on the mattress.

A gentleman's loose nightgown.

Priest had never worn a stitch of clothing to bed. I preferred nudity, as well. But not here.

"Is that for me?" I lifted the hem, rubbing the coarse cloth between my fingers, relieved it wasn't transparent.

"Yes." He flicked a finger toward the privacy screen. "Wash yourself before retiring."

He pivoted and strode toward the dining cabin, dressed in full uniform as if he were going somewhere.

"Ashley?" I waited until I had his eyes. "Where do I sleep?"

"There." He thrust his steely chin at the bed behind me and resumed walking.

"Where are you sleeping?" At his silence, I hurried after him. "Where are you going?"

The click of the exterior door sounded his exit.

A growl of frustration vibrated in my chest. I raced past the desk in the day cabin, around the table in the dining cabin, and swung open the door.

Ashley stood on the other side, boots spread apart, hands clasped behind him, and blue eyes narrowed on mine. Expecting me.

My breath came up short. "You said I could wander freely."

"Not dressed like that." He shifted to the side and motioned at the two lieutenants behind him.

The men bustled in, carrying piles of mismatched fabric. They dumped the tattered garments on the table, along with a platter of sewing supplies, and swept out of the cabin.

"There's enough cloth there," he said. "You will fashion a proper wardrobe for yourself before you leave these quarters."

"I don't know how to sew." I folded my arms over my chest.

He bent toward me and put his nose inches from mine. "Your upbringing says otherwise."

I blinked, searching for the best retort. It was true that Lady Abigail Leighton had taught me how to work with a needle and thread. But the only sewing I'd done in the past seven years involved open wounds and bleeding flesh.

Another man stepped into the room, carrying a small medicine chest that rattled with glass vials.

"Madam." The blond man glanced at my raw wrists, bloody shirt, and throbbing jaw. "I'm Lieutenant Flemming, the ship's surgeon. Let's look at your injuries, shall we?"

Shocked, I watched the wardroom warrant officer stride toward the day cabin. Behind him trailed a younger uniformed man holding a tray of fruit, meats, and biscuits.

After everything Ashley had unleashed on me today, never in a thousand lifetimes would I have expected this level of decency. There must be a catch.

When I turned back to the doorway, Ashley was gone.

Twenty-one

I knew I was tired but hadn't comprehended the extent of my exhaustion until I fell asleep at the dining table while Lieutenant Flemming treated the abrasions on my wrists.

He woke me with a hand on my shoulder, shaking me gently. "Madam? You should lie down."

His soft English accent matched his demeanor. White strands streaked the roots of his blond hair, making him appear older than his forty years. That was my guess, anyway. He didn't talk much.

Ointments and bandages gathered, he stepped out without another word, leaving me alone in the dimly lit cabin.

I ate some roasted meat and biscuits to appease my grumbling stomach. Then I padded into Ashley's sleeping quarters.

Behind the privacy screen, I removed Priest's shirt and held it to my nose. It no longer smelled like him, but I couldn't bring myself to discard it.

Using the soap and water in the basin, I scrubbed the blood from the linen and hung it to dry.

Various supplies filled the cabinet, such as fragrant oils for hair, ambrosial salve for skin, an oxbone brush with horsetail hairs for cleaning teeth, and cutting instruments for whiskers. Did Ashley actually use the latter? After a full day, he still had naught a bristle on his unshaven face.

I washed my hair and body with his cleansers, taking care with the jade stone at my throat. Then I donned the gentleman's nightgown, swimming in the linsey-woolsey as I crawled beneath the counterpane on his bed.

The stuffing was soft enough, the distance between sides wide enough for two. But I felt more secure tucking myself against the wall of the alcove and pulling the blankets up around me.

The ship rocked lazily, lulling me into the space between sleep and wakefulness. But I couldn't turn my mind off. Couldn't quell the churning in my stomach. Couldn't ignore the cedar scent of an unfamiliar man embedded in the mattress.

Slumber came and went in restless fits. The passing hours chased the moon out of the frame of the open balcony.

Whenever Priest arrived, what would I hear first? The hissing sails of his ship? The battle drums of HMS *Blitz*? The command of Ashley's voice from the speaking trumpet?

Something sounded in the dining cabin. The click of the door. Then footsteps.

My breath stalled, my entire being straining, listening to that gait. I recognized it—the confident, unhurried heel to toe rhythm.

How unnerving. I barely knew this man. He wasn't the highlight of my life, something I looked forward to seeing. He'd been the darkest part of one day. So why was I lying here, focused on the cadence of his approach as if I'd been awake all this time, waiting for him?

I shut my eyes as he entered the sleeping chamber. His movements stilled on the threshold, and I imagined him squinting at my prone form in the darkness.

With my shoulder pressed against the back wall of the bed's alcove, I'd left too much room on the mattress beside me, like an invitation to join me. But it was too late to rectify that mistake.

He was already moving, stepping near the armoire. Drawers opened and closed. Fabric rustled. Leather creaked. The glide of laces emitted soft, rapid sounds.

And there went his clothing.

With my eyes sealed shut, I feared what I would find if I opened them. If he believed I was asleep, maybe he would go away.

The mattress dipped, canting beneath his weight.

My lungs tried to push a gasp past my lips. But I measured my breathing and kept the rise and fall of my chest even, subtle, mimicking sleep.

He stretched out beside me and adjusted the coverlet, making no attempt to be stealthy. The heat of him alone could've woken the dead. With less than a foot of space between us, I felt his body warmth as if he were pressed against me.

I wanted to sleep alone.

Except I'd done exactly that for two years, and it had been miserable.

Perhaps I wanted to sleep alone with someone like Ashley Cutler. But that didn't make sense. I would've never considered such a thing with Madwulf MacNally or Lieutenant Flemming or any other lout on this ship.

Priest was the only one I'd ever fallen asleep with. The only one I ever *wanted* to fall asleep with.

Until he hurt me.

I cracked open an eye and glimpsed the bold squareness of Ashley's nude back. Opening both eyes, I traced the line of his strong neck, the muscled slope of his shoulder, the bulge of his bicep. Exquisite. Flawless. Mercy God, I truly had a weakness for cruelty wrapped in a beautiful package.

The residual moonlight blanketed his nude body in shades of gray and trapped puddles of shadow where his lean waist met the edge of the coverlet. He was infinitely more desirable to behold when lying at ease in nothing but his skin rather than standing at attention in a gold-embellished uniform.

Knowing his nudity continued beneath the counterpane, I couldn't have looked away if I wanted to. I should have chastised myself for inspecting him so closely, and I would have if my brain hadn't abandoned me.

"Go to sleep." His thick, rumbling voice stopped my heart.

I glared at his back. "You're naked."

"It's how I sleep."

"There's a woman in this bed."

"It's *my* bed."

"But—"

"Quiet."

I pressed my lips together. Until I imagined his unclothed body tossing up against me during the night. "I don't know what to do with this."

He expelled a heavy breath, and I could practically see those aristocratic nostrils flaring.

With a heave, he rolled over and faced me.

I wasn't prepared for his mouth to land so close to mine. His soft breaths kissed my lips, and his dark blue eyes gave me their full attention. They were the eyes of a man who directed, oversaw, and controlled everything. Eyes that command a woman's soul.

"I've never slept beside someone who I wasn't involved with…amorously." I swallowed. "This… We're not amorous."

"No, we're not." He shifted to turn away.

"Wait."

He waited.

"What will your soldiers think?" I didn't care a whit about my reputation, but I needed to understand the ramifications. "If they believe you've succumbed to a lady pirate's sexual prowess, won't you lose your hard-won status in the Royal Navy?"

I believed him when he said he was the only one standing between Madwulf and me. A mutiny among Ashley's crew would strip me of that protection.

"I'm not commanding a pirate ship," he said. "This isn't a democracy. *No one* on this vessel has the rank to question me, especially not my unruly prisoners."

"Just so. This prisoner doesn't wish to be molested by her captor while she sleeps."

"Don't look for lust where none exists." He returned to his side, giving me his back.

"Then don't jab me with your erection."

"Stop talking."

"Do you always get hard when you truss up and spank rabid animals?"

"One more word, and I'll gag your impudent mouth."

Another threat. I was certain he would follow through on it and grow hard as a rock from the result. The man was in severe denial, which served me well. For now.

In the back of my mind, I understood the likelihood of this situation turning in a direction I dreaded.

Much to my dismay, being rescued by my vicious, relentless husband was my best option. But the odds weren't in his favor. He couldn't just sneak aboard a first-rate ship of the line and carry me off unnoticed. The approach of the smallest, fastest sloop under his command would be spotted.

The terrifying truth was I didn't know how he would battle the heaviest armed warship in the high seas. I trusted that he would try with every breath in his body, but I couldn't wager my life on his success.

Ashley intended to deliver me to England to stand trial, where I would be convicted and hanged. That was a fact.

But *I* held the power to change it.

As a healthy adult woman, I'd won many hearts *accidentally*.

I had a month to win Ashley's heart *intentionally*.

I'd thought of this before I'd taken the plunge off *Jade's* gunwale. Before I'd met the unsmiling, unfeeling commodore.

A heartless man couldn't fall in love. But part of me hoped that a warm, squishy, sensitive organ beat beneath his cold veneer. If a heart was there, I could take it, turn it, and use it to escape.

But the logical part had already considered a third plan.

If I couldn't reach the commodore's heart, I could most definitely reach between his legs.

While I wasn't skilled in fluttering demure eyelashes or wagging my hips like a coquette, I knew how to lace myself into a bosom-revealing gown and touch a man until his eyes crossed and his brain exploded.

A sweaty tumble beneath the blankets with Ashley Cutler wouldn't convince him to free me. But if he believed I carried his babe in my womb, *that* would change everything.

He wouldn't send me to the gallows.

Because he wouldn't execute his own child.

Win his heart or conceive his baby.

For either of these plans to work, I needed to get close to him. Close enough to take his seed into my body.

As I stared at his beautifully sculpted back in the darkness, it shouldn't have felt like such a hardship. He was a gorgeous man, and I'd done worse things to survive.

If I succeeded in bedding him, I would be betraying the husband who betrayed me. The thought made me sick because, God confound me, I still loved the king of libertines.

But if I did nothing, I would hang. I would die. It wasn't the best option.

If Priest were here, I knew what he would say.

The crazy son of a bitch would tell me to lie, steal, cheat, maim, kill, or fuck whomever I needed to stay alive.

As I closed my eyes and drifted to sleep, I heard his growly Welsh accent in my ear.

Survive, my love. No matter what.

Twenty-two

"Ow!" I yanked the needle from the pad of my finger and stuck the bleeding appendage in my mouth.

My frustration with sewing had been mounting all day, but I refrained from tossing the nearly finished garment off the balcony.

I'd woken this morning alone and hadn't seen anyone except the young soldier who delivered my meals. Wherever Ashley spent his waking hours, it wasn't here.

But he'd been ever-present in my mind.

As I measured, cut, and stitched in the chair at his tidy desk, I ruminated the art of intimacy. Touching, kissing, undressing, drawing him into my body… I imagined licentious scenarios in every combination of positions I'd seen performed in cities, gutters, and taverns.

Of course, I had my own experiences with Priest and others to draw on, but I was rusty. And after Priest's betrayal, I lacked the confidence I once had.

Was I still desirable? If I were, would Priest have strayed?

I powered through the negative thoughts and conceived a fantasy where Ashley devoted himself to the service of a lady pirate, where he wanted me beyond all else and became my professed lover. As my fingers worked the sewing needle, my mind erected illusions of us naked, entangled, licking, whispering, caressing, and rutting day and night.

Immersed in my carnal imagination for hours, I allowed myself to feel every reaction—fear, trepidation, doubt, denial, acceptance, hunger, pleasure—until I became…not jaded. I could never become hardened to a man's touch, and when it happened with Ashley, I would experience all these feelings again. But I mentally prepared myself for it as best as I could.

I came to terms with the role I would play as Ashley's prisoner-turned-lover.

Now I just needed my hands to follow my head.

Returning my attention to the garment on my lap, I finished the final touches.

Stays were the foundation of a woman's total look. Whether I went on to knit the fashionable undress of a servant or the stifling gown of the gentry and middling sorts, I had to start with this essential piece.

The boned body was necessary to achieve an elongated torso, cinched waist, and encased bosom. Since I'd worn these contraptions most of my life to support my back and breasts, I'd learned how to make them from scraps.

For the boning, I used narrow strips of pasteboard—thanks to the thick paper I'd found in Ashley's desk. If he'd needed those drawings, he should have been more explicit.

You will fashion a proper wardrobe for yourself before you leave these quarters.

Every time I repeated his command in my head, I grew more irritated. So much so, I raided his armoire, too.

The fine silk of his shirts provided a lovely exterior to cover the stays. And since he owned more gold-embroidered blue frocks than any man required, I tore apart some of those.

The brocaded fabric, with its soft textures, voluminous pleats, and vivid blue dye, would constitute a bodice and skirt that I would later sew together.

It was a lot of work for a single informal gown. But I refused to sit in this cabin for the next month and be petulant about it.

Pushing back the chair, I rose to my feet and wrapped the stays over the shirt I'd donned this morning. Priest's shirt. Since it draped my smaller frame like a shift, the folds of white linen gathered marvelously beneath the bone body.

I left the laces of Priest's shirt open on my chest and cinched the front closure of the stays. To achieve a proper fit, however, the undergarment required a second pair of hands. That would come later.

Returning to the needle and thread, I tackled the skirt.

Sea of Ruin

As the lemon-yellow sun made its descent to the western horizon, I toiled away, my gaze flitting to the windows, my ears perked for the sounds of an approaching ship.

Hope was a dangerous investment. I couldn't control Priest's decisions or the outcome of my faith in him. I could only govern my own actions, right here, right now.

Woman's work.

I sighed. Within three or so days, I would have a functional gown and thenceforth a ticket out of this cabin.

With my head down and another finger bleeding, I lost myself in the task. As dusk mantled the chamber in darkness, I lit the lanterns and pushed on.

Around two bells of the first dog watch, the exterior door opened. From my position behind the desk, I glimpsed the same young soldier setting the evening meal on the table in the dining cabin.

The hearty aroma of baked meat and vegetable lobscouse reached my nose, beckoning me to eat. And I would, after I finished this hem.

Bent over the fabric, I wove the thread in a steady rhythm, listening to the departing footfalls of the soldier. The door shut. Silence settled in. But something niggled.

I looked up and gasped as my gaze tumbled into the gulf of Ashley's dark blue eyes. He stood a cabin away, watching me from the dining table, with his hat pinned beneath his elbow.

Honest to God, he had the smoothest brow and hardest expression of any aristocrat. And with such an innocent-looking face? *Remarkable.*

Perhaps it was the wide, pillowlike fullness of his pink lips. Or the large, round, ocean color of his eyes. Or that perfect, youthful skin that had not a freckle nor a blemish nor a whisker upon it.

His black hair, trimmed by a meticulous hand, fell in tousled, windblown lengths on the crown of his head. It faded perfectly into shorter, more tamed strands on the sides, defying the expectations of his exalted rank and stature.

Longer locks were a status symbol while thinning hair and baldness came with great humiliation. Most noblemen opted to spend a gross amount of coin on bombastic, powdered perukes—yet another scheme to flaunt wealth.

But Ashley had been blessed with thick natural hair, the confidence to show it off, and the resources to keep it trimmed.

Today he wore a white cravat about his neck and a black waistcoat over the silk shirt. His usual blue frock stretched across his shoulders, matching the blue of the fabric I was hemming.

As his eyes widened with the realization of what I'd done, I held my breath, anxious to finally coax a reaction from his impassive mien.

Wait for it… Wait for it… Any second now he would turn crimson and explode.

He slowly set the hat aside. Then his buckled shoes started moving, carrying him toward me with even, resolute steps. With a sluggish exhale, I set the needle and unfinished skirt on the desk and folded my hands on my lap, my gaze never leaving his.

"Explain this." He paused beside me and pressed a finger against the plundered fabric of my sewing project.

"Have you forgotten who I am?" I tilted my head, smiling sweetly. "I raid and thieve wealthy arseholes for personal gain."

"Wretched pirate." His hand twisted into a fist, and he yanked it behind him, his posture as straight as his face. "You were given more than enough fabric to complete the task."

"I was given coarse, unflattering worsted." I grabbed a handful of the itchy wool he wanted me to use and tossed it at him. "I don't see a stitch of this nonsense scratching *your* precious behind."

"You deliberately defied me."

"I did what you asked. Do you know how difficult that is for me?"

"No." He bit out the syllable, pulsing his chiseled nostrils. "Tell me."

I drew my head back, surprised by the command, and recovered quickly. "When I was a child, my mother wanted me to be a harpist. She thought the skill would invite an agreeable betrothal." I slumped in the chair as ancient guilt crept into my shoulders. "During my first harp lesson, I demolished the elegant instrument and used the strings as fishing line."

"Why?"

"I wanted to fish in the pond with the stable boy. That was what nourished my child's heart. *Not* blindly following orders." I lowered my eyes to the unfinished gown. "Conforming to the standards of others goes against everything that I am."

"I shall presume your mother never received an offer for your hand."

"Unfortunately, she did. Unfortunate for him. I broke the betrothal when I opened his bowels with my knife."

He regarded me, unblinking. Following an eternal moment, a small crease formed between his eyes. "You're not jesting, are you?"

Sea of Ruin

"No." I shrugged. "When we arrive in England, you can add the murder of the Marquess of Grisdale to my list of crimes."

"This was the lord with the *unwelcome prick?*"

"The same."

He drifted closer, leaning over me. His hand lifted slowly, stuttering my breath. Fingertips rested against my neck, so soft, so barely there I strained to feel the ghostly touch.

"Where did you get this?" His hand curled around the stone at my throat.

"I stole it."

"And this?" He pinched the linen of Priest's shirt, where it lay against my clavicle. "Who did this belong to?"

"The man I stole it from. I didn't catch his name."

I'd come aboard this ship wearing only two things. Something that belonged to my father and something that belonged to my husband. Sometimes I was so accidentally sentimental it was a wonder I'd survived this long.

His gaze swept over the desk, finding the drawings I'd destroyed to make the boning of the stays.

"Should I possess a harp," he said, "I now know to lock it up."

"And the bristle brush you use on your teeth." I gave him a toothy smile, flashing my sparkling white enamel. "Unless you don't mind me borrowing it again."

"You have no shame."

"None at all."

He had no anger. No emotion. But he must have felt *something*. He was a thinking, calculating man of intellect. It concerned me that I couldn't read him.

"Now you should allow me to ask *you* some questions." I raised my chin.

"Come with me." He turned on his heel and strode into the dining cabin.

Curious, I padded after him.

At the table, he pulled out a chair for me. I moved to sit, but he blocked my path, his eyes fixed on the loose ties of my stays.

I didn't have to follow his gaze to feel my chest spilling from the low-cut neckline. The exposure had been by design.

As I opened my mouth to ask for his assistance, his fingers beat me to it, latching onto the laces between my breasts. Then he yanked. Hard. The stays constricted, cutting my air. He pulled harder until I thought my ribs would crack.

I sucked in my torso and adjusted to the girding pressure, watching his expression, searching for a flush, a heated look, a bobbing throat.

Nothing.

He secured a knot between my breasts, making the stays impossibly close and tight. Strait-laced. Then he patted the surface of the table, willfully mute.

I stared at the gesture, confused.

"Bend over. Face down." He tapped the surface again. "Just here."

"My lord?" My heart rate quickened. "Surely, you don't mean to—"

"You ransacked my personal effects, ruined my clothing, and destroyed my drawings." He folded his hands behind him, shoulders squared. "Despite your childish games, I should hope you have arrived at an accurate conclusion."

"Which is?"

"Your romantic plans to instigate my ire will not come to fruition."

"Yes, you've fallen short of expectations. But honestly, Ashley, you must learn to share your feelings for this relationship to work."

"What…" He breathed in, out. "What relationship?"

"Our captor-captive relationship." I narrowed my eyes.

"Indeed. I was just getting to that." He pointed his chin at the table. "Bend over, if you please. We can do this with your arms free or bound behind you."

"This?" My pulse rammed like a sledge in my ears. "What—?"

In a blur, his hand stabbed into my hair, fingers clenching in the curls at my scalp and yanking my head back.

"Listen carefully, Goldilocks." He forced my eyes to meet his tyrannical glare, his voice chillingly absent of storm or wind. "I will not give you the reaction you seek. But I will always make good on your punishment."

I didn't need the higher learning of a titled lord to comprehend his meaning. Not with my cunt still swollen from last night's smiting.

Reaching back, my shaking fingers closed around the hand in my hair, and I felt the trembling in him, too.

He was shaking. I hadn't invented that reaction nor the hunger pulsing in his gaze. He wanted this. Not just to maintain order. The thought of reddening my backside aroused him.

A shiver ran along my spine and curled into my belly.

"No restraints." I wet my lips, my eyes watering from the smarting pain in my skull. "I'll obey."

Sea of Ruin

His hand vanished. My knees turned to liquid, and I stumbled against the table.

The humiliation from a spanking would hurt more than the physical blows. But with his hand in contact with my arse, there would be a measure of intimacy in that. A step in the right direction.

"How many prisoners have you spanked, Commodore?" I folded at the waist and braced my elbows on the table, holding his gaze over my shoulder.

"None." He stepped behind me and kicked my feet apart, staggering the rhythm of my breaths. "Arms over your head."

My skin heated, and a shiver of uncertainty invaded my nerves. But I did as ordered, sliding my hands across the table and bringing my chest and cheek to the wooden surface. The position prevented me from looking at him, but I felt him everywhere. His muscled heat, commanding presence, penetrating gaze on my bottom…

He lifted the weight of my hair to the side. Then a firm finger touched the base of my skull. From there, it trailed down my spine, over the stays, and pressed low, forcing me into a deeper arch.

His other hand rested on the back of my thigh, the heat of it seeping through the thin linen and making me quake. I didn't want him to know how easily I responded to his touch, but my body didn't understand the wisdom in discretion.

My flesh rose in prickling bumps like the skin of a plucked goose. Noisy gasps heaved from my chest. Tremors danced up and down my legs, shivering the muscle beneath his hand.

Beyond the open door of the balcony, the distant thunder of waves rumbled on the horizon. Wood creaked with the rolling of the warship. And behind me, masculine breaths grew deeper, louder.

"Do you like what you see?" I closed my eyes and ordered my limbs to relax.

"I never imagined," he murmured, "that a view could pertain to the sense of touch. Yet when I look at you, I don't just see beauty. I feel it."

The compliment shocked my eyes open as each word sank beneath my breastbone and saturated the spot where I was the softest and easiest to injure.

"Seeing you like this…" He shifted, leaning along my side and taking in my form. "It's a feeling of such…relief. Like stepping into the rain after years of drought." His gaze strolled along the length of my body, his voice deepening. "The untamed serenity in it, soft as velvet, gentle waves of perfect beauty, glistening with life. One look is a shower that washes the senses anew."

I didn't know if he was talking about the rain or me, but I clung to his voice, to the pledge in it. For a man who didn't express his feelings, he could enslave a woman's emotions through language alone.

If this was a maneuver to knock me off-balance, he wasn't failing. Every wistful particle of my being was on its way to believing.

He straightened and removed his frock. It fell over a nearby chair. His waistcoat followed. Then the fabric on my backside slid upward, exposing me from the waist down.

His breathing altered, and I felt everything inside me accelerate. He was inspecting me, staring hard at my squirming bare arse.

"Don't move." His hoarse command scratched my ears, restraining me without rope or iron.

Through layers of nothing but thinning air, he rubbed his gaze against me, taking his time, stirring me up. Christ, he was a master at this—dominating a woman without so much as a touch.

Shivers of anticipation sprung from each passing second he made me wait. I delighted in the moment, pierced with the thrill of danger as I strained to hear him, see him, and feel his punishment light up my skin.

His patience shocked me with wonder. I imagined he fought battles at the helm of this ship with the same hard, enduring stillness. I fell so deeply entranced by it that I wasn't ready when the atmosphere shifted.

His strike came like deafening thunder, his heavy, unrelenting hand crashing across my buttocks and shaking the dishes on the table. I cried out, stunned senseless, breathless, and burning from cheek to bone.

Before I could manage a gulp, he swung again, setting fire to my entire world.

And he'd only just begun.

Twenty-three

Over the past seven years, I'd been beaten violently by enemies and spanked sensually by lovers. Ashley's strikes slammed through those extremes, erased the line between pain and pleasure, and crashed straight into war.

Most of the blows landed so hard I couldn't squeak out a breath. Others caused my body to brutally flinch beneath the agony as a ballad of vulgarity roared from the back of my throat.

Fewer were the hits that teased stings of pleasure. Those were the ones that made me hate myself for responding as though I were made for his touch.

I didn't want him, but I needed to give him a glimpse of the possibility. I needed to embed the seed in his mind and make him wonder what intimacy with me might feel like.

It wasn't an easy ledge to balance on, but it *was* easy to close my eyes and forget whose hand punished my flesh.

Because he hit like Priest.

The more I thought about that, the deeper I sank into the terrible, wicked intensity of the pleasure-pain. Gradually, my ear-splitting protests melted into raspy whimpers and moans. But even those sounds spluttered with curses at the way I yielded to his imperious discipline.

I was wet. Not from the pain. My body felt as though it were immersed in hellfire, and I wasn't into that.

What aroused me was his undivided attention. For a man of his stature and self-control to gaze upon me like I was his sun, moon, and sea, even if only for a fleeting moment, it made me feel alive. Hungry and hot and vigorously alive.

That was motivation enough to hold my position beneath his strikes.

Aching everywhere, I rocked against the edge of the table. As another open-handed smack collided with my sore bottom, I gasped, shudders seizing me anew. I felt the ridges of my swelling skin as profoundly as I felt the trembling in his palm as he slowed his swings.

Then he stopped.

My mouth opened and closed on an air-sucking gulp. The action pushed my cheek through a puddle of moisture that had leaked from my eyes. I hadn't cried. Not consciously. But I wanted to. God almighty, the pain was all consuming.

"Don't move." His voice shook with the pummel of his breaths.

I couldn't have moved if I tried. My arms felt like water stretched above me. My lower half hung off the side of the table, buckling my knees. I lay there, my eyes drifting shut, as his footsteps treaded aft toward his sleeping quarters.

Then he was standing behind me again, staring at my naked backside. His breaths issued in broken clusters of air, coming hard and fast as an effect of whatever internal force he was fighting.

If he were any other man, I would cover myself in fear of being rutted against my will. But Ashley Cutler hadn't yet reached that level of desperation. Perhaps he was capable of it, of forcing himself on me in a moment of weakness. But I suspected it would take a great deal more than a spanking for him to snap.

I licked my parched lips. "Are you hard?"

Silence extended an eternity before he responded. "Yes. It's an involuntary response to a perfectly red backside." He cleared the scratch in his voice. "It helps that yours isn't covered in hair."

"You see a lot of furry arses?"

"With over four hundred men on this ship, I can say with confidence that yours is the smoothest. And the reddest." He stepped closer and stooped low, crouching behind me. "You're also the first prisoner I've punished who leaked something other than urine down the thighs."

"Don't look for lust where none exists," I said, echoing his words. "It's an involuntary response to a perfectly delivered spanking."

Sea of Ruin

He made a sound in his throat, something between a grunt and a snort.

Setting a small jar he'd retrieved from the sleeping chamber beside my hip, he rose to his feet and rested a finger on my tailbone. I shivered as the touch glided downward, following the cleft of my bottom. He didn't push into the crease, instead keeping the caress agonizing, slow and light as a feather.

"As a liberated woman, I shall presume you've had all your territories occupied." His finger paused directly over my arsehole without sinking between my clenched cheeks. "Tell me, Bennett. Has this domain been pillaged?"

Only a man who was interested in the act would inquire about such a thing. Priest had demanded it dozens of times before he broke down my resolve and introduced me to the sin of Sodom.

To this day, he was the only one who had taken me fore and aft, and he'd done so with a skill that made me crave it relentlessly, thereby damning me for all eternity.

"Yes." I craned my neck and locked onto hooded blue eyes. "I've been plundered forward and backward, with my consent, and only by a libertine who knew what he was doing."

"Does this libertine have a name?"

"I don't recall." I fought the urge to swallow. "How about you?" At his silence, I clarified. "Do you know what you're doing, Ashley?"

"I should flog you every time you disrespectfully address me without my title. Except you love my punishments."

"And you love when I call you Ashley." I squinted. "You're evading my question."

His mouth curved up at the corners. It wasn't a smile, for there were no traces of softness or humor in it. It was the mien of cruelty, and it hit my veins in splinters of ice.

Eyes bolted to mine, he dipped long fingers into the jar and scooped out an oily substance.

Lubrication? To grease a hole I gave him no license to penetrate?

I choked on a spike of fear and pushed up from the table. Until a heavy hand clamped onto my hip, shoving me back down.

"Do. Not. Move." His lubricated palm went to my thigh, gliding upward, unhesitating along my abused flesh.

Cool, refreshing balm penetrated my searing skin, instantly soothing the pain and perfuming the air with the fragrance of garden herbs.

He was treating my wounds? Dear God, would he never stop

deviating from the expectations I'd built up around him? I couldn't read him, predict his actions, or figure out a way to circumvent him. He was an anomaly.

Releasing his grip on my hip, he surrounded my backside with his hands, kneading my aching flesh, rubbing the salve into the burn, and coursing relief and sudden desolation through my limbs.

How long had it been since I'd been cared for this way? Since I felt the attention of a lover's caress upon my body?

I tried not to think about Priest as Ashley worked me into a thrumming, molten puddle of bliss. Talented fingers roved along my hips, waist, and thighs, learning my shape before returning to my bottom.

The friction of skin, even the barest touch, sizzled honeyed pleasure up my legs and into my core. When his thumb hovered over the hidden hole at my aft, rich shivers invaded the muscles there, clenching deep inside.

It was his gentleness that seduced me, his teasing fingers, the tenderness in every diabolical touch as though he trickled thick, hot syrup along my spine and dribbled it down my crack and into the needy gap between my legs.

It wasn't nearly enough. I lifted my hips, urging him to keep stroking, blindsided by the madness of my need. I wanted more than the delirium of his expert petting. I ached to feel his lips mate with mine.

My whimpers found voice as he caressed the arch of my back. His hand tangled in my hair and turned my head. Eyes, so commanding that Satan himself would do his bidding, sucked me in like dark whirlwinds, threatening to swallow me whole.

"Siren." The word came forth like gravel from his mouth, a beautifully shaped mouth befitting the devil, which I stared at quite fixedly.

His features seemed too relaxed to be affected by lust. But I knew better than to trust that handsome face.

I gasped as his weight came down atop my back. He was hard as stone in his breeches, the swollen heat of him intoxicating my blood as if I'd imbibed a cask of rum. I couldn't breathe.

With hair as black as night and eyes bluer than the sea, he smelled like a midnight storm, the kind that infused the air with woodsy loam and turned everything it touched inside out. My mouth watered. My heart shivered.

Sea of Ruin

He gripped the side of my face and tilted my chin up to meet his. Our lips hovered an inch away.

Did he find me pretty? Desirable? Worthy enough to kiss?

To be wanted by a man whose heart didn't belong to another… I would never admit such a vulnerable desire aloud. The desperate, wild hope that fluttered from my thoughts equally mortified and excited me. Oh, how I hated this need to be wanted by him, but it was there, a hunger so deep it clamped down on my lungs.

Kiss me, Ashley.

He trailed a finger along my jaw and traced my quivering lower lip. His mouth parted, inviting mine to edge closer.

I arched my neck, pressing into the hand on my cheek. My nerves buzzed with drunken anticipation as he dipped his head. Closer. Closer. The nearness of his mouth teased mine, trembling, groaning, heating…

Gone.

A chill swept in. Then I saw it.

The curved lips. The humorless non-smile. Eyes as mean as the devil's own.

"You're a pirate whore, Bennett Sharp. Nothing more." He shoved off my body, his tone cutting. "You *will* hang for the crimes you've committed against the crown."

Twenty-four

Ashley's sudden transformation sucked the wind from my sails. A scathing sob rose in my throat, and I trapped it there, humiliated, devastated, and overcome.

The salve on my wounds, the pretty words about my beauty, the almost-kiss... It had all been a ruse to disarm and hurt me.

"Don't move." He straightened the shirt, covering my bare bottom and igniting sore flesh.

I showed no reaction and made no move to disobey. I needed to reassemble my thoughts and rein in the blubbering jumble of emotions unraveling inside me.

He set a chair directly behind my bent position, selected a book from a nearby shelf, and grabbed a bowl of lobscouse from the table. Then he settled in to eat and read as if naught were out of order.

The seething agony of his rejection and outright dismissal of my existence shook me to the core. If I were a cold-hearted woman, perhaps I wouldn't feel so damned hurt. But I wasn't, and I did. A vise of pain shredded my organs to a pulp. Prickling heat seared the backs of my eyes, and my head pounded beneath the pressure.

He couldn't see my face from his position, and that alone kept me in place.

I couldn't hide my true feelings behind a mask like his. Couldn't stifle the spill of tears or the quiver in my chin. Until I fastened a tourniquet around my bleeding heart, I couldn't look into his pitiless eyes.

He'd beaten me with emotional warfare.

Hadn't I considered something as equally nefarious with Priest? I was going to fuck another man in front of him. Probably.

Probably not.

When it came down to it, I wasn't as cruel as I wanted people to believe. But I wasn't a saint, either. I didn't even claim a god. Maybe I deserved this degradation.

Every proud fiber of my being bristled in objection. I was a female prisoner, bent over a powerful man's table for his amusement, after being assaulted to a level of agony that would prevent me from sitting. I hadn't been convicted of a crime, and until then, it was my right to fight.

But to survive this captivity, I needed to adjust, bend with the strikes, and set aside my pride.

So I lay there, deprived of grace and dignity, listening to the clink of his spoon and the rustle of pages turning in his book.

As a king's commodore, he was expected to put country and crown before himself, behave as an officer and a nobleman, and exercise control and order at all times.

But who was he beneath the rank and title? Was he actually reading the words in that book? Tasting the meat he scooped into his mouth? Or was he hiding bawdy thoughts about me and the erection he'd neglected in his breeches?

"Bennett." His English accent—terribly deep and more beautiful than it should have been—curled up my spine. "Stand and face me."

Damnation. If I disobeyed, he would wrench me up by my hair. He'd done that enough times that my scalp shuddered at the sound of his voice.

I pushed myself off the table, discreetly wiping my eyes on my arm. I didn't erase all the tears, but no matter. More fell, trailing itchy rivers down my cheeks. All I could do was remain vertical and hold my head high as I turned.

He closed the book and set it and the empty bowl aside. "Tell me the lesson learned tonight."

"Humility."

He'd been right about me not being frightened enough. While it went against my nature to cower, my ostentatious boldness hadn't helped me, either. His indifference to the suffering of a woman made him a man to be feared. Not that I deigned to be treated differently because of my sex. I just wasn't accustomed to his degree of callousness.

"Bring me the second bowl of stew." He flicked a finger at the table.

I followed his order, grimacing as the muscles in my backside protested the movement. When I returned to him holding the lobscouse, he tossed a cushion between his boots.

"Kneel." He took the bowl, his gaze giving mine an icy reception. "Or sit in a chair."

The ruthless bastard knew I couldn't put weight on my throbbing arse. My hands fisted at my sides, my stomach in turmoil. Would his torture never end?

I lowered to my knees in the *V* of his legs.

Then he fed me.

Spoon to lips, the action felt awkward, but he showed no sign of discomfort. Patient as ever, he scooped, lifted, and served, catching droplets on my chin, waiting for me to chew, and repeating the motions.

I was too hungry and beat down to refuse the hand that fed me. The lukewarm meat melted in my mouth, the broth bursting with spicy flavors. My stomach rolled with pleasure.

Halfway through the stew, he set the spoon in the bowl. "Address me properly, and you may ask your questions."

Let go of your pride, Bennett. It won't save you.

"Why are you so mean, my lord?"

"It's not like me to be so with a woman." He lifted his free hand to my cheek and traced the drying track of tears. "You behave more like a man." He tilted his head, studying me. "Or rather... An animal."

"There's an animal in all of us. Including you."

"Quite so. But the difference, madam, is that I control mine."

"Have you always? What were you doing before you went a-hunting for pirates?"

"I fought in the War of the Spanish Succession." His eyes illuminated as he absently lifted the spoon and resumed feeding me. "The battles that followed kept me occupied in the Mediterranean for five years, where I climbed from the lowest naval rank to my current standing."

"Has the conflict ended there?"

"For now. This ship and my crew celebrated victory in an undeclared war last year when Spain tried to retake Gibraltar and

Menorca. After that, we were sent back to England."

"But you didn't go."

"I command the heaviest warship in the Royal Navy. It would be a shame to moor it." He slid the spoon into my mouth and let the tip linger on my bottom lip, his gaze stuck there. "I found another use for it."

Pirate hunting.

My stomach twisted, and I leaned back, breaking the connection. "I'm no longer hungry."

He set the bowl at his foot and slanted forward, resting elbows on his knees. The position put his gorgeous face so close to mine I had to fight every instinct to remain where I was. I feared him, but I wouldn't cower.

Not even when his hand caught the open neckline of my shirt.

"Do you still love him?" he murmured.

My heart stopped and restarted. "Who?"

"The man who wore this shirt."

All the warmth in my face drained to my knees, replaced by a coldness that numbed my lips. I was too raw, too exhausted to fight another battle, pass another test, learn another lesson—whatever he had in store for me.

I closed my eyes, failing to slow my breaths. Until a curled finger caught me under the chin and lifted my head.

"Yes." My gaze shot to his, hardening with sudden anger. "I still love him, but I'm working on rectifying that. It's a process." I motioned between my chest and head. "In here."

"He betrayed you." The hand beneath my jaw tensed, loosened, and fell away. "Was he involved in the mutiny on your ship that threw you overboard?"

"No." I stared into his eyes, letting him find the truth in mine.

"He bedded another."

"Bedded and *loved*." I wanted to share this. Perhaps not with Ashley, but it felt freeing to voice it to an impartial ear. "He still loves her, but she won't have him. He's alone, and I should be happy about that. I *am* happy about that."

Not really. I was lying through my teeth.

"He didn't maliciously try to hurt you by seeking the arms of another," Ashley said.

"No." My eyebrows crawled together. "I don't see why that matters."

Sea of Ruin

"Love isn't a decision. It arrives unannounced, breeds madness, and leaves a sea of ruin in its wake. Hate him or love him. Either way, he's in certain hell."

My jaw unhinged under the weight of piling questions, but my voice deserted me. As I stared at his detached expression, I couldn't separate the truth from the rhetoric. Was he feeding me what he wanted me to hear? Or was he speaking from experience?

"Close your mouth." He reclined in the chair, regarding me.

"You speak of love from experience?"

"There's a woman," he said slowly. "A lady to whom I'm betrothed."

"Do you love her?" My knees teetered, struggling to hold me up.

"I am here." He spread his arms wide, indicating the ship and the sea. "And she is not."

What did that mean? Did he want her here? Who was she? To be betrothed to a high-ranking officer and son of a viscount, she would have her own titles, family wealth, and obligations.

She would be someone important.

"Does she love you?" I shook my head, changing the direction of my thoughts. "Of course, that has no consequence. She wants to marry you?"

"Yes."

"Tell me about her."

"She's well-bred, titled, educated, modest, kind, beautiful, virtuous—everything a nobleman could want from his betrothed."

There was positively no *want* in his voice or expression. But this was Ashley—buttoned, polished, and starched. Even so, why didn't he race home after the war to see her? She must miss him horribly.

He was an extraordinary catch. Gorgeous. Wealthy. Powerful. As a titled lord, he was required to behave like a gentleman in her presence, meanwhile keeping her in the dark about his unchristian proclivities. Such as restraining, spanking, and sharing a bed with his half-naked female prisoner.

As Lady Ashley Cutler, she would turn the other cheek and focus all her energy on high society. In exchange for his status and affluence, she would only need to open her legs once or twice a year to give him his requisite heirs.

And such was the life of the good and the great.

Yawn.

"Your families want the arrangement," I said. "And you want your career."

"That's the essence of it." He rose to his feet and gripped my waist, lifting me to stand.

I swayed, flinching in pain. "Will you spank her after you marry her?"

With a hand on my arm, he escorted me toward the sleeping cabin. "A gentleman does *not* spank a lady."

He only spanks his whores.

Indignation steamed from my ears, but I kept my voice soft as syrup. "While you spend months or years away at sea, your lady sits at home alone, waiting, starving for attention. Left to her own devices, she'll find ways to pass the time. Delicious, devious ways that involve ungentlemanly spankings from handsome footmen and burly gardeners."

"The nuptials will proceed, with or without her maidenhood intact." He released me in the aft chamber. "Go to bed."

I searched his tone and features and found only the prosaic, unimaginative facts.

What did he feel? It was not fear or dread. Perhaps he felt a whole lot of nothing full of nothing.

Or perhaps he cared very much about his sweet lonely virgin and her potential transgressions. I wouldn't know until I found a way to lift that cold mask. I was tired of seeing it. So goddamn tired.

I peeled off the stays and crawled into bed, face down and bottom up—a bottom that would be black and blue by the morrow.

Ashley left the cabin and returned moments later with the salve. He removed his clothing except the breeches and stood over me, his irresistible physique straight and proud with all those muscled indentations.

I turned my head and faced the wall.

He knelt beside me and, with the dispassionate hands of a doctor, applied more cooling medicinal ointment to my buttocks.

"Lieutenant Flemming treated my wrists last night." I closed my eyes, melting into the glide of his touch. "As the ship's surgeon, shouldn't he be the one doing this?"

His fingers paused on my hips, and a tremor rippled through them.

"I am the *only* man who touches you here." He splayed a huge palm over my sore backside.

The possessive declaration hitched my breath. I expected that nonsense from Priest's mouth. But Ashley's? What the unholy hell?

Sea of Ruin

He yanked down my shirt and climbed off the bed, leaving me whirling in bewilderment.

"What about the forty pirates in the hold?" I listened to him move through the cabin. "Does the threat of *them* touching me still stand?"

"From Monday to Sunday." He dimmed the lanterns and stripped off his breeches.

The bed sank beside me. I kept my face turned away, eyes closed. The coverlet tugged and stretched as he settled. Then silence.

Replaying our conversations, I slipped into drowsy introspection. The matter of his betrothed didn't concern me. If he loved her, he would've put me in another bed. Or on the floor, for that matter.

No, his heart didn't beat for her. If anything, he was looking for a reason to avoid going home.

His career resided on this ship. A warm female body slept beside him in this bed. With the right whispered words, I could move his mind, stir his passion, and convince him that his home was here.

With a pirate whore.

I was a far leap from the noblewoman waiting for him in England. But my gut told me that if it was an obedient virgin that hardened his cock, he would be with his betrothed. Not here with me.

I am the only man who touches you here.

He was the only one stopping himself from touching me everywhere.

Unless my feral, possessive husband showed up. Then my efforts with the commodore would be for naught.

If Priest had his way, my captivity would transfer from Ashley to him. Being Priest's prisoner wasn't favorable, but it was a great deal more appealing than hanging from a noose.

In an ideal world, I would escape both men, recover my compass, and live the rest of my life a free woman, commanding my beloved ship.

But there was so much that could go wrong and so little that could go right.

Those were the thoughts that chased me to sleep. When I drifted, I sank hard. And I dreamed about my mother.

A halo surrounded her, like a blurry ring of light around the sun. Was it her golden hair? Her aura? I wanted to touch it, but I didn't have a body. I wanted to hug her, but I didn't know if she was dead or alive.

None of this was real. Not her smile nor the cliff on which we stood nor the wings that unfurled behind her. No, wait. Those wings were real, for when she

jumped, she didn't fall.
She flew.

I woke gently, quietly, blinking into the darkness and marveling at the discrepancy in the dream. For years, I'd relived the countess falling to the rocks and always woke gasping and shaking with tears in my eyes.

But not this time.

This time I felt warm and peaceful and...

I wasn't the only one awake.

Lying on my side, I stared at the wall. The wild mane of my hair sprawled across the mattress behind me. With a hand tangled in it.

Ashley was petting me.

I held still, measuring my breaths as he stroked the spiraled strands and smoothed out the knots.

The sensation crawled into my veins, torturing me. I didn't know what felt true—my delirious pleasure in the affection or his ability to give it. But it felt right. He felt right. I didn't want him to stop.

His breathing quickened, deepened, and his fingers wandered to my hip. The heat of his hand lingered there, soaking through the blanket and saturating my skin. It was the touch of a man with one thing on his mind.

My body fevered, and my pulse sped up. This was what I'd wanted. But wasn't it too soon?

If he gave me his seed tonight, I could move forward with the pregnancy plan. But shouldn't I try for his heart first? That ruse was easier to play out, less complicated.

If he tried to bed me now, I could deny him, give him the chase men seemed to love. It might make him want me more.

If I denied him, he might force me.

I spent thirty seconds reasoning this out before his hand disappeared.

He slid soundlessly from the bed and strode to the balcony, making the decision for me.

I simmered in frustration and cursed myself for feeling rejected *again* by a man I didn't want.

But I did desire him. For reasons any woman with working eyes desired him. I could look past his pestilent personality for an hour or two if it meant putting my hands all over that flawless, godlike body.

I wasn't usually so lustful and eager. But it had been two years since I'd lost myself on a man's cock, and after spending two days with this one, I was feeling that abstention right where I needed him the most.

My cunt throbbed. My nipples hardened. My entire body strained to sense his movements on the balcony. Then I heard it.

A grunt. A heavy breath. More followed. Then, "Oh, God. Oh, Christ, yes."

I froze, dazed, rendered utterly confused. Those whispered throaty words sounded nothing like his voice.

Sliding from the bed, I followed the string of muffled groans toward the balcony. The loud creaking of the ship deadened my soft steps. His gasping sounds smothered my own labored breaths.

Pausing just out of view, I peeked around the edge of the open door and choked.

Standing in the muted glow of the distant stern lantern, a broad-shouldered silhouette bent at the rail, tall, dark, and gloriously nude. With his back to me, he gripped the balustrade with one hand and stroked his shaft with the other.

My drubbing heart propelled into my throat, and I pressed a hand over my gaping mouth.

Ashley Cutler, you gorgeous, filthy pervert.

His arse was so chiseled and perfectly shaped I wanted to cry. Powerful thighs flexed and contracted as he strained on his toes and worked his muscled arm. And his noises... Those hungry grunts, trapped behind clenched teeth, sent a million shivers up and down and through my body.

Leaning into his impassioned strokes, he was in plain view of the moon and the endless roaring sea. Oh, I envied those waves. He pleasured himself for them, gripping and jerking his long swollen rod.

Earlier, I'd felt the thick length of it through his breeches. But to behold it in the flesh, to feel the weight of it in my hand... My fingernails bit into my palms as bolts of liquid heat pulsed through my blood and leaked between my legs.

His breathing came faster. Mine came harsher. Moisture broke out on my forehead. More trickled down my thigh.

Impressive in size and manner, he loomed on the balcony, absorbing shadows and taking up space. The muscles in his back bunched and played with the dim light, his body smooth and hard, glinting silver like the sea in the moonlight.

Watching him, I felt too little, too delicate to accommodate all that strength and terrifying authority. But I would. I would fit him inside me and wrap myself around that broad chest, those muscular legs, that hard, hungry cock.

And if I stood here another second, I might do something embarrassing like force myself upon him.

Fisting my hands, I slowly retreated and crept back to bed. There, I lay on my side, facing the wall, and listened to him grunt, stroke, and moan his way to release.

The sound of him coming set off a mini-orgasm through my core. I shuddered and shook with my hand over my mouth, trying with all my might to calm myself.

By the time he returned, my eyes were closed, and my breathing had resumed an even tempo. But with my body still on fire, I didn't think sleep would find me again.

Until his hand sank into my hair.

He caressed my locks in a soporific rhythm, flowing with the undercurrent that rocked the creaking ship. It was my undoing.

I fell with him, deeply, tranquilly into perfect slumber.

Over the next two nights, he repeated his erotic performance on the balcony, unaware that he had an audience. I watched from the shadows as he grunted and trembled and squirted his seed into the wind. Then I fell asleep to the soothing cadence of those cock-stroking fingers in my hair.

Sinful. Resplendent. Undeniably wrong. I could spend an eternity with him like that.

But alas, the sun rose each morning, bringing with it his severe, tedious countenance. He spent the daylight hours elsewhere, leaving me alone with my needlework and pent-up frustration. In the evenings, he avoided conversation, and I thereby escaped more spankings.

On the fourth day as his captive, I finished the gown.

At last, I could leave his cabin.

Twenty-five

I woke before dawn, dressed quietly in the dining cabin, and waited for Ashley to emerge. As I tightened the laces I could reach and re-straightened pleats, my spine felt taller, my chin angling higher.

The alteration of Ashley's frocks was the best idea I'd hatched since boarding this ship. Extravagant, brocaded fabric covered my frame from breasts to feet. Practical, sturdy material. Yet so elegant in detail. And something I hadn't noticed until now... The dazzling blue threads matched the color of his eyes.

I couldn't wait to see his reaction, to watch his gaze devour the gold-embroidered whorls that edged the deep-cut bosom, the dramatic tuck where my waist greeted my hips, and the skirt full of turnings and windings that accentuated my curves.

I loathed constricting garments, but this morning, I felt fashionably feminine. Sensual. Better than ordinary.

The reflection in the window caught my eye, and for a poignant moment, I saw the image of Lady Abigail Leighton. Golden hair blazing in the sunrise, huge cerulean blue eyes, regal features, delicate lines... Was that really me? It couldn't be. My mother had been such a gorgeous woman.

Doubt swarmed in, heavy and sticky, clinging to my skin.

Graceful garb, tamed curls, and proper posture didn't change what I was.

Pirate whore.

His mockery didn't hurt me. I was, by my own will, a pirate. And by aristocratic standards, a ruined whore to boot. I owned that.

What had injured me with Ashley had been his timing. He'd told me I was beautiful, touched me with interested fingers, melted me with heated looks, coaxed tendrils of my trust, and... *Rejection.* He'd hit me right when he knew it would hurt me the most.

Movement sounded in the sleeping chamber.

The prick hath risen.

I breathed in slowly and remained out of view in the fore cabin, listening to him urinate off the balcony. Just thinking about his cock in his hand brought to mind other things I'd heard and seen him doing at that rail.

It still scrambled my mind. For a man who was annoyingly strict, over-precise, and more strait-laced than a preacher at Sunday service, he sure did have a lot of pollution to release at the end of the day.

Had he stroked himself to completion every night before he'd met me? Or was this a new habit inspired by my charming personality?

One evening, in the very near future, I would join him on that balcony and take matters into my own hands. In the literal sense.

I hated him, and at the same time, I longed to pleasure him in ways a refined lady wouldn't begin to consider.

He was commodore of HMS *Blitz*, the only one-hundred-gun ship of the line on the sea. But with me, he would be a man, mortal and made of flesh that hardened with the hunger to sink into my velvety sheath and live there until death and beyond.

Or so thought my ego.

As he moved through the aft cabin, grooming and donning clothes, the exterior door to the dining cabin opened. The young soldier who delivered the meals—George was the name I'd pried from him yesterday—stepped in carrying a silver tray. And stopped.

His eyes flitted to me, where I stood beside a chair. They widened, blinked, and darted away. Then he hurried to the table.

"If you have something to say, Georgie, by all means..." I rested a fist on my cocked hip. "Let's hear it."

"Madam, y-y-you look..." The platter of dishes rattled as he set it down, losing his grip and poise. "You're radiant." His gaze snapped toward the day cabin, and his chin dropped to his cravat. "I mean to say, uh— My apologies, my lord."

Without another glance in my direction, George swept out of the cabin.

Sea of Ruin

"And that's how you clear a room." I started to turn toward the reason for his sudden departure. "Your presence seems to have that effect…"

My voice lost sound as I met Ashley's gaze.

Hypnotic, shiver-inducing eyes. How unfair for a man to have eyes like that, with lashes so long and silky they cast crescent-shaped shadows on his cheeks. The black fringes made those ocean blue depths dominate his face and everything around him.

My attention lowered to a perfectly proportioned male chest encased in a red waistcoat of the shiniest silk. He was decked in clothing suited to royalty—an immaculately tailored blue frock, thigh-hugging breeches, and gold-buckled shoes. His white hose, made of woven wool, looked as though they'd been melted onto his defined calves.

I didn't have to stretch my imagination to remember those legs, nude and flexing, as he chased his release.

He openly returned my assessment, his focus caressing my appearance at a leisurely crawl, his expression flat. Empty.

My nerves twisted. As his feet started moving toward me, I stood straighter, preparing for the worst. When he reached my side, his hand went to my hair, his fingers immediately catching on a knot I'd missed.

"I searched for a hairbrush and pins." My cheeks heated. "I couldn't find anything to tame—"

"Be silent while I look at you."

"The laces on the back of my—"

"Quiet, woman."

He paced a circuit around me, touching my body with only his gaze. Examining. Breathing. Driving me out of my skin. I felt like a target in a spyglass, waiting for the lit match to lower to the touchhole and drop thirty-two pounds of red-hot iron on my arse.

If I could only be so lucky.

After a full circle, he paused before me and stepped close. So close the buttons on his coat snagged on the gown's embroidery. My heart stuttered as I stared straight ahead, where his cravat tucked into his shirt.

Lifting a hand, his fingers met the taut cords of my neck. Firm pressure guided my head back, exposing the length of my throat. I swallowed, watching him over the tip of my nose.

His eyes lingered on mine then lowered. His head followed, putting his mouth a hairsbreadth above the hollow between my collarbones, fanning warm breaths across my shuddering skin. He hovered there for the longest minute of my life, tarrying on the edge between impulse and restraint.

My heart worked itself to exhaustion, waiting for him to do something more than just…smell me. But I didn't dare move or speak in fear of breaking the spell.

Incrementally, his hot, wet breaths grew hotter and wetter. The sensation confused me until I realized what I felt was the swirl of his tongue.

With a hand still holding back my head, he licked the ridge of my collarbone. A featherlight tickle. A taunt. Wicked to the extreme.

The torment continued lower, his lips ghosting oh-so softly across the exposed swell of my breast. The barely-there sensation brought my lungs to an abrupt halt, and I gulped, inadvertently causing my trussed-up flesh to rise toward his mouth.

His free hand gripped my waist, and he licked again, hunting for hidden curves beneath the edge of the bodice.

I whimpered, and a groan vibrated in his chest, one I knew he hadn't meant to give.

The invisible wall between us shuddered and bowed.

His mouth slipped to my other breast, followed by a scratch of canines. Everything inside me foundered, spiraling into felicity, into burning, sinful bliss.

As if he sensed my internal combustion, he bit harder, sinking teeth into skin, hard enough to leave an imprint.

Arousal surged, and I trembled for breath, needing, fearing, hoping he would close in for the kill. *Lick me, bite me, suck me.* I wanted to drown in his pleasure.

I wanted to grip his stern face, crush my mouth against his, and render him stupid. But if I initiated a kiss, it would give him another opportunity to reject me.

No, he had to start this, lead it, and control every step thereafter. It was the only way a man like him functioned.

So I kept my hands to myself, and consciously doing so made me realize I'd never touched him outside of self-defense. What did the texture of his hair feel like? Would his muscled torso heat and flex beneath my palms? How quickly would his cock grow in my grip?

Those answers, his tongue on my breast, and the sounds of his gasps slowly invited me beneath the mask and into the secret realm of Lord Ashley Cutler.

Sea of Ruin

He lifted his head and allowed mine to lower. His gaze fell upon my mouth, traced the line of my jaw to my hair, and landed on my eyes. Momentarily unguarded, he showed me everything in those volatile depths—the conflict raging in him, the sweet agitation of potential, the masculine need demanding to be satisfied. It left me thunderstruck.

Curling his fingers beneath the top edge of my bodice, he fished out the laces of my stays and cinched them until they were straight and tied.

With his rigid jawline so close, I couldn't detect a single whisker. His ebony hair combed back in modest waves, his face aglow from washing. Dear lord, he had gorgeous skin, the color of moonlight glinting off pristine sand.

At age thirty-four, he'd been blessed with the beauty of man in his early twenties and the confident carriage of a king at the acme of his reign. I yearned to strip him of his shields, his armor, and his clothes and to do to him what he did to me. I wanted to make him ache.

"Turn around." His voice, winded and rough, affirmed that I wasn't the only one affected.

I gave him my back.

He gathered my hair with unhesitant hands, as though he knew how to handle a thick, heavy mane such as mine. Draping the mass over my shoulder, he tackled the laces on my bodice.

Sharp, distinct tugs wrung air from my lungs. *Yank. Exhale. Yank. Wheeze.* Like a slow burst of gunfire, he mercilessly set the pace of my gasps.

When he finished, my relief was short-lived. He didn't step away, didn't move his hands from the gown. Instead, he went exploring.

Fingers drifted around my hips, finding and caressing my curves through the folds of fabric. His touch echoed everywhere at once, a harmony of sensation rippling beneath my skin and thrumming through my veins.

I wiggled against him, awash in desire. It simmered in me like molten sweet cream, but it didn't suffice. Was he dangling pleasure within reach only to rip it away and frustrate my expectation in the end?

Tantalizing bastard. If he were one of my crewmates, I would punish him for being such a tease.

"We should eat now," I said.

"No." He spoke against my neck, his mouth hot upon my skin, burning me up. "I'm not finished."

Standing behind me, he slid a hand across my chest. The other meandered over my abdomen and sank into the voluminous skirts between my legs. With a firm grip on my nether regions, he pulled my backside tight against his groin.

I hissed as bruised muscles shuddered and clenched in pain.

"You still feel my punishment." He trailed his nose along my shoulder. "Shall I retrieve the salve?"

"I'm fine, thank you."

But I wasn't. Wrapped in his powerful arms, held against the marble slab of his chest, with his finger directly on my clitoris, despite all the pleats in the skirt, I didn't trust my own judgment.

If he took, I would give. He wanted me, no mistake. I couldn't feel his hardness through our clothing, but I didn't need to. I heard his want in the consonance of our panting, felt it in the union of our sizzling energy, and saw it tremble in the fingers that now twisted in my curls.

With his grip in my hair, he spun us both until we stood face to face, eyes locked. Barely a sliver of space separated us.

His mouth lowered. Mine lifted. Straining to meet, our lips parted, floated closer, closer, and paused just before making contact.

Our chests rose in unison. *Inhale. Exhale. In. Out.* Deeper than a lick, more divine than a kiss, we became breaths. Nothing but trembling, heating, mating breaths.

It was a magical, instinctual attraction. I pulled, and he came with me. He leaned back, and I followed. We were joined by sparks that coalesced into one entity, drawn together like magnets, bound by an invisible force.

The fire that burned inside me, deep in the heart of my innermost being, roared into a conflagration, demanding fuel, seeking him. I wanted his mouth to fan the flames. And his hands. His heavy cock.

With his gaze fixed upon my lips, he held me prisoner, a willing captive to his attention. Now he just needed to erase that last inch. It had to be him.

Then he did. He pulled me tight against his hard body. But instead of raiding my mouth, he seized my neck. Licking. Kissing. Vibrating, bone-penetrating kisses that made my heart and blood hum with satisfaction.

My fingers clutched his waistcoat and shirt, clinging to his strength. It was a miracle that my legs remained beneath me. His potency washed unbearable longing through me, rousing a craving I'd held at bay for four days. And he wasn't finished.

Tilting my face up, he put his sculpted mouth at my ear. "You are so gratifying to the senses. So clear and absolute." A kiss at my hairline. "Unrestricted. Unconditional." His lips brushed across my cheek. "Ripe with temptation. Fit for eating." He touched his forehead to mine, breathing heavily. "You're so damn stunning it hurts."

I closed my eyes, shivering at the mercy of desire. Heat gathered between my legs, pulsing, liquefying. If he could do this to me with only his words, what else could his tongue do?

"Ashley—"

"Silence."

"Kiss me, then. Kiss me until I can't speak."

He went motionless, wooden, all signs of lust rapidly evaporating. His arms fell away, and he retreated a step.

My eyes widened, tapered, and glared.

"Don't give me that look, Goldilocks."

"You're attracted to me."

So was my wretched, cheating husband, and look what that got me. *Remember the pain, Bennett? You still feel it.*

But Ashley was different. He wouldn't betray me like that.

"Apples..." He plucked one off the breakfast tray. "They're a rare treat during long voyages at sea. When I see one, it attracts me, makes me crave that which I don't need. If there are several available, I always select the prettiest one. I can eat it. Or I can simply appreciate its beauty and toss it back." He dropped the fruit onto the platter. "Because I know I can live without it."

My nostrils widened with the seething rush of my anger. "You're comparing me to a goddamn apple?"

"Was it not an apple that influenced Adam's fall and introduced evil into human nature? Adam's apple is..." He pulled down his cravat and ran a finger over the bulge in the front of his throat. "Man's *swelling*."

Forbidden fruit and temptation led to sin. *And erections*. Understood.

"Point made." My cheeks rose mischievously. "Challenge accepted."

Twenty-six

After we shared a breakfast of fried hasty pudding, molasses, apples, and tea, Ashley strode aft toward the sleeping chamber. With a sigh, I admired the muscles flexing in his thighs beneath the hem of his blue frock.

My attraction to him was a ball and chain. There was no shaking it. His head-to-toe prettiness made seducing him a palatable plan. But what if this became more than a ruse? What if I lost my grip on what was real and what wasn't?

I needed to remember that I had a violently possessive husband coming for me, and he would rip apart every man who touched me. Ashley could die on Priest's sword. Or vice versa.

My stupid heart constricted at the thought of either man perishing. How did that make sense? They were both my enemies!

Ashley returned, carrying a comb for dressing hair. Where had that been hiding?

Rather than offering it to me, he stood behind my chair and arranged my curls to hang down my back.

Frozen, I sat upon the cushion he'd provided for my sore backside, bracing for the impending pain from his ruthless hands. But it didn't come.

He started at the ends, gently working at knots and moving his way upward. Each gentle drag of the comb sent tingling comfort across my skull and down my neck.

Peculiar. He doted upon my hair every night when he thought I was asleep. Like a secret compulsion. But showing tenderness in broad daylight? And combing with a finesse that rivaled a female hand?

"You've done this before." I relaxed beneath his touch and closed my eyes. "Who is she?"

Not his betrothed. A lady of virtue would require a chaperon. And absolutely no touching.

He glided the tool rhythmically through a section of my locks for several minutes before responding.

"My sister." He divided another portion of curls and crouched to comb the ends. "She had hair like yours. Tight, coiling curls that bounced around her waist. Except hers were black."

"The same color as yours."

"Quite so. She used to cry when the lady's maid took a comb to it. I was many years younger than her, always clinging to her skirts. Very much the annoying little brother." Affection softened his voice. "I hated when she cried. So I took over the task and learned how to smooth the stubborn knots without causing her pain."

I felt my eyebrows shifting from squished disbelief to raised surprise. I was probably the only soul on this ship who'd heard this story. Perhaps I was the only one who knew he had a sister.

He was opening up to me.

But my brief victory didn't taste sweet, for I detected tragedy in his tone and verb tense. "You speak of her as if she's in the past."

He set the comb on the table and proceeded to gather my untangled tresses into a long pleated rope down my back. Deft fingers braided mindlessly and tied the end with a leather thong.

That done, he didn't move, holding his unnerving stance behind me, depriving me a view of his expression.

"There were complications during the birth of her first child." His hand clamped onto my shoulder as if to prevent me from turning. "Neither she nor my nephew survived."

Death. An incurable disease.

I breathed out slowly, achingly. "I'm sorry for your loss. Truly, my lord." My chest squeezed. "What was her name?"

"Arabella."

"Do your parents have other children?"

"Just me."

My feelings toward this cruel-hearted man loosened, just a little. I owed him nothing, but my hand moved anyway, reaching back to wrap around the stiff fingers on my shoulder.

He didn't reject me. Instead, he took my hand in his and pulled me to stand. By the time I turned, he'd erased any sentiment that might have leaked into his countenance.

"Will you tell me about her?" I squeezed his fingers. "Your sister?"

"Another time, perhaps." With a hard stare, he searched my expression as if expecting to find ill intent.

I stared back, daring him with my eyes to say something mean.

His gaze lowered to my lips. His hand wrapped around my braid. The air quivered.

Then he kissed me.

Deep and drinking, his mouth plundered and claimed. The sudden taste of him stole my senses. My pulse stalled somewhere between utter shock and overwhelming delight before bursting into a gallop. I lifted on my toes and gripped his arms, opening for him, greeting his warm tongue, and moaning against his firm full lips.

His muscles hardened beneath my palms, and I clung, holding him, drowning in the fever that surged between us. His fingers curled around my waist, pulling me close, immobile, tight against his grinding hips.

God's teeth, the man could kiss and move his body. His tongue rubbed against mine. His mouth conquered and consumed. His pelvis rotated, subtly, suggestively, stoking fierce flames of longing in my belly.

I shook uncontrollably as he licked the inner flesh of my lips, infusing my blood with potent desire. He tasted exactly how I'd imagined—wet, dark, and masculine—like a devastating storm. His powerful body quaked as his throat produced the deep guttural noises I'd heard on the balcony.

My heart danced. My legs quivered. Then I was moving, being lifted by strong hands and set onto the edge of the table.

He wedged his hips between my thighs, shoving the skirt up and out of the way to make space for his indomitable physique. Through it all, his mouth stayed with mine, refusing to release that glorious, voracious kiss.

Teeming with hunger, I leaned into him and reached for his cheek. His jaw flexed beneath my buzzing fingertips, the skin supple and smooth over unbending steel. He cupped the back of my head and angled my mouth where he wanted it, deepening the crush of our lips.

My hand slipped to his corded neck, caressing the tension beneath his cravat. His Adam's apple bounced against my touch as he swallowed our kisses in greedy gulps.

Tucked into the hollow beneath his iron jaw, his jugular throbbed and swelled beneath my finger. His heart definitely existed. It had beaten for his sister once. And now it pounded for me.

My body thrummed with awareness as he kissed me into oblivion. I was so lost in the intimacy I hadn't realized where my hand wandered until he gripped my wrist, stopping me from seizing him between his legs.

He didn't halt the kiss, though. Guiding my fingers up his body, he flattened my palm against his neck. But I kept going, reaching higher, until I discovered the soft, thick texture of his hair.

With a groan, he expressed his pleasure in the touch. His arm hooked around my back as his mouth feasted and fed with no end in sight.

Gradually, in a melting of lips, the kiss dissolved on its own.

His brow fell against mine, our breaths rushing forth in sharp spurts. My heart dealt blows like a hammer, my entire body trembling in a sheen of restless want.

I'd enjoyed that with a recklessness I didn't want to analyze. But as my pulse slowed, irrational guilt crept in.

I hadn't kissed another man since I'd met Priest three years ago. The betrayal tasted like stale ale in my throat, and this was only the beginning.

I banished the thought before it grew roots.

Ashley leaned back, and his eyes captured mine, intense and dilated.

"You feel this." I glanced at his groin, unable to see the engorged ridge I knew was hiding beneath his frock. "You took as much pleasure in that kiss as I did."

"Relish it." He lowered his mouth and kissed me with infinite kindness, as though for the first time. *Or the last time.* He straightened and retreated a few paces. "It won't happen again."

I slid off the table and abolished the distance, pushing into his space and craning my neck way back to meet his eyes. "Is the view so very different from up there?"

He glared down at me, nostrils pulsing. "What I see is—"

"A whore sleeping beside a naked man every night? Tell me how this cozy situation doesn't become *cozier.*"

In answer, he clutched my waist with both hands, lifting and setting me aside as if I weighed nothing. Then he strode into the day cabin and vanished around the corner.

I simmered until he returned with two cocked hats. One, he jammed onto his hard head. The other, he wriggled onto mine.

After adjusting my braid to drape just so, he offered me an elbow. "Would you like a tour of the finest warship ever built?"

Since talking seemed to get me nowhere with him, I welcomed the change of scenery.

"Yes, my lord. I would like that very much."

Twenty-seven

I didn't feel like a prisoner.

As Ashley escorted me through the passageways of His Majesty's Ship, which stretched nearly two-hundred feet fore to aft, I didn't feel like a pirate or a whore or anything comfortably familiar.

With my fingers loosely curled around his muscled forearm and my skirts swishing over my bare feet, I heard the greetings and commands he gave the sailors he passed. But I focused on what wasn't being said.

I was, on the surface, ignored by all. No one looked at me. Not directly. Yet every man in the vicinity was viscerally aware of the woman on their commodore's arm. I could practically hear their arseholes clenching.

The last time they'd glimpsed me, I'd just been plucked from the sea like a drowned rat, wearing only a man's shirt. Today, garbed in a gown made from Lord Cutler's frocks, I looked refined enough to be a lady.

If I'd wanted that title, I would've followed my mother's rules, married the Marquess of Grisdale, and perhaps both of my parents would still be alive. My rebellion had cost them everything, and I would make damn sure it wasn't in vain.

My pirating career would *not* end in a whimper on the gallows.

The gown, the modest braid, and my delicate hand upon his lordship's elbow were but small steps to freedom. If I embarrassed the commodore in front of his soldiers, I would lose the progress I'd made toward warming more than his bed.

I needed to melt the ice around his heart. So I behaved myself as he guided me through the upper and middle gundecks—I would return to inspect those guns on my own time—the galley, and the infirmary. Somewhere near the stern beneath his quarters, he opened the door to an elegant cabin occupied primarily by a large table.

The wardroom.

Access to this space was restricted to only warrant officers. Its purpose was to provide a private place for high-ranked men to socialize, dine, and conduct business during wartime.

From what I understood, the topic of women—not to mention the presence of one—was strictly prohibited within its walls. So when Ashley invited me across the threshold, I thrilled at the idea of him breaking a sacred rule.

Perhaps there was a little rebellion in him after all.

Several lieutenants sat around the table, which was long enough to serve a dozen officers. Ashley stepped in ahead of me, and all conversations ended. Everyone rose to their feet, clapped up their hands to their hats, and bowed.

"At ease, Lieutenants." He pulled his elbow forward, bringing me with him through the narrow space.

The scent of tobacco and rum sweltered in the humid air. Sunlit windows veneered one wall. Shelves of alcohol, silver serving platters, books, and navigational equipment lined the other.

As he led me past the officers, none of them glanced at me. But their body language, stiff and unwelcoming, threw the entire cabin into a state of brooding dissatisfaction.

Ashley gave their attitudes no acknowledgment.

Arriving at the bulkhead at the far end, he stopped at a small table and poured a cup of tea for himself. He didn't serve me, but I wasn't interested. My complete attention fixated on the sheets of printed paper covering the aft wall.

Each page highlighted a different pirate. Some had sketches of faces and designs of their personal flags. All of them were titled by name.

The first print depicted me. My name. My relationships with Edric Sharp and Charles Vane. No mention of Priest. No sketches or descriptions of my image. And no flag, for I never cared to hoist my own. But the page contained some intelligence about where I'd been and the ships I'd attacked over the past few years.

There were fallacies in the report, but most of it was horribly precise.

Sea of Ruin

Even more harrowing was the sheet that hung beside mine. This one with a picture.

The "Feral" Priest Farrell.

The representation of his features had been drawn by someone who knew *exactly* what he looked like. The artist had captured every gorgeous detail, down to the shading of his whiskers, the braids and beads woven through his hair, and *the look* he wore on his face. The accuracy of those sketched eyes staring back at me, the fearlessness and savage intensity in them, made my heart squeeze.

I tipped my head, angling the brim of the hat to hide my face. Then I quickly scanned his report for my name. Not finding it, I jerked my gaze away.

A dozen of the most notorious pirate captains covered the wall. I knew every name and had met half of them. But the sketches of the ones I'd encountered in person hadn't been drawn with the same impeccable care as the picture of Priest.

Anger ignited beneath my skin and clenched my fingers. I wanted to knock Priest into a cocked hat for being so heedless with his identity. Knowing him, he'd probably posed for that drawing.

The arrogant twat was going to get himself captured. Then I would have to rescue him. *After* he rescued me, of course.

"You know these rogues." Ashley sipped his tea, studying me over the porcelain rim.

Every officer in the cabin stilled, awaiting my response.

Well, now I knew why he'd invited me in here. He wanted me to take a long look at these prints of *the bad and the worse* and help him hunt his prey.

Heat rose to my face, burning my cheeks anew. My chest heaved with indignation, and it took everything I had to control my temper.

Yes, this was Ashley's career, his duty as a pirate hunter, which he put above and beyond all else. But I would never aid him in the mass capture and murder of my kind. Not even for a pardon. It went against everything I was.

After spending four days with me, he should have gleaned that much.

"Everyone out." He set down the cup, never taking his eyes off me.

The cabin vacated. The door shut behind the last lieutenant. Then we were alone.

"You stared at this one the longest." He tapped the sketch of Priest. "He has a dissolute reputation with women. Have you bedded him?"

"Hasn't everyone?" A hollow thud erupted in my ears. "They call him the king of libertines."

"Yes, and you mentioned a libertine the other night."

Me and my big mouth.

He grabbed my arse cruelly through the skirt, wedging invasive fingers into the divide between my cheeks. "Was he the one who took you here?"

A defensive posture and adamant denial would've given away my true feelings for Priest. So I loosened my stance and tossed out the answer he would expect from a pirate whore.

"Yes." I twisted the corner of my mouth into a devious half-smile. "Jealous?"

"How many times?"

"You want a number? Like an actual count?" I blew out a breath, making a splattering noise between my lips. "I don't know, Ashley. It was a very long night, and he had an insatiable staff that stood near as tall as the mainmast. So if I'm counting strokes, do I include every position, fore and aft and—"

"It was just one night?"

I saw the writing all over the wall. He was fishing, hunting for clues about his target. How well did I know the infamous Priest Farrell? Well enough to provide a list of weaknesses, habits, favorite ports, and haunts?

Why yes, I knew him better than anyone. And I just so happened to be wearing his shirt. Because I loved the traitorous bastard.

Unfortunately for me, I would choose endless torture and certain death before I ousted him.

"That feral pirate never beds the same woman twice." I shrugged carelessly and moved away from Ashley's grip on my backside. "I was lucky enough to have him all to myself for an entire night."

I'd had him for a year. Sadly, during my time with him, I hadn't truly had him to myself.

"Where is he now?"

"That depends." I stretched my mouth into a yawn.

"On?"

"Is he your next target?"

"Yes."

"If you go after him, what happens to me and the forty pirates in your hold?"

"You're free to roam the ship, and I'll arrange limited exercise and fresh air for the others. They won't perish if I extend the voyage a little longer."

Perfect.

"Hm." I folded my arms across my chest and tapped my lips, toying with him.

"You're trying my patience, woman."

"Fine. If I tell you what I know, what do I get in return?"

"I can't grant you a pardon."

In 1717, King George issued a proclamation that granted a full pardon to pirates who surrendered themselves to any governor in the colonies. I hadn't wanted it then. I hadn't wanted it when the king reissued his pardon in 1718. And now, three years later, the opportunity was gone.

Well, fair riddance. I would hang myself before I traded my vivacious livelihood for a spiritless existence of conformity.

"For your assistance in this matter, you shall receive a reward." He pointed at one of the royal proclamations on the wall.

Persons who willfully and obstinately persist in their piracies, robberies, and outrageous practices shall be pursued with the utmost severity, and with the greatest rigor that may be, until they and all of them be utterly suppressed and destroyed.

If any person shall discover any other person concerned in the said heinous offenses, above mentioned, so that he or they may be apprehended and brought to justice, such discoverer shall have and receive the sum of one-hundred pounds.

The decree went on to state that pirates themselves would be awarded two-hundred pounds for turning in their own captains.

That amount of coin would provide a luxurious retirement in the West Indies. Yet none of my crewmates had been tempted. If and when I escaped Lord Cutler and recovered my compass, I would find my father's treasure and reward my men for their loyalty.

Until then…

"God save the king," I said dryly. "Tell me about His Majesty's reward. Shall I receive it before or after I hang?"

He slowly released a breath. "What do you want?"

The smile I concealed between my teeth made me tremble. I was going to send him on a wild chase, thereby delaying the journey to England and allowing myself more time to turn his heart. I couldn't have asked for a better boon.

"I'll assist you in this hunt, in exchange for a kiss." I met his dark blue eyes. "It must be equally as passionate as the first one. But this time, you'll give me unrestricted access to touch you anywhere I please."

His pupils flared so wide I saw the reflection of my unbidden smirk in them. A muscle feathered in his hard jaw, and his cravat twitched over the straining sinews in his neck.

Oh, what I wouldn't give to hear the thoughts churning in that gorgeous head.

"I agree to your terms." Miraculously, his voice retained its unruffled smoothness. "Tell me what you know."

"The king of libertines leases a room in New Providence. He resides in a brothel called the *Garden*."

That had been true three years ago when I'd met him. Whether he'd returned to visit his pretty naked flowers during our separation was anyone's guess. What I did know was that he wasn't there now.

"Nassau." Ashley's lips thinned.

"Pirate haven."

It was about a week's voyage away. Considerably closer than England. From his perspective, if he turned the ship about now, he wouldn't be backtracking too terribly far.

"What are the chances he's there?" he asked.

"Who knows? But his doxies adore him and keep careful records of his comings and goings. I'm certain, if you licked their middle parts with the utmost severity and the greatest rigor that may be, you could coax them into sharing their innermost secrets."

He narrowed his eyes. "You seem to know a lot about this libertine for having spent only one night with him. A night that, by your account, wasn't given to conversation."

"Quite true. Due to all the *unnatural* sexual relations." I grinned, trying to raze his stiff demeanor.

He didn't blink an eyelash. "Tell me how you really know Priest Farrell."

This was the tricky part, and I would need to tread carefully. "My quartermaster is Reynolds Farrell."

"Another Farrell?"

"Half-brother."

His head jerked back, his eyes round with disbelief.

"I thought you knew everything, Commodore." I took advantage of his shock and hooked a finger into the front closure of his waistcoat, relishing the pocket of body heat beneath. "Priest has a gaggle of half-blood relations."

"This brother, your quartermaster…" He gripped my wrist but didn't push it away. "Are they close?"

"They despise each other. But Reynolds keeps up with him."

"When was the last time you saw Priest Farrell?"

"The night I spent with him. So that was…" I let my focus blur as if pondering the question at length. "Two years ago."

"Thank you for the information." He lifted my hand and softly kissed my fingers, lingering with the barest touch.

Every iota of my being gravitated toward that beautiful mouth. But distrust kept me rooted.

His warm, masculine scent surrounded me, his hand firm around mine as he regarded me closely.

The rich red waistcoat and blue frock with gold embellishments, chiseled countenance, and physique worthy of envy—he was the paragon of English nobility.

Until he licked my fingers.

His tongue, firm and hot, dipped into the valley between my knuckles, conjuring images of another slit he could have been laving with the same delectable pressure.

"You're beautiful, Bennett." His sensual blue eyes jumped to mine and blinked. "I've never said those words to a woman. Never thought to say them until I saw you."

A sound rose in my throat, one of startled disbelief and abject need. His kisses traveled to my thumb, and he wrapped his supple lips fully around it. I fell into paradise with my mouth open.

His free hand clutched my head beneath the rim of the hat, and he pulled me into him, trapping my knuckle with his teeth. He didn't bite, but he looked as though he wanted to desperately.

He owed me a real kiss, and his hooded eyes told me he was thinking of it. Loosening the clamp of his jaw, he released my thumb. His face drifted closer, his head ducking until his hat bumped mine.

The hand on my head began a slow caress, firm fingers stroking the base of my braid, holding me still, making me wait with shortening breaths. He erased another inch until nothing remained but his mouth and his strength restraining me so close, so exquisitely captive.

His gaze flitted to my lips, adding extra beats to my heart. Then his eyes drifted over my shoulder, snagging on the wall behind me.

I knew exactly where his focus went. I felt Priest's sketched eyes staring at my back. He didn't even need to be present to control my life and everyone in it.

"Ashley." I touched his stony jaw.

His gaze remained locked behind me. I'd already lost him, the moment between us gone, in lieu of a new target, another pirate to catch. Of course, he would choose duty over me.

"Time for you to leave." He clutched my arm and ushered me toward the exit.

I dug in my heels. "Wait a sec—"

"Do as I command and make haste."

"You owe me for that information."

"I agreed to a kiss. Not a time or place."

"You're evil." I jerked my arm from his grip. "Far more wicked than any man on that wall."

"Perhaps you should learn how to negotiate." He slammed a hand into my backside, sending me along. "Go."

"No—"

His fingers closed around my neck, and he yanked my mouth to his, stopping just before our lips touched. "Don't ever tell me *no*."

He opened the door and shoved me huffing and seething into the companionway.

His personal guard, Sergeant Smithley, waited just outside, showing no reaction.

"Gather the lieutenants, Sergeant." Ashley straightened his frock, his expression void of emotion. "We have another pirate to collect."

"Yes, my lord."

The Sergeant departed, and the door shut in my face, leaving me alone in the passageway with thoughts of violence.

The depraved pirate in me wanted to storm through the ship and stir up havoc from stem to stern. At the very least, I wanted to toss weaponry over the bow, cut all the ratlines, and piss on the king's flags.

But all that would get me would be a ticket back to the hold. An impatient temper certainly wouldn't win favors with Ashley.

So I went for a stroll and iced my anger. First stop… The gundecks.

Hammocks slung above the guns on all three decks. Senior officers probably had small cabins of their own, but the majority of the crew slept here. It was also where they ate. Tables hung from the beams of the deck above, making the most of the confined, airless, overcrowded space.

Running my fingers along the snouts of the bronze beasts that crouched along either side, I imagined their mighty booms as they spat

Sea of Ruin

thirty-two-pounders at enemy ships. Galleons like *Jade*. But she would never again sail into the sights of these guns. I trusted Reynolds to hide and protect her and my crew.

As I continued to roam, vigilant eyes tracked my every step. None looked pointedly at me. But there was always someone on my stern or at my beam, following orders. Ashley's orders. It was apparent he'd charged a retinue of men to watch over the wandering prisoner.

I was standing at the rail of the quarterdeck an hour later when Ashley turned the ship around.

Overhead, cables and tackle clattered as rigging lines were hauled. Canvas slowly turned, and HMS *Blitz* swung into the wind, angling for a wide arc.

Plumes of frothy spray flung from beam to beam as she came about, her towering masts heeling out over the sea on a starboard tack. Timbers creaked and shivered. The deck canted, and I braced my legs as her massive hull smashed through the waves.

I missed *Jade*. I missed my compass, Reynolds and Jobah, my trousers, and so many things. But God's teeth, I lived for this. The beat of the sailcloth in the wind, the salty scent of the ocean, the mist of spume upon my face and sleeves… The incomparable unity of the senses.

Squinting through the blinding sunlight, I scanned the decks for Ashley, but I already knew he wasn't topside. I couldn't feel him.

Strange how I had that faculty of perception with a man I'd only known a few days. Yet whenever he neared, I became unmistakably conscious of his presence as if my entire body was attuned to him.

There was only one other man who had that effect on me.

The distant horizon drew my gaze, the sun high over the yard-arm. There were no ships in sight. No signs of Priest.

Changing our route wouldn't throw off his pursuit. If anything, it would make it easier for him to find me, for I was leading Ashley into the busiest port in the West Indies. And it just so happened to be in the vicinity of Harbour Island, where I'd sent Reynolds to hide *Jade*.

In full suits of sail, HMS *Blitz* set a northerly course to New Providence, riding easy on a south-southwest wind.

I had a week.

One week to corrupt the lord of propriety and reunite with my ship.

Twenty-eight

I felt his eyes on me.

It had been two days since he tossed me out of the wardroom, and I hadn't seen him since. He spent most of his time in that damnable cabin with his lieutenants. Evidently, my access to it had only been a one-time event. Every time I approached the door, Sergeant Smithley turned me away.

At night, Ashley slipped into his private quarters after I retired. He was quiet enough to not wake me. If he was pleasuring himself on the balcony, I'd slept through it.

If he was trying to evade me—and that kiss he owed me—he was doing a fine job of it.

Be it as it may, he wasn't ignoring me now. I felt him somewhere behind me on the upper deck, his gaze boring a hole between my shoulder blades. The impulse to look gripped my neck, but I didn't turn, didn't give him the satisfaction of acknowledgment.

Straight ahead, thunderclouds heaped together on the horizon. Their dark undersides scudded along the chopping waves, freshening the wind and injecting enough friction in the atmosphere to prickle the hairs on my arms.

We were headed into the teeth of it. I should take cover since I only had one gown. Though, I'd started working half-heartedly on a second one, needing something to do to pass the time.

Nevertheless, I didn't dare move out of the cage of Ashley's gaze.

With any luck, he would approach and personally escort me below.

The wind rose, warm and damp and thick with brine. Below, white foam broke upon the crests of turbulent waves, flinging the spray high over the warship's bows. Since it had been overcast all day, I'd foregone a hat. My loose curls whipped in the gale, tangling around my arms and slapping my face.

Lightning flashed. Thunder grumbled, and a moment later, great sheets of rain fell from the sky and blew sideways with the gusts. The deck slanted, and I braced against the sudden sway, gripping the rail for support.

So much for Ashley's courtly manners.

I glanced around and couldn't see a tarnal thing through the violent shower. To hell with him.

Hurrying to the gangway ladder, my legs absorbed the roll of the deck. I descended quickly and leaped off the last step.

And landed in pure agony.

The pain shot through the sole of my foot and drove me to my knees. I cried out and fell onto my hip, digging through the skirts to locate the source of my anguish.

A small metal spike protruded from the planks. A boot would have absorbed the sharp tapered end. But since I didn't have shoes, the puncture had gone right through my soft fleshy arch.

I yanked the hem of the skirt away from the river of blood and pushed myself up onto one leg. My eyes closed against the deluge of rain, and my foot slipped, flying out from beneath me.

Strong hands caught my waist from behind. I was lifted, cradled, and carried against a warm chest. That single embrace released all the tension in my body.

I didn't have to open my eyes to know I'd find the brightest, deepest gulfs of blue fringed in black rain-soaked lashes. But I looked anyway, sighing in appreciation of his masculine beauty.

Ashley didn't meet my gaze as he strode toward the main hatch. But he pulled me tighter against his chest and tucked my wet head beneath his jaw.

"Send Lieutenant Flemming to my quarters." His command vaulted over the crash of thunder, scattering men like chain-shot. "And find me the smallest pair of boots on the ship. Make haste!"

My feet were the size of a child's, so best of luck with that. But the thought warmed me.

Down the companionway and into drier depths, he stopped the first soldier he encountered. "Remove the spike on the upper deck."

"The spike, my lord? I don't—"

"Find it!" He spun away, carrying me toward his quarters. "How's the foot, Goldilocks?"

His endearment replaced my needling pain with unexpected contentment.

"I could've limped back to the cabin on my own." With my arms around his broad shoulders, I pressed my face to his neck, relishing his fresh, earthly scent. "But this way is much more enjoyable."

"You're shameless."

"You're delicious. Why have you been avoiding me?"

"I don't meddle with prisoners."

I touched my lips to the dark hollow between his jaw and cravat. "You like meddling with this one."

"You're bleeding." He arrived at his cabin. "Sergeant."

"My lord." Sergeant Smithley opened the door and shut it behind us.

"I'm not bleeding on purpose." I wriggled my toes, igniting stitches of pain. "I didn't see the spike and—"

"It wasn't your fault." He set me on the dining table. "Lie back."

Outside the open window, the rain came down hard, flickering with lightning and flooding the planks inside the cabin.

He lifted my legs to the table and wedged a cushion beneath my knees. I lowered to my back, astonished by how he could be so attentive and aloof at the same time.

"Have you been thinking about me?" I brushed wet hair from my face and neck, shivering in the soaked gown.

His gaze narrowed on my prickling flesh. "Shift to your side."

He rolled me where he wanted, and his fingers tackled the laces on my spine. Moments later, the gown loosened. He dragged it down and off my body.

I bit my lip, captivated. What was motivating him to do this? Was he concerned the wet clothing would ruin the furniture? Or make me ill? Or was something else going on?

His hands returned to my torso. Quick caresses of his fingers here and there straightened Priest's shirt beneath the stays and down my legs. Once he confirmed the undergarments were dry and in order, he positioned me to lie face-up.

His wet frock, waistcoat, and cravat came off next. Everything went on hooks to dry. Then he strode toward the windows to shut out the rain.

"Have you imagined my lips wrapped around your cock?" I asked softly.

The glass rattled beneath his hand, slamming harder than necessary. He disappeared through the day cabin. The balcony door closed with a whoosh, followed by the sound of his returning footfalls. He didn't show it in his features, but his steps landed harder, more agitated than usual.

I stifled a smile. "I'm crawling underneath that steel mask of yours and—"

"Stow it, Bennett."

"I scare you."

"You pester me." His stern, sculpted face appeared upside down above mine, his hands braced on either side of my head. "Always talking and making trouble and…" His gaze slid down my body. "Bleeding all over my table. Where the devil is that surgeon?"

"Here, my lord." Lieutenant Flemming swept in, adjusting his cravat as if it had been haphazardly thrown on.

"She stepped on a spike." Ashley shifted to stand beside me, resting a proprietary hand on my knee.

Flemming sank into a chair near my feet and opened his medicine chest. As he went to work on my wound, Ashley kept the linen shirt tucked around my legs, protecting my modesty as if I possessed such a quality.

"How's the pain?" He focused on the doctor wearing a strange expression. Like he was troubled by my injury.

"I'm not going to bleed to death, my lord."

He didn't glance at me.

"I don't understand." I folded my hands on my midsection, watching him watch Flemming. "You punched my face, tossed me off your balcony, shredded my wrists, bruised my arse and other unmentionables. Yet you're concerned about a gash on my foot?"

That brought his gaze to mine.

"I *control* the pain I inflict. I know where and how hard to strike to avoid permanent damage. But this…" He motioned toward my feet. "I can't control infection should it decide to attack and contaminate your body."

Flemming kept his gaze on his work, pretending to ignore us.

"I should have located boots for you." Ashley ran a hand through his wet hair. "I should have ensured the deck was safe."

Sea of Ruin

"I don't see how any of that matters," I muttered. "You intend to see me hang."

"I intend to see you stand trial."

Same thing. But arguing the particulars wouldn't change the outcome.

"The wound is clean, my lord." Flemming shifted. "But it requires stitches."

"Do what is needed, Lieutenant."

With a needle and thread, the doctor began the painful task of closing up the bottom of my foot. The skin was so tender along the arch that every stab made my teeth clamp together. Muscles contracted without my permission, and I couldn't stop my body from jerking and bowing off the table.

Ashley bent over me, blocking my view of the attacking needle. Blue eyes pinned mine, and his hand sank into my hair, smoothing out the damp coils.

"Lieutenant Flemming revived you the day we pulled you from the sea." He ran a finger along my temple and down my cheek. "You weren't breathing."

I was barely breathing now with his insufferably gorgeous face so close to mine.

"We debated the method of resuscitation." A muscle jumped in his jaw. "I decided the best way to stimulate you was by inserting a pair of bellows into your rectum and thereby fumigating your insides with tobacco smoke."

"Oh, for the love of God." My entire body cringed.

Blowing smoke up the arse of the *suddenly apparently dead* was a treatment I'd seen too many times. It never worked as far as I could tell. So how was I alive?

Ashley drew his bottom lip between his teeth, and that unholy gesture made my stomach dip. Did my eyes deceive me, or was he fighting a smile?

A muffled chuckle drifted from Flemming.

I craned my neck and glimpsed the doctor barely containing his grin.

"You're jesting?" My mouth dropped open as I looked back at Ashley. "You made an actual joke? To excite laughter?"

"You're not laughing."

"I'm too shocked to do anything at the moment."

"That's good."

"Why?"

"All done, my lord." Flemming stood and gathered his tools. "Keep the foot elevated for a time."

He finished? I couldn't believe it. Ashley had deliberately distracted me from the stabbing needle. Why would he do that for someone he was condemning to the gallows? Why engage with me at all?

There was so much more to this man than he allowed to be known.

As Flemming stepped out, Sergeant Smithley set a pair of black boots inside the cabin. They looked small. Perhaps small enough.

The door shut, and it was just Ashley and me, staring at each other.

Twenty-nine

Ashley touched my chin, closing my still gaping mouth. I expected him to pull away, but his fingers stayed, drifted, inching their way to my lips.

"How was I revived when you pulled me from the sea?" I stared up at him, hypnotized.

"Flemming put his mouth on yours." He traced the curve of my bottom lip. "He gave you breath until water squirted from your airway."

"He did *what?*" I'd never heard of such a thing. "That worked?"

"I should say so." His gaze lowered, caressed the rise of my breasts above the stays, and returned to my eyes. "I've never met anyone so full of life. It pains me to imagine your…vitality being choked from your body."

A flutter swarmed my belly as the tips of his fingers touched my throat, tracing my pulse. Choking was exactly how this would end if he continued on his path. But for the first time, I glimpsed a genuine struggle in him, an inner battle that gouged creases into his serious brow.

While his king's desires came before his own, he didn't want to deliver me to England. Deep down, he knew I would be convicted and hanged.

Choosing a pirate over his country was nowhere near a possibility in his mind. But the situation unsettled him. He liked having me around, even if he wasn't ready to admit it.

He lifted me into his arms and lowered us into a nearby chair, arranging me sideways on his lap with my legs propped on the table.

"Relax." He touched his lips to my temple.

I hadn't realized I'd tensed. It seemed my body didn't trust him. As it shouldn't.

Releasing a sluggish breath, I ordered my muscles to loosen one by one. Softly, gently, I sank into the cradle of his brawny frame and dropped my head onto his shoulder.

He stretched out his legs and deepened his recline, letting the cadence of the storm lull us into a profound sense of serenity. Now and then, he indulged in his need to untangle my curls—unraveling the wet strands with patient fingers, smoothing out the tresses from roots to ends, and breathing rhythmically with the movement of his hand.

With each stroke, I snuggled closer until my lips rested against the hard lines of his jaw. He had the smoothest skin I'd ever felt on a man, and he smelled delightful, so clean and virile. I couldn't resist the pull to nuzzle him.

He allowed the intimacy and played in it, too, brushing his mouth across my cheek and against the ticklish place beneath my ear. Off and on, he dropped tender kisses along the frame of my face, seemingly unaware of his effect on me as he absently petted my hair and stared off into the rain.

His affection was neither lust-filled nor expectant. He didn't grab me or grope me or hurry this along to some indecent end. He was giving me a connection, a closeness that was bigger, stronger than bedplay.

We were meaningful together. Intricate. An unlikely bond formed in the dwelling place of souls.

The moment felt unreal, like a dream between time and space, with no boundaries, no titles. We weren't enemies in this sphere. We weren't captor and captive or lord and pirate.

We were but two people who came from and belonged to the sea, reaching for each other because it felt right. It felt natural.

In the security of his arms, I floated into slumber, waking periodically to his lips grazing some part of my face, his breath rustling my hair, or his hands roaming the shape of my hip.

As the rain tapered off, I woke fully and found him watching me with an engrossed expression.

"What is it?" I tried to sit up.

Sea of Ruin

The hand in my hair brought me to a halt and held me there.

"You're fragile when you let your guard down." His voice rumbled, setting my chest aflutter. "This spot... Just here." He touched the curve between my neck and shoulder. "It's so delicate and feminine. Like the softest silk." He caressed the dip again, making me twitch. "You're ticklish. Even when you sleep. It's...remarkable."

I stared up at his beautiful, impassive face where excellent breeding met intelligence and sophistication. Carved and polished from head to toe, he was a nobleman through and through. And a damned good commodore, too, with eyes that missed nothing and an iron will that never bent.

What did he want with me in his arms? What did *I* want beyond my freedom?

There were no painless answers to those questions.

With each passing second, my intent to win his love felt less like a devised plan and more like a fate I couldn't stop or control. I needed his affection. Not to use as a means to escape.

I didn't want to escape Ashley Cutler. I didn't want to betray him or lose him in any capacity. The greedy, unreasonable truth was I wished to keep him and hold him *just like this* every night.

What did that mean for Priest?

Did it matter? Priest irreparably hurt me, and Ashley was betrothed. In the end, I would end up alone. Or hanged.

Which was why I needed to stick to the plan. Love hurt. It betrayed and ruined. My plan was safe. It protected *me*, not Ashley or Priest. It ensured I wouldn't be the one destroyed in the end.

Not only that, Priest was on my tail right now, and he wouldn't be receptive to discovering I'd fallen in love with another man.

Had I fallen?

No, not quite. But as our gazes melded, those eyes held mine with an intensity that filled a terrible void inside me. The way he looked at me made me feel special, desired, almost loved.

I was doomed.

My need for this, for the sort of all-consuming love I could have with Ashley... It was greater than my survival. It was more essential than life. More significant than death. It was immutable. Immortal. Beyond all doubt and faith.

I needed him, plain and simple. Which meant I could never hurt him. I could never let Priest hurt him.

As I slowly came to terms with this, I was fantastically, undeniably terrified out of my mind.

I tried to straighten my twisting thoughts, tried to curve my lips into a casual smile, but nothing worked right. Not my brain. Not my mouth. I was cracking. Weakening. Losing my sanity.

We sat motionless, bodies entangled, gazes locked, sequestered together in the fading light, for no other reason than because we fit so perfectly this way.

It was too real. I wanted this too badly.

Doomed.

I looked away, but his stare stayed with me. His eye contact… Good God, it was more intimate and private than anything I'd ever experienced. Staring at him felt like making love, only closer, deeper, farther reaching.

What was this sorcery?

"Bennett." His accent caressed. A delicious torment. Sensual. Excruciating.

I closed my eyes, trying in vain to draw air. The need he roused in me was so beautiful and frightening it was all I could do not to weep. I felt it rising—the scalding emotion, the swelling in my throat, the wetness behind my eyelids.

Warm hands framed my face. "Look at me."

I placed a palm on his chest to push him away. He covered my touch, flattening it to flexed muscle. His heart hammered, strong and fast, and mine tripped over itself to keep up.

Opening my eyes, I found his lips an inch away, the tantalizing seam parting, drifting closer. "What are you—?"

"Your kiss, madam." He planted it on me, buried it in me, deep and devastating, with a pledge to grow.

His mouth imparted so much passion and potency it stunned my senses. The sensual glide of his lips, the twist of his fingers in my hair, the roll of his tongue against mine—the execution put me to death and brought me back to life.

My chest heaved with the force of my gasps, threatening to tip my breasts over the stays. Then my legs were shifting, readjusting with the help of his hands. We moved together, bringing our bodies as close as possible on the chair.

I settled onto his hard, powerful thighs, straddling his hips—all of which gave his mouth better access to mine.

With my fingers in his hair, and his arms holding me tight, he kissed me through vast, unexplored eternities.

Sea of Ruin

I poured everything into the union. Every part of me filling with heat and giving it back to him ten-fold. He mated with my mouth as though the connection was all he wanted, all he needed. I sank into his passion, welcoming his hard body between my legs as he rotated his hips and ground against my aching.

He felt wonderful, so solid and male and *him*, the man I'd slept next to for a week. I flicked my tongue against his, whirling, teasing, tasting the sky and the sea and every desire between.

"Touch me." He panted against my mouth, his hand sliding down the front of my stays.

His lips feasted, and his palm covered my breast, encouraging me to explore.

I didn't slow at setting my fingers upon the muscled meat of his abdomen, but glided my touch downward, reaching into the space between our spread legs. There, I clutched his throbbing response.

"Christ." His sharp grunt fanned against my lips, and his hand tightened on my breast.

Holy mother, he was enormous. I traced the swollen outline through his breeches, following the hard curve along his thigh. The length of him stretched from my wrist to my fingertips and farther still. He was thick, too. Thick enough to feel for days after he impaled it.

"Are you pleased?" He grasped my arm, holding my hand against his erection.

"What?" I didn't like the sudden clip in his tone or the meanness in his grip.

"Does the size of my hunger meet expectations?"

"Exceeds, I should think." I pulled on my arm. "If you unhand me, I'll show you my appreciation."

His fingers opened, and I lifted my hand to cup his face.

"You feel incredible, Ashley." I searched the chilling blue of his eyes. "Not just the hard parts of you. But the tender ones." I leaned in and tasted his full sweet lips. "I find your softest parts the most pleasing."

His gaze warmed, his chiseled features losing their sharp edges as he kissed me back. He molded his hands around the back of my head and rubbed his mouth against mine, watching me between the unhurried, languid rolling of our joined tongues.

Magic pulsed between us, producing marvels with every touch. My entire being assimilated to the harmony of his, joining us on a level neither of us understood. I knew he felt it. He wore the thunderstruck look of a man who was sinking fast and forgot how to swim.

The temperature of our licking grew hotter, more carnal, and soon the air dripped with fire, spitting sparks across my skin. I wanted to slow it down, to savor the moment and capture the intimacy.

With my hands framing his face, he mirrored my pose, holding me the same way. We lingered in that embrace, kissing, sharing eye contact, as hidden forces bound us closer and tighter together.

Until he pushed back.

His arms fell to his sides, and something snapped between us, twisting a dark, helpless feeling within me. Slowly, our connection frayed and broke. A wall went up, emptying his expression. Then he shoved me off his lap and onto my knees.

"Unlace my breeches and take me out." He rose from the chair, towering over me. "Don't make me wait."

Kneeling at eye level with the erection straining beneath the fabric, I knew what this was. Detachment under the guise of possession. The ugly kind of possession that had no obligation or respect for the object possessed.

A cold sensation, wrapped in hurt, knotted in my belly. I wasn't prepared for the humiliation. Wasn't prepared for my body's trembling betrayal or the tears that swarmed my eyes and cascaded down my cheeks.

He reached down and caught a droplet with his finger. "What's this for?"

"I don't want us to be like this." I flung him a sharp look, and more tears fell. "I don't want to be your whore."

I was ruining everything, sabotaging my own plan.

He rubbed my tear between his fingers, studying me with a tedious mien of righteousness. At length, he gripped me under the arms and set me on the chair. Then he disappeared into the aft cabin.

My stomach sank as I cursed my foolish, irrational behavior. What the hell was wrong with me?

It wasn't long before he returned, clad in full dress—cravat, waistcoat, frock, breeches, buckled shoes. His armor.

As he stepped before me, bending to put his face in mine, I braced for the consequence of my stupidity.

"We're not equals." His mouth, that had kissed me so sweetly, now twisted into an authoritative sneer. "Don't forget what you are or why you're here."

His fingers shook as he grabbed his hat, jammed it onto his head, and left.

The sound of the door shutting gave my body permission to release its pain. I doubled over and clapped a hand against my mouth, muffling the pathetic sounds that erupted from my chest.

If he were any other man, I would never tolerate such indignity. But as my captor, he could speak to me in whatever manner he wanted.

But he hadn't wanted to be so cruel. I'd glimpsed the emotion in his trembling hand. I'd heard the creak in his voice that didn't match his detached proclamation.

Indifference hadn't walked out that door. There'd been regret in his footfalls and a burning in his eyes.

He was fighting this hard and unraveling fast.

What did a man do when he unraveled?

He lashed out.

We're not equals.

Those words were for him. He clung to them, desperate for the reminder, because he knew where this was headed, and he had about as much power to stop it as I did.

Fated. Destined. Whatever name I gave it, I'd felt it the day we met.

But awareness didn't make it hurt any less.

As I stared down at my bandaged foot, registering the smarting throb, I suspected there would be more stumbling and more pain before we found our way.

Thirty

Dawn was a welcome sight as it swelled over the horizon, melting yesterday's gloom. The mingled scents of salt water and fresh air shimmered through my deep inhale, invigorating me.

I slid from the bed—unsurprised to find Ashley's side cold and vacant—and limped toward the open door of the balcony. The foot injury was inconsequential, if not a little sore. I'd received the utmost care and would be walking with a normal gait by the time we reached New Providence.

The other missteps I'd taken, however, still needed mending.

At the rail, I stared out at the empty ocean. The sun glowed in smudges of pink and lavender, reflecting like sparkling diamonds across the water's surface. Warm rays kissed my face and soaked through the loose nightgown. The trade wind sought my hair, tangling the strands as though it had nothing better to do.

What was *I* going to do?

I was married to an adulterer who would never let me go. I wanted a nobleman who would never marry me. If and when the two men collided, they would promptly kill each other. I should hope for that outcome and escape the moment it happened. But I was finding that my ability to exercise logic where they were concerned was nonexistent.

Even if my affection for Ashley was requited, he wouldn't desert the Royal Navy or eschew his family, ranks, and obligations to be with a ruined, untitled woman. Besides, a relationship with him wouldn't sever the one I'd been running from for the past two years.

One thing I'd learned was that love conquered nothing. It would only make my hopeless situation all the more hopeless.

A rustling sound drifted from the dining cabin. Footsteps? I thought I was alone.

Curious, I stepped back inside and followed the disturbance through the sleeping chamber, the day cabin, and… *Oh.* My eyebrows lifted.

Ashley sat at the table, wearing breeches and nothing more. A stout man with crooked legs bent over him, scraping a cutthroat razor along his neck.

"You have whiskers?" I edged closer, squinting at the steel-edged lines of Ashley's jaw. "Since when?"

"Good morning, Miss Sharp." He glanced at me sidelong without turning his head. "How's your foot?"

"Good morning. The foot's fine. But seriously, I didn't know you could grow facial hair."

"Not that it's any of your concern, but I can, and I do."

His barber finished and turned away to stow the tools. As he reached for a towel, I beat him to it.

"May I?" I held up the rag and met Ashley's steady gaze.

He stared at me a moment before giving a stiff nod. "You may go, Sergeant."

The bandy-legged man lumbered from the cabin with his small sack of supplies.

When the door shut, I sidled between Ashley's spread knees and sat on the edge of the table. Leaning in, I ran the towel along the strong column of his neck.

His lips parted, and I sucked mine between my teeth. I could still taste his kisses and feel his hard male body wrapped around me. The magic between us hadn't faded. Every lingering look rushed my blood like a tidal wave bent on ruination.

"I've never seen hair on your face." I dropped the towel to glide my fingers across his rigid jaw and sharp cheekbones. So soft. So impossibly stony.

"It grows slow and comes in patches." His breathing quickened beneath my caress. "Shaving is only needed once or twice a fortnight."

"That's okay." I floated closer, tracing the satiny skin around his wide lips. "I can't grow a beard at all, which makes me dreadfully ill-suited to my role as a pirate captain."

"That so?"

Sea of Ruin

"Truly. Everyone knows that beards incite terror and inspire reverence. You saw Madwulf's horror when you severed his bug-infested pride and joy."

"I think..." His majestic blue eyes glimmered as they dipped to my mouth, and lower still, pausing on my chest. "You possess other, more sufficient assets, so as to strike a man with awe."

I followed his gaze downward, and my heart bounced off the walls. The neckline of the nightgown hung low and gaping in my bent position, offering him a glaring view of my bare breasts.

As I leaned back, his hand caught the loose garment and yanked it down my shoulder. The linen settled at my elbow, exposing one breast entirely. His gaze fixated, his pupils expanding, darkening, and soaking in that bared part of me for the first time.

My flesh ached for the heat of his wet mouth, my nipples tightening with each agonizing second he stared.

For two years, I'd dreamed of being gazed upon by a man who desired me. A man who didn't lie or betray or long for another woman when he was with me.

Ashley didn't just gaze. He narrowed the space between us, enveloped me with his scent I loved so well, and raised a hand toward my chest. Rather than seizing me in a careless grip, he skimmed his palm against me, just a featherlight touch on my nipple.

I whimpered and shivered as a delicious fever sprang to life in my bones, heating deep in my core, and hotter still between my legs. He watched every reaction, his hawk eyes examining my body's answer to his oh-so-soft caress.

"You're exquisitely formed." He molded his fingers around my breast, lifting and testing the weight. "Like a queen."

"I'm certainly no queen." My bosom felt so heavy, so swollen with need.

"No, you're right." He lowered his mouth to my chest and breathed, "You're a goddess. A sea goddess."

He ran the flat of his tongue over the pebbled peak, and my spine bowed in response. A groan vibrated in his throat, and I moaned with him, shaking beneath the heavenly sensations of his warm firm lips. My hands flew to his hair, my nails dragging across his scalp and threading through the glossy black strands.

My head dropped back on my shoulders as he suckled. His hand cupped my backside, and the other plumped up my breast, holding it against his worshiping mouth.

Any second, he would throw up his walls and say something mean to push me away. But for now, I gloried in the unguarded moment, savoring the rush of breaths, the caress of strong fingers, and the masculine sounds of appreciation.

I touched him everywhere I could reach—his bulging shoulders, the hairless bricks of his chest, and the heavily muscled flesh that flexed along his arms as he commanded them to move.

His jaw felt like marble against my breast, where he licked and kissed with devotion. His lips, so soft and full, delivered pure ecstasy when they wrapped around my throbbing nipple.

Fingers fanning down the curves of my waist, he splayed them across my midsection and slowly sank into the valley of my thighs. My bottom teetered on the edge of the table as he teased the dark juncture between my legs, finding my wet curls through the linen.

I realized, truly comprehended, just how very destructive this man was on my life. He hadn't just physically captured me. He'd besieged my emotions, my reasoning, and he was on his way to imprisoning my soul.

As he leaned back to stare at my glistening, swollen breast, his broad shoulders blocked out the world. All I saw was him and the gorgeous planes of his face in facets of light and dark, silk and steel, kindness and cruelty. And I trembled.

With fear.

With desire.

I craved the addictive sensations he stirred in my body. And I feared every second he made my knees weak and my heart yearn for more than carnal pleasure.

He braced an elbow on his thigh and lazily trailed a knuckle around the outer curve of my breast, his gaze pensive as he watched the movement. "Why do you hate England?"

"Besides the fact that everyone there wants me dead?"

"Yes." He cupped me in his palm and ran the pad of his thumb over my nipple.

"England rejected my mother. Banished her." I brushed my fingers through his shiny black hair. "Whenever she was reminded of her home, it made her horribly sad."

"Perhaps she was sad because she missed her beautiful country. Have you ever been there?"

"No. I remained here, in the West Indies, for the last seven years. Before that..." I took a bracing breath and met his eyes. "I spent the first fourteen years of my life in the wilds of Carolina. Charleston. No one knows that."

Except Priest.

Ashley regarded me impassively. "If you were in Charleston, how did you know your father?"

"He visited throughout my childhood. I was closer to him than I was to anyone else. When he…" I placed my hand over his, flattening our fingers against my broken heart. "When he died on the gallows, my mother threw herself off a cliff." My voice stuttered, hitching with old hurt. "I was there when it happened. I lost both of my parents on the same day."

He reached for me, pulling me onto his lap and against his bare chest. "I'm sorry."

His soft, sincere tone swaddled me in warmth. As did his arms and the protective cage of his body. He straightened the nightgown to cover my chest. Then he just held me, watching the sun rise, sipping from a cup of tea, with no sense of urgency to set me away.

So I started talking. I told him about my upbringing, my mother's struggles in exile, my father's secret visits, and their tragic love story. And because he listened with such quiet intensity, I walked through every detail of that harrowing day seven years ago, including the start of my relationship with Charles Vane.

By the end of it, my sadness had settled like the sand in an hourglass, resting quietly but always there, ready to tip and flow again.

"Have you visited Carolina after that day you left with Vane?" he murmured against my hair.

"No. Charleston and England are the two places I intended to avoid for the remainder of my life."

"England is a special corner of the world, Bennett."

"What do you love about it?"

"The rich history. The raw, unspoiled countryside. It glows with greenery, moss-covered moors, and dramatic cliffs along the coastlines. The view from the hill on my father's land looks out onto nothing but sprawling fields crisscrossed in stone walls like seams on a patchwork counterpane." His accent thickened, and his eyes seemed to shine with inner peace. "Since most of our tenants' families have resided there since the fall of the Roman Empire, they've been maintaining the same hedgerows for generations upon generations. I daresay they've perfected the art."

"Does your family own a lot of property?"

"Two estates in London and many along the southern coast. I own several myself. My favorite sits upon a cliff that overlooks the very water that touches your Carolina."

That brought a small smile to my lips. Although he was thirteen years my senior, perhaps at some point during our childhood, we'd gazed out onto the same ocean at the same time.

"Is it cold there?" I asked.

"Depends on the season. It'll be summer when we arrive. Warm and pleasant."

Not on the gallows. No matter the weather, the noose would be as frigid as death.

"Will you watch me hang?" I met his gaze. "Or will you deliver me to the headsman, accept your promotion to admiral, and sail away on your flagship without looking back?"

His expression emptied. "I'll be there until the end."

My throat and stomach burned as he set me on my feet. Then he stood and stalked into the sleeping chamber.

Honestly, either answer would've hurt. Why had I even asked the question?

I swallowed a painful lump and followed him at a distance, remaining quiet as we dressed and groomed for the day.

The things we did by rote—cleaning teeth, donning skirts and shirts, lacing stays and boots—would've been ordinary if done alone. But here, together, every task felt significant. I would wager that he'd never performed his morning routine side by side with another person. A husband and wife didn't even do these things together. Yet we went through the movements as if we shared everything and had known each other our whole lives.

Once my gown was in place, I didn't need to ask for his assistance. His hands were already there, tightening the laces and adjusting the pleats in the back.

Only this time, when he finished, he didn't pull away.

His fingers sifted through the coils of my hair, brushing the tresses over my shoulder. Looming behind me, he set his lips against the exposed side of my neck. Not to kiss. He simply rested his warm mouth there, breathing me in, scenting my skin. *Apologizing?*

His hands curled around my waist, bringing my backside against his groin. A pained noise sounded in his chest, followed by a whisper at my ear. "You're the chief cause of my misery."

I flinched, eyes narrowing.

Sea of Ruin

Not an apology, then.

"You make me hard, Bennett." His cultivated accent cracked like kindling. "So unbearably, ceaselessly hard I'm in agony. I can't think, can't do my job, can't—"

He released me and turned away. I spun toward him, watching the frock stretch across his back as he ran his hands down his face and over his mouth.

"Ashley."

He shifted back and pinned me with an accusatory glare. "I will *not* fall for your trickery."

"Trickery?" I squared my shoulders. "You think I *want* to feel affection for a man who intends to watch me hang?"

Something flickered in his eyes. Then they cleared, and his jaw worked side to side.

"Don't play games with me." He strode toward the exit. *Big surprise.*

"You're the one playing games." I raced after him and caught his arm in the day cabin. "You touch me and kiss me and work us both into tangled knots. Then you run away."

He swung back, his ocean eyes bright and deep, as he clutched my face in his hands. "Who says I'm running?"

I didn't understand his meaning.

Until he kissed me.

His mouth paralyzed all thought as his assertive tongue delved between my lips, past my teeth, and straight through my heart. I moaned at the heady contact, the emotional intimacy, gulping down the force of his ravenous intensity.

Tongues twining, hands sliding, his mouth, his potency, his overwhelming masculine presence consumed me. Then he hooked a knuckle beneath my chin, lifted my face, and did something no man had ever done to me.

He kissed the tip of my nose, soft, lingering, deep in its affection.

"You feel me running, Bennett?" He rested his forehead against mine.

"No." My chest rose hard, my voice barely a whisper. "I feel you falling."

He closed his eyes. When they opened again, he stared at me with sullen austerity. His mask locked in place.

Stepping back, he straightened his frock, turned toward the dining cabin, and left.

I pressed a hand against my mouth, trapping the heat from his lips.

It was hard to love a man—much less tolerate one—who would choose his career over my life.

But it was impossible not to love Ashley Cutler.

He was complicated, iron-bound, steadfast, and passionate. Like Priest in the best of ways. Not better. Just… He was everything I longed for, for so very long. To give up on him would be to give up on myself.

I looked around his empty quarters, debating whether to go topside for a stroll in the ocean breeze. But I shouldn't strain the stitches in my foot. Infection was the last thing I needed.

My gaze snagged on the unfinished gown on his desk. Fabric and sewing supplies scattered every surface. I'd left his day cabin in total disarray.

And he'd left me painfully, miserably, completely unsatisfied.

I sat behind the desk, focused on the sewing project, and tried to ignore the ache. A few stitches here. Some fabric cuts there. But the throb between my legs persisted, accompanied by the tingling simmer that his kiss had left upon my lips.

Damn him and his beautiful pouting mouth. It was the bane of my existence and the only thing I could focus on. So I did what any immoral woman in my position would do.

I propped my bandaged foot on the desk, spread my legs wide, and reached beneath my skirts.

I didn't need him or any man for this, but it didn't hurt to imagine his sensual blue eyes. Hooded, unblinking, unsmiling, gorgeous gulfs of blue. I swirled my fingers around my swollen flesh, stirring my slickness and growing hotter. Until those blue eyes turned silver, sharp and glinting like blades.

Stop.

Concentrating harder, I fingered my ache while imagining Ashley fucking me. Then Priest appeared, pounding his magnificent length between my legs.

Confound it!

I started again. Ashley. His severe expression. That godlike body. Oh, the intensity he would bring as he moved over me, against me, inside me. My head spun with dizziness.

Priest returned, taking over the fantasy. Then they took turns, using my body forward and backward, top and bottom. So indecent. So sinful. So inconceivably good.

I worked my fingers faster, rubbing and thrusting with images of

Sea of Ruin

both men polluting my thoughts. I cried out as I came, my legs quivering and hips twitching through the pleasure.

Slumping onto the desk, I caught my breath. *Much better.*

I cleaned up and went back to work on the gown.

Hours passed. Meals arrived. I nibbled on salt fish and ship biscuits and periodically stepped onto the balcony to escape the swelter of the cabin.

Long after the sun went down, I finished the last detail on the skirt. The gown wasn't nearly complete, but the task had effectively occupied my mind for the duration of the day.

Setting down the project, I shook out my fingers to get the blood circulating. Exhaustion weighed heavily in my bones. I was tired enough to sleep without dwelling on a jumbled tangle of blue and silver eyes.

Twenty minutes later, I lay in the dark, stretched out atop the counterpane. Brutal humidity saturated the night, but I didn't mind the heat. It swaddled me into dreamlessness the moment I closed my eyes.

When I woke, I was drowsy, burning up, and not alone.

A beam of moonlight cut across the bed, illuminating a masculine hand on my thigh. I lay on my side, facing the wall, motionless, listening to the creaking of the ship, the roar of distant waves, and his heavy breathing.

His mouth was close, rustling the hair near my ear. Harsh breaths. Labored. He'd been touching me for a while.

The hem of the nightgown had been pushed to my hips, exposing my backside and the length of my leg. His fingers trailed up and down, delicately tracing the curve of my thigh and the dip between my buttocks. Teasing me softly. Burning me slowly.

My nipples puckered, and the muscles low in my belly clenched lazily, heatedly. It was the best torture. And the worst. If I rolled toward him and let him know I was awake, would he stop?

Please, don't stop.

But he did. Yanking away his hand, he shifted to his back and released a tight breath. My heart thrashed in my ears as I waited, anticipating the heave of his body leaving the bed. In three…two…one…

Right on cue, he rose and treaded toward the balcony.

I understood his conflict. If he made love to me, he would no longer be putting his country before himself. A man of his stature and moral rightness didn't bed his prisoners. I was his enemy just as he was mine.

But that line had already blurred, whether or not we consummated our forbidden desires.

I made a decision.

Quietly, I slipped from the bed and pulled off my nightgown. On silent feet, I crossed the chamber to the balcony and stood a few paces behind the lord and master.

Completely nude, he bent at the rail and stared out at the sea, the muscles contracting in his back as he sluggishly stroked himself. Defined sinews etched his biceps. Cords strained along his neck. Twin depressions dimpled the muscles above his taut arse. The sight of his glorious, battle-honed physique flooded me with need.

Then he paused.

"I know you're there." His voice rasped, thick with lust. "You've been watching me like this most nights."

Languid, slow-burning eddies pooled in every corner of my body. I opened my mouth, yet no sound came forth.

He began to stroke anew, harder, rougher, his deep voice snapping like a whip. "Come here."

Thirty-one

Cautious excitement streamed through my veins, shimmering with barmy bubbles of desire.

As I padded toward Ashley's nude back, he didn't turn, didn't remove his hand from that which he stroked between his legs.

Reaching for him, I ran my fingers across the tight muscles flanking his spine. His breath rushed out, and his body grew impossibly harder, stiffer. Closer, I teased my bare nipples against his back. Then my lips. My tongue.

A violent tremor raced through him, and we shuddered together.

I kissed his shoulder blades, tasting salt mist and lust on his damp, velvety skin. My hand trailed down his bulging arm. I kept going, past his elbow, around to the front of his hips, and gripped him where he gripped himself.

Thick, swollen, masculine need overfilled my palm. He groaned, deep and throaty. My mouth dried. My skin caught fire.

"Bennett..." He twined his fingers around mine and slid our hands along his hardness. "Christ, yes. I've imagined this so many times."

A jar sat to the side on the rail. Whatever it was, he'd used it to lubricate. The glide of our fingers moved deliciously over the shape of him as if stroking liquid satin.

Satin over steel that went on and on forever.

I'd seen a lot of naked men in my life but never one with this much girth and length. And I still hadn't *seen* him.

"How are you so big?" I tightened the circle of my fingers, unable to make them touch all the way around.

"Superior breeding."

I swore I heard a smile in his voice. "Let me see you."

The backs of his legs trembled against my thighs. Humidity clung to our skin. Being this close to him, both of us nude and sliding together… God, I burned, feverish beyond the heat of the Caribbee night.

He turned toward me, crowding my smaller frame. His fingers caught my wrists and held them at my lower back, making my heart thump with dangerous yearnings.

With my hands restrained, he brought our bodies flush together, trapping his arousal between us.

My gaze tipped upward, questing. Blue eyes stared back, steady, unwavering, no signs of running.

He hauled me up his towering body, lifting me onto my toes. Chest to chest, I had nowhere to go as he pried my lips open with the demand of his. Hungry breaths poured into me, his tall, strong build bearing my weight and scorching my skin.

His kiss ate me alive, devouring the recesses of my mouth, licking inside me, and swallowing my moans. I was drunk on it, intoxicated by the intensity in which he dominated every movement.

Sucking at the edges of my lips, he used his tongue like a weapon against my defenses, lashing blow after blow until I gave up all pretense of resistance.

His hands continued to shackle mine behind me, his arms binding us together as his mouth hunted and claimed. His jaw widened my lips so he could sink deeper, farther, twisting my senses into a whirlpool of dark, smothering desires.

I'd never imagined a kiss could be so blinding and incorporeal. Our mouths and souls fused together as though we were melded in a forge and fashioned as one in molten fire.

He transferred my wrists to one hand and used the other to rain insatiable caresses upon my skin. He touched me everywhere, between my face and my hips, kissing me passionately and always returning to my breasts. He seemed to love my sensitive nipples, his fingers tweaking and plucking them into hard, elongated peaks.

But I ached to feel that hand elsewhere, to travel lower, where he'd never touched me bare. I was so wet and wanton I thought I would die with waiting.

Sea of Ruin

By the time he sought the curls between my legs, every nerve in my body was quaking. He rubbed firm fingers along my wet slit and sheathed them slowly, sensually. The pleasure that assailed me was so exquisite I bit him mid-kiss, crying out.

"Dripping." He brushed his cheek against mine and panted at my ear. "You want this."

God confound me. "Yes."

He grasped my shoulders and spun me toward the rail.

"Wait." I swayed, trying to shift back. "What are you—?"

"Don't let go." He forcibly clapped my hands onto the balustrade and gave them a commanding squeeze.

His chest covered my back, his body heavy and rigid as though fighting for every shred of self-control.

"Ashley." I craned my neck, trying to see him over my shoulder. "I want to look at you and kiss you while you fuck me."

He pressed his face against my nape and ground out a sound of mingled frustration and pleasure.

"If you want this…" His mouth moved to the side of my neck, and his teeth clamped down. A threatening, lust-filled bite. "Stop talking."

I did want it, but not if he meant to take me like a whore. Before I'd met Priest, this had been my preferred position, for it was less complicated, less awkward with men I didn't know.

Then Priest showed me the divine pleasure and intimacy in eye contact during lovemaking. I wanted that with Ashley.

But he wasn't having it. With a hand clenched on my hip, he affixed me to the rail and bent over my back. Effectively trapping me, he glided the head of his enormous erection through my slickness from behind.

Beneath the feverish swamp of his masculine heat and the sweet relief of his cock fitting against my cunt, I didn't have the strength to stop this. I wanted him to the point of pain.

Until he shifted his hips and pressed up into my darkest place.

"Wrong hole!" My hands shot out, grappling at nothing, the scream in my throat strangled to silence.

"Mercy God." He pushed past the ring of muscle, groaning low in his chest, his fingers a bruising vise on my hip. "Let me in. Deeper. Deeperaaaaah!"

I bucked, gulping for air, stunned beyond thought, as he worked the enormity of his cock into my arse. He was so well lubricated that he'd already sunk halfway in.

"Ashley…" I breathed through the sharp sting, the searing pressure, and tried to shove him away. "Stop!"

He pulled out, and his open hand slammed against my buttocks, jarring fire into my bones.

"Be still while I use you." Then he was on me again, inside me, impaling his length into my backside. "Take it. Just how you like it."

Something fractured inside of me. A breaking apart of my spirit. By the time he was fully seated, I had no fight left.

With unbending hands and an iron will, he controlled me, and I yielded, defeated, letting the ruthlessness of his lust hammer in and out. He felt terrible and beautiful, wild and experienced, mean and ravenous.

I didn't know how many thrusts he got in, but it wasn't many. He fucked me hard and came fast.

When it was finished, he withdrew from my slumped body. His hands didn't reach for me. His eyes didn't seek. He turned his back and strode away, leaving me to fester in agonizing silence.

I wouldn't chase him. I wouldn't beg for a different outcome. And I would *not* cry in front of him.

Pushing away from the rail, I retreated into the shadows of the balcony and listened as he washed behind the privacy screen. He was cleaning me off him, rinsing every trace of me away. Like it never happened.

It shouldn't matter. I shouldn't care. I was stronger than the cruelty of men.

Footsteps sounded beyond the door. Moments later, he strode past the balcony, dressed in a shirt and breeches, without casting a glance in my direction.

"Why?" I heard myself ask as I stepped back inside. "Why did you take me there? Why like that?"

He stopped, his broad shoulders stiffening, as he assumed the powerful stance of a commodore.

"I know why you've worked so insidiously to lure me. You wanted my seed." He turned to face me, his blue eyes blazing. "So I gave it to you in a place you couldn't use it against me." His nostrils flared. "You will stand trial, Bennett Sharp, and you'll do so without my babe in your womb."

I backed away, my legs shaking as shock and overwhelming sorrow rode roughshod over my insides. Of course, he was right. I'd arrived with several plans of escape. But the one he referenced would've been a complete and utter lie.

"If you had taken the time to look at my body, you would've noticed my scar." I placed a trembling hand over the puckered skin low on my abdomen.

His gaze followed the movement and jerked back to my face.

"Do you know what happens to a woman when she takes a sword through the middle?" I raised my chin, helpless to stifle its quivering. "She loses her female organs, her menses, and her ability to conceive. I will never be a mother, Ashley. Your concerns have been wrongly placed."

I tried to stem the flow of tears. Tried. And failed.

He didn't stick around to witness them. Turning on his heel, he stepped through the chamber, the hem of his untucked shirt just a flick of silk behind him as he vanished beyond the dining cabin.

The exterior door opened, followed by a deafening slam.

My diaphragm convulsed, shoving a sob past my lips. A series of choking, wheezing, wet hiccups followed, and I tried to swallow them. Tried to muffle my cries. But I couldn't. I doubled over and wailed like a pathetic child.

As those wretched sounds met my ears, I clamped my mouth shut.

This wasn't the ferocious daughter Edric Sharp had raised.

This wasn't me.

I slapped at the tears on my face and staggered to the balcony. There, I transformed my cries into rage. Snarling and roaring into the wind, I let the ocean snatch away my heartache and bury it beneath the pounding waves.

For the past seven years, I'd lived among men, fighting tirelessly for every inch of respect in a man's world. I never let their prejudices weaken me. I never swooned, cowered, or submitted in the shadow of masculine strength. I never allowed anyone to see me as anything but a hardened, ruthless pirate captain.

With the exception of two.

I'd let two men inside my very vulnerable, very feminine heart. And they chewed it up, one behind the other.

Hadn't I always wanted to be just like my father? Well, I was as it turned out.

I'd fallen into impossible love.

Twice.

The hardest lessons left invisible scars. At the rate I was going, that was all my heart would be. Just a twisted, hideous, unfeeling knot of tissue in my chest.

But it wouldn't kill me.

At age fourteen, I survived the deaths of my parents. At age eighteen, I survived the thrust of a sword in my belly. At age nineteen, I survived the worst pain of all—the betrayal of the man I loved more than all else in the world.

Now, at twenty-one, I would survive this, too.

Somehow, someway, I would escape the madness of this ship, with or without the arsehole who commanded it. But first, I needed medicine. A healthy dose of rum to heal the pain. There was a whole chest of it in the dining cabin.

Grabbing a linen coverlet, I draped it over my shoulders and lit a lantern. Then I trudged through the chambers, past the desk, around the table, and veered toward the coffer of liquor. As I bent to open it, a shadow moved in my periphery.

My blood chilled.

Near the exit, the darkness seemed murkier. I narrowed my eyes. My vision adjusted. My breath stopped short, and my heart took off.

A silhouette sat on the floor, its broad back against the door and head hanging in the clutch of hands.

He hadn't left.

An eruption of doubt, relief, and distrust ran riot through me. Why was he here? On the floor?

Without his shoes and frock, he wasn't armored to walk among his men. Perhaps he was too shaken to maintain the elegant veneer he wore beyond that door.

Was he wearing a mask now?

I drew in a steady breath and stepped toward him, just close enough to examine him in the moonlight.

His arms dropped to his bent knees, and he lifted his head.

And I saw him.

I really saw Ashley Cutler for the first time.

Thirty-two

I pulled the coverlet tighter around my nude body, shivering in the grip of Ashley's unguarded stare.

More than just his soul shone in those luminous blue eyes. I saw the wreckage of his true self, the terrifying depths of his fears, the corruption of his desires, and his deepest regrets.

He must have heard me sobbing when I'd thought I was alone, and that shamed me deeply. But he wasn't without his own shame. The bewailing, contemptible things he'd done and left undone had bled the color from his face, drawing deep creases there, heavy with shadow.

His expression showed everything. His stately demeanor gone. His armor destroyed. His impenetrable walls floating adrift like flotsam.

I wasn't sure if all that emotional carnage was connected to me. But I'd blown the veneer off his elegantly constructed bearing, and he didn't seem to know how to repair the damage.

As he regarded me, his eyes begged for forgiveness. My heart pleaded for justice. Perhaps we both wanted mercy, but I had none to give.

"I botched this." He scraped a hand through his hair. "Rather spectacularly, I'm afraid." His voice sounded strange as he rose to his feet, holding my gaze. "It wasn't my aim to expose you to my unseemly manners."

"Unseemly manners?" I backed away, boiling with outrage. "You viciously fucked my arse, Ashley. You took care of yourself and just left me there without so much as a pat on the head. Even Madwulf would've shown me more decency than that."

He flinched, his features contorting in pain. It was startling how much he didn't look like himself. Oh, he still had that gorgeous innocent-looking face, but it was softer now, almost younger, if that were possible. He didn't wear the mien of a commodore and lord. He looked like a lost man in the throes of anguish.

He stepped toward me on a whisper. "Forgive me."

Two words and my shields erected. They were no ordinary shields, for they'd been welded in a fire of lies and hammered with betrayal. They'd defended me against those words only a week earlier when they'd dripped from the mouth of the last man who hurt me.

"I will not." I retreated, walking backward.

"I thought you were plotting against me." His gaze dipped to my abdomen.

"I was." I hugged the linen around me, hiding the scar. "I intended to seduce you and convince you I was pregnant. A ruse that would've only worked for a few months since I can't conceive." I stared at my feet, blinked slowly, and looked him straight in the eye. "Then you kissed me, and I knew…" A swallow burned in my throat. "I didn't want to escape you."

Clouds of color filled the hollows beneath his cheekbones, his eyes unnaturally bright. Muscles jumped beneath his skin as he repeatedly straightened his sleeves. Fidgeting. Visibly distressed. So out of character.

A traitorous flutter took flight in my belly, a thrill that tingled through my limbs. I flexed my hands, aching to throw myself into the arms of my captor.

I stepped back.

"I'm a monster." He stayed with me, his deep, resonant voice fraying like rope. "Worse than you can imagine."

"No imagination needed." I continued to withdraw, edging into the day cabin. "I can feel the burn of your latest malefaction in my backside."

"Yes, I hurt you." He stalked closer. "God knows, I'll hurt you again. I'm damned good at it."

Raw masculinity dominated his gait as he prowled after me into the sleeping chamber.

He was a whore for his king. A devout adherent. A rule follower. He wasn't a man who just took what he wanted. But right now, he

Sea of Ruin

wore the look of one. Bared teeth, wild eyes, unwavering steps—he projected an animal instinct, primitive and uncivilized, and the full force of it centered on me.

"Don't come any closer." I held up a hand, warding him off. "Stay back."

"I can't." He kept coming. "This isn't some fickle inclination or casual infatuation. What I feel for you isn't sane or safe or rooted in lust."

My stomach tumbled as I staggered back, seeking distance and bumping into the bed. "What is it, then?"

"It's madness, Bennett. Ruin." He cornered me, imprisoning me with his eyes. "You know as well as I do that this affinity, you and me, is frighteningly, magnificently, hopelessly real."

My heart thundered, shrieking at him for being so cruel and so irrevocably right.

He reached for me, and I fell back, landing on the mattress with nowhere to go. His hand closed around my wrist, and I twisted, swinging a fist and missing him in a haze of panic. Then I went crazy.

Scrambling across the bed, I snarled and kicked and hit every part of him that came near. But nothing deterred him. He caught my leg, then my waist, tackling me to the mattress and driving my heart into exhaustion. In the next breath, I was restrained beneath his substantial bulk with my arms pinned to my sides.

Was the coverlet still wrapped around me? A thin drape of linen wouldn't protect me from him, anyway. At that thought, I renewed my struggling, desperate to escape before he forced my legs apart and violated me again.

But he didn't attack. His arms clasped tight around my squirming, twisting, gasping body and just held me there. *Hugging me.*

Searing pressure filled my throat and hit the backs of my eyes. The hoarseness of my breathing rose over the creaking in the cabin.

His mouth went to my ear. "Shhhhh."

Tears invaded, inwardly, silently. But somehow, he knew. He made more hushing sounds and gathered me closer, embracing me in a cocoon of strength without crushing me.

I didn't know what to do with this. I didn't trust it.

His lips moved to my brow, lingering, softly kissing, and I didn't know how to react to that, either. I wanted it. I wanted him to kiss me and hold me and keep me as his captive, without actually being one.

I shouldn't crave any of those things. I was sick. Mentally unwell.

Emotionally and physically exhausted.

I wanted to return to my ship and my life with Reynolds and Jobah.

He shifted, trailing kisses across my eyelids, down the length of my nose, and around the corner of my mouth. Then he stared at me with a magnetism that made everything else fade into the lantern's backlight.

He was such a distinguished, utterly gorgeous man I never tired of looking at him. Even when he was mean. Especially then. The utter loss of control and wild passion he'd asserted on the balcony would've been sinfully arousing under different circumstances.

If I hadn't been plotting against him, and he wasn't trying to condemn me to the hempen halter, I'd wager that we could have had a lovely relationship seeded in trust, communication, and sizzling love.

Notwithstanding the drastic discrepancy in our social classes.

My face gravitated to the warmth of his chest, my lips grazing the silken neckline of his open shirt. My cheek resting against the knit of bone and sinew on his sternum. My fingers sliding around his lean waist to… I only meant to touch his spine. But my hands bumped against the upper curves of his rock-hard arse.

He stilled. I trembled. Then I surrendered to the impulse and palmed his taut, firm buttocks through the breeches.

His body gave a slow, sinuous flex, rolling against me as he released a rumbling groan.

"I want to start over." The languorous grind of his hips let me feel how hard he throbbed between us. "You don't have to forgive me. But we're not leaving this bed until you come."

My scorn clung, setting my jaw. "If I say *no*?"

"I told you." He gripped my chin and locked our eyes. "Don't ever say *no* to me."

His mouth came down, slanting just right and kissing me soundly. He stroked gently at first, his tongue seeking, hunting. When it finally caught mine, the touch felt like an echo of bees, and I nearly jumped from my skin.

His lips curved against my own.

"Is that—?" I pulled back, trying to see his expression. "Are you smiling?"

His mouth chased, kissing me hungrily. "No."

The devil he wasn't. With effort, I wrangled my arms free and grasped his jaw. I pushed. He tightened the tangle of his legs around mine but allowed the distance between our faces.

And there, caught in the bite of his teeth, was a small, heart-melting smile that pulled so playfully at the corners. I was awestruck by the sight of it, dizzy with reverential disbelief.

"There's magic on your lips." I touched them hesitantly.

The twitching lips kissed my fingers, binding me with a supernatural spell.

"Magic is fake." I lowered my hand. "Love is real. What is this?"

"It's real." His expression sobered, and he caught my wrist, squeezing the delicate tendons. "Do you know how I know that?"

"It hurts."

"Yes. But I can give you more than pain." He let his weight rest fully on top of me, making my blood run as hot as a fever. "Strike your colors, pirate."

"Never."

He clicked his tongue. "You hoisted your white the day we met."

I'd raised that damned flag in a ruse to distract him from firing upon my ship. But I couldn't tell him that. "I won't strike for you again."

His eyes lit with challenge. That look alone sent my pulse into a frenzy.

"Ashley." I grabbed a fistful of black hair. "Don't even think about it."

Slipping from my grip, he shoved down my body.

Thirty-three

My lungs slammed together, and I twisted away. But Ashley quickly yanked me back by my ankle, giving me no time to counter. In a fraction of a breath, his hands spread open my thighs, and his mouth covered the juncture between.

Everything ceased to exist, the distant waves a mere echo of the world around me. All that I knew, all that I felt was the hot caress of lips and the tongue that stroked, dipping inside, licking circles, and teasing all the sensitive edges.

Sublime torture.

"Not fair." I moaned loudly, shakily, rocking against each annihilating kiss.

I wasn't impervious to radiant heat. Nor was I resistant to the destruction of storms. I was only human. A lusty one by most standards, but a mortal, nonetheless. I had no defenses against the whims of a god.

"I'm still..." *Aching.* Heaven and Hell, I ached for this man beyond reason.

"Still what?" His tongue slid upon me in divine torment.

"Still angry." I dragged in air, trembling. "I'm not striking. Not forgiving. Notahahahhhh!"

His mouth plundered, ravaged, and buried itself voraciously. When his fingers joined in and impaled me to the knuckles, I grabbed his hair and cried out. My back arched, and I flexed my hips wantonly, recklessly, beneath the scorching lashes that tore me asunder. I couldn't be still or quiet, too lost in the delirium of pleasure as he claimed another piece of me.

It was far too late to turn back. He'd already scaled my bow and flung me into a sea of pure ecstasy. Hot shimmering sparks burst through me, spasming my insides as I rode his sinful mouth through the torrential waves of orgasm.

Eventually, my shallow breaths lengthened and slowed, finding a safer tempo, and reality crept back in.

"How did you learn how to do that?" I sagged on the bed, dissolving into lethargy.

"Practice." He sat back on his heels and pulled off his shirt. "Before I joined the Royal Navy, I had more free time, in which I spent beneath the local girls' skirts."

"Those poor maidens." My gaze ate up his sculpted chest, my skin heating anew. "Their virtues didn't stand a chance with the likes of you."

"I heard no complaints," he murmured, his eyes glinting with triumph. "None from you, either."

"A lopsided victory." I straightened the coverlet, where it draped around my torso. "You disarmed me unjustly and usurped the advantage."

"On the contrary, Goldilocks. It is me who has been put at a disadvantage for a week and counting." His hand curved around my breast and smoothed down my stomach, drawing back the coverlet to bare me fully. "Your beauty affects a man like potent wine. When I look at you, I'm drugged."

He lowered his head and brushed his lips across my scar. My breath hitched, and my legs quivered around his waist.

"When I lick you..." His tongue trailed a wandering path to my chest. "Taste you..." He drew my nipple between his lips, sucking. "Kiss you..." His mouth returned to capture mine, delving deeply with sweet, languid strokes. "You make my head spin as though I'm drinking from the unholy grail."

"*Un*holy?"

"Filled to the brim with sin. I want to consume every drop."

He set out to do just that, eating at my mouth with an unhealthy obsession. I tasted myself on his tongue, the sharp tang of arousal mixed with the clean mintiness of his breath.

"Do you forgive me?" He suckled my lips.

Sea of Ruin

"No."

With an ominous gleam in his eyes, he ducked his head to lave gentle caresses beneath my ear and along my throat, descending slowly across my chest.

Hard, contoured muscle glided against me as he moved downward, his tongue making whorls on my aureole. I sighed, and he lingered, the heat of his body pressing along my legs, stretching and swelling behind the laces on his breeches.

My hands twined through the silky strands of his hair as his mouth made love to every inch of me. Roving down one leg and up the other, there wasn't a curve or dip neglected by his tongue.

"Life hasn't been kind to you." He was at my scar again, kissing the sad relic with reverence.

"Life isn't kind to anyone. Not even my father, who always seemed so untouchable and free."

"He was a lucky man to have the unconditional love of a daughter."

Something I'll never have.

Watching him stare at my scar, I knew he was thinking the same thing. Even if he decided to somehow look past my rank as a plebeian and criminal, I would never be able to give him heirs.

The odds were stacked so thoroughly against us there was nothing I could do to change our destinies. But I could enjoy the moment. Right here. Right now.

"Ashley." I waited for his gaze to lift. "You've seen all of me. Every scar. Every freckle. It's my turn to look." I gave him a nudge with my knee. "Take off your breeches."

"Tell me you forgive me."

"If you do this for me, I'll think about it."

The corner of his mouth curved into a delectable half-smile. He leaned up, smacked a hard kiss onto my lips, and rose from the bed.

My gaze followed his hands to the row of laces beneath the defined ridges of his abdomen. As he opened the front flap, I pushed up onto my hip, mesmerized.

The long, bulging outline of him twitched visibly beneath the fabric, thumping against his thigh as if attempting to get out. My mouth salivated for a taste, and I shivered. No sane woman would willingly stretch her lips around that beast.

But I wanted it. Desperately.

Finished with the laces, he met my eyes and shoved down the breeches. His bent posture momentarily blocked my view. When he straightened, he lowered his arms, stark naked, and regarded me with an arched brow.

His hair was indecently tousled by my fingers. His teeth caught the corner of his bottom lip, accentuating his innocent-looking face. But there was nothing chaste about the *superior breeding* that hung between his legs.

The most impressive cock known to man jutted outward, hard and swollen with veins. It was too heavy to rise upward, though it tried. Christ almighty, he was sinful. Gorgeous. Insanely, powerfully built from head to toe. He looked good enough to eat.

I shifted to the edge of the mattress and sat nude before him with my feet on the floor. Without preamble, I slid my fingers along his length, stroking lightly. His breathing grew, fast and shallow, speeding up my pulse.

Another stroke and his hands flew to my tangled mop of curls. He gave my head a slight pull, asking for my mouth, not demanding it. That was a nice change.

I lowered to the deck and knelt before him.

"Wait." He lifted me to wedge a pillow beneath my legs, his hands trembling violently as they returned to my hair.

"Has anyone ever done this for you?"

"It's been a very long time." He closed his eyes, his expression taut.

"How long?"

"Two years."

"Since you've had *any* sexual relations?"

"Yes." He bit out the syllable, jaw clenched.

I thrilled at the thought. It empowered me, made me ravenous, perhaps because I despised the idea of anyone else touching him.

Lowering my hand to his heavy testicles, I fondled the smooth skin and set the flat of my tongue against his broad crown. A deep masculine groan vibrated the air, low and continuous, as I painted a long, wet lick from the plump tip to the thick base.

Tremors shook his legs. Blue eyes burned down at me, and he shored up his grip on my hair. Dear lord, he was beautiful.

Scattering caution to the wind, I drew the head of him into my mouth. He pressed in, forcing my tongue and teeth to make room. When he hit the back of my throat, I swallowed, breathed through it, and began to suck.

"Bennnnnnett! Goddamn!" Grunts plummeted from his mouth. His chest heaved. His fingers clenched, and he couldn't control the thrust of his hips.

I rolled with it, slurping and swallowing as much length as I could. I fed on him so greedily I would question my sanity later.

As the first pearls of his seed slid over my tongue, I lapped him up and sucked harder, faster, drawing more salty essence from his leaking tip. My palms traveled up the backs of his thighs and clutched his firm arse. Then I pulled him deeper into my mouth, licking along his shaft.

He shook and panted and rocked his hips, his backside clenching drum-tight in my hands. "Slow down, damn you."

Not a chance. I held him to me, pouring every ounce of experience and instinct I had into bringing him to his knees.

"I won't last." Sweat broke out on his brow, and his mouth hung open to accommodate labored breaths. "The sheer agony, woman. I can't take it."

I grinned around his girth, flicking my tongue. Then I fisted his root with both hands and stroked, sucking him hard, harder, hungrier, making him sway. His sounds grew louder, wilder, alerting me that he was close. His toes curled against planks. His fingers dug into my scalp, and the thrust of his hips lost rhythm.

I pulled back, letting him pop from the seal of my lips.

He released a furious growl and tried to yank me back. I ducked low and scrambled out of his reach.

"Get your arse back here." He squeezed the base of his cock, glaring at me.

"I think…" I leaped to my feet and backed away. "I haven't forgiven you."

"Bennett." A low warning snarl. "We're not finished."

Heart racing, I took off and fled the sleeping chamber.

Footsteps charged after me. I would've been disappointed if they hadn't.

Veering past the desk and into the dining cabin, I made a full circuit around the table before the long reach of his arm hooked my waist. My feet left the floor, and he twisted me, wrangling my body until I was pressed against him, chest to chest.

"Caught you." He held me tight, his mouth a kiss away.

"Let you." I wrapped my arms and legs around the tall column of his physique and wriggled my hips, taunting him.

He gripped his cock, where it throbbed beneath my thigh, and set the tip at my slick opening. "You forgive me."

"Only if you use the other hole this time. And you better make it good, Ashley Cutler."

His mouth crashed onto mine, and he pushed himself inside.

I whimpered at the stretching intrusion, gasping uncontrollably by the time he wedged all that thickness to the hilt. Oh, the floating fullness, the bursting stars, the ultimate state of bliss… I might have heard angels singing.

He groaned. I shivered, and his arms tightened around me, eyes fixated on mine. Our lips pulled apart but stayed close, hovering in an almost-kiss.

He drew back his hips and slowly thrust again, digging all the way in. I felt him pulsing and heating against my walls, and it brought another glorious shiver, another wave of tingles swarming through my limbs.

Our foreheads drifted together, our bodies locked in the most intimate way. Beyond the quaking and heavy breathing, neither of us moved. Something held us in its mist. Something big and profound and terrifyingly monumental. I couldn't see it, but it was glaring, deafening, thudding in my ears.

Instinct was said to be blind. The same was true of love. Both were upon us, and though the end wasn't understood, I comprehended the connection and knew it was extraordinary.

"What are you doing to me?" he breathed against my mouth.

"Same thing you're doing to me."

"You feel this." He nudged his pelvis tight against mine. "I'm inside you, madam. Deeply. Completely." His voice rasped, hoarse with need. "Are you well?"

No, I wasn't well or good or fine at all, and that was perfect. *This* was perfect. He was doing it right, taking care, showing me respect, and looking at me in the eyes.

"Fuck me, my lord." I skimmed my fingers along his stony jaw. "I'm ready for your unseemly manners."

"Good because you feel entirely too pleasing for me to carry on like a gentleman. I do hope you're not tired."

"Would that stop you?"

"Not in the least." Feet planted and back straight, he began the rhythm of times long past, sliding his cock in and out, moving naturally, impulsively, driven by that which underlies the heart of every man. Sexual hunger.

Standing as he was, he didn't stagger or flag with fatigue, attesting to the graceful mastery of a seaman accustomed to using his strength and balance on the rolling decks of a warship.

And the man could move. Thrusting at a sensual pace, he rotated his hips and worked my body in measured strokes. Breathless gasps tumbled from my lips, and he fed on them, kissing me, watching me, and setting me afire.

Gradually, our passion built into a roaring flame. My hands clawed at his back, my nails sinking into muscled flesh as I clung to him, biting and groaning with my legs clamped fiercely around his waist.

He fucked into me harder, deeper, heightening my need for completion. I arched to meet him, holding his gaze as my insides convulsed with a violence that shook me to the core. He was right there with me, his kisses losing precision and careening into the wilds of madness.

When his legs began to shake, he spun, and my back hit the nearest bulkhead, jarring an *oomph* past my lips. His hand flattened on the wall, and he used the leverage of that hard surface to tunnel inside me with unrestrained savagery.

Senses heightened. Fingers clawed. Gazes held, and we exploded into urgency, possessed by passion, grinding and gripping, lips reaching and missing.

My vision clouded, and a primal noise wrenched from my throat.

"I'm going to come." I bore down on his cock, trying to slow the detonation.

"I'm with you. Jesus Christ, Bennett. I'm… Goddamn—" He jerked, lost his breath.

I peaked. He followed, and I kept coming and coming, hurling my screams loud and wide as I chanted his name and stared into his eyes.

Watching him fall apart was the most erotic thing I'd ever seen. Throaty male groans hissed past clenched teeth, his head thrown back and cords stretching along his throat.

I felt him releasing—the intense throbbing of his shaft against my muscles and the molten wash of fluid spurting deep within. He held my gaze and clutched me hard in the flex of his arms, rocking into my body as if trying to milk his pleasure to the last drop.

Then he expelled the low humming breath of an exhausted, thoroughly satisfied man.

"Incredible." He slid a hand into my hair and kissed me lazily, deeply, sweeping his tongue through my mouth. "Nothing compares, Bennett. Nothing."

Hard to argue. I felt so peacefully content. There was no room for regret. Not even thoughts of Priest could wreck the moment.

Ashley continued to hold me against the wall, his hands roaming around my face and along the curves of my body.

"I daresay…" He kicked his hips, still full and very hard inside me. "You'll be enduring my unseemly manners for another round. And a few more after that."

He wasn't jesting.

As he carried me toward the sleeping chamber, he stopped in the day cabin and fucked me on the desk. Afterward, when I crawled onto the bed, he grabbed my hips and took me from behind.

Following several more orgasms, my hearing went fuzzy, and my muscles lost coordination. Any limits my body might have imposed had been eradicated by the endless stamina of a commodore thirteen years my elder.

His strained male gasps of exertion couldn't be trusted. Just when I thought he'd worn himself out, he broke me all over again.

As the sun crested the rail of the balcony, yellow-pink fingers of light crept over our tangled, sweaty limbs. We lay naked on our sides, face to face, waning in the softness of a new day.

He twisted a coil of my hair around his finger, regarding me with the grin of a sated wolf.

It made my heart dance, and I couldn't stop myself from touching that curved mouth. "So this is what you look like when you smile."

"I haven't…experienced this in a long time."

"Smiling?"

"Feeling. You make me feel again."

"Why ever did you stop?"

"Titles. Ranks. Responsibility." His gaze roamed my face. "But you…with your unrehearsed words, bold touches, fierce eye contact, raw, untamed beauty… God help me, everything about you is such a welcome freedom from the tedious, rigid order of my life."

"Then change it."

"Change…?"

"Your life. Remove the things that confine you. You can do anything you want."

"Like your mother did?" he asked gently. "She was the daughter of an earl, and *one time*, she ignored the rules and followed her heart. How did that work out for her?"

My stomach hardened. In fourteen years, I'd never once seen her smile. She'd been utterly and completely miserable. Because of her mistake. Because of *me*.

I hooked my leg over his hip. "Have you ever been in love?"

"I'm betrothed."

"And?"

"It's a sensible contract. Business. Love is unneeded, and frankly, unwanted."

"You're a fool."

His eyebrows formed an angry *V*. "Careful…"

"Surely you see the gross stupidity in forsaking your happiness for that which is perceived as *sensible*. Nobility as a notion is objective and impersonal. What a horrible doctrine to live by. From where I stand, aristocrats rob the world of pleasure."

"Says the woman who chose a dangerous career that put her constantly on the run. Tell me, Bennett. In your life beyond the reaches of laws and social constraints, have you been happy?"

I'd been happy for a year. In the arms of a libertine.

"No." I sighed, feeling the press of exhaustion. "But at least I'm free to love who I want."

But I wasn't free.

I was a prisoner, facing an uncertain end.

As if he read my mind, he tucked my head beneath his chin and stroked my hair. "You need to sleep."

"I can't."

"All right." He released a slow breath. "Then I'll tell you a true story." He leaned back and ran a knuckle along my jaw. "I met your father once."

"What?" My eyes widened, my pulse hammering. "When?"

"I was around your age so… Thirteen years ago. I was a sergeant then, taking a short leave in Nassau with some mates." His thumb rested against my neck, softly caressing. "He was in a brothel."

My throat convulsed.

"It was attached to a tavern, and that's where I saw him—sitting alone, staring into a tankard of ale, while his crew of scoundrels spent their coin on painted women."

"Did you know who he was?"

"Indeed. Everyone knew. The island was more or less overrun by pirates at the time, and I was but one English soldier among dozens of rogues in that tavern."

"What did you do?"

"I sat beside him at the bar." His lips twitched. "And he bought me a drink."

My heart swelled, and a tingling burn rose to my eyes. "Did you talk to him?"

"No. We sat in silence, just two sailors enjoying their drinks." He brushed a curl from my face. "Women approached him, doxies and ladies alike, and he turned them all away. He wasn't there for that."

"He loved my mother."

"And his daughter." He kissed my forehead, my nose, my lips. "Time to close your eyes."

As I drifted to sleep, his sensual smile was the last thing I saw.

When I woke later that afternoon, it was the first thing that filled my vision. He lay beside me in the position, as if he'd never moved.

"What are you doing?" I yawned, stretching my lovingly abused body.

"My second favorite activity."

"Watching me sleep?"

"Yes." The delicious curve of his lips deepened as he rolled on top of me, both of us nude, and wedged my legs open with his hips.

"What's your first favorite activity?"

He reached between us and parted the dampening folds between my thighs with the head of his erection. Then he slowly sank inside, showing me what he favored above all else.

We didn't leave his private quarters for the next two days. We ate, bathed, slept. And fucked. Made love. Hard and soft, sluggish and rabid, lazy and impassioned. In every position, bottom and top, fore and aft. In the bed, on the chairs, over the rail, against the walls, on the floor—if the surface was strong enough to support us, we broke it in.

We were so caught up in each other, we lost time, lost our bearings, lost our sense of the end. In the back of my mind, I knew it was coming. New Providence couldn't have been more than a day's journey away.

I'd been on this ship for twelve days. Long enough for Priest to seize a fast sloop, take over its command, and catch up to HMS *Blitz*.

I knew in my bones that he was close. I also knew it was time to press Ashley about what needed to happen next. Whatever that was. I didn't have a plan, and that terrified me.

We'd begrudgingly dressed that morning, knowing a third day secluded away in his private quarters would raise suspicion.

Sitting on his lap, I finished a quiet breakfast with him, my belly filled with clam fritters and sour milk biscuits with blackberry

Sea of Ruin

preserves. I set down my napkin and pulled in a bracing breath.

"Ashley…" I shifted on his hard thighs and met his stunning eyes. "We need to…"

His lips twitched, his gaze dipping. "You have…some…" He slid a finger along the corner of my mouth. "Preserves." The finger went into his mouth, and he licked it clean, casting me an innocent grin. "What?"

I was going to say something, something important, but my brain broke.

"Sugary sweet." He was still staring at my lips. "Addictive."

Then he put his grin there and kissed me senseless. I twined my fingers in his hair and yielded beneath his irresistible mouth. How could I do otherwise? I'd been collecting his smiles for two days. Smiles he gave to me and no one else. Each one made me feel like anything was possible.

Until an urgent knock pounded on the door.

"Lord Cutler?" Sergeant Smithley called from the other side. "Lieutenant Wallers is here with urgent news."

My pulse exploded. Was it news of an approaching sloop? Had Priest been spotted?

Ashley stood abruptly, holding onto my waist until I found my feet. He gave my gown a quick inspection, ran a hand through his hair, and turned toward the door.

Shoulders squared, hands folded at his back, feet braced apart, expression blank—the transformation of his demeanor completely rebuilt him from top to bottom in less than a second. I'd forgotten what this fine-mannered commodore looked like. And *felt* like. His severe presence choked the air.

"Enter, Lieutenant." His aristocratic voice made me shudder.

An older man in a white periwig stepped in and clapped a hand to his wrinkled brow. "Good morning, my lord."

"Good morning, Lieutenant. What news do you bring?"

"A ship approaches off the larboard bow."

I drew in a quick, silent breath and gripped the top rail of the chair beside me.

"One of ours." Wallers lowered his hand. "A command flag flies at the fore-topgallant masthead."

"Which command flag?"

"Admiral of the White Squadron, my lord."

"Sir John Dycker." Ashley's fingers twitched at his side.

"Who?" I asked quietly.

He pretended not to hear me as he collected his blue frock and shrugged it on. "Prepare to receive him and his lieutenants."

"Yes, my lord."

Wallers stepped out, closing the door behind him.

"Who is John Dycker?" I gripped Ashley's arm, startled by the tension in his muscles.

"Admiral of HMS *Ludwig*. My superior." He pulled away and grabbed his hat, his tone calm, void of emotion. "Play-time is over."

He headed toward the exit.

"Ashley." My heart ached as I waited for him to turn. When our eyes connected, I stood taller, my voice fierce. "Change your course and set me free. This is *our* happiness. Yours and mine. Take it."

"I cannot." He opened the door and swept out in a blear of royal blue. "Sergeant, escort Miss Sharp topside if you please."

He vanished around the corner, without a backward glance at my fractured expression.

Thirty-four

There were three things certain in life—disappointment, death, and the pompous presentation of English admiralty.

Sir John Dycker strutted his important self across the upper deck of HMS *Blitz*, paying no attention to the rolling drums, strident pipes, and booming cannons that lit up the overcast sky in his honor.

His superior rank allowed him to walk among these men as if he were the king himself. Adorned in rich silks, brocades, and embroideries of gold and blue, he reeked of wealth and status.

Lines of soldiers stood in perfect formation around me, regarding the admiral with unconcealed awe and great fear.

As the sailors had escorted me topside, I'd heard their whisperings about the sort of discipline Sir Dycker meted out. One sergeant claimed that the admiral carried a rattan cane so that he could whack slow-moving crewmen across the head. Another said Dycker was known to make his lowest-ranked man run the gauntlet, forcing him to walk naked between parallel lines of soldiers while everyone flogged his back with knotted cat-o'-nine tails.

Ashley would have a better idea than most as to how his admiral governed men, but his expression gave nothing away. He stood off to my right at the end of the line with a row of lieutenants separating us. I'd been shuffled toward the back as if my presence put a moral stain on the proceedings.

I watched Ashley in my periphery, only glancing in his direction when I was certain no one noticed. But he never met my eyes or acknowledged my existence in any way. I reminded myself he was the commodore of this ship, and this was his mask. The veneer he wore among his men.

Deep down, however, I didn't believe that was all this was. Something had changed between us the instant that knock had sounded on his door.

That *something* had to do with HMS *Ludwig*.

The admiral's flagship made an impressive sight where she was braced onto the opposite tack. Beneath a cloud-stuffed sky, her stately masts towered protectively over the sea, her gunports open to breathe in the lazy breeze.

The admiral himself didn't tower over anything. He was a head shorter than the shortest man on board. Yet he wore the tallest, highest high-parted periwig I'd ever seen. Perhaps an attempt to make up for his lack of height.

The stiff-lipped little man was around forty years old and did, in fact, carry a cane, which he swung from a loop on his stubby middle finger.

Maybe he was a loving husband, generous commander, and all-around decent fellow, but I disliked him instantly. I didn't know why. Just a feeling in my gut.

Ashley greeted him with all the required formality, and they launched into a discussion about Dycker's purpose here. I caught bits and pieces of the conversation over the roar of waves. Evidently, Dycker had been sent from England to Nassau at the earnest request of the colony's governor to hold a conference on some private matter. That was now concluded, and HMS *Ludwig* was on course to return home.

When it was Ashley's turn to explain his whereabouts, he spoke of the forty pirates he'd captured and currently held below. Then he mentioned the Feral Priest he was soon to collect in New Providence before sailing back to England.

The admiral's gaze wandered toward the sea as if he'd lost interest in Ashley's plans. As his attention circled back, he went still. His head turned, and his eyes landed directly on me.

Pulling himself away from Ashley without a word, he strode down the line of soldiers and paused before the men who stood in front of me. "What is this?"

The throng of seamen parted, putting me into full view of admiral's inspection.

"A prisoner, my lord." Ashley didn't move from his position or look my way.

"This charmingly small little confection is a prisoner?" The glittering beads of Dycker's brown eyes danced over me, making my skin prickle with unease. Then he drifted closer, reaching out to touch my hair.

"Mind your fingers, my lord," Ashley said. "She bites."

I gritted my teeth. So his lordship *was* watching. I couldn't tell, given the way he stared straight ahead as if he couldn't stand the sight of me.

"She's Edric Sharp's daughter." Ashley's accent thickened with something akin to pride. "Bennett Sharp."

"Well done, Lord Cutler. A fine prize, indeed." Dycker gave me another skin-crawling appraisal. "But why, pray tell, is she not confined in the hold with the others?"

"I wish to deliver her to England alive and in one piece. My hold is crammed with savages. She lasted less than a minute in there before they were upon her."

"I see. So she's sleeping where?"

"In my quarters, my lord." Ashley's tone hardened, leaden with challenge.

"Good heavens, that is highly irregular."

"So is the capture of a female pirate."

"It's unbeseeming. Intolerable." Dycker tapped his cane hard against the planks. "The Royal Navy is not running a brothel aboard its ships. If the First Lord of the Admiralty heard of this—"

"He would understand my quandary and appreciate my willingness to be flexible."

The air stretched with nervous strain. Anxiety rippled from the rank and file of soldiers and quickened my own breaths.

"Just so." Dycker sniffed. "There is no further need for you to thwart the boundaries of propriety and risk your reputation. The hold in my flagship is empty. I shall transport this prisoner to England in your stead."

My objection exploded in a plaintive, horrified gasp that quickly turned into an enraged growl. A smirk stole across Dycker's face.

Ashley's hand balled and released at his side. "I appreciate the offer, but she is *my* prisoner. As thus, I intend to deliver her myself and collect the due recognition."

My heart shriveled. He wanted his promotion. Of course, he did. And perhaps a part of him wanted to keep me close for the duration of the journey so that he could continue to use my body until he handed me over to the headsman. There might have been an even smaller part of him that wished to keep me forever. But in the end, when forced to decide between his career and my life, I knew he wouldn't choose me.

My thoughts twisted to a dark place, one that painted the aristocratic world in shades of liquid red.

Dycker strolled back to Ashley. "We're only a day from New Providence. I don't have the space to confine forty prisoners, but I can hold the woman while you capture your feral pirate. I shall take her off your hands and moor along the eastern coast of Eleuthera, just a few hours from here." He thrust his chin in a southwesterly direction. "I'll wait for you there, and upon your return, I shall sail in consort with your ship back to England. There, you can collect your prisoner from my hold and deliver her to the authorities yourself."

I stopped breathing, my pulse shivering and gaze locked on the man who held my heart and my life in his hands.

His expression showed no creases, no tension, not a twitch of an eyelash as he spoke in a steady, unconcerned voice. "Very good, my lord. I'm most grateful for your assistance."

"Excellent." Dycker snapped his fingers at the lieutenants behind him. "Transport her to the flagship. Make haste." He turned back to Ashley. "How about a drink in your quarters? I shall like to hear the story of how you captured Edric Sharp's daughter."

"It would be an honor." Ashley turned and led the admiral to the companionway.

Everything inside me cried out, begging him to meet my eyes and reassure me that he had a plan, one that wouldn't end us. Not like this.

But he didn't. He didn't look, didn't try to send me a hint or give me a sign. Nothing.

It hurt. God's wounds, it hurt far more than I thought it could. This didn't even feel like a good-bye. I just felt...forgotten.

Fingers curled around my arms and wrenched me toward the stern, where the ladder to the jolly boat waited. Fighting my escorts and the hundreds of other armed men around me would only speed up my execution. I had no choice but to comply.

As I was ushered off HMS *Blitz*, I twisted my neck, trying to find Ashley among the scattering of soldiers. When I spotted him, it was only his back, where he vanished below deck. He hadn't glanced back to check on me, hadn't waited to see me off his ship and out of his life.

As I slid over the gunwale and descended the ladder, I couldn't feel

Sea of Ruin

the rungs beneath my hands. As I was rowed to the flagship, I couldn't hear the waves over the drubbing of my heart. As I climbed aboard my new prison, I couldn't see the horizon through the blurry smear of wetness in my eyes.

Priest wouldn't know to look for me here. This wasn't the ship he was hunting.

Every plan I'd made to escape lay in ruin.

Because I'd fallen in love with yet another man who would never choose me first.

The desolation was all-consuming, unfathomable, dragging me into the unsearchable depths of the darkest abyss. And that was nothing compared to what was coming.

Little did I know, I'd just been delivered into an infernal hell that would surpass the very limits a human soul could withstand.

Thirty-five

I was immediately put under the decks by two of the admiral's lieutenants, who looked like brothers with their matching stern expressions and white periwigs. They handled me with less care than one would give a goat as they kicked, shoved, and dragged me to the bilge.

I'd expected the rough treatment but not what followed.

A wad of cloth was forced into my mouth. A ring of iron went around my neck, attached to a chain. Shackles were clapped onto my wrists and ankles. My boots came off. Then I was stripped to my skin.

They didn't bother with the laces on my bodice and stays. Steel blades ripped through the fabric, removing the gown in strips. Thankfully, they left the jade stone on the choker at my throat. Perhaps because they didn't see it beneath the iron collar.

My stomach plunged to my feet as I stood before them, naked, gagged, and shaking in the suffocating heat of the climate, trapped in the airless belly of the flagship.

The leg and arm irons connected together by a short chain, preventing me from lifting my hands or removing the gag. Why did they think I needed to be restrained so drastically? And without my clothing?

Perhaps I could've outrun them through the hold, scaled the ladder, climbed through the hatchway, and locked them down here. Then what? I couldn't sneak through multiple decks undetected. Even if I did make it topside, where would I go? Jumping into the sea was only an option for those who preferred death over life.

Was that a possibility? Would I reach a point where I'd rather die than endure whatever awaited me here?

My trepidation heightened as they escorted me toward a door in the hold behind the mainmast. It opened without a lock, and they pushed me into the pitch-dark space.

I received such a greeting in my nostrils as I had never experienced in my life. The loathsome stench surged bile to my throat, and the gag prevented panting through my mouth.

A ruthless boot knocked me down upon the deck, and the very planks themselves reeked of grisly things—excrement, despair, death. I became so unbearably sickened by the smell that I couldn't focus beyond the violent urge to vomit.

Until they brought a lantern into the compartment.

The glow didn't stretch all the way into the corner. But the edge of light that did reach… Oh, merciful God, I wished it hadn't.

Skeletal legs extended from the darkness—bloodied, unmoving, human, *female*. My stomach twisted painfully as the officer with the lantern turned in that direction and held up the light, illuminating the cargo.

Three nude African women lay on their backs, glassy eyes staring at the deck above. Their emaciated bodies were restrained in the same manner I was, only they didn't move. Didn't breathe.

The abdomen of one protruded with a small, round bump. The undeniable swell of a babe that would never be born.

A low, unpreventable wail erupted against the rag in my mouth. Tears seared my eyes. Tremors overtook my limbs, and ice-cold fear sat like iron in my stomach.

I knew I was to be transported to England to hang, and if my demise had been no worse than death, I could've faced it with some semblance of courage and clarity. But my situation wasn't that merciful.

As I took in the scars and open wounds that covered the women, the layers of gruesome bruises on their upper thighs, I was forced to acknowledge precisely what would assail me before I crawled out of this hole. *If* I crawled out.

The soldiers stepped toward the bodies and kicked at the torpid legs. The youngest-looking woman lay in a state of rigor, suggesting she'd died recently. The one beside her had shriveled to a stage of death that was beyond human recognition. The third one…

Sea of Ruin

"Still alive." The man kicked again, prompting a jerking twitch from the pregnant body that now showed signs of breathing.

Matted black hair hung over her face in clumps, but her eyes were in there, bright and desperate and staring directly at me as she tried to lift an arm to defend herself. I scrambled toward her—awkwardly and ineffectively with my ankles and wrists shackled as they were—and threw myself onto the soldier's ramming boot. A foolish decision, for the next kick sent me careening into the wall.

I hit so hard that black spots stole my vision. Pain stitched through my skull, and a loud ringing swallowed my hearing. I climbed through the fog, clinging to consciousness. After several attempts to sit up, the agony dissipated, and my eyesight returned. But I was too late.

Across the hold, one of the officers held the pregnant woman's head in a bucket of water. I screamed against my gag, scrabbling toward her as her arms flailed weakly, uselessly. Then she fell limp.

Dead.

Gone.

She'd suffered only feet away, and I'd been helpless to stop it.

The horror that swamped my senses was unlike any that had come before it. My lungs burned with the frantic gasps of my shallow breathing. My jaw clenched so tightly I couldn't unlock it, and the pain in my chest and throat tried to black out my awareness.

I knew this level of evil existed. I'd glimpsed it beneath the rutting body of the Marquess of Grisdale. I'd felt it in Jobah's stories of his months aboard a slave ship. Hell, I'd battled it on the high seas in all forms of demons and monsters.

But to drown a dying, defenseless woman without reason or care? My mind couldn't process it. My soul couldn't bear it.

I lay in a state of traumatic shock, staring at their lifeless bodies.

And I was next.

Before I reached England's shore, I would be defiled in so savage a manner I would likely die in consequence of it. Just like those women before me.

Being unaccustomed to wearing irons, I naturally feared that particular infliction as the officers turned their attentions on me. Could I have twisted my arms free, I would've gone for the knives on their hips. But I could not, and besides, I still had the ring around my neck to contend with, which they now secured to a hook on the wall and locked with a screw key.

Then, to my surprise and relief, they left.

The door closed, and the stark absence of light swarmed in around me. Within that terrible gloom lay the miasma of sluggish heat, the creaking of an unfamiliar ship, and the bodies of my cellmates.

The odor of decay had lived long in this grave, inhabiting its walls, arising from the deck, and floating in the atmosphere. It was old death, the aroma of it suffocating the confined swelter, making the air unfit for respiration.

Trapped in this forsaken place, sharing this nightmare with three women I would never know… It was inenarrable. Inexpressible. Every inch of me trembled, rattling the chains as my heart screamed in grief.

The women were in a better place now. Wherever that was, it had to be easier than what they'd endured in this pit. Still, I wished they had lived. I would give anything to have them here so I could tell them we would get through this, overpower our captors, and escape this ship of horrors.

I would've believed those words for them. I would've vowed to save their lives with every breath in my body.

But it was just me, all alone. I didn't know how to make brave promises for myself.

Although the officers had left me inviolate, I still feared I would be taken by force and raped to the point of death. They had looked and acted as though they were capable of such brutal cruelty. Not just with Africans, whom the English had no compunction over enslaving and abusing. But also with me. I supposed they valued the life of a pirate the same as a slave and would treat me with equivalent savagery.

In the dark, I contorted my body as such to put my face near my hands and feet so that I could use my fingers to work the gag from my mouth. Then I gave into an overwhelming need to wiggle toward my recently departed companion. When I found her in the desolate blackness, I lay my cheek on her still warm hand in the shackles.

And I cried.

These women had been stolen from a place of innocence and freedom and, in a barbarous and heartless manner, conveyed to a state of horror and slavery. They were lost to their dear parents and relations, and they to them. No one knew they were dead except me and the evil that had caused their suffering.

All I could offer them were my tears, and these could not avail, for there was no hope for them anymore.

I felt little hope for myself.

My abandoned thoughts grew murkier as time fell stagnant in the

Sea of Ruin

stifling abyss. Had it been hours? Days, perhaps. I'd felt the flagship heave from its mooring long ago and knew we'd already sailed to the coast of Eleuthera.

As an added torture, I thought about how close I was to *Jade*. I'd sent Reynolds to Harbour Island, which sat on the northern tip of Eleuthera. If the flagship anchored close to the shore, I could make the swim and walk to there. How long would Reynolds wait for me?

How long had we been waiting here for Ashley's return?

He was hunting the pirate who hunted him. How would that end? While Ashley stormed the brothel in New Providence looking for Priest, would Priest sneak aboard HMS *Blitz* in the harbor? Would he kill Ashley when he learned I'd been imprisoned elsewhere? Or would he die during the confrontation, surrounded by hundreds of Ashley's soldiers?

That terrified me more than anything.

It had been *my* choices in life that brought this situation upon me. Not Priest's. If he died trying to rescue me, the guilt would destroy me. The possibility of any harm coming to him or Ashley hurtled my pulse into hopeless panic.

From the time Ashley had handed me over and thence—in the brutish but fashionable way of the Royal Navy—consigned me to this hole of death, the grief I'd felt then still panted in my heart. Though my tears over his rejection had long since subsided.

I couldn't blame him for doing his job to the utmost. I couldn't accuse him of betrayal, either, for he'd never promised me freedom or happiness or even life. How many times had he told me I would stand trial? He'd specifically warned me he would hurt me again.

There had been no trickery or lies on his part. He'd voiced exactly how this would end and followed through on his word.

I hated him for it. Despised him to the depths of my heart. I had no choice. I needed an outlet for my helpless rage, and he was it. The longer I sat in solitary darkness, the more my thoughts suffered for it until one succeeding woe swelled up another and another and another and…

To my horror, the two lieutenants returned.

They forced the rag back into my mouth. A cravat was wrapped around my eyes and head, hindering my eyesight. Then I was conveyed from the foul-smelling hole and into fresher air. They didn't take me far. Only a few feet beyond the door of my confinement.

Without my sight, I tripped over planks and cables, stumbling in the shackles. My pulse thundered frantically. My breath beat wetly against the gag as fear ruled every step.

I tried to fight, but one of them held me fast by the hands and laid me face down upon a barrel. He secured the restraints on my wrists and ankles to something on the floor, while the other man dumped water onto my back and callously scrubbed me from head to toe.

The scent of vinegar burned my nose. My skin caught fire beneath the harsh solution, my eyes watering as the fumes stole beneath the blindfold.

There was only one reason they would take the time to wash my body.

Blind and shaking, I tracked their footsteps up the ladder behind me. The door to the hatchway creaked open, sounding their departure. Then another pair of footfalls entered the hold.

These were different. New. The tread sounded softer, the steps lighter. My pulse raged, thrashing hollowly in my ears, as the stranger grew closer, breathing heavily. Sucking the air with excitement.

My fear was so sharp and cold I didn't think my bladder would hold. I didn't care. Panic was a separate entity inside me, skittish and slippery, jumping at every sound.

Where was he? Behind me? In front of me? Was he holding a dagger? I blinked rapidly, straining to see through the blindfold.

"Let me see, you coward!" My scream garbled, my voice indiscernible behind the gag.

The vulnerability of my bent position, with my bare bottom in the air and my body stretched over the barrel, sent me into a fit of convulsive thrashing. But the shackles did what they were meant to do. I went nowhere, and the violent jerking and bucking soon exhausted my already weak muscles.

Male hands gripped tightly to my hips.

For a moment, I imagined they belonged to Ashley or Priest. One of them had come for me, and the worst of this nightmare was over.

But the fingers were too thin, the skin too soft and cold. I didn't know these hands or this man. As if to confirm my thoughts, he forced my thighs apart and groaned in an unfamiliar voice.

A sob broke behind my gag, and my legs quivered brutally beneath his heavy weight.

There would be no courage here. No strength or inspiration. I couldn't fight in shackles. Couldn't voice my adamant objections. I couldn't even see the face of my tormentor. But I could smell the stink of onion on his breath.

And I felt him.

Deeply, traumatically, he used his body as a weapon, one violating stab after another.

Parts of me broke away. I tried to cast aside the physical pain, but the agony punctured through, reaching me where I hid inside my mind.

I felt myself crying as he took what wasn't given. Bent over that barrel, my insides splintered as he forced his corruption everywhere he wasn't permitted.

He stole from me. Plundered. Thieved in the most barbaric way a man could hurt a woman.

Burning and ripping, the cruelty pierced deep, beyond the limits of my physical self, all the way to my soul. There was no moment in time, no piece of me, that didn't know pain.

Unable to use my eyes, my limbs, or my voice, I held the worst of it inside. The edges of my mind withered. My belly filled with liquid fire. My muscles moved with the speed of molten lead as my bones and joints crumbled like crushed stone.

Three dead women lay in the hole only a few feet away with ungodly bruises covering their thighs. I now knew exactly how they'd acquired those injuries. With every agonizing second, I felt the skin, tendons, and vessels in my own legs smash and break against the barrel.

He'd hurt those women here. Just like this. He'd hurt them until they'd died.

Every moment beneath him devastated more flesh, thrusting me deeper, further into a place where the spirit stopped living. The pain was of the lowest, most wretched kind, the anguish so constant and complete it became the only thing that existed.

I took a breath. Breathed again. It was all I could do, and so it was all I focused on. I breathed through intervals of him finishing and starting again. Each inhale was a grapple for sanity, each exhale a stumble to retain it.

My tears gradually dried, my body too exhausted to produce them. But I didn't stop breathing.

I was a pirate captain. The ferocious daughter of Edric Sharp. If my tormentor meant to break me, he would need a sharper, stronger, more significant weapon than his body.

That was what I told myself.

Amid the pain, time moved at an agonizing pace. Sometimes it didn't move at all. But eventually, he gave a final heave and walked away, his footsteps retreating up the ladder and beyond the hatchway.

If there was any relief to be had, I didn't feel it. He'd left me on the barrel, drenched in his sweat and other fluids. I couldn't move, couldn't see, the rag in my mouth softened by spit and tears.

I lay there for an infinite eternity, forced to think about every inch of flesh he'd touched, every muscle he'd bruised, every opening he'd stretched and bled. Time became a torture on its own, until I lost track of it, sinking in and out of consciousness.

At some point, the two lieutenants returned.

They removed the gag and blindfold and pushed me to my knees on the planks. Eatables were offered. Salt fish and water.

Nausea rose at the sight of it, my stomach refusing to accept sustenance. But I didn't know if or when the offer would come again. So I choked down the food and drank the fluid without tasting it.

Then they returned me to the black hole, locked my chain to the wall, and left me with the rotting, nidorous corpses of my predecessors.

I curled up on my side as much as the shackles allowed, shaking in the rancid heat. And I slept.

Until they came again.

Thirty-six

Again and again, the officers pulled me from the hole and restrained me on the barrel. Over and over, the man who reeked of onions returned and defiled my body. Sometimes his visits were quick. A few thrusts and done. Other times, I thought the never-ending torture would rip me in half.

Whenever the officers came, I fought and screamed and begged for news about Ashley. Had he returned? Was he well? Did he find his feral pirate? How long had it been? I pleaded for answers until they stuffed the gag into my mouth.

They never spoke. Not a word between them and certainly not one offered to me. But I didn't need conversation to understand the intentions of men.

Women existed to them as nothing more than vessels for pleasure. Worthless slaves for whomever they answered to. It didn't matter how much pain they caused me. My health was of no concern as long as I was breathing when we reached England. If I died incidentally... Well, they would still have a body to deliver. Ashley would still receive his promotion.

They would never be punished for the horrendous murders of my fellow captives. The laws of Englishmen didn't protect African slaves or rebellious pirates. There would be no justice.

Every time they returned, they restrained me, gagged and blindfolded, to the barrel and scrubbed my body with vinegar water to kill the stench of death. Then the other man would come, and it would be only him and his terrible cruelty. Afterward, I was chained in the black hole with the decaying bodies.

As the days passed, the air became absolutely pestilential. How many days? How often did they come? The displacement of time had a way of fracturing the mind. Some days, I struggled to hold onto a thread of rational thought.

They fed me bites of fish after every violation. My hunger pangs remained the least of my torments, and my throat never felt parched beyond what I could handle. They came often enough to keep me hydrated.

Daily visits, I decided. The constant pain between my legs suggested that some of those visits occurred multiple times a day.

I'd been in here long enough that my stitches needed to be removed. When the tight, itchy skin became unbearable, I spent hours twisting unnaturally in my shackles and using the broken edge of a fingernail to pick the threads from the underside of my foot.

Giving up would've been so much easier. But I didn't know how to do that.

By dint of stubborn will, I thrashed and snarled every time they came. Twice, they struck me so hard I lost awareness and woke in a fog upon the barrel. Each time they sent me back to the hole, I was weaker, more depleted, the desire to live gradually draining from my bones.

When they weren't abusing me, they kept me shackled in the blackness. It wasn't long before I looked forward to their visits if only to escape the suffocation of rot and loneliness.

The stench was so intolerably loathsome it was dangerous to breathe. I craved fresh air and would take the pain that accompanied it over spending another second inside these walls.

Isolation was my enemy. It had a gravity to it that dragged me down, a choking sadness that warped the mind. Made worse by the galling of the irons on my wrists and ankles and the filth of the planks beneath my nude body. My head grew fuzzy with poisonous thoughts, and my brain began to fail me. I wouldn't be able to hold onto my sanity forever.

With every bleak hour that passed, I expected to share the fate of my cellmates. Sometimes, I pleaded for the last friend, Death, to relieve me.

But there were still small pockets of time when I hoped for a miracle.

Sea of Ruin

I created fantasies in my head, my favorite being a gallant rescue where Priest and Ashley took down this ship and killed everyone on board. In reality, Priest would do it without hesitation or question. If he were still out there, fighting to rescue me. I didn't know.

Ashley, on the other hand, would always choose his career first. But could he ignore the evil that took place here? Would he let the admiral's officers live if he knew what they'd done in the hold of their ship?

I didn't know that answer, either. It didn't matter. Neither Ashley nor Priest had come for me. I didn't resent them for it. I'd never been a woman who depended on a man to save her. This wasn't their fight. It was mine.

At age fourteen, I could've chosen any path. I picked this one, a life of crime and dangerous risks. I lived for pirating, and in the end, I would die for it. I'd always known that. I just hadn't expected it to end in rape and torture aboard the ship that would carry me to the gallows.

As certain doom descended heavier and harder upon me, I turned my mind to the past, seeking a happier, freer place. I thought of my father often. My mother, too. And I indulged in reminiscences of *Jade*, Reynolds, Jobah, and the glorious years we sailed together. I missed them terribly. I missed my life. But more than that, I missed Priest and Ashley.

Even as I knew contempt for Priest's betrayal and Ashley's rejection, I had a lot of time to sit with my remorse and re-examine it from a new perspective. Ironic how things looked clearer in the dark. Sharper. More poignant.

Despite their faults, I knew they loved me, each in his own way. That meant something.

It meant *everything*.

Because I loved them, too.

I loved a libertine *and* a pirate hunter. Of course, I did. Insanely, shamelessly, irrefutably.

Could love exist without forgiveness? I didn't think so. It was time that I removed my invisible chains.

In the tenebrous, rotting heat of my prison, I let go of the scorn, freed the bitterness, and relinquished the anger. I forgave the two men I loved, completely and unconditionally. Not for their sakes. I did it for me. A final gift to myself.

I felt stronger for it, lighter, braver. It gave me an overwhelming sense of solace, even in this deathly place.

When my captors returned again, I didn't fight them. Instead, I focused the last of my energy on holding my head high.

If they were to remove the gag and blindfold, they would find neither shame nor fear on my face. They would see relief, for I'd been reduced so low in the hole that I basked in every gulp of uncontaminated air I breathed.

But it was more than that. They'd taken so much from me, tried so hard to break my spirit. But I was still me. Only bolder. Sturdier. Shatterproof. I was a woman who loved and forgave and found peace in her darkest hour.

I was the pirate captain Bennett Sharp.

When the faceless man fell upon me, like all the times before, I appointed him no identity. No name. No rank. He was an inanimate object. Meaningless. Powerless.

As he rutted and grunted his onion stench atop my body, I didn't cry. Didn't make a sound. He seemed frustrated by this, his hands ripping at my hair. His knuckles pounding against my back. His hips ramming harder. More brutally. More bruises. I bit down on the rag and bore it. I held onto my peace.

Until the door of the hatchway creaked open.

Boots pummeled down the ladder. One pair...two pairs... Three...?

My breath froze, and my tormentor fell still, impaled inside me.

Not once had anyone ever entered the hold while I was being abused. This man worked alone. No witnesses. But whoever was down here charged straight toward him and forcibly wrenched him off and out of my body.

Then the world erupted in chaos.

It couldn't be well described, for I lacked sight, voice, and movement. But I heard horrifying things—boots frantically scuffing, fists smacking flesh, bones crunching, and the gurgling cries of dying men.

Was it the admiral? One of his soldiers? Were my abusers not supposed to be down here hurting me?

Or had Priest found me and sneaked aboard the ship?

My heart thundered as a battle waged behind me. The metallic stench of blood flooded my nostrils. A man began to scream, but the roar cut off. A heavy thump slammed against the planks, followed by the continuous sound of something being pounded with a heavy object.

Sea of Ruin

Oh, dear sweet God, please don't let that be Priest beneath those blows.

Over and over, the dull striking noise repeated, echoing through the hold. The longer it lasted, the wetter it sounded. Like the smack and crush of blood and organs and other vital things.

There were no grunts. No whispers of life beyond my muffled wheezing. Just the ominous *thump, thump, thump.*

Dread twisted knots in my stomach. If Priest were only feet away, he would've come for me, reassured me. He would've called out and said something to calm my hysterics.

I jerked harder against the barrel, rattling my shackles and screaming against the gag.

The thumping sound stopped.

My breath seized.

Boots creaked as someone shifted. Then footsteps advanced.

A warning chill shot up my spine as I listened to those steps. They grew closer. I listened harder, *really* listened, recognizing the confident heel to toe rhythm.

My entire body came alive, tingling, gasping, *shaking.* Christ almighty, I shook so hard the tremors struck agony through every muscle and joint.

He was the highlight of my life, someone I looked forward to seeing desperately, frantically. As I lay strapped to the barrel, concentrating on the cadence of his approach, every second felt timeless. Endless. *Hurry.*

Hands swept through my hair, long fingers stiff and *trembling.* He was shaking as viciously as I was, worse even, as he unraveled the blindfold and removed the gag.

I blinked rapidly against the sudden light, impatient to see him. Then I did.

Cold blue eyes.

Full lips pulled back into a snarl.

A savage expression bathed in so many layers of fresh blood it was unrecognizable.

"Ashley."

Thirty-seven

"How many times?" Ashley's voice scrubbed against my raw senses, grinding like jagged rocks.

He didn't sound like himself. Didn't look anything like the man I knew.

Gone was the demeanor of an aristocrat. Not just because of the thick blood dripping from his face. Or the sanguine clots of gore that clung to his silk cravat, fine frock, and gold embellishments. It was his bearing, the wild aura that surrounded him. He wore the reckless, uncivilized countenance of a pirate, every muscle in his body emanating a dangerous combination of madness and savagery.

His hands shook so uncontrollably he struggled to unlock my shackles with the screw key. A key he must have taken off the bodies of my abusers.

With a grimace, I twisted my neck to see the source of all the blood. But he grabbed my hair, stopping me.

"How many times, Bennett?" His terrifying expression, buried under all that filth, looked like it might fall apart any second. "How many times did that monster hurt you?"

"I don't know." I trembled beneath the glare of those murderous eyes. "I lost count. I don't even know who he is. Because the blindfold…"

Something fractured in the abyss of his gaze. A breath barreled out of him. And another. Thoughts churned in his eyes, and I knew he was imagining what I'd endured.

Oh, Ashley. No. He looked so horrified. So bleak and devastated.

"You didn't know." I released a sigh of dawning realization. "You didn't know what would become of me here."

"I should have. I should have never left." He freed the shackles on my arms and legs, removed the iron neck ring, and pulled me onto his lap. "By God, I never wanted to leave you."

His embrace and the vehemence of his words centered me in a way nothing else could. I hadn't realized how badly I needed his protective strength until I felt it embrace me again.

My hand went to the jade stone at my throat, touching it for the first time since I'd been transported here.

"I thought this would be the safest place to keep you while I…" He hugged me tighter against his blood-soaked frock and choked on a pained sound. His huge hand cradled my wrist as if it might break, his gaze fixated on the chafed, angry red skin. "I failed. Goddammit, I failed you so fantastically."

"Ashley." My mind hung onto his unfinished sentence. "You wanted me safe while you did what? Did you find Priest Farrell?"

Please, say no. Please, say no.

"I found the brothel." He gently set me on the deck and leaned back to remove his soiled frock and cravat. "He used to live there, just like you said. But…" His gaze moved over my nude body in starts and stops, and his jaw grew impossibly more rigid. "You've lost so much weight. Your goddamn bones are protruding."

He yanked off his linen shirt, which had avoided most of the blood. I looked away and wrapped my arms around my torso, feeling repulsively unattractive and hating myself for that shame.

"Don't do that." With a knuckle under my chin, he lifted my head and searched my eyes, letting me see his sincerity, his undeniable reverence. "Perhaps you have new cracks. Way down deep. Cracked but not broken. Look at you, Goldilocks. You didn't break."

"I'm not a warrior. Confound it, you saw me on that barrel…" I shook my head vigorously. "I just did what I had to do, and most of the time, it was nothing. There was nothing I could do but breathe."

"I wager that breathing hurt the most."

Heat swelled behind my eyes, surging tears.

"Christ, your courage and resilience are awe-inspiring." His thumb stroked my cheek. "You've never looked more beautiful than you do now."

Sea of Ruin

"Thank you."

"That doesn't mean I'm letting anyone else see you uncovered." He pulled the shirt over my head, tenderly guiding my arms through the sleeves.

Was this really happening? Was he truly here? Or was it just a figment? My brain felt foggy and full of shadows.

I cleared my throat. "What happened with Priest?"

"He hasn't visited the brothel in years." He gave me another concerned inspection. "Can you stand?"

"Yes." With the help of his hands on my waist, I climbed to my feet. "He lives, then? Priest?"

"I didn't kill him or capture him."

Relief soared in my chest.

"But that was never my aim." He strode toward the ladder.

"What do you mean?"

He retrieved a bowl of salt fish that one of the officers had brought down. That was when I saw them. The two men who had hauled me in and out of the hole.

They lay in a pile of lifeless limbs, throats cut open and eyes unseeing. That would explain some of the gruesome noises when Ashley had entered. The other ominous sounds I'd heard became apparent as my gaze landed on the third man. The one who'd raped me.

A concave hole hollowed out his head. All that remained of his face was a bowl of splintered bone and red mush. The skull, the eyes, all of it was crushed, completely pulverized beneath whatever had caused the repetitive *thump, thump, thump*...

I looked around for the weapon and paused on Ashley's broken, bloody knuckles. "Did you...?"

"If I could kill him again, I would. But I would slow it down. Draw it out. Make him suffer for weeks." His teeth ground together as he set the bowl of salt fish in my hands. "Eat. I know it's the last thing you want right now, but you need your strength." His eyes narrowed coldly. "Who else hurt you?"

"Just him." My stomach tightened.

The mutilation extended beyond the face. Multiple stab wounds covered the abdomen so as to permit the bowels to fall out. A knife protruded from where the genitals used to be, the hilt jutting upward like a crude erection. A few feet away lay the severed flesh that had hurt me so brutally.

Sick satisfaction hummed through my soul. Ashley had disemboweled, castrated, and defaced this man in a matter of minutes. The only person I'd ever seen do something so swiftly and grotesquely was Priest.

"Who else knows what was happening in here?" He collected the knives from the bodies of the officers. "Be very certain, Bennett, because I will slaughter every man on board this tarnal ship."

"Only these three as far as I know." I swallowed down a sour bite of fish and fought back nausea. "Did you recognize the man who raped me? He always smelled like—"

"Onions. He ate them raw." He cast the body an intense, fevered glare. "Sir John Dycker."

"The admiral? You killed your superior?" I clutched my forehead, whirling beneath the implication. "They'll execute you, Ashley! They'll hang you right alongside me!"

His gaze narrowed on the hatchway as if daring it to open. "Neither of us is hanging."

A flutter tingled in my belly. That was the first time I'd ever heard a promise of my survival from his mouth.

"I have a great deal to tell you." He paced around the bodies, his expression pensive. "First, we need to get off this ship. Finish eating."

I choked down the remainder of the fish in seconds. "How do we get out of here?"

"I'm working on that." He handed the knives to me and scanned the space. "When I opened that hatch and saw him with you…" His eyes burned with renewed fury, his lips twisting back from clenched teeth. "I had no plans beyond beating his face into the back of his head."

"You achieved that quite successfully."

He lifted the admiral's shoulders and began to drag him toward the black hole. "I left you here, thinking you were safe, so that I could find Priest Farrell and ask for his help." He paused, growling angrily. "I never found the bastard."

"Wait. You wanted *Priest's* help?" My pulse quickened. "For what?"

"To free you." He resumed moving the corpse, presumably to hide it. "I was going to make him an offer."

"What offer? Ashley, forget the body. You need to clean the blood off your face and—"

"Any second, a soldier is going to come through that hatchway looking for his officers, his admiral, or perhaps even me, because I've been down here longer than acceptable. I spent the day arguing my way through a dozen different lieutenants before I reached the lower deck. It's not normal for a commodore to visit his prisoner." He glanced over his shoulder at the black hole and scowled. "What is that smell?"

My heart sank. "That's where they kept me."

A vein bulged in his scarlet-smeared forehead. He dropped the admiral's body and spun toward the hole.

"Ashley, wait!" I planted my feet, refusing to go anywhere near there. That stench would forever haunt me, and I wasn't brave enough to breathe it again.

He crossed the threshold and staggered to a stop. His head swung toward his shoulder, and he buried his nose there, gagging and coughing.

"How long have I been down here?" I asked softly.

"Two weeks." He gripped the door, his fingers digging into the wood, his accent slurring with rage. "You were in there for two weeks with what I can only imagine is a dead body. Two weeks I spent hunting a pirate who might as well be a ghost. No one has spotted Priest Farrell in months. I should have turned back the first day when I learned he wasn't at the brothel. Had I done that, you wouldn't have suffered for so goddamned—"

"Ashley, stop this. And get away from that compartment."

"Who's in there, Bennett?"

"Three African women." With a boulder of grief in my chest, I rushed through an explanation of what I'd experienced in that hole the first day. "They were abused the same as me. One of them was pregnant."

"I didn't know." His hands clenched, and he tilted his head to one side, staring intensely at me over his shoulder. "You have to believe me, Bennett. I would've never allowed you on this ship had I known."

"I believe you." I stood taller, tightening my fingers around the hilts of the daggers. "I forgive you. For all of it. Everything. That forgiveness came *before* you showed up. Now tell me what your purpose was with Priest Farrell?"

"I don't deserve your forgiveness, but we'll discuss that later. And Priest... God's teeth, if I only knew where he was hiding..." He swiped a hand down his face, making the blood smear. "I was going to offer him my protection in exchange for kidnapping you."

My jaw dropped.

"I couldn't free you." He turned toward the admiral's body, staring down at it with unbridled wrath. "Not without losing my career, shaming my family, and getting us both sent to the gallows. The day Dycker showed up, I decided to carry out my plan to find Priest Farrell. Only instead of capturing him, I was going to convince him to rescue you and make it look like a raid."

My mind spun at the irony, and my mouth opened to tell him everything. But no words came forth. Where would I start? The compass? My marriage? Priest's betrayal? My rescue plan? There was too much to explain and too little time.

"You trusted him with your body once." Ashley watched me carefully, misunderstanding my reaction. "He would've remembered you. No man could forget."

Oh, dear God, I needed to tell him.

"If I thought he'd hurt you instead of help you…" Possessiveness growled through his voice, but there was something else. Something desperate and strange darkening his eyes. "I would've killed him. I swear it."

My gaze drifted toward the hatch. Did I just hear a creak? Footsteps on the deck above?

"Tell me you have a plan." My nerves rioted.

"I have a plan." He yanked the knife from the admiral's groin.

"Be more specific."

A transformation swept over him, his expression emptying before my very eyes. No emotion, not a trace of humanity as he stabbed a finger at the barrel beside me, silently ordering me to hide.

Then the door to the hatchway opened.

Thirty-eight

My pulse detonated as a pair of boots sounded on the ladder.

I crouched behind the barrel, completely concealed, and tightened my grip on the daggers. Any second, our visitor would turn and see three dead bodies and one very bloody commodore holding a knife.

Trembling, I gathered the hem of Ashley's shirt high on my legs so that it wouldn't hinder my movements if I needed to fight. Then I waited.

The door to the hatch closed, and footsteps descended into the hold. *One man.*

"My lord? What are you—?" His unfamiliar voice gasped and stuttered with the stumble of his boots. "Is that—? Pray, sir, put your hands where I can see them!"

I peered around the barrel, and my heart turned keel-up.

A head taller, the soldier towered over Ashley, holding a cocked pistol to Ashley's head. The man was bigger, probably stronger than Ashley. But he trembled so miserably his finger bounced against the trigger.

Ashley's face was one sneeze away from looking like the admiral's.

He didn't move. Didn't appear to be breathing. His aristocratic mien smoothed his features, his unfeeling voice showing no traces of fear or guilt. "Lower your gun, Sergeant, and I'll enlighten you on the situation."

There was no explaining this. The blood of three officers coated his face. He murdered an admiral of the Royal Navy, for Christ's sake.

"Do not presume to give me orders." The sergeant stiffened his stance. "Your privileges are presently revoked, by God! Where is the prisoner?"

A chill hit my core.

"In the compartment behind me." Ashley cocked his head. "Did you know the admiral was raping her?"

Oh, no, Ashley. Let it go.

"She's a pirate. And you, sir, are a *murderer*." The sergeant craned his neck, trying to see into the darkness. "Miss Sharp? Come out, if you please."

"She's gagged and shackled. See for yourself."

"You first." The soldier thrust his chin. "Go on."

Perhaps Ashley had this under control. But *perhaps* wasn't good enough. I couldn't leave his survival to chance.

Rising slowly, silently, I curled my fingers around the daggers and sneaked up behind the sergeant. Ashley didn't glance at me as he stepped backward, following the soldier's orders.

Together, they shuffled into the tenebrous hole. When the soldier coughed, distracted by the stench, I charged.

Blades out, I swung them with all my strength. The steel slid easily into either side of the man's neck, the tender flesh giving little resistance. A gurgling sound bubbled from his mouth. Warm blood spurted over my fingers, and Ashley caught the waving pistol, wrenching it away.

The man dropped. I pulled the daggers free and heaved a shivering exhale.

Another soldier dead. Another body to hide.

"Thank you." Ashley's gaze latched onto mine.

I nodded, breathing heavily. "You were saying…"

"My plan was to acquire clean frocks and breeches." He stepped to a bucket of water and washed his face. "If we lure two soldiers down here and subdue them *without* bleeding them"—he cast me a narrowed look—"we can walk out wearing disguises."

"Oh." I grimaced at the gore saturating the sergeant's frock. *Blast it.*

"We're going to take care of each other, Bennett. You and me, from now on. No matter what happens. We'll get out of here. I promise."

His vow flowed through my veins, warmed my blood, and penetrated my heart. But I knew, even dressed as the admiral's soldiers, we wouldn't make it off the flagship without inquiries and detention.

Sea of Ruin

"We're even." I squatted before him and cleaned my hands in the bucket. "You saved me from the admiral. I saved you from the soldier." I closed my eyes against the resolution hardening his face. "I need you to go. Leave. *Now*."

"No."

I made a sound of frustration. "*Think,* Ashley. I'm a savage. A murderer. My fate is decided. This ends with me hanging, and you know it." I met his searing gaze. "You are going to walk out of here. Right now. Tell them I murdered these men, and you managed to escape. Do it. *For me*. It's the only way."

"Never." He rose in a blur. In the next breath, he pinned me against the wall beneath the furnace of his hard, shirtless chest. "If you ever suggest a preposterous idea like that again, I will punish your lovely arse until you can't sit for a week."

I sighed. *That* was the commodore I knew and loved.

Confident, stalwart nobleman.

Irritating pain in the arse.

Tipping my head back, I gazed into his beautiful, passionate blue eyes, and *whoa*. I was dizzy. Head-spinning, heart-racing dizzy. Probably stress and nerves. Or hunger. Or perhaps it was the floating, mystical magic I always felt in his presence.

Honest to God, if we weren't surrounded by the stench of death, I would've planted an adoring kiss on his lips.

"We're not equals." He cupped the side of my face and brought my cheek against his warm chest. "And we're not even close to being even, madam." His mouth lowered to the top of my head, his breath rustling my hair. "I'm beneath you, less than you, in every way that transcends this world. Perhaps someday, I'll do something great and good and *earn* your forgiveness."

"You *are* great and good." I circled my arms around him and squeezed tight. "So good, in fact, it's positively annoying and not at all attractive." Pressing my face into the chiseled heat of his torso, I found heaven. "Damn, I missed you."

"I missed you, too, but we need to—"

A deafening boom exploded above us. The detonation hit so hard it blew me out of Ashley's arms and across the hold.

The wind knocked from the lungs. The keel of the ship canted with a mighty groan, and the world slanted to the starboard, rolling every barrel, cable, and body in the hold to one side.

I must have hit my head, given the colossal pang hammering in the back of my skull. I couldn't find my bearings, couldn't see anything through the cloud of smoke that engulfed the space.

"Ashley!" The stench of sulfur burned my nose, my eyes stinging as I searched the gray haze. "Ashley! Where are you?"

"Here." His voice came from behind me, right at my ear, and his arms hooked around my waist.

"What happened?"

"The flagship's under attack. Don't let go of me." He lifted me up in the air and tossed me over his shoulder.

Then he took off. I clenched my whole body around his shoulders and back and held on as he scaled the ladder and shoved open the hatchway.

Another eruption shook the ship, the magnitude of it so loud it felt like a sledge in my chest. Shock waves rippled outward, and his boots lost purchase on the rungs. We started to fall, my stomach plunging. But his hands caught the deck above, and he pulled us up.

"Let me walk!" I shouted over the din of shrieking men and distant gunfire.

"Quiet!" He heaved me through the hatchway.

I had no choice but to hang on as he ran through the lower decks. All around us, sailors scurried left to right, paying no attention to the shirtless commodore and his female prisoner.

Gunfire grew louder, erupting overhead. Screams and curses chilled my skin. The stench of sweat, smoke, and fear congested the air. Mayhem ensued, and we were headed into the thick of it.

"I hope you have a plan." I hung upside down with my face against his back, wishing I'd had the foresight to grab a knife from the hold. "Where's your ship?"

"With any luck, she still sits a hundred feet off the flagship's larboard. My plan is to get us to her."

That didn't fill me with hope. If the flagship was under attack, Ashley's ship would be, as well. The admiral was dead. The commodore of HMS *Blitz* was with me. Who was commanding these ships? Who was attacking?

In the back of my mind, I wondered if Priest was responsible for this battle. It would be just like him to make an appearance now with guns blazing.

Ashley burst out of the final companionway and onto the upper deck, holding fast to my lower body. The bulkhead beside us exploded in a shower of wood, but he didn't flinch or slow his sprint.

Sea of Ruin

Black obscured the sky and sea. Not just from the smoke. The hours of darkness were upon us.

I clung to his broad frame, blinking in the haze of sulfur, unable to believe my eyes. Bodies lay everywhere, some dismembered by chain-shot, others still alive and crushed beneath overturned cannons. Many were so mutilated there were only pieces left.

The gangways and foremast were gone, smashed by massive, hard-punching cannons. Thirty-two-pounders if I had to guess. But that wasn't possible unless HMS *Blitz* was shooting at this ship.

Gunfire ricocheted, and fires burned, the smoldering haze so black it made visibility impossible. I scanned every direction, searching for the attacking ship. Men continued to drop to their deaths, the shots coming from somewhere off our larboard.

Ashley seemed to share my thoughts, for he raced in that direction. On his way, he ripped a spyglass from the hands of a lieutenant, not waiting for the protests.

He reached the larboard bow and set me under it, out of the line of fire.

"Don't move!" Standing over me, he raised the glass to his eye. "God's wounds, I can't see!"

Cannon thunder vibrated across the sea, up through the deck, and into my rattling bones.

"My lord?" A sailor appeared at Ashley's side, bleeding from a wound on his face. "Why are you *here*?"

I tucked myself against the bow, trying to remain out of view.

"I've been here all day." Ashley dropped his hand to my head as if making sure I hadn't moved. "Is my ship firing at this one? Who's attacking?"

"It's Madwulf MacNally, my lord. He and his men escaped the hold and overtook HMS *Blitz*. They're attacking us, using the guns on *your* ship."

My face went cold, and my heart sprinted out of my chest. I wanted to deny what I'd heard, but as I took in the carnage and destruction, it made terrifying sense. Only a one-hundred-gun ship of the line could do this kind of damage.

Ashley's ship was the deadliest on the sea, and it was now under the command of a violent, deranged pirate.

"May God be with you, my lord." The sailor ran off to help a fallen comrade.

Ashley didn't move.

Reaching out, I touched his leg and felt a tremor run through the muscle. "Ashley?"

Was he in shock? Or was he thinking through a plan?

Another boom barreled through the smoke, the horrendous sound ringing my ears. I hunched low as a cannonball careened across the deck and took out a row of starboard guns. Gunners exploded into meaty fragments. Some were still alive, still screaming and kicking as blood spurted from irreparable wounds.

Beside me, a man leaped overboard as the ship burned around us.

"Ashley!" I punched his knee.

He tossed the telescope and crouched before me, his eyes wild and glowing in the shadows.

"I can't stop this ship from sinking. She's mortally wounded." He gripped my face, locking us together. "We must get back to HMS *Blitz*."

"How?" I jumped at a nearby explosion and hugged my ears. "How will we get over there?"

"Longboat." He gripped my hand, rising to his feet.

And with a deafening boom, he was gone.

Gone in a gale of fire and debris that hit so soundly it sucked him away from me and into the night.

I screamed, arms reaching, scrambling in the direction he was blown. But I didn't know where that was. I couldn't see through the smoke. Couldn't hear over the rage of battle. Couldn't breathe beneath the horrific fumes of death. Oh, God, where was he?

"Ashley!" Panic drove me forward, disregarding the dangers around me.

A ball whizzed past my head, so close it singed my hair. But it didn't halt my mad rush across the splintered deck, my tear-soaked eyes frantically searching the carnage of dismembered extremities.

"Ashley! Where are you? Ashley, please!" My voice bled, cracking and raw, but I kept screaming. Kept searching.

Another shot rang out, knocking me onto my back. As I pushed myself up, a terrible sound buzzed in the distance, growing closer, faster, louder. White-hot terror turned my limbs to seaweed.

Overhead, the storm of a thousand fiery bees swarmed across the ship, smothering lanterns, snuffing out sounds, and spitting iron at the decks and rigging. The attack of gunpowder blew in and blasted over in a roaring fire, taking everything with it—sheets, spars, sailors, chunks of the mast, the entire forecastle, and most of the hull beneath it.

Sea of Ruin

I took cover under a bulwark as violence rained down like angry fists, hurling burning pieces of canvas, cables, and timbers onto the cracked and burning upper deck.

Men cried out in agony, screaming for their mates. I was right there with them, crawling through rivers of blood and scattered bodies, searching for Ashley with shrieking desperation. Terror gripped me so brutally my insides became a single pulsing, ice-cold spasm.

From the sky fell an armless corpse, and it landed beside me with a bone-breaking crunch. A severed section of a backstay tangled around the leg, suspending the body feet over head. Shielding my face, I followed that line up, squinting heavenward at what remained of the crosstrees.

Nothing. There was nothing left of this ship. No one left to watch it sink. No one to hear my cries as I went down with it.

Except Madwulf MacNally.

If Hell existed after this life, I would find him and become his own personal devil, his eternal punisher. I looked forward to death if only so that I could revenge whatever had befallen Ashley.

Returning my attention to the deck, I resumed my search for him. But there was no time left.

The flagship heaved in a great groaning roar of snapping timbers and rushing water. The stern rose heavenward, tipping shoulders over the nose as it began a vertical dive into the sea.

I tumbled downward along the sharply sloping deck, shoved by gravity and banging into debris. The descent was unpreventable, terrifying, stealing every ounce of breath from my lungs. Even so, I swung my head left and right, looking for Ashley, desperate for a last glimpse of him.

The waves rose up and grabbed my legs, drenching me in salt water and tossing me into the flotsam of netting, chunks of wood, dead bodies, and chaos.

I tried to stay afloat and evade the line of cannon fire coming from HMS *Blitz*. My lungs seethed with smoke. Busted casks slammed into my head, and the ocean rolled over me, pulling me under.

Warm currents surged from every direction, driving water into my nose and eyes. Pieces of shipwreck arrowed through the water like bullets. I pumped my arms and legs, trying to avoid the volley while swimming toward the surface. But I was too deep.

Far above, the ship exploded in orange balls of fire, lighting up the sea. The hull's broken skeleton dove into the abyss, clouding the water in boils of smoke as it dragged canvas, spars, and cables down with it.

Ashley's shirt fluttered around my upturned legs, contorting my view of the devastation. As the warship plunged to its death, following me into the nether world, it felt dreamlike. Fantastical. Beautiful even.

But it wasn't. I'd lost Ashley and Priest.

All had been taken from me, and soon my last breath would be taken, too.

My lungs began to give out. Something crashed into my head from behind. Pain shattered. My heartbeats slowed, and the inevitability of the end fell upon me.

I wasn't ready.

I wasn't ready.

I wasn't ready.

Thirty-nine

I was floating.

Not in water.

Not on a ship or a piece of flotsam.

I floated in the air, held up by an unseen heavenly force.

It must have been a dream. Certainly not death, for when I departed, my destination would be far below the seabed, down in the infernal regions of torment for the bad and the worse.

A breeze kissed my face, warm and briny. It felt so unreal I didn't want to open my eyes to reality. But my lashes lifted on their own, pulling against the weight of a strange drowsiness. My head felt achingly heavy, my lungs bruised and eyes bleary.

Sprinkles of light filtered in, dominated by one brilliant color.

Blue sky.

Blue water.

Blue eyes.

My heart missed a beat.

I struggled to sit up, but there was nothing beneath me.

Except arms. Strong, masculine arms.

Salt stung my skin and burned my nose. I gulped in air, coughed, and blinked rapidly, trying to focus past the daze. Then I saw him.

"Welcome back, Goldilocks." Ashley smiled down at me, his full lips tipping wearily amid a glow of blinding light.

"What?" I wiggled and twisted, unable to find purchase, swimming in confusion. "You died."

"Did I?" He was standing, cradling me against his bare chest and controlling my movements with his hands. "Calm down. You hit your head rather spectacularly."

"We're alive?" I squinted against the brightness of the sun, trying to see where we were and who was with us. The light tortured my eyes, igniting agony in my skull. "Are we safe?"

"For now." He glanced around, his expression tired and perplexed. "I believe we washed ashore on the southern coast of Eleuthera."

We escaped the battle? And Madwulf? And the murder of the admiral? How did we not drown or get blown apart by gunfire?

My vision blurred with tears. Through the wet sheen, a pink sandy coastline took shape, stretching left and right.

This was real. He was alive. We were on land.

My heart took flight, bursting from my chest and soaring over the sea. I threw my arms about his neck, inhaling his clean scent. He was breathing, standing, sweating, alive!

"I thought I lost you." I kissed his throat, his hard jaw, his beautiful mouth. "I watched you get ripped away from me. I couldn't find you. I looked everywhere. The ship, the bodies, so much blood and—"

"Shh." He kissed me back, his lips soft and chaste. "You've been in and out of consciousness all morning. I'm concerned about your head."

I touched the back of my skull where it throbbed and found a swollen bump amid the salt-encrusted tangles. "No broken skin? Are *you* hurt?"

"Not one open wound between us. Do you have any pain?"

"Just a megrim. I'll be fine." I hugged him tighter, afraid to let go, terrified this wasn't real.

He seemed reluctant to release me, too. How long had he been standing here on this beach, cradling me in his arms?

Behind him, nothing but dense wilderness was exposed to my view. I didn't know what inhabited this island other than a few farmers. Were there wild beasts within those woods? Other extremities likewise? If there were a weapon left between us, I would be shocked.

I shifted in his tight embrace, following his gaze to the sea. Floating wreckage and cargo scattered the rolling waves. A great many bodies and busted barrels bobbed amongst the flotsam.

I looked up and down the shoreline, scanning for signs of life. "Are there survivors?"

Sea of Ruin

"Just us."

The admiral's flagship was gone. I'd watched it burn and sink and take hundreds of men with it. But what about HMS *Blitz*?

"Where's your ship, Ashley?"

"Besieged." His jaw clenched. "She's an unthinkable prize for a pirate like Madwulf. I imagine he's on his way this very second to plunder every treasure ship on the high seas. With one-hundred guns at his disposal, it'll take an entire fleet to stop him."

Madwulf would offer Ashley's crew democratic freedom and a share of the spoils in exchange for their loyalty. No one in their right mind would turn down an opportunity to be rich *and* free. Most pirates were, after all, deserters from one navy or another. Those who refused to convert to piracy with Madwulf would be put in the hold or killed.

While Madwulf turned Ashley's soldiers into outlaws, Priest would still be pursuing that ship. Only death or capture would prevent my husband from hunting me.

"I'm sorry." My heart constricted in terror for Priest and sadness for Ashley.

"Yes, well, I've proved to be a rather incompetent commodore. I allowed the heaviest ship in the Royal Navy to fall into the hands of a pirate. For that, I shall be the target of mockery and ridicule for an entire nation and will never again be able to show my face in society." He paced along the shore and set me down. "But I'm not sorry."

Reeling with dizziness from his words and the haze in my head, I realized I was sitting on the bow of a beached longboat. I wore the tattered remains of his shirt and nothing else. On that thought, my hand flew to my throat.

"You didn't lose it." He crouched before me, his gaze fixed on the jade stone beneath my fingers. "See? Still there."

I released a breath. "My father gave it to me."

"When you said you stole it, I knew better. I don't think you realize how often you touch it."

"It's scary how perceptive you are."

"Not perceptive enough. My men were extorted by Madwulf right under my nose. It's the only explanation for his escape. He must have bribed my wardens into setting him free."

"Recruited them more like. He would've offered them a share of the spoils if they joined his band of thieves. You're not sorry for that?"

"If Madwulf hadn't escaped when he did, you would still be in the custody of the Royal Navy." His eyes locked with mine, the depths rotating with hot, resolute emotion. "You're free, Bennett."

"We're both free. No one will ever know you killed John Dycker and his lieutenants."

"I don't care about that." He looked away, the muscles tensing in his gorgeous face. "I'm losing my mind thinking about what Madwulf will do with a weapon like HMS *Blitz*." His stare returned, harder and brighter than ever. "But I can't regret Madwulf's attack on the flagship. The admiral's soldiers knew about the depravity happening to you and those women, and they did nothing." His accent thickened, growing deeper. "They deserved to die."

"The sum of a man's actions determines his future, right? The same can be said about me. I'm a pirate. A thief. A murderer." I gripped his flexing fist and held it on my lap. "I went down with that ship. By English law, that's a fate I deserved. So how did I get *here*?"

"I was blown toward the stern, and that's where—"

"The longboats were stowed." I glanced down at the one I sat on, unable to imagine how he'd deployed it during a battle.

"This boat found me. It was just…there. Then I found you. Christ, it took an eternity in the smoke and chaos, and I died a million deaths thinking I lost you. But when I saw you going down with the ship, I knew my purpose, *my* fate." He squeezed my hand, his Adam's apple bouncing. "I was meant to be on this longboat exactly where I was when you fell into the sea. It was as if every decision I ever made led up to that moment when you fell, and I dove in after you."

"Don't be ridiculous." My chin quivered, ruining my scolding tone. "You risked your life."

"A life that's worth nothing without you."

"Ashley…" I leaned forward and rested my brow against his. "Was I breathing?"

"No." One syllable wrought with anguish.

"Did you put your beautiful mouth on mine like Lieutenant Flemming showed you?"

"Yes." His hand slid into my hair, bringing our lips together. "After I pulled you into this boat, I gave you my air over and over until you breathed again. It was the longest hour of my life."

I smiled against his frown. "If saving drowning women is your way of soliciting female companionship for dinner, you're trying too hard."

He choked on a laugh. "I fell in love with you that day."

"You say?" My head jerked back, and I scrutinized his expression, finding the bluest, most honest eyes I'd ever seen. "That was the first thing I said to you aboard your ship."

"I remember it well. If you only knew what was going on in my head…" He cleared his throat. "And in my breeches."

"Now you *must* tell me."

"I was equally terrified and aroused by you. The intensity of feelings you stirred in me was unlike anything I'd experienced. I wanted to strap you to my bed, redden your arse, climb inside you, and confess my deepest desires. What really tormented me was that I knew you could handle my unseemly manners—the indecency I hid from the world. I knew you would enjoy every form of immoral pleasure ever invented, welcome it even, if you trusted me. I met my match the day I met you, and it took every ounce of training and self-discipline to keep those sentiments off my face."

I touched his steely jaw, foundering beneath the fire in his eyes.

"Had I taken you to my quarters straight away," he said, "every man on my ship would've known I was compromised. Putting you in that hold with Madwulf…"

"I was your enemy. You were doing your job."

"I regret it. Listen to me, Bennett. I will *never* forgive myself for allowing Madwulf to touch you and…" His hand clenched in my hair. "The admiral. What you endured in that monster's custody—"

"Cracked but not broken. That's what you said." I kissed his seething mouth. "I lived, Ashley, and I'm stronger for it. Thank you for coming for me."

An angry sound vibrated in his chest, and he leaned back to caress his thumb around the shape of my mouth. "Your lips are dry. You're dehydrated." He shoved to his feet and stepped a few paces away, probing the trees that fringed the shore. "We'll find fresh water in those woods."

His white breeches, now brown with dirt and sand, frayed at the waistband and calves. Bloody gashes glistened through ripped holes. Scrapes, gouges, and other reddening bruises marred his muscled torso and arms. He donned no shoes or weapons. Nothing but the breeches and all that carved brawn. I couldn't imagine the strength and balance that was required to pull my limp body into the longboat without oversetting it.

Stripped down to his skin and tattered rags, he looked like a warrior of the Roman Empire. Fashioned of iron and ferocity, his masculine beauty alone would excite a hungry crowd. He needed naught a weapon, for he was one. The breadth of his shoulders and the well-thewed power in his arms and legs attested to his competence in battle.

The man had pulled me from the ocean, right out from beneath a burning, sinking warship. He'd more than earned my respect.

Gradually, I dragged my gaze from his magnificent physique and found him regarding me. "What?"

"You're staring."

"I'm admiring."

He took my hand, and my body shivered from the heat of his touch. Then he bent to lift me.

"Wait." I pushed against his chest, stopping him. "I'll walk."

"You have a concussion."

"You're not a doctor, and besides, while I slept for the past however many hours, you didn't shut your eyes once. Am I right?"

"I'll sleep when we find water and food."

I stood, fighting a sudden onslaught of vertigo. With a hand shielding my eyes, I marked the location of the morning sun. "We're on the eastern side of the island. The southern tip, you said?" I started the walk toward the tree line.

"Yes." He drifted right up against my side as if expecting me to fall. "Where are you going?"

"Eleuthera is quite long and skinny. Less than two-hundred kilometers from end to end." I picked up my pace to escape the burning sand underfoot. "If we head straight through these woods for three or four kilometers, we'll arrive on the western shoreline. There's a small farming hamlet somewhere on that side, and if we're nice…" I gave him a pointed look. "The farmers will feed us and give us a place to rest." I stepped into the shade of the woods, instantly relieved by the drop in temperature. "What I don't know is if there are poisonous creatures or man-eating predators here."

"None that I'm aware of."

"One less thing to worry about." I picked along a narrow path, quickly navigating around brush and low-hanging trees. "We'll head toward the hamlet and—"

"You're trying so hard to be the captain of this expedition. It's adorable."

"Don't mock me, Ashley Cutler. I *am* a captain."

"Yes, but I outrank you."

I cut him an incisive glare, which he returned with a teasing glint in his eyes.

"As I was saying…" My lips twitched. "We'll stop at the hamlet for food and rest then make our way north."

"North?"

"Harbour Island. Look!" I pointed at a shallow creek. "Barely enough water to wet the stone bed, but if we follow it, we'll find the source."

In favor of drinking water, he didn't pursue the topic of Harbour Island. Three kilometers or more from whence we started, we located a freshwater pool attached to a small waterfall.

The water tasted so crisp and refreshing I submerged my entire body in it.

"I haven't had a bath in…" I dunked my head and came up to find his face inches from mine. My breath stammered. "I don't remember."

"The next time I have access to soap, I'll wash every inch of your body myself."

I'd said those words to my husband the last time I saw him. How long ago was that? Three weeks? A month?

Too long.

Oh, the irony. I ran from that man for two years. And now, I missed him horribly.

My throat closed, my world stilling to a dismal, eye-opening view of my situation. For the first time since jumping from *Jade's* bow, I was looking at the real chance of survival. That meant I had to consider the future.

I was married to a man I loved. I loved another man who didn't know I was married. Choosing between them wasn't an option. I couldn't. I wouldn't. I'd rather drown beneath a burning ship.

Ashley wrapped his wet body around mine and pulled me close to all his tempting male heat. His lips fell upon my neck, kissing, nuzzling, and governing the rhythm of my pulse. I melted into the velvet blanket of his chest, so firm and hot, not a dream but real flesh and blood. *My man.* He belonged to me and no one else.

Heat tangled between my legs. His mouth ravished my skin. I sank into it, into him, and froze.

It felt wrong.

I felt like a fraud.

Pushing at his arms, I wrenched myself away and climbed out of the pool.

I had to tell him about Priest.

I needed to tell Priest about Ashley.

Unless Priest was dead.

A lump lodged in my throat. No, I couldn't think that way. I would never give up on my husband's life. He'd outsmarted and outlived every person who'd ever underestimated him.

"We should get moving." Stomach in knots, I wrung the wetness from my curls and started walking west.

Water splashed behind me, and strong fingers caught my arm, swinging me around.

"I wasn't trying to…" Ashley raked a hand through his wet hair, and his gaze dipped, roaming over my shredded garment, which was now soaked, transparent, and clinging to my body.

My nipples, the shadow of curls between my legs, everything was on display.

I cocked my head, trying to read him. Was he repulsed knowing another man had defiled me so despicably?

"I want you." His throat worked for a moment, seeming to push forth words that wouldn't come. His hand, still scrubbing over his hair, wilted to his nape. "God help me, how could I not? You're painfully, inconceivably the most stunning woman I've ever seen. I'd be lying if I told you I didn't want you in every way, right now, right there in the water, despite the horrors and abuse your body has endured over the past two weeks. I. Want. You. Selfishly and completely. I want to fuck every torment out of your mind and soul until I'm all that's left." He took a breath, his voice softening. "But I would *never* expect you to want me in that way so soon after…*him*."

Something shifted in my chest, locking in place. "Ashley—"

"Be silent." He held up a finger, glaring at me. "When I pulled you against me in the pool, I wasn't trying to take from you. I love you. That goes beyond lust. It surpasses carnal pleasure. What I feel for you is deep and fierce and so strong, Bennett. I finally have you back and…" He pressed a fist against his chest. "My heart knows it. And my body knows it. So when I feel your beauty beneath my hands, I harden, thinking about you taking me where you're deep and fierce and strong." He straightened, his expression stony. "Damn it all, I'm not saying this decently. I was bred to be a damned gentleman, and I don't know how to be gentle."

"Right." I blew out a breath, my pulse humming through my veins. "First of all, I love you, too. Second, you've never been gentle or decent with me. Never treated me like a fragile maiden. Don't you dare start now."

"Is there a third point?"

Sea of Ruin

"No, I—"
He was on me before I could blink.

Forty

Ashley's mouth collided with mine, his warm lips parting seductively with the drive of his urgent tongue. He was an assertive kisser before, but now, his passion felt reckless, desperate, as if every stroke was a command to forget, every lick an insistence that I heal.

I surrendered willingly, my body throbbing to give where it had been defiled, all those delicate parts aching to feel his fullness. By the time he let me breathe, I didn't want air. I just wanted him.

"Fuck me, Ashley." I palmed the thick, hard swelling in his breeches. "Fuck every torment out of my mind and soul until you're all that's left."

A ragged groan tore from his throat, and he dropped his forehead to mine. "I will. I'll bed you so often and thoroughly you'll grow tired of looking at me. But not here. Not until I have control of our situation." His hand shook as he gripped my fingers and slid them away from his erection. "You stand much in need of nourishment, proper clothing, and a closer inspection of the contusion on your head." He glanced around at the surrounding wilderness. "We've moved some distance through the wood, whence we know not. We need our wits about us as we approach the other shore."

I groaned, dropped my head to his chest, and sighed. "You're right."

After another long drink from the lagoon, we resumed our westerly expedition. Other than the chatter of birds in the canopies overhead, the walk was relatively quiet. Until he remembered what I'd said before our hunt for water.

"Harbour Island…" He plodded ahead of me, using a branch to clear away the foliage. "Tell me why you want to go there."

"Um… Yes, about that… I haven't been completely honest with you. The day you captured me—"

"You told your crew to wait for you there?"

My knees turned liquid, and I stumbled, catching myself on a tree limb.

"Are you well?" He glanced over his shoulder.

I glared at him.

His lips tilted into a gentle arc at one side, eyes gleaming. "You think I didn't know that you organized that jump from your ship?"

My mouth opened and closed like a dying fish.

"Oh, Bennett." His chuckle shivered through me. "I do love to stun you speechless."

"How?"

"The pirate who pushed you…" He held out his hand, waiting for me to take it.

"Reynolds." I stepped toward him and gripped his warm fingers. "Priest Farrell's brother."

"Yes, well, the poor fellow wore the most dreadful look as he shoved you over. I watched him through the glass, and I daresay there were tears in his eyes."

"Overprotective idiot," I muttered. "Exceptional quartermaster."

"Not just him. When you fell, your entire crew held a collective, horrified breath. They *mourned* you so deeply I felt it across the water. It was really quite something."

"Damn those blasted fools. They were supposed to cheer and behave as if the mutiny was real."

"They quickly pulled themselves together and put on a show of clapping and whistling. My lieutenants believed the ruse."

"I can't believe you knew this whole time." I stepped over a fallen tree, keeping my senses locked on the distant waves. "Why did you let them go?"

"I only wanted *you*. From the moment you stood upon that gunwale, half-dressed and shouting profanities at His Majesty's Ship, I couldn't look away. I was completely taken with you. To hell with everything else."

"Good lord, I had no idea." I pushed a twig out of my way, studying him as we walked. "What else did you figure out about me?"

"What else are you keeping from me, you deceitful woman?"

Too much.

"I had some escape plans." I peered up at him, dreading the conversation about Priest.

"Yes, your siren tactics were strikingly successful. Tore my heart out in pieces when you plundered it. Well done."

"A much better scheme than the fake pregnancy."

He twined his fingers around mine and held my gaze. No need to belabor the topic of my infertility. We'd already said all there was to say about that.

My first plan of escape was still out there somewhere, tirelessly hunting me.

As we made our way through the thick brushwood, my stomach tumbled. The sounds of the tide breaking on the western shore grew louder, closer.

I needed to tell him about Priest. I couldn't put it off any longer. "Ashley…"

"Is that…?" He yanked my hand, dragging me behind him as he hurried through the woods. "Look!"

Following his gaze upward, I gasped at the sight of innumerable oranges. We'd stepped into a grove of citrus trees. Christ, this would feed a village. Unless they shared Priest's strange affliction to the fruit.

Ashley plucked a ripe one from a low branch and quickly peeled it. After test sniffing a huge juicy wedge, he offered it to my lips, which I ate with a great appetite.

The overwhelming sweetness burst across my tongue, making me moan and nod for more. Within minutes, we greedily devoured four oranges between us.

He gathered as many as he could carry, gripped my hand, and resumed walking. The sustenance in his belly should have raised his spirits, but he seemed deeply reflective, sullen even.

"Ashley?"

"I need to talk to you about Priest Farrell."

"What?" The hairs on my nape erected.

His feet slowed, his gaze fixed in the direction of the sea. "He's not who you think he is."

"What do you mean?" I glanced at the oranges he held, my throat tightening with suspicion. "Why are you mentioning him now?"

His head turned slightly, his face averted and suddenly pale. Then he went chillingly still. *Distracted.*

My nerves turned inside out.

"Do you see that?" Eyes wide, he stared off in the distance at something I couldn't see.

"No, what are—?"

He clapped a hand over my mouth, and the oranges tumbled to the ground. With a hard look in my direction, he held a finger against his lips. My bones fused at the joints with fear.

Moving slowly, soundlessly, he crept away, angling his neck to see through the trees. Whatever alarmed him contracted his muscles, straining every sinew and tendon in his bare back.

Pulse racing, I leaned forward and squinted through the foliage. And gasped.

Was that a ship? The hazy silhouette of rigging and masts looked so far away, but not inconceivable if the shore lay beyond those trees.

The ground cover stirred behind me. The crunch of leaves, the snap of a twig… *Footsteps.*

Ashley spun toward me as I twisted to look back.

A fist cracked across my face, jarring my vision and hurling me to my knees. I thought I might pass out until Ashley's enraged roar shattered my stunned fog.

I snapped my head up as two shaggy white men attacked him. They held his arms and neck, attempting to restrain his body. But he broke free and rushed forward, his expression seething with unleashed violence.

Halfway to me, the men leaped onto his back. He dragged them several more steps, his teeth bared and eyes locked on mine.

"Ashley!" I grabbed a heavy branch to use as a weapon and tried to stand. But my legs failed me, my entire body pulling downward if I were submerged in mud. My head didn't feel right, and it messed with my coordination.

A few feet away, Ashley swung his fists and elbows, knocking off the men only to be attacked and overpowered again. They wrestled him to the ground, and his gaze stayed with me, his fight driven by one single purpose. I saw it in his eyes. His determination to protect me.

Then his attention jumped to something over my shoulder. His expression warped, transforming from a man into a savage animal as he bellowed and wrestled, attempting to crawl forward.

In a flash of steel, a blade caught me under the chin. My stomach plunged.

Sea of Ruin

"I'll take her head." The unfamiliar English accent came from behind me, deeply male and decisively triumphant. "Move a single muscle and she dies."

Ashley's face went ghost white, his fingers digging into the dirt. Lying on his chest on the ground with two roguish brutes on his back, he had no choice but capitulate.

My lungs panted as I strained my range of sight to the side. In my periphery was the solid cupped hilt of a cutlass, held fast by a calloused seafarer's hand.

Pirate.

As the blade pressed against my throat, I knew I'd lost my freedom the very day I'd gained it.

"State your purpose, pirate." My voice splintered, and I coughed, fighting dizziness. "Who are you?"

"You don't remember us?" The bearded bastard holding Ashley threw back his head and laughed. "I look forward to reminding you."

Ashley stared at them, his eyes shining with recognition and horror. Then his entire demeanor hardened with raw, bone-chilling rage.

"The ship…" Without moving my neck, I flicked my gaze toward the shore, shaking with fresh outrage. "It's HMS *Blitz*, isn't it?"

"She's *Blitz*, all right. But no longer His Majesty's Ship." The man with the cutlass gave me a nudge in the back. "On your feet. The captain's not going to believe his eyes when he sees you."

Captain Madwulf MacNally.

Nausea rose, roiling with dread.

I didn't look at Ashley as I stumbled to stand. I couldn't bear to see the misery, fury, grief—whatever must have been twisting his expression.

My captor held me up and helped me walk, for my head weighed too heavily on my shoulders. They used sashes and leather straps from their waists to bind our hands at our backs. Ashley was kept behind me, both of us escorted with pistols and blades. Weapons they'd pilfered from the armory on Ashley's ship.

The march through the wilderness passed in a blurry fog. At some point, I emptied my stomach, losing every bite of orange I'd ingested. Consciousness floated away, pulling, but I hung onto it by a thread.

Soon the low-growing plants beneath my feet gave way to sand. Sunlight pierced shards of agony through my eyes as I took in the coastline. And there she sat, far off down the beach.

Blitz.

From stem to stern, the one-hundred-gun beauty stretched smooth and sleek, her hull, sheets, and masts in top order. She didn't appear to have a scratch after last night's attack on the flagship.

I dared a glance at Ashley behind me, but he wasn't looking at her. He stared directly at me, his eyes glinting with bloodthirsty promises. Wordless vows to destroy everyone on this island.

Good because I was eager to shed some blood, too.

Perhaps, if I weren't stumbling and dry-heaving and fighting double-vision, we might have been able to overpower our captors. But my weakness served to keep Ashley in line. If he tried to overpower the men holding him, the pirate at my back would kill me.

I needed to get my strength back and my head in working order. Then I would figure out a plan.

The pirates shoved us forward. Onto the beach we went, staggering toward the ship for longer than I thought I could walk.

"How did you escape the hold?" I licked cracked lips, parched and overheated under the unbearable Caribbee sun. "Did you bribe the wardens?"

"Stop talking." A boot slammed into my back, knocking me onto my face in the sand.

"Don't touch her!" Ashley roared and charged toward me, yanking uselessly at the bindings at his back.

The cutlass reappeared beneath my chin, and he skidded to a stop.

One of the rogues removed his sweat-stained neckerchief and tied it around my head, gagging me. Another one laughed and followed suit, silencing Ashley, too.

And that was the end of conversation.

We trampled along the coastline in silence, each step carrying us toward *Blitz*. Ashley showed no remorse or reaction at seeing her anchored so close. Perhaps because she was still so far out of reach.

Eventually, we arrived at the farming hamlet. It comprised of small cottages strung along the tree line connected to pastures of livestock and crops. An ideal target for a pirate ship looking to pillage supplies, restock food stores, and rape farmers' daughters before continuing on to bigger prizes.

I never claimed to be a decent pirate, but my crew and I followed some rigid rules of conduct. The Articles we'd drawn up on board *Jade* prohibited raids against unarmed persons, farmers, commoners—anyone who didn't fall into the *wealthy arsehole* and *king's men* categories. *Jade* had sailed past this hamlet a few times over the years, and not once had we considered attacking it.

But that was exactly why *Blitz* was here.

Amongst these farming families, Madwulf could muster another fifty males as reinforcements for his militia.

As my captor shoved me forward along the beach, I watched pirates come and go on longboats between the warship and the shore. They were plundering the inhabitants of their liquor, whale oil, and as much livestock as could be carried away, no doubt crowding the warship's decks with live chickens, pigs, goats, sheep—the makings of a feast.

Ashley and I were ushered into one of the humble, single-room dwellings. Upon entering, the air went taut, stifling in the humidity.

At least a dozen pirates had already made themselves at home, lounging on the beds, sitting around the dinner table, and sprawled on the modest furnishings.

A crawling sensation rippled across my skin and burrowed into my stomach.

Were any of these men Ashley's soldiers? Where was Madwulf? On the ship? In one of the neighboring cottages? Perhaps he was out back, violating the women who lived here?

I shared a look with Ashley and knew he had the same dark thoughts.

"She lives?" One of the pirates jumped up.

"And the commodore." Another spat through the gaps in his teeth.

Laughter and malicious cheer pressed against my bones, stretching my raw nerves.

Before the day ended, I would serve as entertainment for these bawdy rakes. They were all thinking it. And during the impending debauchery, Ashley would be forced to watch, tortured, and gutted, in no particular order.

I needed my voice, but they gave no indication that our gags would be removed.

We were led to a beam in the center of the cottage. Rope replaced the bindings on our wrists, and we were positioned on the floor, shoulder to shoulder with our hands tied to the post.

The impulse to rest my head on Ashley's arm rode me hard, but I remained stiff and obtuse, giving nothing away. They didn't need to know I loved the commodore. They certainly didn't need to know I would die for him.

Thankfully, he followed my lead and didn't drift closer or cast affection in my direction. For all they knew, he still wanted to deliver me to England to be hanged.

"Where's the captain?" someone asked.

"Heading this way now." A skinny, awkward, loose-jointed fellow leaned in the doorway, picking his teeth with a blade. "Captain! Come see what we got!"

Outside, two voices approached the cottage. One was too soft to hear clearly, but the other drawled in a brogue that hailed from Scotland. As the inflection hit my ears, my entire body shook with fear.

"I dinna ken anything about that," Madwulf snarled. "I was told the admiral hanged her from the yard-arm. She's dead."

Who was he talking to? I leaned forward, heart pounding, hoping, pleading…

"She was spotted on the upper deck of the flagship while you were blowing her rigging to bits against my will!" That voice. The rage. His vicious, gravelly Welsh accent.

My breath left my lips on the wings of salvation.

Priest was here.

Forty-one

The booming pulsation in my head consumed the sound of Priest's unforgettable accent. I pressed my lips together and silenced my gasps, straining to hear him.

Beside me, Ashley went inhumanly still as if his entire being was focused on the conversation beyond the door.

"*Who* spotted her?" Madwulf's Scottish brogue thickened.

"One of Cutler's soldiers. Why am I *just* learning this?" Fury roughened Priest's voice, every syllable boiling with vehemence. "Mark me, Madwulf. If she's dead because of your actions, I'll need something to stab repeatedly, and your face will become my favorite target."

"Uh, Captain MacNally..." The duke of limbs in the doorway held up a loose-jointed finger.

"I dinna understand the problem," Madwulf said, ignoring his crewmate. "You told me you *wanted* her dead."

"I wanted to kill her myself!" Priest roared. "Me! No one else. That was the agreement."

Agreement? My mind spun, trying to fit the pieces together. How did Priest get here? Had he arrived with Madwulf? Did that mean he was on HMS *Blitz* when it fired on the flagship?

All at once, everything clicked.

Priest must have sneaked onto HMS *Blitz* while Ashley anchored in Nassau to search the brothel. Ashley was there for two weeks, so I couldn't be sure about the timing. Evidence suggested that Priest freed

Madwulf from the hold after Ashley sailed back to the admiral. Because the pirates overtook HMS *Blitz* while Ashley was with me on the admiral's flagship.

Apparently, no one had told Priest I was alive and imprisoned on the admiral's flagship. The omission was deliberate, to be certain, for it would've been in Madwulf's interest to sink the flagship without Priest stopping him to look for me.

My ears thudded wildly with the drum of my overtaxed pulse. I'd been so heartsore over Priest's perfidy, but that was nothing compared to what he must have felt when they told him I was dead. *After* he'd already freed them.

Madwulf wanted Ashley's ship. Priest wanted me. They'd lied to each other to protect their agendas, and here we were, teetering on the cusp of full disclosure. I felt the impending bloodshed in my bones.

"What's done is done," Madwulf growled. "Dinna threaten me again, Priest."

"Actually, Captain…" The lanky, ill-made fellow in the doorway interrupted again. "She's here. Look." He motioned inside the cottage.

The sound of footsteps exploded into a flurry outside. A second later, several men burst in, but my world narrowed to one.

Priest's silver eyes shot straight to mine, his expression awash with everything I felt—shock, confusion, relief, and savage determination.

As his gaze frantically swept over me, hunting for injuries, I gave him the same inspection.

He wore a baldric of blades and pistols over his shoulder. A cutlass hung from straps of leather around his waist. My father's black jackboots covered his feet, and leather braces adorned his forearms. My examination traveled over the snug brown breeches and loose black shirt before landing on the compass.

My compass.

Wedged beneath his waistband and secured to his many belts, it was a glorious shock to the heart. I thought I'd never see it again, yet there it was. Safe. Whole. Precious. Impossible to replace. Just like my husband.

He hadn't moved from the doorway, his rugged physique so stiff and hard it was as if the sight of me had turned him to stone.

His intense gaze held mine. His breaths came faster, and in that sublime moment of eye contact, everything felt right in the world. With Ashley at my side and Priest armed to the teeth, I knew we would survive this. All three of us.

Sea of Ruin

But those thoughts evaporated the instant Priest turned his attention on Ashley.

Priest's countenance clouded, his entire demeanor taking on that of a stranger. He seemed taller somehow, broader, his shoulders rolling back into a fighting stance. Why? Did he recognize Ashley as the pirate hunter who had taken me into custody? He couldn't have known about my intimate relationship with Ashley.

The creases about his mouth and brow confessed nothing. Was it anger? Suspicion? Resentment? He normally expressed his feelings so clearly on his face, but this wasn't anything I could interpret.

He's not who you think he is.

Thank you, Ashley, for planting that seed of doubt. Now I wondered if they knew each other.

Ashley was probably spinning on his carefully controlled axis, wondering why the Feral Priest was hunting me.

What a monumental disaster.

Movement pulled my attention to the man beside Priest, and I shuddered.

Captain Madwulf MacNally stood with his boots braced shoulder-width apart, his hands clasped behind him, and his eyes ticking between Priest and Ashley. Intelligence fired in those eyes, and that scared me more than the brace of weapons he wore across his chest.

It didn't matter how much help he'd received in his escape from the hold. The fact was he'd managed it. He'd broken out, seized command of a Royal Navy ship of the line, and sank HMS *Ludwig* with both the admiral and the commodore on board.

This wasn't a man I wanted as an enemy, but I'd foolishly cemented that given how my hands were bound, my mouth was gagged, and he was staring at me with a look one would give a smear of manure on the bottom of a boot.

I annoyed him. It must have been the beard incident. Evidently, he still blamed me for that unfortunate show of disrespect. If I had my voice, I would explain to him that I wasn't his enemy, and I wouldn't interfere in his plans to raise hell on the high seas with *Blitz*. I couldn't, however, speak for the man beside me. Ashley wanted his ship back.

Perhaps it was for the best that my stoically simmering commodore was gagged.

"Do you ken this officer?" Madwulf thrust his chin at Ashley, his question directed at Priest.

"I know he's the reason I lost her trail a month ago." Priest prowled toward me, but his glare was all for Ashley. "I was so close to catching her. So. Damned. Close. I daresay I wasn't keen to learn that the Royal Navy had plucked her right out of my reach."

Ashley glared at him, emotionless. Utterly unmoved. Meanwhile, my vital organs worked themselves into a frenzy.

Whatever game Priest was playing, I would go along with it. I trusted him with my life. It was Ashley's odds of survival that shook me to the core. Priest wouldn't protect him. If Priest discovered our relationship, he would gut Ashley himself.

"Let's hear the story, Priest." Madwulf walked a circuit around us, watching, analyzing. "What did this puny bit of skirt do to drive you to the extremes of a murderous desperado?"

"She killed my father."

Well, that much was true. Priest would've done the deed himself. I'd just happened to thrust the blade first.

Madwulf narrowed his eyes, pouted his lips, and gave a sharp nod. Kin was invaluable to the Highlanders. It was a Scotsman's duty, a war cry in his blood, to avenge fallen family members.

Priest knew that as he stood over my outstretched legs and leaned down. With a hacking sound, he expelled a wad of spit onto the floorboard between my thighs, missing the hem of the shirt by a hairsbreadth. Then he backhanded my face for good measure.

Despite the ringing in my ears, I had to give him some merit. His stellar performance sent the room into cheerful approval.

Beside me, Ashley didn't move. He'd been under the impression that I'd spent one night with Priest Farrell two years ago and hadn't seen the libertine since. Hopefully, we would live long enough for me to explain.

With any luck, the audience of ten or so armed pirates would move out soon and finish plundering the island. Priest could overpower and kill a few men by himself. But not this many.

Madwulf knew this, and it was unlikely that he would give Priest any advantage. Based on my last encounter with the Scotsman, he probably wouldn't leave without taking a bit of revenge for himself. I'd embarrassed him in front of his men. He might seem amicable now, but he was only biding his time before he made me pay.

"She looks like an emaciated whore." Priest strode away.

I snarled behind the gag, playing along.

"What are you doing?" Madwulf tilted his head, tracking Priest's movements near the table.

Sea of Ruin

"Feeding the bitch." He returned with an earthen jug and bowl. "I didn't come all this way to punish a corpse."

He crouched beside me and set the stoneware on the floor. His hand went to the back of my head, his fingers instantly finding the contusion there.

I stifled a whimper, but he sensed it, his expression losing its savage depiction in favor of genuine concern. My pulse ramped, for I knew Madwulf was watching every interaction with suspicion.

Priest quickly blanked his face, but his tender touch remained, his fingers circling the circumference of the swollen knot, inspecting the condition of it. Then he removed the gag.

I stretched my jaw as a million questions and declarations rose in my throat. I knew better than to blurt any of it. One wrong word could expose Priest's sham, cost him his life, or at the very least, my mouth would irritate Madwulf enough to gag me again.

So I shoved down everything I wanted to say and opted for something mundane. "How did you find me?"

Priest sat beside my hip and held the jug to my lips. Warm milk washed over my tongue, which I readily drank. Then he offered me boiled rice with his fingers. I choked down the mush, wishing he would give Ashley the same nourishment. He wouldn't, and I couldn't ask.

"Your crew happily directed me to HMS *Blitz*." Priest's mouth curled into a devilishly alluring smile.

There was another smile hidden within it. A private one just for me. He knew my crew released him from the hold and told him exactly where I was, on account of *my* orders.

I ached to tell him I forgave him, that no matter what happened, I loved him and needed him and missed him. God almighty, I missed him.

Instead, I had to feign disinterest and disgust. I was never good at dissimulating. But that would need to change, for Madwulf sprawled in a nearby chair, watching and listening with rapt attention.

Priest launched into a narration of his activities over the past month, confirming everything I'd already assumed. He'd followed HMS *Blitz* to New Providence on a stolen sloop. During the night, he clambered up the side and jumped aboard. Quickly and silently, he made his way to the hold, assuming I was imprisoned there, only to find Madwulf and his unkempt band of ruffians. When Priest was unable to locate me anywhere on Ashley's ship, he struck an agreement with Madwulf through the iron bars.

Priest promised to free them and help them overtake HMS *Blitz*. In exchange, they would assist Priest in hunting me—with a strong emphasis on Priest being the only one who would kill me.

During his dialogue, I listened for hints about the status of my ship and crew. Had Reynolds followed my orders and sailed to Harbour Island? Were they there now? Less than two-hundred kilometers away by land? That was only two days' travel by horseback, and there were plenty of horses in the nearby pastures.

Unfortunately, Priest and I couldn't discuss any of this in present company.

"I didn't know Madwulf intended to *sink* the flagship." Priest clenched his jaw, twisting to glower at the Highlander. "I wanted to search it first and look for proof of her death."

"You had no chance in hell of sneaking aboard that vessel, and you ken it," Madwulf said.

"I waited to free you until HMS *Blitz* returned to the flagship. Why do you think that was?"

Madwulf reclined in the chair, arms crossed. "I presumed you were just being a vexing cunt."

"While your pack of rogues was storming the gundecks, seizing the arms, and killing every Englishman who withstood you, I was going to use that distraction to steal aboard the admiral's flagship. That was my plan until you started blowing the tarnal thing to splinters!" Priest's pretense slipped beneath his rising fury. "You told me she was hanged."

"I dinna see why—"

"You knew she was there." Priest shot to his feet, nostrils flaring and neck corded. "You knew she was alive when you destroyed that ship!"

I agreed that Madwulf was lying, but the past was in the past. We needed to secure our future, and that wouldn't happen if Priest continued down this path.

"Madwulf." I waited for his gaze. "I'm not your enemy. I'm a pirate captain, same as you."

His hand went to the short red hairs on his chin, his fingers grasping at a phantom beard. "There's nothing personal between you and me, lass. But after the disrespect your lover gave me, the lads and I will be wetting our cocks between your bonny thighs."

Ashley made a pained sound, radiating tension beside me.

My insides shriveled, and my face went cold, bloodless.

Sea of Ruin

"Lover?" Priest glared at me, his eyes swirling with dark, twisted threats.

Madwulf's attention stayed on Ashley, his tone goading. "She took up with Lord Cutler in his cabin for nigh two weeks. His men—who are now *my* men—claim the two of them fucked like rabbits."

My heart hammered so hard I saw black spots.

Priest's head snapped toward Ashley, his ruse of revenge morphing into blatant jealousy. I'd seen him castrate men for touching me without my permission. He would have no qualms about killing Ashley first and asking questions later.

Except he didn't go for any of the weapons on his person. His hands didn't even twitch for them. If he had, one of these pirates would've ran a blade through him. There would be a vote on who got the privilege of murdering the commodore.

Even so, Priest never exercised self-control in these situations. How was he reining in his jealous, impulsive reactions now? I didn't know what it was, but something about this niggled.

I needed to send a message to him without Madwulf suspecting our relationship. I had to get through to my husband the same way he'd tried to get through to me a month ago.

My mind sprinted through every argument Priest and I had exchanged about his adulterous relationship. I'd asked him why he protected his lover and remembered his response.

"Yes, he's my lover." My voice drew his eyes to mine. Then I threw his words back at him. "I protect what I love. Simple as that."

We stared at each other, entangled, inseparable. I watched him recall our conversation and slowly process what I hadn't said aloud.

I love Ashley Cutler. Killing him would be the same as me killing your *lover.*

Comprehension flashed across his face, there and gone in a blink.

Message received.

He stood and paced toward the table, running a hand down his face, hiding his expression.

Ashley sat stiffly beside me, eyes straight ahead and lips clamped around the gag. I couldn't imagine the state of confusion he was drowning in right now. He didn't have a clue about my history with Priest. Christ, he didn't even know we were married. No one in this room knew.

With our hands bound to the beam at our backs, he stretched out a finger and hooked it around mine. The gesture meant more in that moment than anything else. We were a unified front. We'd get through this.

Across the room, Priest bent over the table, glaring at a plate of cut oranges.

Lounging idly around the cottage, Madwulf's men talked amongst themselves, the din of their overlapping voices clustered with questions and speculation. With every second, the air thickened, filling with uncertainty. Madwulf watched it all with a calculating glint in his eyes.

I saw the moment Priest made a decision. The muscles in his beautiful face slackened. His shoulders relaxed, and he straightened.

"She took my father's life and plundered his ship. My inheritance is gone." He turned toward Madwulf. "I demand restitution from her. Following our agreement, I'll kill her myself, but not before I exact my pound of flesh from her *and* her lover. Days, weeks… I want her to suffer for as long as possible." He paused to draw a breath. "I'll take both of them, a couple of horses, and find an isolated cottage farther up the coastline, where I can take my time fucking her to the point of death while her fine-mannered lord watches."

"No." Madwulf freed a dagger and proceeded to clean his nails with it. "The commodore is mine. I've been dreaming about his tears since the day he captured me."

"No one touches him!" Horrified, I threw myself forward, jerking against the restraints. "If any of you so much as—"

Warm fingers curled around my mouth and shoved the neckerchief between my lips.

I glared up at Priest, and he glared back, wordlessly warning me he would do more than gag me if I had another outburst.

"You can have Edric's daughter," Madwulf said. *"After* the fellows and I take our turns with her. She was a real bitch when we met, and as it happens, we like them mouthy and kicking. Isn't that right, lads?"

Whistles, stomping boots, and boisterous shouting erupted around the room.

Ice crystallized in my chest.

Priest clicked his tongue. "I'm not sticking my cock anywhere your diseased, unwashed pissers have been."

Silence descended, constricting with unease. That was the thing about disease. When it attacked, it was one against all, and very few escaped. No one joked about it. No one uttered the word *disease*.

Except Priest.

"Pox on the lot of you. Her cunt is mine." He strolled through the room, scratching his whiskered jaw. "You like a little fight in your

Sea of Ruin

women? Some fearful, virginal resistance? You'll find that with any number of the daughters on this island."

Oh, Jesus, Priest. Please, stop.

"I claimed the right to break this one when she killed my father." He flung a scowl in my direction. "She's *my* prize. And her lover, too. It's a fair trade, Madwulf. If not for me, you would still be locked up on HMS *Blitz*."

"If nae for my attack on HMS *Ludwig*," Madwulf said, "she would still be in the admiral's custody. The lads and I will be taking our turns with her. Then you can haul her anywhere you want on horseback. The commodore stays with us."

Fear, cold and sharp, penetrated my gut and chilled me to the bone. I expected to see something similar materialize in Priest's expression, but he remained calm. Confident.

He had a plan.

Some of the tension loosened in my shoulders.

"No." He stalked across the room and lifted an object from a small table. "There's only one way to settle this."

"I'm listening." Madwulf cocked his head.

"A game of chance." He turned, holding an hourglass in his hand. "If I make her come on my finger before the sand runs out, I will fuck her first. If not…" He shrugged. "We'll go with your terms."

Forty-two

I will fuck her first.

A shiver of dread dragged down my spine.

Why had Priest phrased his conditions that way?

Fuck her first? That implied Madwulf and his mates would go next. Priest wouldn't want that. He would cut off his own arms before he let that happen.

Given the banter of lewd comments and vulgar smiles around me, the pirates had interpreted Priest's offer the same way I had. Worse, he hadn't stipulated Ashley's fate in his conditions.

My stomach dropped, and my breathing careened out of control. Amid my unfurling panic, Ashley's hand strained in the restraints behind us until three of his fingers captured mine.

I squeezed back, hanging on. He was lending me his strength, letting me know he was here. It helped me to focus past the fear.

Whatever Priest was planning, it wouldn't end with me being passed around to these scoundrels. I trusted that. I depended on his unwavering, overbearing possessiveness.

Madwulf rose from the chair and strolled toward Priest. "That hourglass measures ten minutes?"

Priest nodded, handing it to him.

"I dinna care how skillful you are with the lasses, libertine." Madwulf cast a thoughtful look at the sand in the glass. "Ten minutes isn't enough time to bring a woman to the acme of excitement."

Priest could do it in two minutes. *Under different circumstances.*

He said nothing, waiting.

"She'll fight you to the death before she surrenders." The uncertainty in Madwulf's eyes belied his smooth smile. "But it'll be fun watching you try. If you fail, we go first. If you succeed, you fuck her in this room while we watch. *Then* we all get a piece."

A muscle flexed in Priest's jaw, and he gave a stiff nod.

Vicious chills attacked my circulation as excitement charged the air. A rippling current of hunger swept through the gathered men, intensifying with the tempo of their breaths.

"Lads?" Madwulf looked around. "Do we accept this proposal?"

A chorus of *Aye's* rang out.

"She doesn't leave the cottage until we're all finished." Madwulf lowered onto the chair closest to me and stretched out his legs. "Go on, then. Finger the cunt."

My insides jumped as Priest approached. He wasn't the only one who had to perform. Whether I faked this or truly surrendered, I would have to make a good show of it.

From Madwulf's perspective, I didn't have a stake in this wager. No matter who won, my outcome would be the same—rape, torture, death. If I looked like I was trying to help Priest win, the ruse would be over.

Damnation, I wasn't on board with this. My body was already trembling, shaking the hell out of my clammy hands.

Ashley held on, his fingers repeatedly clenching and loosening around mine, telling me he was at my side. I didn't know if his proximity would help or hinder my ability to perform. Guilt was already pressing in.

Priest knelt between my legs and gripped the backs of my thighs. My breath hitched.

Leaning around me, he glanced at my bound hands. Ashley didn't release my fingers. Priest showed no reaction to it.

"Ready?" Madwulf balanced the hourglass on his thigh.

"Give me a second." Priest scowled at him. "And stop talking, arsehole."

Sounds of snickering wafted through the cottage.

I hated this. Hated every second that coiled my insides tighter and harder. I couldn't breathe.

Priest sat back on his heels, hooked my legs around his waist, and lifted my thighs so that they rested atop his. Discreetly straightening

Sea of Ruin

the hem of my shirt, he kept me covered as he inched closer on his knees.

The position raised me higher up his muscled thighs until I straddled his lap. He kept an eye on my hands behind me, ensuring the rope didn't tighten and dig into my wrists.

I was entirely at his mercy, with my legs spread around him and my arms bound. A month ago, I would've resented him for this. A month ago, he was the one in restraints. So much had changed since I'd last seen him, but the one true constant was and always would be his obsession with keeping me safe.

He softly glided his hands up my thighs, causing my breaths to quicken. Ashley squeezed my fingers and made a deep threatening noise in his throat. A sound meant for Priest's ears only.

I couldn't look at Ashley, couldn't think about him if I wanted this to work. He would die if Priest failed. I didn't know what the plan was, but it obviously required Priest to fuck me first.

The shaking in my limbs worsened. I bit down on the gag and met his eyes, pleading, soundlessly screaming. For what I didn't know.

Enforced contact with his masculine heat and chiseled physique softened me a little. But what if I couldn't do this? What if he couldn't make me come?

He leaned in between Ashley and me and put his mouth at my ear. "Relax." A guttural whisper. "We've done this hundreds of times."

Not with an audience. And certainly not with a protective lover trussed up beside me.

Hundreds of times. Confound it, Ashley had heard that. He didn't react, didn't move a muscle, but his ear was right next to mine. He now knew that Priest and I had shared much more than one night together.

But one thing I could count on was Ashley's unnatural ability to only show the face he wanted people to see. No one in this room would guess what he was feeling or thinking. *Or hearing.*

I gave his fingers a hard hug with mine, and he squeezed back.

"Time starts now." Madwulf tipped the hourglass.

Ten minutes. I drew in a breath and stared into the molten silver of Priest's stunning eyes.

Never had there been a pirate more gorgeous or seductively built than him. He exemplified manly beauty and virility. Staring at him this close, I was immediately overcome, shook to my soul with love and longing.

Hypnotized, I lost myself in our connection, sinking fast and deep into the mystical alchemy that bound us together so intensely.

Light fingertips tickled between my legs, stirring nerve endings. Calloused fingers. Familiar. Comforting.

"One finger." Madwulf's brogue broke through the spell, tensing my spine. "And I require proof of her lust."

"Every time you speak," Priest snarled over his shoulder, "the sand begins anew. Start it over!"

"Fine." Madwulf reset the hourglass. "Carry on."

Sweat slicked my hands. Ashley's sweat? Mine? We were both perspiring in the clasp of our entwined fingers, the tension unbearable.

Priest set his mouth on my jaw, breathing easily, patiently, as his finger slid along the slit between my legs.

I felt dry down there. Perhaps too dehydrated to produce natural lubricant. But for Priest to succeed, it wouldn't be the physical pleasure that sent me over. It would be our emotional connection. I needed him on that level more than any other.

So I focused on his dependable gaze, on the thoughts he couldn't voice that swirled so turbulently in those eyes. He penetrated me completely, without so much as the tip of his finger in my body.

He penetrated me with his adoration, the force of his steadfast tenacity.

He'd been inside me for three years, stretching out, rearranging things, and making a home for himself. He was stronger than my heart, bigger than my soul, and more powerful than my mind. He symbolized the deepest level of love. Not because he was kneeling beneath me and fingering my cunt, but because he never gave up on me.

I knew he would find me. Never doubted it. I shouldn't have run from him two years ago. I'd been too narrow-minded, too narrow-hearted to hear him, to understand his tragedy in loving two people.

I'd been wrong.

His finger circled my center, never dipping, never entering. The motion was exquisite, overwhelmingly tender, lulling me under his sensual spell.

The heat of his body made my breaths tumble, and his heavenly scent wrapped me in memories of home. My home on *Jade*, surrounded by the sun and sea, with Priest at my side and the aroma of his skin in my lungs—hot and male, leather and sin, everything I craved—imprisoning my senses, possessing me.

He owned me, and he proved it with a single finger as it descended upon my clitoris. His caress enveloped the erectile bud with perfect pressure, diabolical warmth, and uncanny rhythm. Every particle of my being gravitated to him, captivated.

I imagined us together on another plane, in a different realm, united, intertwined, untouchable. *Safe.* I yearned for the feel of his lips, the beat of his heart, and the security of his arms around me. But I couldn't have those things. Not here, where I played the part of a woman paying the price for killing his father.

How much time was left?

My gaze drifted toward Madwulf, but Priest grabbed my throat, forcing my eyes to his.

"Give me your come, Bennett." He rubbed his finger through my growing slickness, arousing and stimulating my body with extraordinary mastery.

But it was that raw, devoted gaze that held me immobile. He loved me with an intensity and forcefulness that ruled him. It was there in his eyes—his instinctual attraction to me, selfless affection, and divine magnetism that went beyond science and nature.

His love was the impetus that opened me to his touch, relaxed me in a way I didn't think possible. I felt the give in my body, the languid loosening of inner muscles beneath the strong, deep throb of desire. A rush of heat rolled forth, my cunt clenching and sucking to be filled and satisfied.

If he were to sink his finger in now, he would find all the drenched proof he needed. But he stayed with my clitoris, working it into a swollen, thrumming knot.

I hovered on the edge, rising, trembling, panting, rocking against his hand, and chasing the high. I couldn't quite get to the ultimate peak. I was close enough to feel the shimmering edges of it, but relief danced just beyond reach.

"Bennett," Priest breathed against the gag in my mouth. "The commodore has a rather large erection in his breeches."

Unbidden, I moaned at the mental image, my attention turning to Ashley. I didn't look at him, but my God, I heard him.

His shallow breaths seethed past the cloth in his mouth. At first, I thought it was rage. But after a closer listen, I detected a low, nearly imperceptible groan. A hungry, continuous groan. It didn't make sense.

Except it did. He understood the stakes, knew I had to achieve climax, and sensed I was close. He was feeding off my arousal and growing hard because he was in this with me, joining the fight instead of fighting against me.

I rebounded off that knowledge, imagining him stiff and engorged in his breeches. Another swamp of heat flooded between my legs.

Priest slid his finger downward and hooked the tip just inside. From there, he slowly circled the sensitive inner rim of my opening, stirring, escalating the hum of sensations. I felt my arousal dribble out, and Christ almighty, it turned me on knowing he felt it, too.

Like a cable pulling too taut, the pressure inside me snapped, shattered, and came crashing down in a glittering shower of star-shine. I threw my head back and moaned as loud as I could past the rag.

"That's my girl," he whispered, his finger swirling lazily, stroking me through the twitching, muscle-heating spasms.

His arm supported my back as I sagged, the hand between my leg still concealed by the shirt. Did we do it in time? My gaze shot to the hourglass on Madwulf's thigh.

Only half the sand had trickled through.

Five minutes.

If Priest wasn't a god, he was damn near close. The entire room held its breath, waiting for proof. No believers here?

"Forgive me for this." Priest moved his mouth against my ear in a hush. "And for everything that comes next."

I'd already forgiven him, but his words made me tense.

He pushed his finger all the way inside me, collecting my arousal as it leaked out over his knuckle. Then he shoved me off his lap as if he couldn't stand the sight of me.

I fell against Ashley, the rope tearing into my wrists. With a furious yelp around the gag, I twisted and jerked into a better position, hoping my drama appeared genuine.

No one paid attention, for every head in the room tracked Priest as he approached their captain. Extending his soaked finger, he held it out for Madwulf's inspection.

Madwulf straightened in the chair and gripped Priest's wrist. He examined *every* finger, confirming that only one had been used, which was undeniably coated in the slippery white proof of my release.

Then he took it a step further and brought it to his nose, inhaling the scent.

Depraved goddamned animal.

"Unbelievable." Madwulf laughed and shoved Priest's hand away. "As a man who's known for his sexual prowess, I daresay you've earned the reputation, king of libertines."

He laughed some more, roaring manically as his men joined in.

Sea of Ruin

My hackles bristled, and old resentment rose to the surface. Priest had been with more women than I cared to estimate, but it didn't matter. Not here. Not ever again.

"I want *that* bed," Priest barked over the commotion and pointed at the small mattress in the corner of the cottage.

There were four beds in total, but the shadows attached themselves to that one, for it was the farthest away from the windows and the congregation of pirates.

Priest turned back to me, stepped over my legs, and crouched before Ashley.

My heart hammered as they stared at each other for a timeless span. I couldn't read either expression, which only heightened my panic.

"I want the truth." Priest grabbed a fistful of black hair and wrenched Ashley's head backward, glowering with a viciousness that scorched. "Do you love her?"

My pulse roared. My teeth sawed against the gag, and my hands wrung in the rope.

Ashley's face remained empty, calm, *fearless*, making Priest wait before he contemptuously thrust his chin up then down, his gaze hardening with a challenging, resounding *Yes*.

Priest released him and stepped back, his carriage taut and rigid as he turned to his audience.

"You want to see what happens when someone wrongs me?" His hands went to his many belts, removing weapons. "Put them both on the bed."

Forty-three

After some shuffling—with Ashley and me fighting through every bruising shove—Madwulf's scoundrels succeeded in putting us on the bed. There were too many hands, too many zealous touches, making my skin shudder. All the while, Priest stood off to the side, instructing them on how to position us.

"Depraved bastards," he mused, casting the comment out as a compliment rather than an insult against anyone's proclivities.

It was true. The pirates damn near trembled with anticipation to witness Priest dole out whatever vile, twisted revenge he had planned. They were so eager, in fact, they hadn't questioned his demand to include Ashley in this sick game. A game that would unquestionably involve Priest's cock and my unwilling body.

Madwulf himself didn't argue when Priest repositioned our restraints to *properly administer the torture*.

Ashley lay face-up on the bed. I straddled his hips, with our hands shackled in front rather than at our backs. We weren't tethered to anything, but it wasn't necessary. Every brute in the room was armed with pistols and blades. The only way we were getting out of this was if half of them vacated the cottage.

That wouldn't happen until everyone had a turn.

With Ashley still in his breeches and me in his shirt, we remained covered and gagged. Priest had removed his weapons, leaving them in a pile on the floor beside the bed. The compass still hung from his many belts. He hadn't parted with it or his clothes, thank God.

Beneath me, Ashley's eyes blazed with rage, his chest riding on labored breaths. Setting my bound hands against his heart, I absorbed the pounding source of his torment.

He didn't deserve this. He'd only been doing his job. If I hadn't entangled Priest in my rescue, Ashley would still have his ship. Madwulf would still be locked up, and Priest would be safe somewhere else.

I'm so damned sorry.

I leaned down, softening my gaze with apologies and choking on a torrent of despair. Ashley's mouth was so close, if not for our gags, I would've felt the velvety warmth of his lips against mine.

His shackled hands lay trapped between our hips. He shifted them, reached down, and curled his fingers against the apex of my legs, cupping me in a startling show of possessiveness.

A chill dripped down my spine. I lifted my head, turned my eyes slowly over my shoulder, and found Priest climbing onto the bed behind me. He knelt between my legs, between Ashley's thighs, forcing us to spread around his muscled lower half.

My pulse lost its rhythm, and the taste of sour milk washed over my tongue.

He untied the flap on the front of his breeches.

This was happening. He was really going to do this with Ashley beneath me. Horrified, I shook with panic and angrily growled my objections behind the rag in my mouth.

"Leave your hands there, Cutler." Priest bowed over my back and grabbed Ashley's throat, pinning him to the mattress. "I want you to feel me when I impale her."

Ashley seethed, his body bucking under mine. Until I felt the cold press of metal against my temple.

Priest's flintlock pistol...gripped in his free hand... He was holding a gun to my head.

Enthusiastic voices raved in the audience, but I didn't hear anything they said. My mouth filled with hot sand, my mind blank with incomprehension.

Why was he doing this? Was this a private war in which a jealous husband wreaked vengeance on his wife and her lover? Or was it part of his plan to help us escape?

I had to trust him. No matter what, I had to believe he wasn't here to hurt me.

Sea of Ruin

"Hold this, would you?" Priest said to the man-eating giant leaning against the wall.

The bearded ogre approached and took the flintlock.

"Careful with the trigger. It's loaded." Priest gripped the barrel, pushing the man's hand farther away from my head. "I just cleaned the flint. It'll spark with barely a twitch. If you spray my face with powder, I'll open your throat before I die, no mistake."

The ogre chuckled in a deep baritone. "I know how to use a pistol, mate."

It wasn't loaded. I couldn't tell by looking at it, but Priest would never take such a risk with my life. No one here knew that, though. Including Ashley.

Priest released Ashley's throat and gripped my hips with both hands. The gravity of what was about to happen crushed my lungs in a vise grip. If we lived, how would we move past this? What did my future even look like with a husband and a lover and...

Stop. Not helping.

I slowly lowered my chest to Ashley's, tucking my bound hands beneath our chins. Priest followed me down, his weight pressing against my back.

"You've put me through hell, sweetheart." His hand slid beneath the shirt covering my backside and moved around near his groin, presumably lining himself up with my body. Then he rested his mouth against my cheek and spoke so quietly I barely heard it. "It's been two years since I've fucked you, Mrs. Farrell."

My heart stopped, and my gaze flew to Ashley.

His eyes widened. His chiseled nostrils pulsed, and his entire body flexed beneath me. Then he slid his hands away from my cunt.

"Scream," Priest whispered and thrust his hips.

Every muscle between my legs clenched, bracing for the burning, stretching agony of a dry invasion. His pelvis rammed into my backside. He groaned with wicked pleasure, and I felt... Nothing.

No intrusion.

No forceful stabbing.

No penetration.

Was he even hard?

Realization punched me in the gut, and I screamed, cursing my delayed reaction. The sound muffled through the gag and shattered the air. He thrust again, and I drew out my cries, sobbing and stiffening as if I were dying of trauma.

He never intended to rape me. Of course, he didn't. The shadowed corner, the positioning of our bodies, the placement of Ashley's hands—all of it had a purpose. To what end, I didn't know. Perhaps he was buying time.

Ashley furiously growled his misery, his eyes wild with madness. But he knew it was all a ruse. His hands fisted between my legs, awkwardly and undeniably, in contact with Priest's cock.

Priest proved to be a remarkable actor. He groaned lewd promises of torture for the room to hear and worked his hips like a savage in the throes of rapturous violence. With his fingers curled around my hips, he kept his groin tight against my backside and roughened the sounds of his breaths.

My shirt covered my thighs, and he still wore his breeches. No one was the wiser from any angle they viewed us.

And view us, they did. The revelry of whistles and stomping grew louder, every man in the cottage saluting Priest's conquest with shouts of encouragement. The ogre wasn't even training the gun on me anymore, his attention absorbed by his friends as they bantered back and forth.

Amid the noise, Priest leaned down against my back and gripped Ashley's hair.

"She didn't tell you, did she?" He pressed closer, making sure Ashley could read his lips. "She's mine, Cutler." He thrust, jarring me against Ashley. "*My* wife."

I sobbed harder, forcing the sounds and faking the tears. But the pain was real. I knew what it felt like to be betrayed and didn't wish that on Ashley. I never wanted him to learn about my marriage like this.

It could've been avoided. I should have told him when I woke on the beach or in the lagoon or while we were still on his ship. There'd been hundreds of opportunities, and I'd put it off like a coward. I was wretched.

His eyes shifted to mine, and what I saw there wasn't resentment or hatred. His gaze moved over my face, warm with understanding. He looked at my shirt, the jade stone at my throat, and returned to my eyes.

I knew in my gut that he was thinking about the conversation we'd had when I was clad in another man's shirt.

"Do you still love him?"

"Who?"

Sea of Ruin

"The man who wore this shirt."

"Yes. I still love him, but I'm working on rectifying that."

"He betrayed you…He bedded another."

"Bedded and loved."

I gave him a discreet nod, silently telling him that Priest was indeed the man who'd betrayed me, the one I still loved.

He turned his attention to Priest, and they exchanged a look I couldn't read at this angle. Maybe not at any angle.

Where was the animosity? The possessive, primitive chest pounding? This was certainly not the time for that, but what passed between them was something akin to an alliance.

Ashley's hands jerked beneath me, the motion of his wrists confusing. One arm slid upward. The other remained stretched toward our legs. Did he…?

Good God, he'd removed his restraints. My heart panted. Not only that, he held something in the hand that fisted between my breasts. The weight of Priest's body kept us pressed together, and flattened along the center of my torso lay the broad, curved shape of steel.

Thunder drove through my veins and crashed in my ears. Priest had given Ashley a blade. It must have happened when he'd untied his breeches. He kept knives beneath his loose shirt and all those belts. It would've been feasible to slip one out and pass it between my legs.

That was why he wanted Ashley's hands there.

Priest continued the pretense of violating my body, stirring a crescendo of huzzahs and applause amongst the unruly onlookers.

With his voice smothered by the noise, he met Ashley's alert gaze. "Just like our ruse with Arabella."

I stopped breathing. Arabella? Ashley's sister?

Ashley's eyes glittered with comprehension. Good for him because I didn't understand any of this. God's teeth, Priest knew Arabella?

My mind spun. He and Ashley shared a history *and* a plan I wasn't privy to.

"Give him your hands," Priest breathed at my ear and pushed off my body with a pained roar.

My heart beat in rapid-fire as I shoved my wrists toward the knife Ashley held between us. No one noticed, for all eyes tracked Priest's strange grunting and stumbling beside the bed.

He tucked himself into his breeches, groaning as if the action pelted him with agony.

The pirates fell quiet.

"You dinna finish." Madwulf's skeptical voice broke from the crowd. "What's wrong with you, lad?"

"Nothing," Priest snapped, fumbling with the laces at his groin.

I realized that the grinding friction against my backside hadn't made his body respond at all. Hard to orgasm without an erection. I didn't believe for a minute that he couldn't perform in front of an audience. Something else was going on. Was it related to the burn scars that covered one side of his body?

"Captain..." The ogre stepped forward, staring at Priest's lower regions. "It's his pisser."

The rope around my wrists frayed and fell away. *Hallelujah.* Now that I was free, it would only take a second to go for Priest's blades on the floor.

"Show us." Madwulf stood and prowled toward Priest. "Let's see your cock."

"I'm not showing you a tarnal thing." Turning away, Priest continued to clumsily lace his breeches, deliberately drawing out his efforts.

Madwulf motioned to the ogre, who trained the flintlock at Priest's head. *Priest's* flintlock, which wasn't loaded.

Priest had planned for this.

"Open your breeches." Madwulf glared, his face turning crimson.

Beneath me, Ashley's empty hand moved between our hips. He inched it out and to the side near the wall. Wait, no, it wasn't empty. His fingers opened, and the smashed wedge of an orange rolled off the mattress and into the shadowed corner behind the bed.

The plate of oranges on the table, Ashley's hands between my legs... My senses heightened with comprehension. Priest had given Ashley the fruit while opening his breeches behind me, and somehow Ashley had known what to do with it.

Priest grinned, an impish curve of sensual lips. "I didn't realize you fancied me that way, Madwulf."

"If I dinna see your cock in the next two seconds, there won't be any of it left to hold onto."

I held my breath as Priest dropped the smile and exposed himself beneath the barrel of an unloaded gun.

"Syphilis." The ogre made the sign of the cross with three fingers and backed away.

Not syphilis. The same red blisters that I'd inflicted on Priest's hands a month ago now covered his groin. Christ, it looked excruciating. No wonder he hadn't gotten an erection. He must have been in horrible agony, burning and inconsolably itchy.

Ashley's features gave no reaction. Except for the glint in his eyes. He definitely knew about Priest's affliction from oranges.

"What have you done?" Madwulf gripped his brow and retreated, too. "You're infected. You… You contaminated her!"

Everyone knew about the infinite numbers of syphilis patients clogging hospitals and infirmaries throughout the West Indies. Without a cure, the plague tortured its victims with pestilential rashes and sores, facial disfigurement, blindness, madness, and hair loss.

Fear of baldness swept the high seas, and that was precisely the concern among every sea robber here.

Faces glistened with nervous sweat. Eyes widened. Hands flew to beards and long braids of cherished hair. No pirate wanted to be bald. It was a fate worse than losing a limb.

Priest fastened his breeches, his expression strained with pain. That part wasn't fake. He'd hurt himself to protect me. None of Madwulf's men would touch me now.

Every pirate in the room was standing, looking at the exit as if ready to bolt.

"Captain." An older man burst into the cottage, oblivious to what was unfolding inside. "Cargo's loaded. She's ready to weigh anchor, and we got a perfect wind to let her sheets fly and push us straight past the island."

Madwulf's glare swung coldly to Priest as he spoke to his crew. "Tell everyone to return to the ship and prepare to weigh. Four of you will stay with me until I finish this."

No one argued. Most of them looked relieved to not have to handle the *diseased* prisoners.

As the room scattered, my muscles and joints locked up, bracing for battle. Five of them against the three of us? We could overpower them, especially with the element of surprise. If we killed them quietly, without gunfire, we had a real chance of escape.

"Do you ken what she did the day I met her? When I grabbed her filthy cunt?" Madwulf yanked the neck of his shirt to the side, revealing the fading pinkish imprint of my teeth marks. "I was looking forward to collecting my retribution." He spat a wet clump of phlegm on the floorboards at Priest's feet. "You tricked me, libertine."

Priest stepped over the spittle and bent to collect his weapons. "Perhaps you should learn how to negotiate."

Ashley had said those exact words to me once.

Careful with the knife, I gripped Ashley's hands between us and soaked in the calmness on his face. Whatever Priest was up to, Ashley showed no signs of concern.

Warmth filled my chest as I pressed my gagged mouth against his neck in a gesture of oneness. We would live together or die together. The three of us. Their happiness would be the most important thing I ever fought for.

"We had an agreement." Securing his daggers to his baldric and belts, Priest met Madwulf's stare. "Fuck her or leave. Either way, the prisoners stay with me. I'm nowhere near finished with them."

"Cutler is mine. He was never part of the agreement." Madwulf turned and strolled toward the door, addressing his men. "Kill the pirate hunter."

"Without a vote, Captain?" the ogre asked.

"Vote if you want. I'm leaving this bloody island."

My fingers twitched to curl around that bastard's neck until he soiled his breeches with the stink of fear. I tracked his gait through the cottage, hoping he would stick around long enough to fight me.

The ogre turned toward us and raised the flintlock. "Better move, Miss, or you'll be eating powder, too."

He didn't wait. His fat finger squeezed the trigger. The flint struck the hammer, and nothing sparked. Just as I thought. Not loaded.

Confusion gave the giant pause, and that was our cue.

Ashley and I bounded off the bed.

Forty-four

Pulse booming, I yanked off my gag and scanned the floor for a weapon. *Gone. All of them.* With a savage curse, I whirled, stumbled, and came face to face with Priest. He tossed me his cutlass and slammed a second blade into the giant's eye socket.

The clang of steel against steel rang out behind me. Ashley was already engaged in battle.

Raising the heavy cutlass, I searched the cottage for my target, didn't spot Madwulf, but a nasty-looking fellow was scowling right at me. He would do.

We charged at the same time. As he reached me, I ducked, spun, and sliced the blade across his throat, just like my father had taught me. A second spin, however, had me staring down the barrel of a musket.

This pirate laughed like a rabid dog. I would stab him low, right beneath the ribs. But before my arms were in motion, blood sprayed across my chest.

Priest slid his dagger from the man's throat, leaned over the falling body, and smacked a hard kiss on my lips. "Missed you terribly, my love."

"Missed you—"

He was already gone, leaping over another corpse and racing toward the last two men standing.

It was Ashley, still wearing his gag and fighting for his life with a honed intensity that stole my breath. He battled a lean, agile blackguard, who refused to go down. They flew at each other with lethal arcs, hacking, chopping, and wielding their blades with savage purpose.

This wasn't a nobleman's sport. It was life and death. Sweat beaded Ashley's brow. Tendons flexed in his forearms. He was fighting the strongest, fastest pirate I'd seen in years and holding his own impressively.

Priest rushed in behind Ashley, who punched out a bare foot and collided with the enemy's groin. The kick sent the man stumbling, but he remained on his feet. Ashley renewed his attack with Priest at his side.

It was a beautiful thing to watch—the two of them together, thrusting, grunting, and putting those mouthwatering muscles to practical use. Their physiques were so much more than just an indulgence for the female eye. Strong as oxen and skilled with weaponry, together, they were a mighty force to reckon with.

How did they know each other? Had they met through Ashley's sister, Arabella?

I desperately just wanted to take a moment and appreciate the view, soak them in, and commit every gorgeous detail to memory. But as Ashley's blade came up and knocked the blackguard's dagger from his hand, I knew they had it under control.

Turning toward the door, I headed out to look for Madwulf. If he was already off the sand and on his way to the ship, I'd let him go. But I also needed to see who was lingering out there and clear the perimeter for escape.

Clutching tight to the hilt of the cutlass, I crept on silent feet and picked through the sounds of waves crashing on the shore, seagulls screeching overhead, and in the distance, Madwulf's crew laughing on the ship.

I cautiously stepped over the threshold, my senses on high alert. The angle of the doorway faced away from *Blitz*. I needed to round the corner to view it.

"Priest...Ashley," I whisper-hissed over my shoulder. "Let's go."

A muffled feminine cry hit my ears, spiraling tingles across my scalp.

The sound came from around the side of the cottage, garbled as if a hand was smothering her mouth. Then another wail joined in, higher-pitched, younger, female.

A child.

My heart felt the chill of winter in Carolina, my limbs frozen in

Sea of Ruin

horror. I hadn't had time to ponder what might have become of the women on this island, but I was about to see it firsthand.

With a shake, I pulled myself from the grip of fear and started forward. Until a hand grabbed the back of my shirt.

Over my shoulder, I found Ashley's eyes harder than I'd ever seen them, his teeth bared now that the gag was gone. Beside him, Priest's mean mouth anchored itself in a scowl.

I didn't have to tell them to listen. The sounds of crying grew closer, louder. Seconds later, Madwulf emerged from around the corner, dragging a petite blond girl who couldn't have been older than thirteen.

With a fist in her hair and a knife against her tiny throat, he jerked his chin at something out of view.

Footsteps advanced. Pirates rounded the corner, and I found myself staring at the six or so men who had left the cottage only minutes ago. One of them restrained a sobbing woman in her thirties, presumably the child's mother, with his hand covering her mouth.

My hopes for escape sank like a burning ship to the bottom of the sea.

I tightened my grip on the cutlass. Priest and Ashley flanked me, fisting knives in both hands.

"What do you want?" Ashley shifted closer and slightly in front of me as if preparing to shove me back. "You already have my ship and my soldiers. My career is ruined. I won't be able to show my face in London again. My life is over."

He didn't cant the words in a whining, pompous voice. He spoke coldly in a tone he reserved for low-ranking servants. Or for fools who made the mistake of inciting the murderous side of his unseemly manners.

"Your life isn't over," Madwulf said, "until your head is separated from your body. Set down your weapons." He wrenched hard on the girl's hair, making her sob. "Or this pretty little lass won't see her next sunrise."

The mother shrieked behind the pirate's hand, her fear trickling sparks of pain through my chest. Madwulf hadn't made a hollow threat. His eyes burned with vindictive anticipation in cutting the child while we watched.

With effort, I loosened my grip on the cutlass enough to drop it. But Priest and Ashley didn't move.

"Do it," I said to them. "He'll kill her."

The potent masculine energy on either side of me held still.

Twisting my neck, I found Priest staring furiously at me with those blade-sharp eyes. Yes, he despised this as much as I did. But he didn't have to hammer the point home with his withering, belligerent glare.

I refused to back down and returned his scowl with one of my own.

At last, with an enraged grunt, he surrendered his weapons.

Meeting the same resistance with Ashley, I stood my ground until he dropped his blades. Between the two of them, I'd never seen such torment. It was true that, disarmed and defenseless, our chances of survival were slim to none. But I had a plan.

"Release the girl, Madwulf." I crossed my arms, shielding the rapid rise and fall of my chest. "We did what you asked."

Without warning, a new swarm of pirates spilled out from around both sides of the cottage. All at once, we were overrun with nowhere to go. The hostile mob fell upon us too fast, with too many weapons. Some held us down. Others restrained our arms with rope.

Outrage and helplessness swept through me. I kept my eyes on the child, knowing that one wrong move would end her life.

Within seconds, Priest, Ashley, and I were shoved to our knees, hands bound behind us, in the horrifying custody of Madwulf MacNally. I ordered my damned tears not to fall, even as they clogged my eyes and turned my captor blurry.

He shoved the girl into the arms of a nearby pirate and stared at me in a way that could only be defined as evil. "Kill them."

In my periphery, a cutlass reared back, aiming for Ashley's head.

"Noooo! Wait!" The hysteria in my voice pierced the air. "I have something you want!"

Madwulf held up a hand, staying the man with the blade. "You have nothing left, Bennett. Nothing to barter. But tell me this. Why would the Feral Priest surrender his life for the woman who killed his father?"

The truth. I still had that, and it would work in my favor. "Priest Farrell is my husband. And he loathed his father."

Madwulf narrowed his eyes, sharp and disbelieving.

"What are you doing, Bennett?" Priest growled behind me. "Shut up and let me handle—"

I talked over his fury and told Madwulf how I arrived in this unfortunate position between my lover and my husband. I explained Priest's infidelity, his two-year hunt for me, how I came into Ashley's custody, and ultimately fell in love with him.

The one crucial detail I left out was my ruse on *Jade*. I led Madwulf to believe that my crew tossed me overboard and fled without looking

Sea of Ruin

back. I did *not* want him to know that my galleon was waiting for me on the opposite end of this island.

"So you're married to the libertine." Madwulf paced in front of me. "You love them both. They both love you, and if I dinna kill them, they'll probably kill each other?"

"Probably."

Maybe. Maybe not. The question of how they knew each other still clawed in the back of my mind.

With a disgusted expression, Madwulf stared me up and down. "If the libertine loves you, why would he expose you to syphilis?"

"I already had it, and truly, Captain, that's the least of my concerns." I poured the sincerity of that declaration into my voice and eyes. "I would die for them. Spare their lives, and I will give you more wealth than you would ever acquire with *Blitz* under your command."

"Where is your wealth, lass?" Madwulf looked around, laughing. "You have nothing!"

"I'm the daughter of Edric Sharp, you ignorant tar. Where do you think all his spoils went?"

"She's lying!" Kneeling beside me, Priest bellowed and jerked against the hands that restrained him. "Don't believe anything she says."

Stillness fell over Madwulf as he watched us closely. I had his attention.

"There's an invaluable compass attached to Mr. Farrell's person." I pulled in a deep breath and released it. "Relieve him of it, if you please. It belonged to my father."

"With pleasure." Madwulf nodded to one of his men.

Everything inside me stopped as my most cherished possession was wrenched from the body of my seething, snarling husband. My gaze clung to the polished brass casing while it passed from one hand to the next, ending with Madwulf.

"It's a puzzle." I swallowed down the knot in my throat, refusing to let my grief shine. "My father hid all his treasures, locked the map of the location in that compass, and gave it to me the day he hanged. The keyhole will reveal itself with the correct combination of movements. I wear the key around my neck."

The sudden glare of a dozen pairs of eyes seared my throat.

"You can't open it," I said hastily. "Not without the secret instructions, which are locked inside my head. If I die, the combination dies with me. If you kill Priest and Ashley, I will die with them, for it would be too painful to live. You can torture me for the instructions, but I swear to God, Madwulf, if you hurt them, there will be nothing left of me to break."

"She doesn't know the combination. It's a trick." Priest tried to stand and rush forward, only to be shoved face-first into the sand.

"She never mentioned a goddamned compass or a secret map." Ashley gnashed his teeth. "She's leading you on a wild chase. Same thing she did to me when she sent me after Priest in Nassau."

I fisted my hands in the rope. *Irritating, overprotective arseholes.*

"Gag the husband and pirate hunter and string them up to a tree," Madwulf said absently, his gaze locked on the compass in his hand. "This opens with that green stone on your neck?"

"Yes, the key *and* a combination of movements."

"All right." He prowled forward and crouched at eye level with my kneeling position. "Open it, and I'll let your lads live."

A few yards away, Priest and Ashley roared and snarled behind their gags, uselessly fighting the men who trussed them to a palm-tree.

I blocked their torment out of my mind and focused on Madwulf's offer.

Firstly, he couldn't be trusted. Even if I could unlock the compass straight away, he would take the map, kill all three of us, and claim my father's treasure. Secondly, I'd spent the last seven years trying to unlock the instrument without any luck.

But that was before my last conversation with Priest. Before he'd shared what he'd learned from the compass maker's son.

Every instrument was built with a key and a list of verbal instructions. Something to hide on your body and something to hide in your mind.

The answer was buried in my head. I was certain my father had given the instructions to me. But how? In a riddle? A song? Christ, he'd taught me so many things over the fourteen years I'd known him, so much of it through lyrics and storytelling. I couldn't remember half of it.

Right now, all that mattered was getting Madwulf and his band of outlaws off this island without killing the two men I loved.

"I don't trust you, you scurvy dog." I glared at the brass instrument held out in his hand. "You want that open? Here are my conditions. No one else dies here. Not that little girl or her mother. Not Priest or Ashley. Take me with you. When we weigh anchor, I want visual proof that Priest and Ashley are still alive. Then I'll need some time to unlock the puzzle. Once I do, you can take the map without showing it to me and put me ashore on any island you please."

The last part wouldn't come to fruition. Madwulf would kill me to ensure I never tried to reclaim my father's spoils.

"How long will it take to open?" he asked.

"I don't know. I have a lot of combinations in my head." I quickly explained to him how I'd only just learned the details about the use of a key and a list of instructions.

"You're certain you can unlock it?"

"I swear it." I set my forehead upon his thigh and held it there, knowing the submissive gesture would move him.

He rose, pulling me to stand with him. "Let's weigh, laddies!"

With his hand on my arm, I stumbled after him, trying to keep up with his gait. The beach lay barren around us, all the farmers and fishermen either hiding in their dwellings or dead.

As we passed the palm-tree, the vibrations of gagged, wrathful shouting from Priest and Ashley tightened my insides. I sucked in a breath and bolted, erasing the distance between us in three long strides.

Footsteps gave chase, but I made it to the tree and crashed onto Priest's lap, landing ungracefully with my arms bound.

"The bird island," I whispered in a panic. "Find me there."

Arms wrenched me away, and a hand grabbed my throat, choking me.

"What did you say to him?" Madwulf put his face in mine, seething.

"I forgive you." I twisted my neck, locking onto Priest's blazing silver eyes. "All my resentment and scorn… Honest to God, Priest, it's gone. I love you." I turned my gaze to Ashley, shivering at the cold, hard anger icing his expression. "I love you both."

"That's enough." Madwulf laughed and shook his head. "Let's go before I shed a tear."

The force of rage and unholy violence wafting from Priest and Ashley caught my chest on fire. My gaze didn't stray from them as Madwulf hauled me away. I would see them again. I had to believe that.

If they traveled by horseback, they would reach Harbour Island within two or three days.

If *Jade* was still anchored there after a month of waiting, they would have a ship to hunt me down.

If I could trick Madwulf into plotting a course to the tiny uninhabited island north of Anguilla—the home of more nesting birds than I'd ever seen in my life—Priest and Ashley would find me.

Maybe.

Hopefully.

That was a lot of *ifs*. Too many.

My heart constricted so painfully I felt a sickening crunch as it collapsed in on itself.

I'd conceived many wild plans in my lifetime. Some worked. Some failed magnificently. This might be my flimsiest, most hole-ridden scheme yet.

As Madwulf dragged me toward the longboat, I cursed my lack of clothing. Once again, I would be boarding *Blitz* wearing only a man's shirt and the jade stone. *Ashley's* shirt this time. And it was much worse for wear, hanging in tatters around my thighs.

The crew wouldn't rape me, for fear of contracting syphilis.

But there were endless other ways to hurt a woman.

Forty-five

Standing at the bow of *Blitz*, I held a spyglass to my eye and sank into the overwhelming relief in my chest. The distant palm-tree, with two savagely determined men tied to it, filled the spherical field.

They were still alive, and in a few minutes, the greatest threat against them would sail far away from this cay.

Behind me, seamen strained at the capstan. Others hauled lines and howled with excited laughter. The anchor heaved from the water. Yards swung. Sheets hissed, and the mainsail turned hard, thrilling with the power of the trade wind. A mist of warm spray slashed my cheeks as the warship luffed away from the sand and cast a wide arc toward the blue swells of the open sea.

A tingle raced up my spine, and the glass was yanked from my grip. An iron shackle went about my ankle, connected to a short chain that secured me to the foremast on the upper deck. There, I sat, awaiting my fate amid a menagerie of live chickens, goats, and pigs.

Ashley would have a fit if he saw his ship in such filthy disarray. To think that only yesterday, most of these men had reported to him with the utmost discipline and respect. I supposed the promise of riches and merriment could buy just about any soul.

I depended on that as Madwulf prowled toward me.

He crouched within arm's reach, joined by two beastly pirates standing at his back. I emptied my expression, squared my shoulders, and met his hard stare with one of my own.

For endless seconds, he held me in deliberate discomfiting eye contact. A tactic meant to intimidate. I sat taller, unmoving, and waited.

"We can be friends, Miss Sharp." He held out the compass, daring me to grab it. "Just give me the combination."

"I'll give you something, darling." My mouth twisted. "How about an oozing rash? Or a bald head? Just come a little closer."

He hissed past his teeth and reached for the red beard that no longer hung from his chin.

"Oh, for the love of God." I leaned back against the mast behind me, reclining. "The big brave Highlander can't take a joke?"

"Not about that." His gaze dipped to my throat, narrowing on the jade stone. It was useless to him without a keyhole. Perhaps that was why he hadn't taken it from me yet. "Tell me everything you ken about the puzzle."

"Well… When my father gave it to me," I said without emotion, hoping he wouldn't smell the lie, "he talked about an island of birds."

"Where?"

"Near Anguilla, I think." I blew out a sigh. "I don't really know. I was young."

"What else?"

"Truly, Captain, I need time to sift through my memories and figure out the combination. But I *will*. I'll unlock the damned thing if you get out of my face and leave me alone."

I needed to give Priest and Ashley time to race to Harbour Island and sail *Jade* down the coast of Eleuthera to my current location. If they didn't encounter any delays, they would only be three days behind *Blitz*.

"You need an incentive." Madwulf stood and clasped his hands behind his back.

Incentive? I tensed, every muscle on high alert. His two rogues rushed forward and towered over either side of me. I didn't flinch, didn't look away from the Scotsman.

He flicked his gaze at the men, and a second later, they had me on my feet and held between them.

My pulse accelerated. My legs felt like water, but I refused to avert my gaze from Madwulf.

A third man from Madwulf's crew appeared at my side. In his fists, he held a broad, flat wooden plank like a sword.

I swallowed, unable to feel my tongue or my face or the deck beneath my feet.

In a blur of movement, the pirates manhandled my arms, jerking me

Sea of Ruin

this way and that. The iron on my ankle galled my skin as I tried to kick and twist away. But they overpowered me by sheer strength and numbers.

As they held me where they wanted me, I had no choice but to tuck my elbows in tight and protect vital organs.

The plank swung, colliding with the front of my thigh. My teeth slammed into my tongue. I cried out, and my entire body jolted with inconsolable agony.

My head dropped forward as I sagged and grunted with excruciating breaths, moaning, pleading with the pain, begging it to stop. It felt as though my leg had been ripped from my body.

The tars tossed me onto the deck, sending another wave of anguish through my thigh. I lay there, gasping through the splintering torment.

It took a minute before I could push up to sit. Resting on the opposite hip, I met Madwulf's pitiless gaze with the bravest face I could muster.

"On the morrow, at eight bells of the morning watch, I shall return." He dropped the compass onto my lap. "If it's not unlocked, I'll provide another incentive. I'll do this every morning, and each incentive will become increasingly more convincing. I do hope you solve the puzzle before you're too broken."

He ambled away, and I hugged the compass to my chest, realizing my shirt was still awash in the sticky blood from the man in the cottage. I felt sick. Scared. Angry.

Daily beatings.

The horrendous pain in my thigh would be less pronounced by the morning. I could do this. I'd endured a fortnight of torture on the admiral's flagship. Blows against my bones with a wooden plank were less intrusive, less damaging to my psyche. I would survive this.

I wanted to see Priest and Ashley again too badly to give up.

Gripping both hands under the knee of my injured leg, I dragged it out in front of me. My choked whimpers couldn't be helped. The agony swept through me like fire, but the limb didn't look broken. No visible bones protruded. No unnatural angles. Just muscle and ligament damage, perhaps.

As the Caribbee heat blazed down upon my pale skin, I scooted into a patch of shade cast by the rigging. Over the next few hours, I moved with that shadow, desperate for its cool protection as it crept across the deck with the passage of the sun.

Blitz headed east. The bird island was southeast. If Madwulf had taken my bait, we would be headed there. But it was too soon to know.

That night, I lay on my back on the deck, staring up at the starlit sky and thinking about my father. I'd toyed with the compass all afternoon without any real commitment to opening it.

It was time to solve it. Shackled to the foremast, I faced certain torture on the morrow. At some point, I would have to give up the combination in exchange for mercy. But I needed to figure it out first.

So I closed my eyes and mentally recited poems, songs, and rhymes that I remembered hearing in my father's Irish brogue. God's wounds, I missed him. If he were alive today, perhaps he would be disappointed in me for taking so long to solve his puzzle.

When you're ready, you'll know what to do.

I didn't know what he'd meant when he said that, but his compass had saved the two men I'd left on the beach. I didn't think he would mind that I'd bartered his treasure in the name of love.

Maybe, if I unlocked it at the right moment, it would save my life, too. I just needed to be strong and patient.

My strength, however, waned miserably over the next few days.

Each day, at eight bells of the morning watch, Madwulf emerged from the lower decks. "Unlock the compass, lass."

"I'm trying."

Standing calmly before me, he signaled to his brutes and watched coldly as the plank of wood damaged another part of my body. It struck my ribs on the second day, my shoulder on the third. By the fourth morning, the pain was so tremendous I hadn't slept.

I couldn't stop shaking. Couldn't stop whimpering. Couldn't eat or breathe or focus on anything beyond the terrible, constant agony that decimated every muscle and bone.

My leg had swollen into a contusion of black and blue damage from hip to knee. Though I couldn't stand on it, it was the least of my tribulation.

The ladder of bones beneath my left breast had broken in several places. I was certain of it, for every breath made me cry out and wheeze. And my arm refused to respond. It wouldn't lift or move in any way. Dislocated shoulder? Possibly worse.

My teeth rattled endlessly, my nerves and sinews ceaselessly twitching and convulsing. The pain governed me, overtaking my motor functions, and the dread was more than I could bear. Could I withstand another blow from that plank?

Adding to the misery, the moon and stars had abandoned their

Sea of Ruin

watch over me. Clouds crowded the sky, black and brooding, rolling alongside *Blitz* as if set on the same course.

Where were we headed? The compass said south. The direction of the bird island. But after four days, we should have already arrived. I feared we'd gone too far east and overshot the destination. *Jade's* destination, if all had gone as I hoped.

Madwulf never mentioned a route, and the crew didn't speak of it.

Throughout the voyage, they lived loudly and boisterously, soaring with high spirits on board Ashley's ship. Heavy drinking ran rampant day and night. The supply of farm animals dwindled as they gorged on freshly slaughtered meat. Sometimes, they tossed raw scraps to me, laughing and keeping their distance as if *I* were the feral dog.

As if.

As a result of their excessive drinking, eating, and overall misbehavior, they failed to do much of anything for the better part of a week. Madwulf didn't partake in the merriment. He didn't discourage it, either. Remaining below deck, he presumably indulged in the luxuries of the private quarters and slept in the bed I'd shared with Ashley.

It became my practice to block it all out. I sat with my back to the unruly festivities, turning the compass on my lap and reciting every rhyme I knew. All the while, I strained my eyes on the distant horizon, watching, hoping, wishing for sails to appear.

The prospect of *Jade* coming near this one-hundred-gun warship again scared me to death. But my crew knew what they were dealing with this go around, and Priest and Ashley would be with them. Ashley knew *Blitz's* weaknesses. If anyone could defeat her, it was him.

More storm clouds rolled in, stealing my view of the horizon. The heavy overcast forced me to stare at the deck, the gunwale, anything or nothing at all, as long as I didn't glance down. One glimpse at my abused body shoved me into the shadows whereupon the pain resided, dark and hopeless.

On the fourth morning, Madwulf paced before me, visibly agitated. "You look like death's head upon a mop-stick. Ghastly, truly. I wouldn't ride you into battle."

"Rot in hell."

"Open the compass, Bennett."

"I said go to he—"

Hands shot out from behind me and wrenched my injured shoulder backward. The joint screamed, shooting blades of racking pain through my neck and chest.

My attacker was joined by another, and together, they pinned my elbow against the foremast, holding it with my forearm extending past the timber. The agony in my shoulder throbbed so brutally I drowned in the nauseous, spinning dizziness. Black dots peppered my vision. Acid seared my throat, and excess saliva filled my mouth.

The brute with the wooden plank approached.

"No." I shook my head wildly and dropped the compass in a useless effort to jerk free. "No, no, no, no! Please! I'll unlock it right now. I promise."

The two men restrained me as the brute with the board swung it hard and fast at my forearm. The blow hit like lightning, snapping my arm backward at the wrong angle. Bones cracked from elbow to wrist.

I screamed, choking on the anguish. Ice surged from my feet to my chest, chased by a boiling eruption of vomit.

The contents of my stomach expelled past my lips. That was the last thing I remembered before passing out.

Forty-six

I floated back to consciousness on the wings of my father's words.
Start and end north.

His warm, soothing brogue began to sing to me from somewhere behind, overhead, and all around…

Oh, sad fellow, by the thrust of my blade
North to south, click, click
South to east, one tick

I remembered it as a cheerful melody with morbid lyrics. It had been so long since I'd thought of it. How did the rest go? I crawled through the strange wet fog around me, humming along and searching for the words.

Until a sharp, stabbing throb caught me unawares.

With a gasp, I found myself lying face-up, choking, drowning as if submerged in the sea. The deck stretched out beneath me. The stink of farm animals flooded my nose. My limbs felt weighted, my entire body soaked. If I had to guess, someone had dumped a bucket of water on me to rouse me.

Sounds were distant. Garbled. Voices. Someone was talking to me, saying my name over and over. That English accent didn't make sense. I recognized it and turned my head, seeking its face and blinking through sheets of misery. Christ almighty, I hurt…everywhere.

My eyes opened, and I stared up at the concerned mien of Lieutenant Flemming.

Bending over me, the blond doctor reached down and gently tipped my chin side to side. Creases fanned from the corners of his miserable eyes, his face pale with fear.

Given his crestfallen expression, he wasn't here as a willing new recruit. He was a captive, just like me. Because every pirate crew needed a doctor, and Flemming happened to be the only ship's surgeon on *Blitz*.

"Where are we?" I croaked.

His head angled down, shaking slightly as his eyes lifted to the pirates lounging, drinking, and belching around us.

"The arm will need to be set and braced, sir." Flemming sat back and looked up at whoever stood outside of my view.

"I dinna care about fixing her." Madwulf's voice sieved through my chest like ice water. "Just keep her alive long enough to open that compass."

The task of solving the puzzle suddenly felt too big, too impossible, and it grew more so as I turned my neck and saw the mutilated wreckage of my arm.

A splintered white bone protruded from a bloody gouge near the inside of my elbow. My forearm curved outward in an unnatural angle, lying like a dead, displaced thing on the deck.

I gagged and released a soundless scream as my stomach clenched and heaved. Viscid, bitter fluid projected from my mouth, and the shivering… God save me, the tremors were overpowering, uncontrollable. As the magnitude of my injury forced itself upon me, I shook with a violence that engaged every muscle and ripped apart every nerve.

No need to look at Lieutenant Flemming's grim face to glean my fate. I wouldn't survive this. My heart had known that all along, but the bulwark of stubbornness within hadn't allowed me to accept it.

As Flemming tipped a medicine vial and poured a sizzling liquid over my exposed bone, the unholy pain tried to drag me into its darkness again. Blood ran cold through my veins, and my breaths hissed wetly past my clenched teeth, each exhale riding on the lamenting sounds of my cries.

Through the haze, a final wish rose to the surface. A wish I'd carried with me since the day I found my father hanging on the gallows.

Before I died, I had to see inside his compass. I desperately needed to hold and smell and read whatever he'd left for me.

Flemming squeezed a water-soaked cloth over my mouth, offering fluids. Then he padded away, disappearing below deck with his chest of supplies and flanked by two pirates. Madwulf moved in, taking his place.

Refusing to be goaded, I pressed my lips together and glared mutely up at him.

"It's all good, lass." He touched a jagged fingernail against my cheek and softly cleared wet locks of curls from my face. Then he set the compass on the deck beside me, his eyes hard, intent, determined. "Unlock it, and all the pain goes away."

"Aye." My teeth chattered, slicing up my tongue as I tried to roll into a sitting position. "Can…y-you…help…?"

He gripped my good arm and hauled me up. The sudden movement hurled me into a spinning, blinding vortex of queasiness. I dry heaved through the misery until my back settled against the foremast.

Weakness, pain, and fatigue plagued my body, pushing me down into an awkward, uncomfortable slump. I couldn't straighten or move without blacking out, so I remained where he left me, dragged the compass closer to my hip by the chain, and threw every ounce of concentration into solving the puzzle.

Hours passed, and night fell too soon. I lost precious time during bouts of unconsciousness, but I was getting closer to remembering the song my father had taught me. It was the only rhyme I knew that mentioned navigational points of direction. But no matter how many times I turned the instrument along with the chant, nothing happened.

The darkness didn't help. A thick black blanket of dreary fog hung over the ship, snuffing out the moonlight, the lantern light, and everything around me. I couldn't see the dial on the compass, and with every passing minute, my body began to give up.

Morning arrived with a horrifying awakening. I'd evaded sleep, but my mind wasn't working right. There were moments when I remembered the entire song, but the compass didn't respond to the combination of steps. I was doing something wrong.

I was out of time.

Amid the damp, dense mist, Madwulf's silhouette appeared.

Right on cue, someone struck the ship's bell. Once… Twice… Between each of the eight resonant rings, I swore I heard the squawking of nesting birds. My heart jolted.

Madwulf nodded at something behind me. I didn't see it coming, but I heard the swing of the plank whistling through the air before it collided with the side of my face.

The force of it sent me flying sideways, rupturing my ear and jaw in a jarring clap of thunder. I collapsed on the deck, clutching the compass and swimming in a smothering, crippling pool of pain.

Blood spurted past my lips. My mouth gaped open, and my throat burned raw with my screams. The vibration of my shrilling voice battled the explosion of anguish in my skull. But I couldn't hear it. I couldn't detect a single sound.

Swallowed whole by the agony, I wept in the startling silence. The deck was hard and sticky beneath my cheek, the constant punch of pain swarming from every direction, tearing through my ribs, chewing at my arm, and piercing my head like the tireless stabbing of a sword.

Sanguine droplets spluttered from my mouth and stained the deck. All I could do was stare at those red beads of blood, and in that moment of noiseless clarity, I mentally hummed.

Oh, poor fellow, your life will end
And I say so, and I know so
Oh, sad fellow, by the thrust of my blade
North to south, click, click
South to east, one tick
I'll cut you thrice, east to west
I'll spear you once, west to north
Say I, dead man, you met your end
I'll drop you down to the depths of the sea
Where the sharks'll have your body
And the devil'll have your soul

The *clicking, ticking, once, thrice* verbiage hadn't made sense before, so I'd ignored those parts. Perhaps that was where I'd gone wrong.

Determination took over.

Sprawled on my side with my weight on my uninjured shoulder, I exerted more energy than I thought capable as I dragged my hand—which still held the compass—toward my face.

A smear of something thick and dark blurred my right eye. Swollen skin? Broken vessels? I strained to see through the partial vision. Worse, I still couldn't hear a single sound. Even my breaths had been silenced.

It didn't matter. Listening wasn't required as I dug down deep and

Sea of Ruin

gathered the last vestige of my strength. I just needed enough grit to stay awake and turn the dial.

The world narrowed to my father's song and the rotation of the brass casing in my hand. *North to south.* I depressed the center pin on which the needle turned. *Two clicks.* Did I just feel a spring release inside? My pulse quickened.

Carefully, hurriedly, I followed the series of steps in the rhyme, gritting my teeth as pain swept up and down my body, wracking me from the inside out.

When I reached the end of the song, the needle felt unsteady as if it had been ejected from its housing. I slowly lifted it away, shaking with shock. It had *never* done that before. Whatever had held the dial onto the compass had been rotated away like a vise opening its toothy grip.

My fingers trembled as I untied the leather thong around my neck and inserted the stone in the hole in the center.

It fit.

Start and end north.

I turned the compass north.

A series of springs vibrated inside the casing. Without my hearing, I couldn't detect mechanical movements, but I imagined a stack of wheels turning in the chamber, or gears with teeth, sliding levers into notches and shifting pins. Maybe it wasn't that complicated, but the damned thing had eluded me for seven years.

Until now.

The seal around the casing parted, and for a moment, I didn't believe my eyes.

It was unlocked.

Painful breaths rushed forth as I cracked it open and found two miniature scrolls of paper within, each no larger than the jade stone.

With only one usable hand, I placed it over the little rolls of paper and worked my fingers in an agonizing attempt to unfurl one of them. The grueling effort became worth it the instant I saw my father's handwriting.

My beautiful daughter,
If you're reading this, I'm probably gone from this world and waiting for you in the next. I have so much to tell you, starting with

The tiny paper was snatched out of my grip. With a bellow I couldn't hear, I scrambled after it. Only my limbs wouldn't cooperate.

My body was too broken to seize the hand that stole my father's letter. More hands fell upon me, taking the compass, the jade stone, and the second scroll.

The grief that assailed me was unwieldy and devastating. It replaced my blood with poison, my air with smoke, and my limbs with lead weights. I couldn't breathe or move. Still, I tried.

I reached through the haze, shaking violently, seeking anyone who would listen.

"Please. My father's letter… I beg you." I pushed the words out, but not one reached my ears. "I can't hear. My ears… Something's wrong. I just want to see the letter. Please."

The dense mist glowed in pale shades of gray, swirling around me as I lay on my side, bleeding and cracked in so many places. From this angle, with my cheek on the deck, I watched innumerable black boots stepping around me. One pair stopped an inch from my face, and Madwulf lowered into a crouch.

He held one of the tiny scrolls and unrolled it between his big fingers. Then he started reading.

I focused on his lips and made out the word *daughter*. He was reading the letter out loud, reading my father's words of love, and I couldn't hear any of it. I couldn't interpret the heavy brogue that shaped his cruel mouth.

"Please, Captain." I tried to lift my hand toward him. "That was…written…for me. I can't hear…"

He dropped the paper on the deck, and it furled into its original rolled-up shape. His boots pivoted, and he walked away, his attention locked on the second scroll in his hand.

The letter lay only two…three paces away. The chain on my ankle would reach.

Try, Bennett. You can do it.

I rolled to my chest, swallowed my cries, and pushed the blood-soaked curls out of my face. Bearing down against the dizzying agony, I dragged myself forward on my elbow. Shoved another inch with the toes on my working leg. Scraped the raw bone of my arm across the deck. Hacked up blood. Bit down. Pushed again.

Oh God, give me the strength.

I just needed to reach the paper before it blew.

Just help me reach it. Dear God, it's all I'll ever ask.

I heaved my broken arm forward, followed it, lugged it again, catching the exposed bone on the seams in the deck. I cried out. Kept

Sea of Ruin

moving. So close.

The toe of a boot pressed down on the rolled letter. My insides shriveled.

A hand grabbed the tiny scroll away.

Madwulf bent down and met my eyes. Whatever horrible thing he uttered stopped at my ears. Holding my gaze, he slowly, deliberately ripped the letter into tiny pieces, walked it to the bow, and flicked the remnants over the side.

Gone.

Destroyed.

It would never come back. I would never know the words, never read them, or hear them.

The pain was so powerful, so monstrous, I collapsed beneath the gravity of it. All I had left was the grief burning inside me, my twisted little friend with arms that embraced me in fire and teeth that sloughed the meat from my bones. I sank into its constricting grip and begged it to end me.

Still, my body refused to die.

Madwulf's men hauled me up and strung me to the foremast. Without the strength to stand, I buckled against the rope that caught me around the thighs, hips, and ribs. My arms were forced at my sides, punishing me with another layer of agony as every broken bone and shredded tendon rubbed and pushed against the squeeze of the restraints.

Then they walked away.

I didn't need my hearing to know their intent. They'd left me here to die.

Meanwhile, they slaughtered the last goat and passed around the dregs of the wine casks. Ashley's men had deserted the Royal Navy in hopes of living merry and acquiring riches. Now they would.

They had my father's map.

As the crew's morale took flight with smiles and dancing, mine plummeted.

Swelling had set in on the side of my face, pinching my eye shut. My jaw, cheek, and ear felt like a massive knot of fire, pulsing and stretching. My broken ribs turned every breath into a battering strike, and I refused to look at my arm. I couldn't without passing out.

I went mad with the urge to claw my way out of these ropes and throw myself overboard. I wanted to be anywhere that wasn't here, hanging from a mast and awaiting my death.

Would the pain follow me when I left this place? I imagined it would, if I never saw Priest and Ashley again. I imagined the pain would be worse.

Hours felt like days, and I still couldn't hear. The bells of the afternoon watch must have rung, for the watchmen changed. Unlike the dreary weather.

The fog around the ship seemed to thicken. We weren't moving.

The wind had dropped off. The sails hung loose. I didn't need my hearing to sense there were no waves. No tide. The ship wasn't rocking. Were we close to land?

The pale, obscuring mist prevented visibility beyond the bows. I tilted my eyes up and focused on the crosstrees. If I could hear, I imagined I would be listening to my rattling teeth, whimpering gasps, and the dying pulsation of my heart. I could feel the latter like a thudding drum, slowly losing energy.

The decks lay quiet to my broken ears. The glow from a pipe, the flicker of a lantern… Nothing else caught my eye in the gloom. Another hour passed. Two. Still, I kept my gaze on the crosstrees.

The watch changed again.

I felt myself fading, my limbs chilling in the oppressive humidity. Fever setting in.

Then something fluttered overhead. Feathers. Wings. A flash of a red beak. And another.

I knew that species of seabird. They flocked to the low, rocky cliffs of the bird island.

My heart restarted, pushing through the exhaustion of stress and pain.

Madwulf had taken my bait.

Minutes later, in a fleeting moment of lucidity, I glimpsed a vessel breaching the fog off the starboard bow.

Her silhouette split a hole in the vapor and emerged from the haze like a phantom ship. The bank of mist flinched away from her hull as if shuddering in fear.

I pinned my lips together, trapping the flood of my frantic breaths.

Amid the sound of silence, the air didn't stir, the wind chillingly dead. She slid across water that was as smooth as glass. Dew glistened along the lines of her rigging. Her decks bristled with armaments.

I would recognize her mighty masts anywhere.

Jade had arrived for a fight.

Forty-seven

Jade crept in, stealthy and dark, sliding board-to-board with *Blitz*. Whorls of mist curled around her spars, her masts looming overhead like the tentacles of a giant monster slowly rising from the sea.

The fog, the sinister stillness, the promise of devastating retribution—all of it shook me to my soul, slaying me at my most tortured, vulnerable depths. I wanted to sob at the sight of her. At the same time, I'd never been so furiously hungry for bloodshed.

By the time Madwulf's drunken rogues noticed her in the mist, it was too late for them.

Within seconds, my crew threw over pikes and planks and swarmed aboard, their eyes wild and mouths agape. I wished I could hear their unified roar.

I wished I could stand and fight with them.

May the sins of Thanatos grace their hearts and bloody their swords.

Aboard *Blitz*, they immediately met resistance from the Madwulf's pirates. But his soused bastards weren't prepared to thwart the ambush. As they pawed through their weapons chest, my men fell upon them with blades, flintlocks, and boarding axes.

Through the blur of my one working eye, I spotted Reynolds and Jobah as they cut down every brute in their path. I searched the throng, fighting to stay conscious, desperate to glimpse the two men I loved.

More and more of my crew joined the fight, parrying enemy bayonets, cutlasses thrusting, flintlocks firing, blades clashing in the air, and bodies falling and thrashing in death. The smoky aroma of spent powder stung my nose, and the reverberation of so many boots shook the deck beneath my feet.

I experienced it all in chilling silence.

Were Priest and Ashley calling my name? I wouldn't know. I couldn't make out the faces of the men storming across the planks between the ships. The fog made it impossible to identify those who remained on *Jade* to repel unwanted boarders.

Then, amid the noiseless chaos, the haze of smoke and mist shivered, parted, and a beast of a man emerged from the cloud.

His shirt was shredded and filthy, the lacing gone and front edges hanging open to his belts, revealing a wall of rippled brawn from throat to waist.

Skeins of his hair, the color of chestnut, were braided and adorned with shell beads, the top half scraped away from his face and caught in a seaman's queue. The rest curled around his loose collar and thick neck, and I longed to feel it sliding between my fingers. I missed my husband dearly.

He held his arms stiffly at his sides, fisting two cutlasses. I recognized the brass grip on one. It belonged to me, and my father before me. I'd taken it off the beach the day he'd hanged.

Head lowered, chin to chest, Priest set his silver eyes on mine. Eyes that glared from beneath a darkly savage brow, the depths blackening like rain-heavy clouds as they took in my appearance.

It must have been difficult for him to see me like this—a half-naked corpse tied to the foremast with bones exposed in my arm and every inch of my flesh beaten and swollen in various colors.

When his gaze finally returned to my damaged face, his demeanor had taken on so much pain something inside him seemed to have snapped. His arms bulged with tension, his shoulders lifting and spreading out. He opened his mouth, lips curled back, teeth bared. Then he *roared*. I couldn't hear it, but I felt it with my entire body. His torment. His intensity. The feral eye contact. The foreboding. I got chills.

Terrible things were about to happen, for he wasn't angry. He was deeply, spectacularly, viciously enraged.

He charged toward me with all that ire, never looking away. Around him, the battle waged, but he didn't stop. Didn't flinch when a blade swung close. He was too focused, too determined to reach me. He erased half the distance before someone broke from the fray and ran at him, wielding a sword.

Priest didn't twitch a muscle to evade the attack. He didn't need to.

Ashley came out of nowhere and struck like a thunderbolt, cleaving the assailant nearly in two with the hack of a sword. Then he turned and met my regard.

His blue eyes were the calm to Priest's storm, the ice to Priest's raging fire, his expression blank and smooth, his brow fraught with restraint. But I saw past that mask. Everything I felt with him, everything I wished for, spilled out between us.

I saw the man beneath the rigid armor. He was bellowing in there. Thrashing and stabbing and pounding fists into flesh. A cold, calculating man held my gaze on the surface, but underneath that severe discipline, he wanted vengeance and blood and everything Priest wanted.

He wanted *me*.

The bandages I'd repeatedly wrapped around my heart over the past two years peeled away. I didn't need them anymore. God, I was so horribly, foolishly, completely in love with both of them.

Ashley looked taller standing next to Priest, and though he held fast to his stoic demeanor, his appearance was a far leap from the aristocrat I'd met on this ship five weeks ago.

Covered in blood and stripped to the waist like a common pirate, his body gleamed with muscle, flexing beneath two thick leather bandoliers that crisscrossed his torso. They held four pistols. Two more dangled from around his neck, one of which Priest grabbed and fired at someone approaching my side.

The two of them battled their way to me as fast as they could, stopping every second to fight off more attackers. I had to rely on my waning vision to follow the commotion. I didn't know when a blunderbuss or flintlock fired until I saw the bits of black powder, shower of sparks, and pool of blood.

If Priest or Ashley got hit, I wouldn't hear it coming. I wouldn't know until they fell.

My chest squeezed painfully, my entire being locked on their progress as they edged closer and closer. My body wouldn't hold out much longer. With each breath, the pain grew bigger and sharper, consuming my ability to think. I could no longer hold up my head.

When they finally reached me, Priest swept around the foremast, sawing through the rope that suspended me to the timber. Ashley sheathed his sword and held his trembling hands near my waist, hovering, as if unsure where to grip without causing me pain.

Everywhere hurt. There was no part of me that wouldn't protest the press of hands. Even his. But I wanted off this ship, even if it killed me.

"Do it." My throat burned, dry and sandy. "I won't bite."

A rabid pirate ran up behind him, poised to thrust a rapier into Ashley's back.

"Behind you," I tried to shout.

But Priest was already there, cleaving the man across the face. Then he used the pirate's own rapier and plunged it into the belly, jerking upward on the blade until it opened the stomach and part of the chest. The man dropped.

Pivoting aft, Priest screamed something at someone, raging, spitting, his face contorting with feral madness. I'd seen his temper at its most dangerous peak, but never this. His wild eyes, demonic expression, and mercurial bearing embodied a violent storm. A savage war. A roaring, consuming fire of wrath.

He was terrifying.

Returning to my side, he yelled at Ashley, who calmly answered, seemingly unruffled by Priest's rage. I tried to read their lips, but my focus was ebbing, the darkness pressing in at the edges.

Priest slid a knife beneath the rope around my midsection and paused. His hand shook. His chest rose and fell. He desperately needed an outlet for the fury that snarled inside him.

Ashley touched my waist, fingers featherlight, and his mouth moved through a string of words, of which only a few were discernible at the end. "…I'll hurt you."

"Already hurt."

I could no longer see the blue of his eyes, for the dangerous shadows that lowered over them were too dark and stricken.

"Can't hear. No…sound." I wasn't sure how well I could talk. My face was swollen, and my voice didn't reach my ears. "Find Madwulf. Below deck. He took… Opened compass. Tiny map. My stone…"

My father's letter.

A tear leaked from the corner of my eye.

Priest set his jaw, nodded, and cut the rope.

The fetters unfurled, and I fell into Ashley's arms. He caught me as delicately as he could, but everything inside me moved at once. Bones shifted. Muscles engaged. Weight displaced. The shocking, wracking pain was too much.

Sea of Ruin

Nausea invaded. My stomach heaved. I drifted in and out of awareness.

I tried to stay alert as Ashley carried me across the planks to *Jade*. Over his shoulder, I spotted Priest at the bow of *Blitz*. He glowered with a shivering lust for death, his expression boiling, creased, cemented in an unblinking grimace. Once he saw me safely aboard my ship, he would go after Madwulf, no mistake.

A new pair of arms slid beneath me, along with a new level of hell as I was hauled over the gunwale. The pain came in constant waves, piercing and gnawing so deeply I couldn't stop crying.

Ashley didn't follow me over. He leaned in and spoke quickly to those on *Jade*, presumably giving updates and instructions on my care.

Bending down, his warm fingers found the hand of my uninjured arm, and he lowered his brow to my knuckles. I felt the love he poured into the gesture before he straightened and hardened his expression. Then he drew his sword and raced back across the plank to *Blitz*.

Neither he nor Priest would return until every man involved in my torture was dealt with brutally and without quarter.

Except Madwulf.

When they found him, his demise wouldn't end in a few hours or even a few days. They would torture him for as long as they could keep him breathing.

As another surge of anguish battered my body, I stared up at the man who held me, blinking through the fog of pain. Jobah's dark warm eyes stared back.

Dear God, it was a relief to see him.

Missed you, Captain, he mouthed, carrying me slowly, gently into the companionway.

"You, too, Jobah." More than I could voice.

The last time he cradled me like this, I was bleeding out from a sword wound in the gut. Too bad my present injuries hurt a thousand times worse. I faced a long, rocky road ahead and wasn't confident I would survive the battle this time.

Today, Jobah said, slowly shaping his lips around each syllable, *isn't your day.*

He was reminding me of my favorite motto.

If I had the strength, I would've laughed. But he was right. Today wasn't my day to die.

Tendrils of determination wound around my chest. For as long as I lived, I was still the captain of this ship. So I put on a tough face and swallowed down my pain. "How…are…new passengers?" *The two badly beaten men? The slave ship?* Did he understand what I was asking?

His smiling lips created a clear answer. *Healed.*

Good. Christ, that was great news. My old surgeon, Ipswich, while ever sour and rude, had an impressive success rate with saving people.

As Jobah conveyed me through *Jade's* lower decks, a sense of peace penetrated the torment in my bones. I was finally home. If I died, it would be on *my* ship surrounded by loyal friends.

Dammit, no. I wasn't going to die. I'd come too far. I had a ship to command, a map to my father's treasure, and a crew that depended on me. I. Would. Survive.

I must have passed out before Jobah reached our destination. The next thing I remembered was bolting upward in sharp, wrenching pain. It felt as though something was digging around in my broken arm.

My spine bowed as soundless howls spluttered past my lips. Numerous hands pinned me to a flat surface. I recognized the rafters overhead. The wall of windows. The Caribbee chart tapestry on the wall. I was in my private cabin, lying face-up on top of my desk.

Priest and Ashley stood on either side of me. Reynolds held my feet. Lieutenant Flemming was here, looking on as Ipswich tortured my arm. Something hard and metal scraped against the raw bone, sending me into another thrashing fit.

They were helping me. Knowing that, I tried so hard not to cry or move. But the pain… God's blood, I couldn't take much more. I trembled with it. Shook. I'd been shaking since Madwulf had taken me.

Huge blue eyes appeared above my face. Compelling eyes, chiseled jaw, muscular shoulders, and so many other gorgeous body parts that I hoped to admire again someday.

Ashley watched me as I watched him, unwavering, locked. In my periphery, Priest spoke to the doctors, his words heated and firing with threatening fury.

I focused on Ashley, on his carefully controlled reserve. It bothered me how close he was staring. Oh, how my appearance must sicken him.

"I look…" I pinned my lips and silently whimpered through a fresh twist of pain. "Dreadful."

His gaze didn't leave mine as he gave a hard swallow. A dip of his head. A slow blink. Then he mouthed, *Strong. Fierce.* His brow furrowed. *Too beautiful, Goldilocks.*

"Liar," I said.

Sea of Ruin

But his words reminded me to give myself some merit. I'd suffered an unimaginable amount of torture over the past few weeks. I was still alive. Still fighting. My father would've been proud of me.

"Madwulf?" I gulped through an insufferable sweep of spasms as something was tied around my arm.

Ashley's mouth shaped the word, *Contained.*

His gaze flicked to Priest, who shifted out of my view and returned a second later, opening a leather pouch. From within, he removed my compass, the jade stone, and the tiny scroll that presumably held the location of my father's treasure.

"Thank you." I tried to make my lips smile, but I couldn't breathe without crying.

His features turned stony as he pulled out a rag stained with blood. Unfolding the cloth, he tilted it downward so I could see what it held.

A severed hand.

Pale, freckled skin. Jagged fingernails.

Madwulf.

I closed my eyes and nodded, knowing that was the first of what would be many gifts. In my present condition, I couldn't partake in Madwulf's torture. But I could count on Priest to bring me all the bits and pieces.

Perhaps that made him an animal. I was accustomed to his feral behavior. In fact, it endeared me to him. Maybe that made me an animal, too.

Ashley showed no revulsion to it. Not that I was surprised after witnessing the brutality he'd inflicted on the admiral.

Over the next few hours, Ipswich and Flemming worked feverishly on my injuries. I blacked out through most of it, my awareness coming and going in fits of seething pain.

When I could talk, I answered their mimed questions on how each injury had been inflicted. Amidst my delirium, I might have fixated too much on the loss of my father's letter, but Priest and Ashley understood my grief. Every word fueled the rage radiating off them.

I had so many questions for them. How did they know each other? What were their plans for tomorrow? And the next day? And next year? What did they discuss together over the past week? Did they share everything they knew about me? About my history with each of them? Did Ashley tell Priest that I'd started our relationship as a ruse to escape? That I hadn't set out to fall in love again? Did they fight? Work things out?

They seemed tolerant of each other at the moment. I didn't know what that meant and didn't have the mental capacity—or the hearing—to interrogate them.

Exhaustion pulled at me, dragging down my limbs. I just needed sleep, and it heard my plea. It reached up from the depths and took me.

When I woke, the cabin was dark and empty, save for the glow of a single lantern. And Priest and Ashley.

I lay on the desk in a vacuum of unnatural silence. Ashley sat on the edge beside my head, washing my face and hair. Priest leaned over my lower half, running a warm, wet towel over my nude body.

The pain had ebbed into dull clenching convulsions, concentrating in my arm, my ribs, and the side of my head. I didn't move, didn't try to speak. The caresses of their hands felt too precious, each touch a heavenly balm on my battered spirit.

Priest took his time cleansing every bruise, contusion, and abused inch of flesh. There wasn't a part of me he didn't inspect and tenderly wash before he draped a sheet over my hips and stood.

Ashley finished with my hair, his fingers sliding unhindered through the long spirally curls. He'd removed every tangle, a task that would've taken hours.

From what I could tell, they didn't speak to each other or make eye contact. Was jealousy simmering beneath the surface? Were they behaving themselves for my benefit?

I didn't know what they were doing while I was unconscious. Trying to kill each other, perhaps. But I appreciated *this*. Everything. All of it. Just having them here was more than I could ask.

For the first time in weeks, I felt clean. Loved. *Safe*. Maybe I would survive, after all.

A glance at my arm confirmed it hadn't been sawed off. *Yet*. It lay strapped to a brace of wood. Jagged lines of stitches closed the flesh over the bone. Infection could still arise and require amputation. Or worse, it could kill me.

"What is my diagnosis?" I asked into the empty hush. "Broken arm and ribs?"

Above me, Ashley nodded and gently ghosted his fingers across my forehead, his mouth wrapping around the word, *Concussion*.

"Anything else broken?"

No, he said without sound.

"And my ears?"

Sea of Ruin

When he didn't answer, it was Priest who shook his head, his expression grim in the lantern light. Then he started talking, his features growing harder and meaner-looking with every word.

"What? I can't..." I couldn't even hear my own voice. "What are you saying?"

He made a face that usually accompanied a low growl. He was frustrated that I couldn't hear him. Frustrated *for me*.

"The doctors can't fix my hearing," I said.

His nostrils flared, confirming my assumption. My heart sank with sadness and anger, but I was too tired to cry.

I'd lost my hearing when the plank of wood slammed into my head. Was it a brain injury? Or something torn inside my ears? Perhaps it would heal on its own. My mind seemed too lucid and focused for the damage to be brain related.

Or so I thought until I woke again that night.

Within hours, I plunged into feverish confusion. Lethargy sank into my muscles. Chills wracked my body, and fuzzy vision disoriented the world around me.

Infection had set in.

Forty-eight

I succumbed to delirium.

Time slipped away. Conscious feeling spooled in starts and stops. The doctors hovered at the edges of the murky silence, conversing and administrating medicine, but I couldn't make sense of it. Couldn't concentrate enough to read lips or body language.

Someone had moved me to the bed in my cabin. Drenched in sweat and confusion, I was given draughts of laudanum for the pain and blood-letting treatments to purge the infection from my veins.

The bleeding and opium rendered my incoherency worse. I lost days.

Either Priest or Ashley was always stretched out beside me on the mattress. Always. Even if I couldn't see or hear them, I *felt* them. A hand in my hair, fingertips on my skin, lips against my neck, comforting, reassuring. I never slept alone.

Their constant presence gilded my darkest hours.

Amid intervals of fogginess, I found new gifts from Priest waiting for me on the table beside the bed. Severed fingers and toes. Two ears. An entire foot. Then the stump of another. Most of the extremities had been flayed to the bone—likely *before* they'd been sawed off.

As the body parts arrived, I wondered if my arm would meet the same fate. I checked it often, relieved to find it still attached and lying beside me on its brace.

Sometimes I was lucid when Priest delivered his grisly spoils. He brought me an entire arm once, with the bone protruding like mine had, only this limb was missing its hand. He studied my reaction to it, his gaze gloriously dark and rotating with violence. A skirt of bloody knives draped about his waist, his face and chest dappled in sanguine spots of gore.

He exemplified a barbaric warrior. Not just of body. His heart bellowed for revenge.

Revenge in my honor.

I didn't think I could love him any more than I already had.

Eventually, the gifts stopped coming, and I knew Madwulf had succumbed to infection or blood loss.

To watch one's body being hacked away bit by bit was a positively grueling way to die. Perhaps I wouldn't have been able to exact a better punishment myself. Still, I wished I'd been there. I wished it had been me who'd swung the fatal blow.

But alas, I was bedridden, and Priest was indeed a terrifying executioner. I tried to express my gratitude to him in my eyes, but I couldn't make my face work right. So I settled on a weak, "Thank you."

With Madwulf dead, Priest didn't leave my side again. He and Ashley took turns feeding me, bathing me, and holding me on the chamber pot. Not my finest moments as a pirate captain, but I didn't have the wherewithal to care.

Priest slept here every night. Sometimes in the bed with me. Other times I woke to find him in the chair beside the mattress, his weary frame bent over his knees, with his head hanging in his hands. It hurt my heart to see him so troubled. Worse, I didn't have the strength to comfort him.

Ashley spent his evenings on *Blitz*. When he wasn't here with me, he was trying to take command of what was left of his career. While I'd been shackled to the foremast, Madwulf's men had boasted about all the soldiers they locked in the hold—all the men who had remained loyal to Ashley.

The pirate hunter still had a crew and a Royal Navy warship depending on him. With the admiral dead and his enemies destroyed, he could return to England, marry his betrothed, and carry on like he'd never met me.

If he did that, I would fight for him. But first, I needed to fight this infection.

Despite my fuzzy head and lack of hearing, I knew *Jade* was on the

Sea of Ruin

move, sailing to some unknown destination. Since I still saw Ashley every day, *Blitz* must be sailing with us, plotted on the same course.

Where? My questions were met with shaking heads and silent reassurances. They wanted me focused on regaining my health rather than trying to command the ship from my bed.

Reynolds popped his head in frequently. In my feverish daze, his face looked like a blurry dream in front of me. But I knew he checked on me often, even as he was busy commanding *Jade* in my absence.

He was here now, in fact, sitting at the table with Jobah and Priest. I watched the three of them together, their camaraderie, their brotherhood. Priest smirked at Reynolds and smacked Jobah over the back of the head. Jobah laughed and hit him back.

Priest had missed them, and the realization spiked a new pain in my chest.

I hadn't just deprived him of his wife for two years. I'd deprived him of his family. His brethren. I'd turned his closest mates against him and made them choose sides.

I hated myself for that. When I'd discovered his infidelity, I shouldn't have left him in Nassau. I could've let him remain on my ship as part of my crew while keeping him out of my bed. I could've handled it like a captain instead of an emotionally scorned woman.

That night, when he crawled in bed beside me, I told him all these regrets. I rambled on in a silent, feverish haze, my disordered stream of thought losing focus as I spoke. But he heard the gist of it.

His arms came around me, holding without hurting, and his lips moved passionately against my cheek. I felt the rumble of his *I miss you's* and the heated breaths of his *I love you's*. His tender kisses traced my jaw in a language without words. It was more potent than sound, more profound than speech.

Every declaration was a sensation produced, not through the ear, but through the soul.

It brought to mind something he'd said the night he found me in Jamaica.

No man will ever live up to the ideal you hold for Edric Sharp.

"You were wrong about something." I shifted my head so that I could watch his lips move.

Just one thing? he asked.

"Well, no. But..." I drew a ragged breath, my entire body afire and shaking in a cold sweat. "I left you. Tried to give you up. Yet you never gave up on me. Never stopped pursuing me. You came for me when I needed you the most. Priest… You've far surpassed the ideal I hold for my father."

He and Ashley both. The commodore risked his career, his family, and his life to remove me—a pirate prisoner—from the admiral's flagship. Now he was commanding a two-thousand-ton warship with only a fraction of the crew needed to sail it. The deepening creases around his bloodshot eyes attested to the sort of sleepless pressure he was under. Yet he still spent hours here with me every day.

He and Priest had sacrificed so much. I owed it to them to recover.

I needed to pull my damned self together, harden my bones, and drag my battle-scarred body from this bed. The sooner I did that, the less of a burden I would be, and the quicker I would find my father's treasure and repay my crew for their loyalty.

But the infection wasn't finished with me.

My acute pain combined with continued strong fevers was to be dreaded, no mistake. The danger that I would fall into deep delirium and die loomed in the tired eyes of Priest, Ashley, and my doctors.

As the fever wore on, chills overtook my senses and smothered my consciousness, leaving me to wander alone in my mind. I found myself back in the hole on the admiral's flagship, surrounded by the stench of death.

Whenever I woke, it was in flickers of warped reality. I was still in that black hole, watching a door open and close only feet away. Priest and Ashley flashed in and out of the doorway, talking to me without sound, reaching for me, always too far away.

Shackled and weak, I couldn't crawl toward them. My legs wouldn't move.

Gradually, the door opened less often, and the murk around me grew darker, stretching longer. Flashes of Priest transformed. His cheeks hollowed out, narrowing his face. Whiskers thickened, lengthening into a short beard. I barely recognized him.

Where was Ashley?

I called out for him, but he stopped appearing in the doorway. Sometimes Priest was there, his silver eyes ablaze with grim emotion. But Ashley was gone. I sensed his absence like a missing limb.

Perhaps that was the impetus that drove me from death. From within the suffocating black hole of silence and decay, I clawed my way out. Hands scrabbling, muscles writhing, and lungs panting, I woke on a gasp in the blinding rays of sunlight.

There was no motion. No rocking or waves. I was on land?

Sea of Ruin

My surroundings came in bursts of hazy images—silk fabric, sumptuous wood furnishings, embroidered brocades, silver sconces, and mullioned windows that yawned open to a cerulean sky.

As the mingled aromas of brine and sweet grassy fields tickled my nose, I had no sense of people. No sound. No movement.

Where the devil was I?

Forty-nine

"Ahoy? Anyone there?"

Faster than the words could leave my mouth, Priest was in my face, climbing onto the bed and leaning in with bright gray eyes and a freshly shaved jaw.

Everything rushed at me at once—questions, breaths, dizziness, joy, and pain. Yes, the pain persisted. But it didn't consume. It felt nothing like before.

"Where are we?" I tried to sit up, commanding muscles that refused to respond. "How long has it been? Where's Ashley? My ship? Reynolds and—"

He pressed a finger against my lips and pinned me with his steady gaze, calming me, compelling my lungs to slow down. His touch lifted to my forehead, his palm flattening to test my temperature.

I didn't sense a fever. Just dull aches beneath healing wounds. And fatigue. I'd never felt this exhausted and feeble in my life.

He didn't need to ask if my hearing had returned. Since I couldn't judge volume or pronunciation, my voice would sound ill-fitting to his ears.

I love you. Sculpted lips gave shape to those three syllables a second before they claimed my mouth.

The scent of sea and leather saturated my senses as he sipped with warm, unhurried licks, kissing me sweetly, without tongue or expectation. His hands rested on the mattress on either side of my head, his arms bracing the weight of his upper body.

The reunion of our lips freed a solemnity of emotion I'd kept buried and guarded for so long. I melted beneath the sheer force of it, surrendering to the love and longing that buzzed through our breaths.

His tongue played along the seam of my mouth but didn't force its way in. This wasn't a kiss that took and controlled. This was his devotion reaching out and caressing me, giving and nourishing, making me strong again.

He shifted, trailing his lips across a cheek that no longer throbbed with pain, roaming down my neck to my arm...

The arm was still there, the brace and stitches gone. It felt strange, itchy, sore... Whole. My relief was unwieldy as he kissed a wandering path over the crisscrossed scars near my inner elbow, the flesh pink and bubbled.

No more infection. His mouth fashioned the words against the healing wound, and I felt his smile, his relief, curving upward, tickling the tender skin.

A leather thong held the top half of his hair at the back of his head, but a few strands had fallen free, framing a face that was accustomed to being regarded with feminine pleasure.

He'd thinned out a little, but his complexion glowed with health. I wanted so badly to slide my hands over his sloping shoulders, up the column of his neck, and across his defined cheekbones. My fingers twitched, and he caught them, lifting them to his jaw.

Instant heat hit my palms. So hotblooded, this man, with a temper that always simmered just below the surface.

He'd shaved only hours ago, for there wasn't a trace of stubble on his satiny skin. A shirt and breeches clad his muscled frame in his preferred pirate style, only these garments appeared cleaner. No rips or bloodstains.

I still didn't know where we were.

My arms trembled with fatigue as he lowered them. Then he stepped away, widening my view to the bedchamber.

It reminded me of the one I'd occupied as a child in Charleston. I lay in a bed with four large wooden posts. Tiers of dark silk draped the rails overhead. Wool carpets, a table set with porcelain plates, silver sconces to provide light—the room glittered with wealth and elegance.

Off to the side, a wide doorway led into what looked like a bathing chamber. At the entrance, a cheval mirror stood next to an elegant dressing table. I looked away, fearing the reflection it would show me. I

Sea of Ruin

couldn't even bring myself to shift the sheet off my body, knowing I was nude, scarred, and emaciated.

A sitting area surrounded a stone fireplace that spanned the length of one wall. Windows lined another wall, opening to a balcony that overlooked a landscape I couldn't fathom.

"Where are we?" I tried to sit again, shaking with the effort.

He hooked an arm around my back, adjusted some pillows, and maneuvered me into a quasi-sitting position. My ribs ached with the movement, but it was manageable.

"You've been doing this a lot," I muttered. "Taking care of me."

Gladly, he said without voice and laid his lips against mine.

Dear lord, again with that mouth. More than a kiss, it was a promise. A flutter of hope.

Leaning back, he stretched toward the table at the bedside. My compass was there, along with the tiny scroll and jade stone. He reached over those and grabbed a piece of parchment. A letter.

He held it out for me to read, and I instantly recognized Priest's bold, slanted handwriting.

This is Ashley's private manor on the southwest coast of England.
Yesterday marked five weeks since we found you near the island of birds.
The commodore is in London, settling matters with his crew and ship.
He shall join us here when he's finished.
When you're well enough, I will convey you to the windows.
There, you will see Jade anchored in the private harbor below, sheltered by cliffs.
Your crew is enjoying the township, stirring up trouble at the tavern and debauching the local maidens.
The servants and tenants on the property are discreet and loyal.
We are safe here.
Your men are safe and merry.
The only priority is your return to health.

I read it twice, nodding my approval. It didn't answer every question, but the immediate ones had been addressed.

So this was Ashley's manor. I looked around the bedchamber with new eyes, assuming it was the estate on the cliff that he'd said he favored. Strange that he'd allowed us to stay here—his lover *and* her husband—in his absence.

I didn't know how I felt about that. "When did we arrive?"

Yesterday. His voice stopped at my ears.

Priest and Ashley had spent a week together when I was on *Blitz*. And another five weeks while I convalesced. They should know each other quite well by now. But they'd been already well acquainted, hadn't they?

"How do you and Ashley know each other?" I pitched him my stormiest glare.

He looked away, staring at nothing. When he met my gaze again, his mouth gave life to a string of noiseless statements. With each rapid word, he grew angrier and more agitated. Since he wasn't trying to slow down and help me understand, I suspected he was venting rather than giving me any real answers.

I could tell him to write it all down. But I was too impatient to wait when I had questions he could answer with a single syllable.

"Over the past weeks, did you talk to Ashley about us?" I stiffened, uncertain how to proceed in foreign waters. "Did you discuss…everything? Our marriage? Our separation? Did he tell you how I tried to use him to escape?"

He nodded through every inquiry, his expression hard and unflinching.

"He didn't know you were in *Jade's* hold when he captured me." My mind raced to make all the connections. "Did you tell him? Does he know that's why you hunted HMS *Blitz*?"

Another nod.

"I didn't fall easily into his bed. I swear it." A swallow stuck in my throat. "I was angry with you, and I needed a backup escape plan. And…I was attracted to him. *Am*. Still. I love him, Priest. But when my relationship began with him, it was fraught with pain and distrust. Until he saved me from the admiral. Did he tell you about that? About my imprisonment on the flagship and the violation that happened to me?"

Aye. His teeth clenched in what I assumed was a hot hiss of sound.

He stood and turned away, hiding his expression as his fingers stabbed through his hair, flexing and releasing.

"Priest…" I didn't wish to hurt him. Not anymore. I didn't know how to fix this.

He made another turn, hands on his hips, head bent, pacing forward, walking aft, pivoting forward, eying me. Then he looked at the table beside me.

I followed his gaze to the tiny scroll. "Did you read it?"

He stopped pacing. Nodded.

I crossed my arms, finding the pain from the motion bearable. "Tell me it's a map."

A grin startled at the corner of his mouth, struggling to pull free. I stared at those lips, my own twisting into a smile as he said, *Aye.*

"Tell me something." I narrowed my eyes. "Where did you hide the compass on my ship?"

Now he grinned with abandon, damn near laughing out his response. *Jobah.*

"Jobah?" I couldn't have read that right. "That goddamned traitor had it the entire time? I'm going to kill him."

You won't. He shook his head, trying to rein in his smile.

He was right, of course. I had a terrible weakness where my helmsman was concerned. I let him get away with all manner of insolence, only because he had the purest heart of any man on my crew. But I would still give him my mind on the matter.

Priest returned to my side and twined his fingers around mine. As I stared at our hands, dizziness threatened, my energy already draining.

"Put the map in a safe place," I said. "Don't let me see it or know its secret until I'm out of this bed, walking without assistance, feeding and bathing myself."

I didn't need the motivation, but I liked goals with scintillating rewards. I was a pirate, after all. I seized and savored the riches.

I love bathing you, he mouthed.

"I can't imagine why. I'm repulsive." I sagged against the pillows, struggling to hold my head up. "I think I need a short sleep now."

He scowled threateningly and yanked off the sheet that covered me. I jerked my head away, but he grasped my jaw and forced my eyes downward, showing me my body.

As expected, the bruises were long gone. But my muscles had wasted away, leaving a gaunt, rawboned ghost of the strong, battle-honed woman I'd once been. Even so, it wasn't as wretched as I'd imagined. Priest and Ashley had kept me nourished. I remembered the forced feedings, the constant flavor of broth on my tongue. They'd kept me alive.

Priest skidded his hand down my throat to my breasts. I'd lost weight there, too, but he didn't seem to mind. His fingers lingered, molding around the nipples, and his breaths increased the lift and fall of his chest.

He licked his lips and continued lower, resting his palm on my ribs. I tensed, bracing for the agony that I'd lived with for weeks. The pain had anchored itself there, but the weight of his touch didn't make me flinch. The ache seemed to only flare with muscle movement.

"All right." I sighed. "You made your point."

But he kept going. Prodding here, caressing there, he slowly, masterfully, turned me into a languid mixture of drowsy content. After five weeks of taking care of me, he was more acquainted with my body than I was, and he proved it with every touch.

He saved the juncture of my legs until the end. His fingers skimmed the tuft of curls and traced the slit beneath, cupping me possessively.

You. Are. Stunning.

I read his lips clearly as he lifted his gaze to mine, his thick dark lashes drifting upward. Perhaps there was lust in those silver eyes, but it wasn't the chief emotion. His intimacy with my body ran deeper, his hand between my legs more profound than carnal intent.

It was an act of love. Of acknowledgment and acceptance.

Ashley had pleasured me there. The admiral had abused me there. Priest knew this.

He knew that not all my wounds were visible.

"We need to talk about Ashley," I said.

Not today. A firm response as he rose from the bed and covered me with the sheet. *Sleep.*

"How did you get your burn scars?"

Later.

I hated those soundless words. "I want my hearing back. I miss your voice."

He kissed my brow then my lips. Soft, warm, whispering kisses that gradually lulled me into the sweet surrender of slumber.

The next few days passed in a flurry of activity—meals, medicine, exercise, and a parade of liveried servants. Ashley's manor was fully staffed, and every seamstress, housekeeper, cook, and maid seemed to know my husband on a smiling, tittering, intimate level.

While I slept often and needfully, Priest must have made himself well acquainted with the resident females. I daresay most of the women were twice my age, but that wasn't the reason for my indifference about it.

He'd proved his loyalty to me so many times over the past few months, I knew in my heart he wouldn't betray me again.

My rigorous exercise began in bed with his hands supporting my limbs as I repeatedly sat up, lifted small objects, flexed joints, and stretched muscles. I put myself on a strict tiresome routine that lasted hours several times a day. When I wasn't sleeping and eating, I was

Sea of Ruin

sweating, shaking, grunting, and oftentimes screaming at the rafters in agony and frustration. But I was growing stronger.

Servants came and went. Meals were delivered. Fabrics were hauled in, cut, and sewn to fit my measurements. The ship's surgeon, Lieutenant Flemming, had returned to London with Ashley. But Ipswich was here. *Lucky me.*

I sat on the edge of the bed as he waddled around me, probing tools in my ears, thumping at the bones in my arm, poking, prodding, and running his mouth with a sour look on his wrinkled face.

"I might be as deaf as an adder." I stared into his cloudy eyes. "But I can hear you insulting me, you senile old curmudgeon."

He grinned without teeth.

Perhaps I should have punched his impudent mug. But I owed him my life. After everything he'd done for me, I could only shake my head and laugh.

By the end of the week, I walked on my own. The steps were few but strong. I paced the bedchamber, lifting brass candlesticks, one in each hand. Back and forth, I went. Panting, trembling, and soaked with sweat, I worked my muscles until they limped. Then I plucked one of the swords from the stand in the corner and used it as a crutch to power through.

Sometimes I stepped out on the balcony and gazed upon my majestic galleon far below, where she moored in Ashley's private bay of cliffs. I missed her and my crew.

More than that, I missed my pirate hunter.

Was he visiting his betrothed during his time in London? Courting her while he kept his dirty secret hidden away in his coastal estate? Those thoughts chased me relentlessly. The only way I found I could outrun them was through endless, rigorous exercise.

Priest trailed me through the corridors of the manor for two weeks, huffing and seething and scolding me for pushing too hard. Perhaps that was an advantage of being deaf. I didn't have to listen to his ribald speech.

My body was healing, slowly coming back to life. I sensed it when Priest kissed me, when the heat of his rock-hard physique pressed against me, making me ache for him.

Every night, I slept in the security of his arms, his chest against my back, the nude length of him steeling along the nude length of me. Skin to skin, hips together, with his swollen hardness trapped between us, it was heaven and torture.

I wanted him deeply and basked in his affectionate kisses. But, for the first time since we met, I had the strength of will to refuse him when he pressed for more. I wouldn't betray Ashley, and Priest wouldn't discuss their history. He was hiding something.

Until I understood *their* past and *our* future, I put the present on hold.

It wasn't difficult. By the time I collapsed into bed each night, I'd exerted every ounce of strength I had into rebuilding my body. I had nothing left to give a passionate coupling.

One night, three weeks after my arrival in England, I stumbled into bed beneath the weight of such heavy exhaustion my muscles throbbed. My head pounded, and my ears buzzed with the need for sleep.

No, my ears were *ringing*.

The noise threaded through the thumping pressure in my skull. As I drifted to sleep in Priest's arms, I decided the sensation was just the overworked pulsations of my heart.

Until I woke to the sound of voices.

Fifty

"Rot in hell, you pompous cunt!" Priest roared so loudly I felt it rattle the rafters.

Not only that, I *heard* it.

In my ears.

His Welsh accent penetrated with clarity, volume, and unbridled rage.

Stunned, I lay motionless on the bed, unable to believe the sounds coming at me. The beat of my heart, the rush of my breaths, the tread of pacing footsteps…

And the elegance of Ashley's aristocratic voice. "Your anger with me is misplaced."

Blanketed in shadows, I pushed up on my elbows and waited to see if they noticed me stirring.

Across the room, Ashley leaned a shoulder against the fireplace mantle, hands clasped behind him, head lowered, and blue eyes fixed on Priest. He'd traded his seafaring frock for a somber black coat. Lace at the cuffs and collar matched the white waistcoat and breeches.

Droplets of dew gleamed on the toes of his black boots. A three-cornered hat lay upside down on the table beside him, his inky hair tousled and windblown. He must have just arrived.

Like Priest, his muscular frame appeared leaner, his shoulders twitching with harnessed energy, hinting at the careful calculation of his every action. Such a gorgeous man at once confident in his body and stifled by his nobility.

"Misplaced? I've spent the last few months fighting the impulse to carve out your liver." Priest wore a path across the wool rug, shirtless and seething, his hands clenching at his sides. "I can think of at least ten reasons why I should do it now. First and foremost, let's not forget that you intended to *hang my wife*."

"Ah, but she's the one reason you will leave my liver precisely where it is."

With a quickening pulse, I slid my legs off the side of the bed and leaned forward, deciding to listen to the conversation rather than interrupt.

By God, I could hear!

"If you hadn't captured her…" Priest spun and charged toward Ashley, bellowing, "She wouldn't have suffered so!"

"Don't put that on me." Ashley went deadly still, his voice terrifyingly calm. "Don't you dare. Damn you, I would give my life for that woman."

His declaration filled me with warmth, but Priest wouldn't appreciate it. This wasn't going to end well.

I grabbed a nightgown from the floor and yanked it on.

"She almost died because of you!" Priest shouted inches from Ashley's face.

Calm as a windless sea, Ashley slammed a fist into Priest's jaw. I hurried toward them as Priest countered with a brutal punch to Ashley's mouth, bloodying his lip.

Confound it! I circled back to the bed and snatched a full bucket of water.

"One, you never told me you were married." Ashley tackled Priest to the floor, face-down. "Two, I was hunting you so that I could put her in your protection."

"You captured her to take her to London and secure your bloody promotion!" Priest exploded with fury, knocking Ashley off with an elbow to the head. "Then you fucked her!"

Fists flew. Grunts echoed off the walls. Extravagant baubles crashed to the floor as they rolled through the bedchamber, grappling, cursing, and taking out more furniture. I stormed toward the chaos, intent on dumping the contents of the bucket on top of their foolish heads.

Partway there, I slowed, stumbling to a halt. The room went silent, the air taut and still. They weren't moving.

Ashley lay atop Priest's supine body with a hand around Priest's throat. They didn't look at me, didn't even notice me standing off to the side behind the armchair.

Their tense, rigidly hard frames heaved from exertion, chest to chest, hip to hip, as they stared at each other, locked in some sort of emotionally charged eye contact. Priest lay on his back, restraining Ashley by the hair, wrenching his head back, and holding their mouths a hairsbreadth apart. They were so close they would've tasted the mingling of their labored breaths.

Ashley glared down his nose at Priest, maintaining his imperious demeanor, despite the awkward angle of his neck.

The nonverbal battle lasted longer than was comfortable. I couldn't breathe. I was afraid to make a sound.

Gradually, Ashley released the vise of his hand from Priest's throat. But he didn't push away. Neither did Priest. All at once, they both seemed to relax.

Then, before my very eyes, Ashley sagged, letting the full weight and length of his body sink onto Priest in a confusingly beautiful gesture of trust and familiarity.

My jaw hung open, my thoughts fraying. What the devil were they doing?

The fist Priest held in Ashley's hair loosened, sliding to the back of Ashley's head to draw their foreheads together.

"I love her." Ashley closed his eyes, his jaw tight. "It can't be helped."

"I know." He sighed against Ashley's mouth. Not a kiss. But it wanted to be…something…

I was so enthralled, the bucket slipped from my fingers, splashing water over my feet as it hit the floor.

Their heads turned in my direction, the spell broken.

Ashley stood and removed his cravat, using it to wipe the blood away from his lip. Then he straightened his garments and met my eyes, his expression empty. Chillingly composed. "Good evening, Bennett."

Since he believed I was still deaf, he pronounced his fine-mannered greeting carefully and slowly. As if I cared a whit about formalities.

Had I remained in the bed, the angle would've prevented me from witnessing…whatever that was. They'd assumed I'd slept through it since I couldn't hear. Or perhaps they hadn't assumed anything because they'd been so caught up in each other.

"What were you doing?" I motioned at Priest on the floor. "Just now. What was that?"

Priest's gaze shot to mine, his eyes narrowing, searching, then glimmering with realization. *Ah.* So my voice sounded normal now that I could hear it?

I arched my brow at him, smirking. *Yes, I can hear again.*

His face broke out in a wide, joyful grin. "She asked a question, Lord Cutler." He rose to his feet, all grace and confidence, his accent taunting. "What were we doing just now?"

"It's late. We're not doing this tonight." Ashley looked at Priest behind him, hiding the movement of his lips. "She doesn't need this right now. I'll tell her when she's recovered and—"

"I can hear you, Ashley, and I'm well on my way to full health." I anchored my hands on my hips. "Tell me now."

He whipped his face back to mine, his blue eyes stark with disbelief. "Truly? You can hear?"

"As of five minutes ago, it would seem."

He prowled toward me, his gaze roving up and down, taking me in. Moonlight from the windows dashed across his striking features, highlighting his relief at my healthy appearance. He was so beautiful, especially when he stared at me like that, like I was his favorite view, his only destination.

"Look at you." He stepped into my space, his hands finding and inspecting the condition of my injuries. "So bloody beautiful. Strong. *Glowing.* I knew you were out of bed and pushing yourself. Priest sent letters every few days, boasting about your progress."

I shot Priest a startled look. He narrowed his eyes.

"I wished I would've been here, supporting you." A spark of regret lit Ashley's eyes. "Of course, you managed just fine. Extraordinarily so." His hands slid to my face, framing it. "Your strength of will astounds. Truly an intimidating woman, and God help me, I've gone mad without you."

He cupped the back of my head and drew my mouth toward his. And froze.

I leaned back to find a blade poised across his throat.

"Priest." I gritted my teeth and met his angry eyes over Ashley's shoulder. "You're not going to cut him."

He bent in, setting his mouth at Ashley's ear. "Tell her."

"Tell me what? About your history together? Your relationship with Arabella?" My pulse accelerated as I backed up and lowered into the armchair, glaring at Priest. "Is that how you and Ashley met? Is she the one you…you betrayed me with?"

Sea of Ruin

Ashley sucked in a hard breath, his mouth a grim slash of pain. I'd never asked *when* she died. I only knew it had happened during childbirth.

"I can smell your shame, my lord. It sickens me." Priest stepped away and tossed the blade toward the fireplace. "You've let it rule you your entire life. I've stood by you, honored your wishes, and protected your secrets at the cost of ruining my marriage!" His accent thickened, rising in volume with the force of his rage. Then he pounced, grabbing Ashley by the collar and hurling him to his knees before me. "Do you know that I have not made love to my wife in over two years?" With a hand in Ashley's hair, he leaned in and snarled, "Tell her now or so help me God, I will break my vow and tell her myself."

As Priest released him, my mind swam to keep up, creating and rejecting assumptions with the rapid beat of my heart.

"All right." Ashley bent over my lap and gripped my hips, his muscles hot and coiled with tension. "Christ, I don't know where to start."

A flash of sympathy softened Priest's features. "Tell her who I was with in Nassau two years ago."

Everything inside me stilled. The room melted away until all that existed was Ashley's strong, stern, beautiful face as he lifted it to mine and said, "Me. Priest was with me."

My head jerked back, ice in my veins. "What? No, that's not—"

"I wrote the letter, Bennett." Ashley straightened on his knees, forcing his way between my legs. "Priest told me you memorized it. The one you found that morning."

"Why?" I pressed my back against the chair, seeking distance, not understanding. "That letter confessed intimacy. Love. Passion. *Orgasms*. Why would you…write…that…?"

My gaze flitted between him and Priest, back and forth, over and over, as I tried to imagine them together. Naked. Fucking.

The concept of two men having relations didn't shock or offend me. I lived on a ship with a hundred lusty pirates. I witnessed all sorts of bawdy, creative, man-on-man action, especially during long months at sea.

But Priest and Ashley? No. I couldn't fathom it.

Except only minutes ago, there had been a moment, a seed of suspicion…

Priest lowered into the chair across from me, sprawling like a watchful predatory cat. "Get to the part where I swore on my life to be your dirty, shameful secret."

"I think she can figure it out." Agitated, Ashley rose and shrugged out of his coat, tossing it over the couch. "I'm betrothed. I have a career and a family name to protect. Duty, honor, heirs, obligations, expectations—my entire life was put before me the moment I drew my first breath. I didn't choose this path. I was born into it. Bred to serve and thrive as a peer of the realm." He flicked a hand at Priest. "If he and I were discovered…"

"You would both be executed," I said on a dazed whisper.

Priest was a commoner *and* a criminal. Not only did he lack the required wealth and status, but he was an enemy of England. A relationship between him and Ashley was forbidden for all those reasons. But there was a far greater danger.

Romantic attraction between two men was considered a serious offense. If they were discovered, they would be hanged for sodomy.

"So you ended things with Priest in Nassau two years ago." My head throbbed, mind blown. "You spent the night with him, wrote him a letter, and left before he woke."

Priest watched us quietly from beneath dark brooding brows.

"Yes." Ashley stared at his hands, his sculpted nostrils pulsing. "One of the many reasons Priest wishes to cut out my liver." He paced to the unlit fireplace and braced his forearms against the mantle, his gaze on the floor. "That night in Nassau, I saw him in the tavern. You weren't with him."

"She went back to the ship to check on the crew," Priest said. "While I waited for her ashore, I had a dram of rum. It was a stroke of luck that you spotted me."

"A coincidence I can't bring myself to regret." Ashley's broad, powerful shoulders rose and fell. "It had been two years since we last saw each other."

"I remember."

Ashley turned back to me. "Since he was a known pirate and I was a naval officer, we couldn't be seen together. I discreetly told him where I was staying so we could have a private visit."

"A private visit?" I blew a harsh sound through my nose. "You mean a visit of flesh."

"No." Priest leaned forward, elbows on his knees, and met my eyes. "Ashley and I have been close mates since childhood. Our relationship isn't carnal at its foundation. When I went to him that night, I did it in secrecy out of concern for his association with me—an outlaw. Not because I intended to bed him."

"You could've told me." I straightened, frustration rising. "We were married. You should have trusted me enough to say where you were going and who you were with."

"I gave him my word, Bennett. Long before I met you, I vowed to him that I would never tell a soul about our relationship. Same vow I made to you. I kept our marriage a secret, *protecting* you, just like we agreed." A muscle bounced in his cheek. "Then I broke that vow on Eleuthera when I told Ashley you're my wife."

Fine. I was a reasonable woman. Reasonable enough to appreciate, albeit angrily, his reasons for the secrecy. He hadn't tried to be malicious or deceitful. He'd only meant to keep Ashley and me safe.

"But," I said, "you broke your marriage vow when you bedded Ashley in Nassau. Do you not see it that way?"

"Aye. I do." Guilt drew up his shoulders as he glanced at Ashley and returned to me. "He and I spent hours talking that night, catching up. Like he said, two years had separated us. But when the conversation ended, I walked to the door, prepared to leave…"

"I told you to go." Ashley leaned against the mantle with his arms crossed, the hint of a frown bleeding through his stoicism.

"You didn't mean it."

"No. Of course, I didn't want you to leave. I missed you terribly and had no idea you were married. Regardless, what we did was reckless. It's *still* reckless."

"Reckless and indecent." Priest's eyes flared. "I was always the one thing in your life you couldn't polish or beat into obedience. So you ended two decades of friendship like a coward in a letter."

A letter that destroyed Priest's marriage. I'd left Priest that same day, crushing him beneath a double layer of pain.

"Two decades…" I did the calculation in my head. "You've known him since you were twelve?" I turned to Ashley. "And you were fourteen?" Good God, I would've only been a year old. I rubbed my head, overwhelmed, uncertain. "How did you meet?"

"Here at Ashley's childhood home." Priest gestured around us. "This was his bedchamber until he joined the Royal Navy at age twenty. When my whore of a mother sent me to England for work, the viscount hired me as a hall boy."

"Ashley's father."

Priest nodded. "As I showed steady ambition, I worked my way up to a footman and ultimately secured my position as the Groom of the

Chamber. I was Lord Ashley Cutler's personal valet and whipping boy for six years."

Tingles of shock swept through me. I knew Priest had held various jobs as a boy, doing this and that for the gentry. It wasn't until he was eighteen that he found Reynolds and joined the ranks of the Brethren of the Black Flag. So hearing he'd been a male servant was no surprise.

But Ashley's servant? Here? That was difficult to process. By God, was that why the household staff knew Priest so well? Because they'd worked together?

"He's twisting the truth," Ashley said to me, his bearing stiff and severe. "Priest was my *companion*."

"The companion of the master of the house. I saw to your every personal need." Priest cocked his head, idly rubbing his chin without a trace of resentment in his gravelly accent. "I dressed you and styled you, accompanied you to every tedious formal engagement, and attended to your private arrangements. *All* your private affairs. How many times, my lord, did I personally wash that sizable cock between your legs?"

My indecent mind hungrily grasped at the sensual image he evoked, my insides fluttering and knotting.

"It wasn't like that, and you damn well know it." Ashley prowled toward him, seemingly unmoved, save for flexing of his hands at his sides. "You were my best friend. My *only* confidant. Because of you, I learned how to laugh and play and take risks. You understood me like no one else could. Because you valued me as something other than a rank or a title." He towered over Priest's chair, glowering down at him. "You can talk about my cock and try to degrade our relationship, but I *know* that everything I just said… You felt the same about me. It went both ways, my friend. When we were together, in *any* capacity, we were well-matched. A perfect pair on level ground. Always *equal*."

"Aye," Priest whispered. "I know."

They stared at each other, eyes hard and unblinking, and within the poignant, private space between them, I felt their conflict, their longing, their tortured breaths. I imagined they were thinking about the moments they'd shared. All the time that they'd lost. The rules of society that undoubtedly forced them apart.

My heart wept for them. At the same time, I felt sick with dread.

Where did I fit in? Priest was my husband, and he cheated on me with my lover. But *cheated* didn't sound right. It didn't make sense in my head or my heart.

Sea of Ruin

All that mattered was that I loved them, and they loved me.

Except what they had together, the history they shared, the fraternal companionship… That was something else entirely. It didn't include me.

I struggled to reckon all the strange, intense reactions I had to this. I was positively blindsided.

And terrified.

Fifty-one

My chest squeezed as Priest and Ashley stared at each other in a way I'd never seen them look at anyone else. What radiated from them was more than desire and masculine heat. It went beyond the habits of possessiveness and dominance. I saw it in their eyes—their unconditional love. It blazed with a magnetic force that was too powerful to be controlled or ignored.

I clutched my throat, breathing through the terrible tightness. I was jealous. But also aghast with awe and envy. I coveted what they shared. I wanted that history with them. That brotherly bond. Without it, I felt like an outsider looking in.

With each passing second, the emotions that Ashley kept so well hidden began to surface. Muscles twitched in his clenched jaw. The hands at his sides opened and closed. His entire body seemed to lean toward Priest, his strength visibly contracting, fighting against the pull.

As his control unraveled, I tried to embrace my conflicting feelings about their relationship. I wanted them together. They would never be truly happy apart. But I yearned to be part of it, of them, of whatever they were within the walls of their stolen, private moments.

"Stop looking at me like that." Priest's eyes didn't waver from Ashley's as he rose from the chair and leaned into Ashley's face. "Unless you intend on sticking around this time."

"That was low, even for you." Standing an inch taller than Priest, Ashley pivoted and strolled aft toward the bathing chamber. "I'm drawing a bath."

A bath? At this hour?

The moonlight, skittish now beyond the windows, wouldn't be returning tonight. Dawn was approaching. None of us were going to sleep.

Ashley moved through the bedchamber with natural grace and balance—the gait of a man accustomed to the rolling decks of a ship. But I marked the fatigue in his broad shoulders and the sheen of dust on his white breeches. He'd just arrived from London and probably made the multi-day journey astride a horse to get here quicker.

A bath was exactly what he needed.

"You can hear." Priest appeared before me, crouching at eye level, his hand soft against my cheek. "Every word?"

"My hearing's returned to normal." My brows furrowed, my thoughts elsewhere.

"Talk to me." Elbows braced on the arms of my chair, he let his hands dangle on my lap, trickling light caresses against my thighs. "Tell me every thought in that beautiful head."

"All right." I cleared the scratch in my voice. "I want to understand. I'm trying. But I feel like I don't know either of you. I'm in love with two men who are living this whole other life."

"That's not—"

"Be quiet and let me speak." I breathed in slowly and released my lungs. "For two years, I believed the author of that letter was a gorgeous, intriguing noblewoman, who was torn between her duty and her heart."

"You weren't entirely wrong. The noblewoman just happens to be a noble*man*."

"The same nobleman *I* fell in love with." *What were the odds?*

The sound of water pumping from cisterns drifted from the bathing chamber.

I dragged my fingers over my hair, unable to find my bearings in this new reality. "I have so many questions."

"Ask them." His hand found mine.

I met his adoring eyes and steeled my spine. "Have you been with other men?"

"No. Neither has Ashley. The physical aspect of our relationship didn't surface until he joined the Royal Navy. As we grew older, time and distance separated us, and within that loneliness, our longing evolved into something more primal." His dark eyebrows crept

Sea of Ruin

together. "Perhaps lust is a symptom of the trust we built together as boys. But it's never been a driving force between us. Nor have we ever sought sexual relations with other men."

I nodded. Then shook my head. "I don't know how I fit into that."

"Well, Ashley and I prefer the softer, lovelier, fiercer sex... As it happens, we prefer one woman in particular, who is eager to do more with her life than breed heirs and attend society dinners." He smiled softly. "You're the glue, Bennett. The reason we're here. Think about it. Ashley and I fell in love with the same woman. Was that coincidence? Or something more profound? You know what I think?" He traced his thumb along my bottom lip. "You're the overruling destiny that he and I have been traveling toward our whole lives. Our paths forked, veered, crossed, and forked again a dozen times. And here we are, right where we started. *With you.*"

I loved the sound of that. So much. My hand went to my mouth as a hot rush of tears swelled.

"Damn you." I slapped at the trickle of moisture that leaked from my eyes. "I don't want to cry anymore."

"They're bold tears. Dauntless. God knows you've earned them." He slipped the backs of his fingers along my cheek. "So resilient and tough, yet at the same time, beautifully delicate."

"I'm none of those things, Priest. I'm scared. I remember the devastation on your face in Nassau when Ashley left you. Losing him ruined you so completely you drowned yourself in drink. I knew then that I couldn't compete with your lover. And I know it now, seeing the way you look at each other. I'm so afraid of being shut out."

"The night I stole your compass, we were in your private cabin, and you asked me why I was there. Do you remember what I said?"

"Why are you here?"
"You know why."
"You want to fuck me."
"That's a given, but not nearly the heart of it."
"What, pray tell, could be the heart of your intentions, if not to wet your cock?"
"It's really quite simple. I want to take care of you."

I leaned into the hand he held on my cheek. "You want to take care of me."

"More than anything. I want to spend the rest of my life protecting and worshiping you." His fingers shifted to my hair and clenched with shocking assertiveness. "I want to make love to my wife. It's been two years, Bennett."

A flame of desire, that which lay dormant for so long, stirred between my legs.

I glanced toward the bathing chamber, searching for Ashley, and there he was. Leaning near the doorway, wearing only his breeches, he watched us with a dark, heated look that spiked the temperature of my blood to dizzying heights.

"The bath is ready." He pushed away from the wall and vanished inside the chamber.

Priest slid his arms beneath me and drew me to his chest as he stood.

I'd put in an ungodly amount of work over the past three weeks into ensuring I could walk on my own two feet. But he wanted this. *He wants to take care of me.*

So I circled my arms around his strong neck and offered a prayer of gratitude unto the higher powers for giving me another chance to experience his love.

He set me down in the bathing chamber. Aglow with candlelight and lavishly decorated, the space paid homage to the large rectangular bath in the center. The first time I walked in here, I tripped and fell on my face, thunderstruck.

Constructed from gleaming marble, the bath was finely veined and made smooth. Deep as my middle on the outside, with steps on the inside that descended into the floor, it was big enough to accommodate four people.

Faucets arranged overhead, connecting with pipes that led to a cold water cistern, a copper one in which water was heated, and a sophisticated drainage system.

Steam rose from the water, and within that vapor, Ashley sprawled, his body submerged and head tipped back on the edge, facing us.

"This chamber is…" I shifted my weight, looking around. "It's unlike anything I've ever seen."

"You should visit the city of Bath, just west of London." He swirled a lazy finger through the water. "It's named after its fashionable Roman-built baths. My father had this chamber erected in the likeness of the architecture there."

Another doorway stood closed behind him, which I knew led to the rooms his parents once occupied. Now they sat empty and vacant.

"Do your parents ever come here?" I asked.

Sea of Ruin

"No. They rarely leave London. Even when I was a child, they were never here." His eyes met mine. "Get in the water, Bennett."

My nerves twitched. I didn't know why. I wasn't restrained by a sense of modesty, and over the past two months, they'd attended to every bare crevice, crease, and shadow of my body. But this was different. New.

I shifted to Priest and gripped the nightgown. His hands went to mine, taking over the task. Lifting the linen, he pulled it up and off.

The impulse to cover myself beckoned, but I'd put a lot of effort into not only rebuilding my strength but also my confidence. I looked down at my pert breasts, trim waist, flat belly, toned hips and legs.

Had I returned to normal? Not quite. My muscles needed more strengthening. My elbow smarted when I moved it. My ribs protested twisting motions. But I didn't stumble. I didn't whimper. I was pleased with my progress.

The worst of my injuries, old and new, drew jagged lines across my abdomen and up my forearm. I owned those marks because I was a pirate. We wore scars and wooden limbs the way soldiers wore medals and ribbons.

My blond hair hung in wild, heavy coils to my waist. When it was wet, it was even longer. And shiny. Healthy.

I was healthy.

"Your skin is like alabaster." Ashley's eyes fevered as he blatantly stared at my naked flesh, which hadn't seen sunlight in two months. "You're a raving beauty clad in any garment. But one glimpse of you without clothes is enough to send a lethal jolt along a hungry man's cock."

I sighed, biting back a smile.

"I love her mouth." Priest clasped my hand and led me to the bath. "It's not like that of a sweet girl in her first bloom. Bennett's mouth is impish, seductive, and full of teeth, made for biting, licking, and sucking all rationale from a man's head." He gave my bare backside a hard slap, making me yelp. "In the bath, madam."

I lifted my legs over the edge and into the warm water, craning my neck to look at him.

He untied the flap on his breeches and pushed the material to the marble floor, exposing his relaxed cock, the full length of his musculature, and the scars that had burned most of his left leg.

His eyes caught mine, warning me not to ask about the injury.

I shifted and met Ashley's gaze. No surprise or horror there. He already knew about them.

"Did he tell you how he got them?" I asked Ashley.

He nodded.

"This is exactly what I was talking about." A stab of pain hit my stomach, like a tiny knife sinking its way in. "You share things between you. Secrets, friendship, childhood, trust… Since I'm not part of that fraternity—"

"It happened in Nassau." The water splashed beside me as Priest slid into the bath.

His arm hooked around my back, taking me with him. The steps were designed for sitting, and after a few adjustments, he had us positioned on one with me on his lap. I leaned back against his chest, letting the surface of the water rise to my nipples, lapping at the sensitive tips.

He held me close, his mouth beside my ear, and told me the story.

"You saw what I looked like when Ashley left me. But you didn't witness my self-destruction when I realized I'd lost you, too." He found my hand beneath the water and moved it to the bubbled flesh on his thigh. "I rowed a jolly boat out to sea and set it afire."

"What?" My pulse exploded as I tried to push up. "While you were in it?"

He trapped me against his chest, the bar of his arm like iron across my midsection. "I wanted to die. Positively the least manly thing I've attempted in my life. The fire only consumed one leg before the boat overset and doused me in the sea. I was content to drown there, but a fisherman pulled me out."

My stomach plunged with overwhelming guilt. I should have never left him. I should have been there.

"I ended up at the *Garden*," he said, "with a dozen prostitutes nursing me back to health for six miserable months. And before you ask—"

"I'm not going to ask."

"I'm saying it anyway for both of you to hear. Ashley is the last person I fucked, and that was over two years ago. Now…" He glided his hand across my abdomen and sank it between my thighs. "You're going to promise me that you will never feel guilty when you look at my scars. My actions forced you to run, and *I* set that fire. I vow to you that I will never do those two things again." He caressed his fingers along my slit, distracting me with the blissful sensation. "Promise me, Bennett. You will not blame yourself. Ever."

Sea of Ruin

"I promise." A gasp caught in my throat, and my gaze darted to Ashley.

He sat across from me, his chest and shoulders stiff above the water, and his hands… I couldn't see them, but I knew he was holding himself, touching and stroking that giant cock as he watched me.

His expression was serene. Gorgeously untroubled. I didn't have a clue how this three-way intimacy would work, but he liked seeing me with Priest. Or perhaps he loved seeing Priest with a woman.

"Have you…?" I licked my lips, hesitating. "Have you ever shared a female?"

"No," they said in unison.

Priest hardened and swelled against my backside, his breaths shortening. "Not once, in the twenty years I've known him, have we ever *planned* to fuck."

Fuck. I loved hearing that word on Priest's sinful, accented tongue. Chills. Every. Time.

"You're telling me," I said, "that you've never sought each other out just for pleasure?"

"Never. That part is always spontaneous between us." Ashley held Priest's gaze. "Usually angry. Often the result of a fight. It just happens. Then it's over, and we don't analyze it."

I valued that insight. It helped me understand the physical nature of their relationship.

It also aroused me. I could imagine it vividly. Just like they'd been in the bedchamber, punching and wrestling on the floor. Then the shift in the air. The change in temper, passion heating, consuming. Had I not dropped that water bucket, would they have fucked right there on the floor?

Curling two diabolical fingers, Priest slowly dipped them into my aching. My body's wetness was softer, thicker than water, easing the glide of his penetration. I dropped my head back on his shoulder, gripped his powerful thighs beneath me, and moaned.

"There's a voice in Ashley's head." Priest fingered me wickedly. "The voice of his father or mother, or perhaps it's God, telling him to be ashamed for loving a man. So whenever I take him to the ground and bury myself inside him, he fights it. Christ almighty, he loves to fight me."

Ashley's mouth parted on a groan, his face taut with strain.

My cunt clenched around Priest's fingers, pulling tighter, hungrier… Sweet mercy, I needed him. I dug my nails into his thighs, my legs spreading wider, nipples hardening, insides spasming for relief.

Ashley leaned back and stretched an arm along the edge of the bath, supporting his upper body as his other hand worked his lower half. I wanted to see his cock, thick and pulsing, in the grip of his fist. I ached to feel it, to taste it.

"On Ashley's ship…" I turned my mouth toward Priest, tasting his panting lips. "I watched him touch himself like that. Every night, he stood on his balcony and stroked his cock."

"He told me." A smoldering smile burned in Priest's eyes. "He told me every detail of every interaction you shared, and we'll do the same with you. We'll tell you anything you want to know about us. But right now, I need to fuck you."

Pushing up, he lifted us until he sat upon the top stair, which was level with the surface of the water. As he lowered me back to his lap, he shifted his hips and set his cock against my entrance.

Then he thrust.

I'd never been more grateful for my hearing than in that moment when the sound of his deep, guttural groan of pleasure hit my ears.

He palmed my breasts and moved his hips with a skill that made me want to weep. The sheer ecstasy of having him inside me was incomparable. The thrusting, the stretching, the slap of water, and the glide of heated skin—the man knew how to move inside a woman.

But this went deeper than pleasures of the flesh. The emotional connection fulfilled me beyond the tingling rush of orgasm. I was reunited with my husband, surrounded by his glorious scent, and reawakened by the rumbling, growling noises vibrating in his chest.

He gripped my face and dragged my mouth to his, plundering with lips and tongue. I fell into his kiss, riding his cock, feeding on his masculine beauty and strength, his lips as soft as warm silk, and his taste the flavor of fury.

The kiss was feral as the drive of his hips slammed harder, faster, chasing his release. The water splashed in my periphery, and moments later, a shocking breath of heat smothered the place where we were joined.

I tore my mouth away to find Ashley kneeling between my legs, his mouth on my cunt, and his hand around the root of Priest's cock. The unholy onslaught of stimulation shimmered through me, shaking me from the inside out.

He devoured us from below, burying his face, lashing his tongue, and working his full lips where Priest stroked his length in and out.

Sea of Ruin

My fingers tangled in Ashley's soft hair, holding his sinful mouth against us. Their hands slid over me, touching everywhere as if unable to get enough. I wanted more. Deeper. I needed the connection of their hearts and souls bound with mine as our bodies came together.

When the orgasm hit, it slammed into me with showers of sparks and waves of trembling pleasure. I moaned their names, grinding my hips, and seconds later, Priest joined me.

"Bennett!" His arms wrapped around my breasts, holding me against his chest as he used my body, stroking me up and down his length, thrusting erratically. "Ah, Christ, you feel good. So damn tight on my cock."

Ashley licked us through the peak while stroking himself beneath the water. Then he kissed his way up my front, lingering on my breasts and nipples before crushing his lips against mine.

I tasted myself on his tongue, so wildly turned on knowing his mouth had just been on Priest.

Then I felt his hand there, his fingers slipping around my opening, where Priest was still seated.

"God's teeth." Priest eased out and rammed back in. "Incredible."

Ashley pressed closer, kissing me passionately while inching his fingers into my body, sliding alongside Priest's cock.

"Think you can take both of us?" He nipped at my lips, groaning, panting, his entire body shaking. "I bet you can fit two. But not tonight. I'm not going to last long."

He lifted me off Priest, just high enough to pull me against him. My legs gripped his hips. My arms clung to his muscled shoulders. Then he impaled me where Priest had just been just seconds before.

I cried out, instantly feeling the size difference. Where Priest was big, Ashley was massive. He stood still in the water, his hands palming my backside, and gave me a moment to adjust. Then he unleashed his hunger.

"Missed you so much." He pounded with hard need, pushing to drive deeper, to get closer.

He leaned forward, and I felt Priest encompass us both from behind, my back against Priest's chest, trapped. There was no escaping this forbidden union. None of us were letting go.

I found an evil amount of satisfaction in watching Ashley's unseemly manners obliterate his starched, aristocratic mien. His features were scandalously stunning, his lips parting with shuddering grunts, his brows pinched, and his gaze never straying from mine.

He fucked me through two more orgasms before surrendering to his own.

Leaning my head back against Priest, I twitched and shivered through the remnants of bliss. Ashley bent in, catching his breath, his cock still pulsing inside me.

His gaze shifted to Priest, both of them panting, staring at each other that way they did. Then their faces drifted closer, their foreheads coming together, and before I could blink, their mouths collided.

They lifted their arms, reaching, grabbing, with me caught between them. I couldn't peel my eyes away from their kiss. They inhaled each other, their jaws hard and grinding. Priest wore a day's worth of rough whiskers, and I heard that stubble scratching against Ashley's soft skin.

I gloried in it, knowing I would never experience anything so beautifully intimate as this tender, unguarded moment between my pirate and my pirate hunter.

The kiss gradually dissolved with a masculine hum of moans. Ashley gave a lazy thrust of his hips, his *superior breeding* still hard, charged, and loaded inside me. Behind me, Priest rocked against me, grinding his lust against my backside.

"Are you well?" He kissed my neck.

"Quite satisfied, thank you."

Hungry, competing cocks threatened to take me fore and aft. But after several minutes of teasing pleasure, they didn't attempt something so new at such a late hour.

But they certainly satisfied me again.

Fifty-two

The next morning, I woke to the sublime sensations of four hands and two mouths idolizing my body. Fingers scattered sensual energy. Arms snaked around me. Palms glided down my front and back, immobilizing my hips. And I felt them. God help me, I felt the hard steely jabs of their lust fore and aft.

Delirious pressure built, channeling all the heat between my legs. Everything ached with restless desire.

Crushed between the marble slabs of two chests, I'd never fathomed waking in such an indecent position, never imagined wanting to remain here forever.

"I want this every day." I kissed the lips directly in front of me. *Priest.*

"I want all of you at once." He reached between us and found me wet. "I want your tight, hot cunt. Heavy breasts. Silky legs. And Christ, I want your impudent mouth."

He kissed me hotly, deeply, as Ashley's hand crept around from behind and joined Priest's fingers between my thighs.

Their bodies hardened and gathered against me, pressing in. The combined virility, the feverish hunger, the savage back and forth rocking of their battling hips… I trembled between them, quaking straight to the marrow of my bones.

My flesh came alive with raw, liquefying tingles as they teased me, played with me, and saw to my every need.

Spreading me open, twisting me around, beam over beam, they plundered my body. A pirate in my backside. An English officer down my throat. Stem to stern, they splayed my limbs and stretched every hole, pinning me, fucking me, and filling me with seed.

For hours, I received them. Separately. Two at the same time. Swarthy muscle, heated breaths, men moved in alternating strokes inside me. Ferocious men. Warriors. Friends. Enemies. Lovers.

Their cocks slid together. Their bodies rubbed with friction. Their hands overlapped and tangled, and sometimes, amid the wanton frenzy, their tongues collided in a kiss of dark masculine potency.

But they never showed an inclination to fuck each other. I was their one and only focus.

They set the staggered, frantic rhythm of our unholy trinity while I kissed their mouths, worshiped their cocks, and gasped *I love you's* from the depths of my soul.

Afterward, we lay in a sweaty pile of entangled limbs. Every inch of me felt sore. Lovingly used. Happy.

I smiled. Honest to God, I smiled so big and deep my face hurt. It was a smile unlike any that had come before it.

Curling up on my side in Priest's arms, my back to his chest, I listened to his breaths as he drifted in and out of sleep.

My scarred arm rested across the hard surface of Ashley's abdomen. He sprawled on his back, staring at the rafters. His cock lay across his thigh, thick and long, even in its flaccid state. Ridiculously gorgeous man.

"When we were in the cottage on Eleuthera..." I circled a finger around the small flat shape of his nipple. "Priest slipped a knife and an orange wedge into your hands, and you knew exactly what to do. Well done on that. The two of you managed to execute a plan, right between my legs of all places, without anyone catching on. And despite what happened to me on your ship with Madwulf, that plan with the orange saved me from a much darker fate."

Ashley gripped my hand on his stomach and closed his eyes, his expression pained.

"During the orange incident, Priest said something about your sister." I laced our fingers together. "He said, *Just like our ruse with Arabella.* What did that mean?"

Shifting to his side, Ashley graced me with his deep blue stare. "Arabella was in love with Priest. To be clear, every maiden, widow, and married lady within a hundred kilometers wanted Priest in her bed.

Sea of Ruin

But Arabella was cunning, lovely, and *relentless*. For years, I ordered him not to bed her."

"I didn't touch her, my lord," Priest muttered drowsily behind me.

"I know." Ashley reached over me and rested his hand on Priest's thigh, his thumb stroking the burn scars. "Priest rejected her at every turn," he said to me. "She desired him so badly she didn't care if the affair ruined her. But neither he nor I wanted that."

"Arabella was a spitfire." Priest chuckled. "Christ, I miss her."

A quiet moment passed between them before Ashley continued. "My sister was in her twenties and still unwed. She refused every offer, waiting for Priest. By this time, Priest and I were sixteen and eighteen, respectively. We were young, restless, and strung tight with sexual energy, of which we put to use on the local girls."

"But we spent most of our time alone in this manor, especially during the winter months," Priest said. "Curiosity and tedium brought forth…experimentation."

"You touched each other." I smiled softly, captivated by this side of them.

"Aye." Priest nuzzled my neck. "Hands reaching into trousers. A few strokes here and there. It felt good. Never awkward. We both preferred females, but more than that, we preferred each other's company. When those interactions led to opening our breeches and spending our seed together, it didn't bother us."

"Did Arabella know?" I asked.

"No." Ashley moved his hand to my face, clearing away a few wispy curls. "I overheard her talking to her lady's maid, plotting how she was going to sneak into Priest's room that night and seduce him. I knew my sister. She would've succeeded."

"So little faith in me," Priest drawled.

"She was wearing you down. You said so yourself." With a straight face, Ashley said, "I ate an orange, swished the juice through my teeth, and smeared it on my lips."

"Oh no." I gasped. "You didn't."

"He did." Priest chuckled. "The arsehole sneaked into my bed and put his mouth on me. Sucked my cock right down his throat. No one had ever done that before, and I only lasted—"

"Less than a minute. I daresay he embarrassed himself." Ashley smiled a rare smile, holding my gaze. "My tenacious sister crept into his room an hour later to find her dear Priest nursing a vile rash on his groin. Needless to say, she believed he had syphilis and thereby swore him off once and for all."

Just like our ruse with Arabella.

"You're an evil genius, Ashley Cutler." I leaned forward and kissed his sculpted lips.

"The evil part is right." Priest gave a halfhearted grunt. "I still don't trust his mouth near my cock."

I recalled what I knew about Ashley's carnal nature, his *unseemly manners*. The first time he was intimate with me, he brutally took me in my backside. Before that had been a string of merciless spankings.

"Do you spank Priest?" I fought a smile.

Priest tensed behind me. "I'd like to see him try."

All right. That answered that.

"What happened with Arabella?" I asked.

"She found another fellow to besiege. A fisherman. Of course, my parents did *not* approve." Ashley looked at me with his heart in his eyes. "He didn't show her the same respect Priest had. She got pregnant, banished from society, and you know the rest."

She'd died in childbirth.

"I was twenty when it happened. This house wasn't the same without her." Ashley idly stroked my collarbone. "So I left. Joined the Royal Navy, much to the despair of my parents."

"And me. I demanded he stay." Priest lifted on an elbow and curved a hand around my waist. "We fought about it. Beat the hell out of each other right here in this room." He cut his eyes to Ashley, narrowing them to slits. "He fucked me that night. It was our first time…" His nostrils widened. "The prick fucked me and walked out. I didn't see him again for a year."

I looked down, my chest aching and heart raw. That seemed to be a habit of Ashley's. The first time he'd fucked me, he'd left. Though he hadn't made it past the door of his cabin.

"You must have kept in touch over the years," I said.

"We wrote to each other." Exhaling, Priest rolled onto his back. "Without Ashley, I had no job here. Over the following year, I hopped from ship to ship, doing various work, making my way to the West Indies, and looking for my father. That's how I found a brother I didn't know I had."

"Reynolds." I smiled.

"Aye. We joined a pirate crew. Ashley called upon me between wars. Sometimes we met here. Other times, we reconnected in ports along the Western Ocean. Those infrequent visits were all he offered me."

Sea of Ruin

Until Nassau, when Ashley wrote Priest out of his life completely.

"During those times," Ashley said, "it was more important than ever that we kept our distance. You were making a notorious name for yourself, Priest. And I was an officer in the navy and—"

"You were my best friend."

Priest had every right to be furious. He'd been rejected by both Ashley and me. Yet, as he lay beside me, his fingers absently twisting through my hair, he seemed content. Peaceful.

It became suddenly apparent why he had a sheer lack of interest in hoarding spoils and ships from his plundering at sea. He had all the wealth he could ever need right here.

All he truly wanted, what he *needed*, was someone he could take care of. And perhaps someone to do the same for him.

"You told me on your ship," I said to Ashley. "that it had been two years since you bedded anyone. It was Priest, wasn't it? In Nassau? He was the last person you were with?"

"Yes."

"And before that?"

"I don't recall. Commanding His Majesty's Ship and fighting in wars didn't allow time for such affairs. Meanwhile, Priest spent the past fourteen years fucking every skirt that crossed his path."

"Until I met Bennett." Priest cocked a brow, its sharp downward tilt highlighting the languid dip of his eyes. "There will never be another woman for me."

My heart squeezed and expanded. "When you told me you loved two people, I didn't understand it. I didn't think it was possible. But I was wrong. Clearly." I picked at the ticking on the bed and lifted my eyes to Ashley. "I should ask you about your visit in London, but the only thing I want to know is if you saw your betrothed."

"Yes. I called on her. That *is* what's expected. Had I not, I would've been interrogated and harassed by every meddling lady in society."

Anger and jealousy coiled up my spine as I rose to a sitting position. "What's her name?"

"You intend to kill the lovely girl?"

I struggled in my rioting emotions when it came to these two men, but I did *not* struggle in this.

"Yes." I met him stare for stare. "If you marry her, I will gut her. A knife in the belly. Thrust. And *twist*. No hesitation. So I should hope that while you were in London for three damned weeks, you had the wherewithal to break off the betrothal."

"I did no such thing." He grabbed my throat and in the next breath, had me on my back with his weight atop of me. "I was in London to explain why I didn't arrest the despicable pirates Bennett Sharp and Priest Farrell whilst they were in my grasp. With a ship full of witnesses, I had to spin lies and exaggerate truths to avoid a court-martial and demotion. I was *not* in London to deal with personal matters."

"Break off the engagement." I pushed against his chest, a useless effort. "Tell him, Priest."

"I've been telling him for years." Frustration simmered beneath Priest's voice as he stood from the bed. "Let it go, Bennett."

"I will not—"

"For now." He tipped his chin at Ashley, his eyes fixed on me. "We have a gift for you."

Ashley grabbed my hand and drew me up. All at once, the mood shifted. The men exchanged a look, and something akin to excitement passed between them.

"What?" I asked, impatient. "What is it?"

"A surprise. We need you dressed for it." Ashley ushered me toward the bathing chamber as he said to Priest, "It was important to me to be here for this. Thank you for waiting for me."

"I told you I would."

Their cryptic conversation prompted a fleet of questions from my mouth, of which they ignored. We bathed, dressed, groomed, and broke our fast in the dining hall. All the while, I pressed them for answers and was only met with irritating smiles.

I'd learned early on that the meals at Ashley's manor were unhurried, leisurely affairs. Servants drifted around the table, setting out silver platters of cured bacon and kipper, boiled eggs, kidney offal, blackberry flummery with whipped syllabub, and scores of produce from the manor's gardens.

As the kitchen maids answered to the demands of the dining table, they stole heated glances at Priest. He'd mentioned that the staff had been employed here for most of their lives. Now that I knew he'd been employed here with them, I could only assume that he'd bedded every maid at least once over the past twenty years.

I couldn't care a whit. He was mine now. I had his loyalty, and it seemed that he had theirs.

"You trust them." I nodded at the door as it closed behind the last kitchen maid.

Sea of Ruin

"Unquestionably," Priest said. "They know what I am. But before I was a pirate, I was their friend. Their kin. Still am. No amount of reward will turn their allegiance."

"They've known about Priest's relationship with me since it began." Ashley leaned back in the chair. "They would defend us with their lives."

Relief descended, and more questions bubbled up. "When you captured me, you truly didn't know about my relationship with Priest?"

"No." Ashley released a slow breath. "I had no idea. When you fell into my custody, it was pure coincidence. Or *fate*."

As I finished the remainder of my meal, he talked through his change of heart over those first couple of weeks. Yes, he'd initially hunted me with every intention to turn me in and further his career. But he'd agonized over the idea every day. By the time he'd taken me into the wardroom and shown me the sketch of Priest, he'd already decided. He'd only wanted to track down Priest for help in staging a believable escape for me.

Once I had all my answers, he read from a newspaper, catching up on the day's news, while holding a tedious conversation with Priest about his business in London. Given my huffing and their twitching mouths, I knew they were deliberately dragging out the anticipation for my surprise.

Eventually, Ashley stood and held out his hand to me. "Shall we?"

They took me to my ship.

The manor sat high on the cliffs, overlooking the private bay. Rather than navigating the rocky paths to the shore below, Priest and Ashley led me through a maze of winding stairs and tunnels beneath the estate. The glow of a torch led the way. At the lowest level, an exterior door opened to a dock and a waiting jolly boat.

And across the bay sat *Jade* in all her glory.

The shadows of her soaring masts fell across the nearby cliff, her yards clewed as she patiently waited to weigh.

She was a fighter. A survivor. She'd faced off against a warship with twice her weight in guns. When my father had seized her, she was the only galleon in the Spanish treasure fleet that hadn't sunk in the hurricane. *She was spitting fire and laughing at the storm,* he'd said.

As Priest and Ashley rowed me toward her mighty stern, I couldn't stop staring at her sleek lines and winking gun ports, admiring, smiling. Despite myself, I felt a shimmering surge of pride.

My crewmates greeted me with revelry. Cheers, whistles, and rib-crushing hugs carried me across the upper deck. Amid the fray of merriment, I lost sight of Priest and Ashley. The sailors swarmed me with smiles, the air leaden with sweat, brine, and sunshine, as they pulled me through the throng, spinning me this way and that.

A huge pair of hands caught my face, and hard wet lips smacked hard against mine. When I leaned away, Reynold's glittering brown eyes smiled back.

"Your brother will kill you for that." I laughed.

"And I shall die a happy man." He gripped my arms and held them out. "Pray, Captain, look at you!"

I wore a blue gown that clewed up at the hips, exposing the striped seaman's trousers and black boots beneath. The corset accentuated curves and musculature that hadn't rounded my frame a month ago.

The jade stone dangled from my throat. A brace of knives hung about my waist, along with my compass and cutlass. I hadn't fully regained the strength required to wield such a weighty weapon. But my father's blade belonged there, on my hip, close at hand.

"Your hat, Captain." The cabin boy stepped forward, holding out the three-cornered hat.

I jammed it on my head and tilted up my chin to meet his eyes. "D'Arcy, I daresay you've grown a fathom since I last saw you."

Twin stains of scarlet bloomed on his smiling cheeks.

Three months ago, Reynolds had pushed me over the bow and tossed me onto a path I would've never imagined. A lot had changed since I last stood on this deck as Captain Sharp. But my favorite things had remained exactly the same.

"Captain." Jobah strolled toward me, his long arms drawing me into a hug. "Welcome home."

I squeezed him tight and rose on my tiptoes to put my mouth against the black skin of his cheek. "I know about the compass."

His laughter rumbled through me, and I shoved him away. Shoulders back and spine straight, I tried to stand before him as his captain. But he couldn't stop laughing.

Neither could I. "Next time, I'll punish you."

"Yes, Captain." The bloody bastard didn't believe me. Not for a second.

I looked at Reynolds, sobering. "Thank you for waiting for me at Harbour Island."

"Anytime, anywhere, Captain." His eyes drifted over my shoulder toward the companionway. "Priest and Ashley are waiting. You must

Sea of Ruin

be here for your surprise."

"Evidently." I started to turn then glanced back at Jobah and Reynolds. "Are you coming?"

They shared a smile, and Reynolds said, "We wouldn't miss it."

Moments later, I stood in my cabin and stared at the tiny scroll on the desk.

"That's not the surprise." Leaning against the wall beside Jobah, Priest rubbed his whiskered jaw. "Go ahead. Every man in this room has already peeked at it."

I glanced at Jobah, Reynolds, and Ashley, their blank expressions giving nothing away.

"I had my reasons for not telling you about the map," I said to them. "It was my most safely guarded secret. I presume Priest told you its history."

Reynolds glanced down at his boots and nodded. "While we sailed from Harbor Island to the island of the birds to get you back, he told the crew everything."

The moment I'd made the map known to Madwulf and his pirates, it was no longer a secret. Priest had done the right thing.

"Good." I drew in a breath and snatched the scroll from the desk.

The room fell silent as I unrolled the strip of parchment that was no wider than my thumb. Squinting, my eyes swept over the tiny image of a map at the top.

The island of oaks? Christ, the print was so small I would need a magnifying glass to read it. "I can't—"

"Oak Island. It's near the Sholes of Acadia," Jobah said. "I already plotted the course, Captain."

"Acadia? Isn't that north of the Great Western Ocean?"

"Far north. Between New England and Newfound-land."

"What the hell was my father doing all the way up there?" I scanned the rest of the parchment, finding detailed descriptions of the treasure's hidden location on the island. "Have any of you ever been this far north?"

A chorus of *No's* resounded.

"Well, then we're in for an adventure." With a thrill in my blood, I gestured at the gold hoops in Reynold's ear. "If we succeed, you won't be needing those."

Like most pirates, he wore the ornaments as a means to pay for a respectable burial at sea when he died.

"You'll have gold on your fingers and dangling about your neck," I said.

"Aye." He flashed me his barracuda smile.

"When do we sail?" I looked directly at Ashley.

He glared back, and I knew he wouldn't consent to join us. Not easily. Before we departed, he would learn to never say *No* to the fury of a woman.

"We'll sail when you're ready, Captain." Priest clasped my hand and led me out of the cabin. "First, we have something to give you."

I followed him through the lower decks, down hatchways, and deeper still, until we arrived at the bilge.

My stomach hardened. The last time I stood here, Priest was down below, clapped in irons, his hands blistered, because I'd cruelly exposed him to oranges.

"Is it my turn?" I laughed, a strained, humorless sound, and met his eyes. "Are you going to shackle me down there and stroke yourself while I watch?"

"Jesus." Reynolds coughed into his fist.

Jobah chuckled, and Ashley arched a brow.

"As much as I love that idea…" Priest brought my hand to his mouth and kissed the knuckles. "Your present is of a very different nature."

He glanced at the brace of knives around my waist, confusing me. Then he opened the hatch and led me into the bilge.

At the bottom of the ladder, I didn't know what I expected to find. But as I turned and lost my breath, it wasn't this.

Madwulf was chained to the wall.

Alive.

Fifty-three

My heart luffed, turned about, and plowed into a vicious storm. I drew the cutlass from the brace around my hips, my wounded arm trembling beneath the weight of steel, as I growled at the monster before me.

"Easy, Goldilocks." Ashley stood at my back, close enough to breathe against my ear. "Ipswich didn't keep him alive for two months for you to strike him down in one swing." His voice dipped, deliciously dark. "Savor it."

Madwulf hung from chains, nude, mutilated, and glaring out of pained, bloodshot eyes. His mouth gaped and drooled as he screamed garbled nonsense. No tongue. His ears were gone. As were his fingers, toes, and one entire arm.

The missing extremities had been treated to thwart infection. Ipswich was a master at that. Many men on my crew hobbled around just fine with wooden limbs after Ipswich's care.

The rest of Madwulf appeared intact. Covered in bruises, old and fresh, his filthy skin crusted with blood. Someone had shaved his head and face, depriving him of that which he cherished.

"All this time..." I heaved through a smothering fog of black memories. "I thought he was dead."

"We let you think that." Priest leaned against the far wall and crossed his arms. "We didn't want his survival to tax or distract you while you worked so hard to heal."

"You brought me severed feet and other body parts that he clearly still retains." I rubbed my head, trying to remember. "Did I imagine that?"

"No. Those belonged to the men involved in your torture. Ashley and I collected their souls with the very plank of wood they used upon your body."

I shivered. Shuddered. Then I smiled. "This is my gift?"

"Aye." Priest tipped his head at Madwulf. "Show him how utterly fierce you are, my love."

Ashley circled me, lifting the cutlass from my shaking hand and passing it to Priest.

"Madwulf knows nothing." He leaned in and cupped my face. "He's been rotting down here for two months with no answers as to how you outsmarted him. Tell him." A shadow passed over his expression, threatening, deadly. "Make him feel the pain he inflicted upon you when he destroyed your father's letter."

My mind ran amok with bloodthirsty plans, my veins sizzling with the depravity of my thoughts.

From my waist, Ashley removed a dagger and pressed it against my hand. Then he lifted my hat from my head, kissed my lips, and joined Priest, Jobah, and Reynolds along the far wall, settling in to watch.

Oh, where to start?

"Syphilis." I prowled toward the Highlander, casually paring a fingernail with the knife. When I reached him, I put my face in his, slanting him my most disturbing look from beneath my lashes. "Priest and I have no infections or disease."

As I told Madwulf about Priest's reaction to oranges, *Jade's* location on Harbour Island, and my bait with the island of the birds, I flayed the flesh from his body, strip by despicable strip. I cut and diced until bones glistened in the lantern light. I removed his nose, carved out his eyes, and relieved him of the shriveled rotten meat between his legs.

I gloried in the flow of blood. It wouldn't bring back my father's letter, but I felt vindicated for ridding the earth of an evil that would never again threaten a farmer's daughter or separate a lady pirate from those she loved.

As he expelled his final breath, I felt purged.

"I didn't rush it, did I?" I wiped the bloody blade on a rag.

"You've been at it for nigh two hours." Reynolds pushed up from his position on the floor and ambled toward the ladder. "I think I'll go vomit now."

"In my homeland," Jobah said, "we lashed our enemies to poles and held them over a fire, just above the lick of the flames, cooking them alive from the inside out for days." He grinned, all teeth and savage loyalty.

"I believe Jobah just volunteered to clean up the gore." Priest clapped the helmsman on the shoulder, chuckling.

In the end, we all carried out Madwulf's remains. The gift, as it was, was fed to the gulls and cold-blooded vertebrates that lived in the bay.

That night, I slept peacefully in the arms of a pirate and pirate hunter. But when I woke, it was still dark, and the arms were gone.

I raised my head, listening to the hushed tones trickling from across the room.

"When?" Priest paced in front of the fireplace.

"Next week." Ashley sprawled in a nearby armchair, sipping from a dram of amber liqueur.

"You're not going through with it." Priest spun, his accent thick and hushed. "I won't allow it."

"Take it up with my parents." Ashley stared at his drink. "It can't be helped."

"You're weak."

"And you're naive. You always have been with your goddamned whimsical ideals." Ashley swilled the rest of his glass. "It's like you never grew up. Never left this room. We're not careless boys anymore, Priest. This is life. The strife of being an adult. We always knew what we had…" He straightened. "We knew it would end eventually."

"Happiness. That's what you speak of."

"Yes. We were happy." Ashley set the empty glass aside and sighed. "That sentiment doesn't fit into my life."

My muscles gathered and tensed, my breaths rushing out. But I held still, feigning sleep, waiting.

"So what's your plan." Priest whirled toward him, his whisper seething. "Are you going to leave her a letter and slink away like the coward you've become?"

"It's different this time." Ashley dragged a hand down his face, his voice crestfallen. "She has you."

"She wants both of us. Don't underestimate her pertinacity, my friend. She'll cut your pretty rosebud before the nuptials are over."

Nuptials? Was that what Ashley referred to as *next week?*

I set my jaw, fingers twitching.

"Did she tell you the story about the Marquess of Grisdale?" Priest laughed hollowly. "She was only fourteen and—"

"Yes, I know." Ashley stood, his gaze darting in my direction. "I'm going for a walk."

Priest followed him out of the bedchamber.

Had Ashley seen me awake? I didn't think so. Either way, I wasn't about to let the conversation drift away from me.

I pulled on a nightgown and followed the sounds of their voices through the manor. A maze of corridors led me past torches and gilded paintings. The hour was late, and all the servants were asleep in their quarters at the opposite end of the estate.

Through parlors and great rooms, I trailed undetected. When I found them in the kitchen, I slipped into a shadowed alcove across the hall.

"While I was in London, they hanged another couple for sodomy." Ashley stood at the long wooden table, his hands braced on the scarred surface. "The conviction of the two men rested entirely on the hearsay of a landlord and his wife, who claimed to have witnessed the crime through the keyhole of a door. Their testimony described anatomically impossible acts, and there were no other witnesses or evidence." With his eyes starkly staring before him, he seemed to be unconsciously fascinated by the scratches on the table. "The gaoler escorted the alleged lovers to the gallows with twelve other men."

"Stop this." Priest leaned in and got in his face. "That won't be us."

"They were hanged alongside thieves, rapists, and murderers. I read the newspaper report. The crowd of spectators hissed and jeered. Not at the other criminals. No, their loathing disapproval was directed at the two men who committed a crime where there was no injury done to anyone." He straightened and stepped away from Priest, his expression empty. "I'm returning to London on the morrow. I have my wedding and obligations to attend—"

"You fell in love with two pirates." I charged into the kitchen, my hands fisting at my sides. "I know that comes with a slew of concerns and difficulties, so we're going to hash it out right now."

Neither man looked surprised by my abrupt presence. They must have known I was eavesdropping. Ashley moved to put distance between us. But Priest grabbed him and slammed him face-down on the table.

"Concern number one." I stood beside them and bent down to meet Ashley's angry eyes. "Neither Priest nor I can give you children. No heir means your father, the first Viscount Warshire, will be the *last* viscount."

Sea of Ruin

"I don't care about that." With his cheek pressed on the table and held in place by Priest's hand, the candlelight flickered upon him and communicated to his hard, tense features and rumpled hair. It was the appearance of a man desperately trying to control that which could not be tamed.

I'd already gleaned his indifference about children. He never mentioned a desire to be a father. Never showed interest in the matter.

Reaching down, I cupped his crotch, where he stooped over the table, pinned beneath Priest's immovable body. He wasn't hard, but the intimate touch seemed to calm his thrashing. I needed his attention.

"Two." I stroked him with my thumb, making him groan. "You love your career, and to be with us, you must give it up, along with your esteemed position in the *beau monde*. You will become a Royal Navy deserter, a lowly status so far removed from your stalwart character. I understand the quandary, and I'm not making light of it."

"It's a difficult decision," Priest said, his voice a low growl. "But not an impossible one."

Ashley slid his arm onto the table and sank his head upon it. "You're wasting your time."

Priest watched me steadily, his eyes burning with the same ire I felt. But there was something else there. Beneath the anger lay years of disappointment. A man could only be rejected so many times before parts of him started chipping away. He'd lost this fight with Ashley again and again, and he didn't expect this time to be any different.

But it was two against one now. Priest wasn't alone.

"The third concern," I said to Ashley, "is the one that troubles you the most. Choosing us comes with grave danger. Priest and I are wanted for many crimes, sodomy being the least of our offenses."

"Your concern about the gallows doesn't go away if you leave us." Priest shored up his hold on Ashley's flexing arms, driving his point home with the intensity of his breaths. "Bennett and I will be hunted for the rest of our lives."

Ashley stopped struggling and stared at nothing, his eyes unfocused as he absorbed our words.

"I told you my parents' story." I removed my hand from his groin and bent over the table beside him, mirroring his pose. "In my mother's stubborn sense of duty, she forsook my father and left him desolate and forlorn. She thought she was protecting him, that if he stayed with her, she would make him weak and distracted. She believed their relationship would lead to his ultimate execution." My voice broke on a pained whorl of breath. "In the end, my father hanged anyway, and she followed him."

"We're not your parents." With his face inches from mine, his blue eyes pierced, sharp and unyielding. "This manor is isolated, secure, and the staff is loyal. Priest and I have been meeting here for fourteen years without discovery."

"So that's your plan?" I pushed away from the table, my shoulders quaking with rage. "You intend to marry the virgin and keep your immoral lovers on the side?"

Pain burrowed into Priest's features. "He'll expect us to meet him here, in his stronghold of debauchery and filthy secrets, year after year." He leaned down, seething in Ashley's face. "Meanwhile, your viscountess will be oblivious to your unseemly manners while she remains in London and breeds your heirs. Is that your solution?"

"Yes." One syllable, issued with the unrelenting chill of propriety. "It's all I can offer."

I saw red, forced myself to blink, and slowly reined in my temper.

"When you chose the Royal Navy over Priest, you fucked him and left him." Pacing along the back wall, I eyed a row of kitchen knives and plucked a heavy one from its hanger. "I'll be honest, Ashley. I charged in here a moment ago with visions of Priest fucking you over this table and leaving with me afterward. Perhaps a dose of your own medicine would send you running after us. But we don't need any more hurt in this relationship. The three of us have experienced enough pain and loneliness to last a lifetime, don't you think?" I looked at Priest. "Let him up."

They rose at the same time. Ashley straightened his shirt and retreated a few steps, putting his back against the wall. Priest lowered his hands to the table, slightly bent, watching us both from beneath his dark brow.

Ashley wasn't even trying to argue or state his case. His English nobility and fealty to his king were so deeply ingrained he wouldn't turn against it to fight for his own dreams. He would let Priest and me walk out of his life because he genuinely believed he wasn't allowed to have us.

In a way, I was equally narrow-minded and stubborn, for I saw no other plausible future than living on my ship with him and Priest at my side. I would threaten Ashley, and if that didn't work, I would capture him the same way he'd captured me. But first, I would try to reach him with my voice.

Sea of Ruin

Standing beside Priest, I gripped his fingers with one hand and held the knife at my side with the other. Across the kitchen, Ashley regarded me, wearing that starched, impassive mask I loathed so much.

"The great purpose of life is love." I met him stare for stare, my heart beating loudly and clearly behind every word. "To know with certainty that we exist, we must love and be loved, even through the pain. It's the inexplicable fever inside us, which drives us to battle, to sacrifice, and to surrender. Deny it, Ashley, and all you have left is a starving emptiness."

Priest tightened his hand around mine, his fingers hot and shaking. His emotional investment in Ashley was palpable.

"If you leave for London on the morrow," I said, "and marry a woman for whom you feel nothing, you're choosing loneliness. I can't let you do that. Because I love you. I will *not* let you end up like my mother. Fear drove her from my father. Fear for his safety and survival. She chose loneliness over danger and love. In the fourteen years that I knew her, there was no light in her eyes. No smile. She wore a stately mask just like you, but I keenly felt what she hid beneath it. Do you know what that was?"

"A starving emptiness." His wooden voice was an attempt at apathy. Counterarguments loomed on the far side of it. But closer, right there in his eyes, was the man I loved clinging to every word.

Because his heart knew I was right. His thick head just needed time to come to terms with it.

"You will break off the betrothal." I rotated the hilt of the knife in my hand, calculating the weight and length of the blade. "Desert the Royal Navy. Make whatever arrangements you must with your parents to transfer your obligations. I know it's a staggering hell of a lot to give up while I stand here, sacrificing nothing. But I swear to God, if the roles were reversed, if giving up my life—*Jade*, my crew, the sea, my father's treasure—meant we could be openly together in *your* life, I would do it. I would relinquish it all and choose you and Priest, no mistake."

"This is intolerable." He exuded the bearing of a commodore, his voice layered in steel. "You cannot ask me to—"

"I'm not *asking* you to choose us, Ashley. I'm demanding it. If you forsake us, I will hunt you down like an animal."

He straightened, teeth bared and eyes blazing. "Don't you dare threaten—"

I flung the knife. It spun, end over end, across the kitchen and landed with a thunk in the wall beside his head. He froze, breathless, his gaze cutting to the side and narrowing on the blade that protruded no farther than the width of a whisker from his cheek.

He yanked the knife away as Priest strode toward him. Their eyes connected, their postures hard and combative. But as Priest raised his hand, it wasn't to hurl a punch. His fingers curled around the back of Ashley's neck and dragged their foreheads together.

"Perhaps I should have said this years ago." Priest closed his eyes and released a breath. "I didn't know how to put it into words."

"Don't." Ashley gripped Priest's shoulders, neither pushing nor pulling, as he gritted his teeth. "Don't do this."

"I don't know what to call it…this invisible thing that wraps so tightly around us. All I know is that I want to protect it, guard it with my life, and never let it go. This isn't something that needs mending or burying. It's raw and honest and perfect, and you damn well know it." Priest leaned back enough to hold Ashley's gaze. "I love you."

Ashley's chest hitched, his expression so unguarded I felt his longing in my bones.

"You like hearing me say that to you?" Priest tangled his hands in Ashley's hair, holding their faces together. "I love you, and I will keep fighting for us. But this time, we're doing it Bennett's way. And a word of warning. The last time I crossed her, I woke shackled in the bilge of her ship with a vicious bump on my head."

My chest squeezed as Priest released him and joined my side.

"*Jade* will leave at dawn on the day of your wedding." I squared my shoulders and raised my chin. "All three of us will be on that ship."

Ashley glared so hard a vein bulged in his brow.

Without another word, Priest gripped my hand and led me into the corridor.

We took to the stairs and tunnels beneath the manor. Then, in the pitch of night, we rowed the jolly boat to *Jade*. Our weapons, the compass and map, everything that mattered to us was on the ship.

Except Ashley.

But he would come. I'd never been more confident of anything in my life.

Fifty-four

One week later, I stood at the balcony of my private cabin on *Jade*, squinting at the dock that led to Ashley's manor. The crisp twilight breeze kissed my skin, chilling my nude body. But it didn't persuade my mood. I felt hot, restless, anxious to weigh.

Today was Ashley's wedding.

The sun crowned the distant horizon, burning the underbelly of the dark sky in shades of rose and gray amber. As dawn approached, the shadows shifted around the dock. I narrowed my eyes, telling myself a nobleman was standing there as if that could actually make one materialize.

"Come back to bed." Priest's husky baritone floated from the mattress behind me.

I chewed my thumbnail, my eyes glued to the dock.

The ship creaked. Footsteps sounded. Arms came around me from behind, and his warm physique, naked as I was, pressed against my back.

"Too much time has passed between raids." He pulled my hand from my mouth and inspected my fingernails. "You've chewed them down to the quicks."

"I miss the open sea. I *need* to sail."

"Soon." He leaned his hips against my backside, letting me feel the state of his morning hardness.

He was always in a state of hardness. The man had the appetite of a wolf in mating season.

His hands roamed my hips, caressed upward, and encircled my bare breasts. While waiting for Ashley, we'd spent the past week in this cabin—in the bed, on the floor, against the wall, bent over the desk, rocking against any surface that would support us.

I knew he was anxious about Ashley. But rather than talk about his nervous energy, he preferred to fuck it out of himself while between my legs. It was also his way of showing me his commitment. Not just of body but his commitment of the soul. He was here with me, choosing me, no matter what.

"As long as you stare at that dock, he isn't going to show." His mouth inflicted havoc on the sensitive parts of my neck.

Reynolds had spent the past month readying *Jade* for the six-week journey across the Western Ocean. Food, water, wood, everything we needed had been collected and hauled on board. The only thing missing was Ashley.

"It's not dawn yet." I licked my lips, watching Priest's hands, muscled and tanned, knead the white globes of my chest. "He'll be here."

"What's your plan if he isn't?" He tweaked a nipple.

"I'll strap on my blades, steal the fastest horse in his stable, ride like the wind to London, and arrive before he relieves his bride of her maidenhood."

"You'll kill her."

"Depends. If she's curled up on the floor and crying in fear, perhaps I would take pity."

"If her virgin eyes saw the size of his cock, she would undoubtedly be in that position."

"Oh, yes, his superior breeding." I shook my head and laughed. "His words."

"Arrogant prick." His smile tickled my neck. "I think we got through to him."

"You do?" I turned in his arms to see his handsome whiskered face.

"Aye." He dipped his head and captured my lips.

It was a soft, languid kiss, one that drew my mouth to his in irresistible sips.

"You don't believe for a minute that he married her," I said between sweeps of his tongue.

"No. But..." His hand slipped down my flat belly and pressed firmly against the folds between my legs. "One week wasn't enough time for him to disband his life in London and walk away. He won't make it here by your deadline."

He sank his finger inside me. I gulped, tried to fight it. He stroked an explosive rhythm against my flesh. I moaned, tried to fight it. His other arm firmed its grip around my back, and he went about distracting me from my vigilance of the dock.

I tried to fight it until I ended up on the desk in the cabin with his cock buried to the hilt.

His lips lay waste to my focus, kissing and sucking my breasts, as he rocked at an agonizingly slow pace. My hands curled up and around his broad shoulders, my hips straining wantonly toward his.

While I'd regained my strength in the manor, he'd rebuilt his own. It shone in the hard muscles of his chest and abdomen as he flexed into me over and over.

Roguish masculinity radiated from him, especially while in the heat of passion. He embodied primal danger and power and something else. Something that called to the instinctual needs of a woman.

He was a protector, a provider, and an incomparable lover. The way he used his lips and moved his body had been and always would be one of my greatest weaknesses.

"Come on my cock, Bennett." He snarled the heated words into my mouth.

I responded instantly, trembling and gasping and clinging to his handsome hooded gaze. As he followed me with his own release, the sound of *Jade's* windlass groaned into motion.

We froze, sharing a wide-eyed look.

"They're weighing." My chest clamped tight as I listened to the sounds of what was undeniably the anchor being hoisted from the sea. "Why are they weighing?"

The door opened, and we turned our heads.

Ashley stood in the gilded glow of dawn's light, his eyes afire with a sense of autonomy. His posture was properly rigid yet less…stifled. He looked free, independent, and self-governing.

Relief crashed through me in glorious waves of warmth, and Priest's spent cock gave an answering throb inside me. He caressed my thigh absently, his gaze locked on Ashley. Then he pulled out and drew me up to sit on the desk.

Ashley wore a white satin shirt, open at the collar. No doublet or waistcoat. No lace cuffs or jewel-encrusted buttons. Boots covered his feet. *Jackboots*. His legs—long and finely thewed—were cased in brown leather breeches, the likes of which I'd never seen him wear.

The sword he carried at his hip wasn't a cutlass. But it was practical, the kind used for hacking and surviving rather than sport. With his cropped short hair, clean-shaved face, and perfectly erect carriage, he didn't quite look like a pirate.

His muscled physique was that of a seafaring man, to be certain. But he clad it in fabrics from the most expensive haberdashers and bootmakers.

He looked like a pirate prince.

Elegantly masculine.

Strikingly confident.

Gorgeously male.

I perched on the edge of the desk and crossed my legs, poised like a lady, as if I weren't nude and freshly fucked. "You're late."

"Am I?" He closed the door behind him, his mouth twitching in the shadow of a grin, begging to be kissed. "I arrived two hours before dawn. I gave Reynolds the orders to weigh since you were otherwise indisposed. And missing me terribly, I see." His gaze drifted down my body. "Open your legs."

Jade groaned and creaked with the roll of the waves. She was officially in motion, set on a course to my father's treasure.

"You've been here for two hours?" I arched a brow. "What were—?"

"I have some demands in this arrangement." He strolled toward me and flicked a finger in the direction of my cunt. "Open."

Priest pulled on a pair of breeches from the armoire, his eyes alight with amusement. No help there.

Oh, blast it. I leaned back on my arms and spread my legs.

Ashley set the desk chair before me and lowered into it, reclining, his gaze on mine. "I sold my properties. All but one. The manor on the cliff, its tenants, staff, and land remain in my possession. I understand you wish to live on this ship, and I will remain at your side. But I require annual visits to England—all three of us—and so we shall call the manor our second home."

I nodded, grinning, loving him with all my heart.

"What happened with your parents?" Priest sat on the bed, his back to the wall, and an arm dangling over a bent knee.

"They were so absorbed in what I was losing that they never asked what I was getting in exchange. They believe I've gone mad."

"Perhaps, in time, they'll miss you enough to ask," I said.

Sea of Ruin

"Maybe. Maybe not." His expression showed neither sadness nor relief. This wasn't a mask. He was genuinely indifferent about it. "Given the company I now keep, my answers would be lies anyway." He set a hand on my thigh, his thumb absently stroking. "I ended the betrothal in person, and I daresay the young girl looked relieved. The Royal Navy, however, is a different matter. My superiors won't know I deserted until they realized I've stopped reporting in."

My pulse quickened at his somber tone. "Are you going to regret this?"

"What I've given up is a lot." He gripped my waist with both hands and placed a kiss between my breasts. "What I've gained is precious. Inestimable. A value too great to measure." He exchanged a fond look with Priest and returned to me. "Thank you for helping me understand that."

My heart soared, and my mouth trembled. We stared at each other, and dear lord, there was so much love in that look. I felt full and warm with it, bursting at the seams.

"Oh, Ashley, I do love when you're sentimental." I straightened out my smile. "Now tell me what you were doing on my ship for the last two hours."

A blanket of stillness settled over him as his mien took on the severity of man in command of a room.

"This is your ship." He set a loosely curled hand against my cheek, using the backs of his fingers to gently push my hair away. "Topside, you're the captain. I will never undermine you in front of your men." His hand went rigid in my hair, capturing a fist full of locks. "In the privacy of our quarters, I am your commodore and captor."

My chest lifted on a thrill of pleasure. I commanded the ship. Ashley commanded the bedchamber. Priest, on the other hand, was a man of many talents. Skills that had been earned through his roles as a footman, gunner, pirate captain, husband, and libertine. But the one he favored was his position as Groom of the Chamber. He'd taken care of Ashley for years and was blatantly clear about his intentions in doing the same for me. He was the backbone of our three-part relationship.

"She'll go along with that," he drawled from the bed, watching my reaction, "until you try to dress her in ribbons, lace, and other frilly nonsense."

Truth. I bit back a smile.

"I prefer her without clothes." Releasing my hair, Ashley gripped my thighs and spread me wider. "Jesus, you make me hard." His jaw tensed as he stared at my cunt. "I can see his seed dripping out of you. You're a damned sinful sight, one that would make the devil weep."

I waited for him to touch me there, but his expression turned thoughtful. Watchful. He wasn't finished listing his demands.

"I want marriage." His incisive gaze flicked to mine, to Priest, and back to me. "I don't care about formalities or ceremony. I want a marriage that's recognized by both of you." He clasped a possessive hand between my legs. "You will be my wife, bound to me in the same way that you're bound to Priest."

Currents of joy rocked beneath the keel of my heart.

Priest folded his hands over his abdomen, his silver eyes on Ashley. "After everything we've been through, I already consider our triad a binding union. She's *our* wife. Yours and mine. If you need a formal declaration, I'll give it." The corner of his mouth crooked as he looked at me. "She's Mrs. Cutler, Mrs. Farrell, Captain Sharp, Benedicta Leighton…"

"Goldilocks." Ashley studied my face. "I love you. Be my wife."

"Already yours. Your wife, your lover, your captive, a pirate who loves both you and your best friend above all else. And we shall be blinded by our love for life and beyond the ends of the sea."

"By God and the devil, you're such a deliciously beautiful woman I can't think past my need to be deeply entrenched between your thighs." He drew in a breath and rubbed his eyes. "Just a few more matters to discuss, such as what I've been doing for the past two hours." His lips twitched. "I visited Jobah in his cabin."

My head jerked back. "Why?"

"I wish to propose the end to your crew's raiding and plundering of His Majesty's Ships. I may be a Royal Navy deserter, but I'm still an Englishman who loves his country. I understand that all major decisions are made by popular vote and thereby written into the Articles. But that's not why I sought out Jobah. I have another proposal for your men and ran it by him first."

"What proposal?" I asked. "Why Jobah? I'm the captain of this ship."

"I'll tell you once I've worked out the details. Lay aside your impatience and give me your trust, woman."

"Fine." I blew out a breath. "You have it."

"Very good." He stood and motioned at me to turn. "Bend over the desk."

My pulse sped up, and a chill gripped my spine. "Last time you gave that order, you beat my arse until I couldn't sit."

"Then you know what's coming." He clasped his hands behind his back and stared down his haughty nose at me.

"You're going to spank me? For what reason?" I looked at Priest as if he might have the answer.

"Don't make him wait." Priest didn't move from his sprawl on the bed, the bastard.

My blood tingled as I turned and bent over the desk. "Is this you, establishing your role as my captor in the bedchamber?"

"This is me, beating your arse for the unforgivable bargain you made with Madwulf. For putting yourself in his hands and away from our protection. *And* for leaving me a week ago after making demands and trying to run our lives on *your* terms. This relationship is a three-way democracy, not a dictatorship ruled by one insolent woman."

"Says the man who dictated that I bend for his—"

The slam of his palm against my backside shattered my thoughts and stole my breath. Then he struck me again. And again. With a large open hand and a ruthlessly strong arm, he spanked me brutally, passionately, and without quarter. He set fire to my flesh until I felt every ounce of fear and rage he'd experienced as a result of my actions. By the time he straightened and adjusted his clothes, I was properly apologetic and equally aroused.

He wasn't finished.

Before I could rise from the desk, he impaled himself inside me. With his thrusts and his kisses, he demonstrated how much he'd missed me as Priest watched with approval.

Here now, at last, I possessed what Ashley had warned was so ruinous.

Love had hunted me, captured me, bred madness, and yes, it left a sea of ruin in its wake. But the devastation washed away. The skies cleared, and now we were calm, free, sailing on the winds of our hard-won peace.

Later, we dressed, ate, and left the cabin so that I could make my rounds through the decks.

The three of us strolled side by side in the salty air, talking about the weather, my father's detailed map, Ashley's trip to London, and the life he was leaving behind. We laughed and gossiped and basked in the freedom of one another's company.

Freedom. We all felt it.

It was the beginning of a new life, a new voyage, with an exciting destination.

The thrill that hummed beneath my skin was intoxicating. Given the smiles in their eyes, I knew they were soused on it, too.

That night, I watched them reach for each other. Not out of anger or aggression. They came together in a language of closeness, tightening their arms around a bond that had been forged through twenty years of trials and loyalty.

As their hard, muscular bodies joined and moved as one, I was awestruck, mesmerized, unable to look away.

They took turns inside each other, stroking, grasping, mating. They tried to draw me in, but I found an inordinate amount of inclusiveness and pleasure in watching them. It was profound, poignant, deeply beautiful.

When I was a child, I promised my father that I would marry a man of his fortitude and spirit. A man who loved me above all else.

As it turned out, I doubled up on that vow.

I married two.

Fifty-five

October 1721
Oak Island, Province of New Scotland

It took us nigh two months to cross the Great Western Ocean and sail north along the coast of New England. Another month was spent hauling heavy tools and provisions across the uninhabited oak-covered island, setting up camp, and digging. Endless goddamned digging.

My father had always told me I was an adventurous lass. Seven years after his death, he'd gifted me with the adventure of a lifetime.

The map led us deep into the wilderness and stopped at a natural indention in the ground. Excavation was required. Perhaps I'd expected that. But I hadn't realized just how deep we would have to hollow out the forest floor.

My one-hundred-and-twenty-man crew worked in shifts from sunrise to sunset, taking turns shoveling dirt and watching the ship. The air thrummed with excitement with each passing day as we dug through layers of sand, silt, clay, and years of overgrown foliage. With the promise of wealth so close at hand, there were few complaints and a whole lot of smiles.

"We're there." Priest stooped at the bottom of the twenty-foot hole—as deep as it was wide—and swung a pickax at the layer of rocks. "I can feel it."

The dozen pirates around him shook their heads and kept digging.

"You said that a week ago." I strode along the topside of the hole toward Ashley and Jobah, where they were repairing a pile of broken shovels. "I can take over here if you need a break."

Jobah nodded, wiping beads of sweat from his brow. I passed him a bladder of water and knelt beside Ashley, jumping into the repairs.

"What do you think attracted Edric Sharp to this island?" Blue eyes met mine, sparkling in the dappled sunlight.

"I don't know."

This was an ancient place, rich with the history of indigenous people long gone. Massive boulders marked the land with symbols of religious worship, and trenches in the earth indicated the worn tracks of humans from another time. Who had come and gone here? How had my father learned about it? Had he stumbled upon the island during his travels? Perhaps those answers had been in his letter.

A fingertip stroked along my cheek, pulling me from my thoughts. I looked up to find Ashley rubbing a smudge of dirt from my face.

I daresay his emancipation from English nobility suited him. He would always carry himself with the bearing of a lord, but his posture had lost its uncomfortable rigidity. Since leaving England, he moved freely and naturally in his skin.

"I hit something!" Priest bellowed from the bottom of the pit. "Bennett, get your arse down here."

I was already moving, tumbling down the embankment and ripping my trousers in my hurry. At the bottom, I stumbled toward Priest and knelt near his pickax.

"That's timber." I clawed away dirt and clay and ran my hands over the wooden surface beneath. "Man-made. Some sort of hatch. Throw me an ax!"

Three hours later, we broke through a wooden fortification that stretched six-feet wide and two-feet deep. As the last of the shelf was ripped away, everyone gathered around, breaths held, the very air silent and waiting.

I expected to descend into a cave the likes of a royal palace that overflowed with treasure chests, carved silver, gold jewelry, baubles, Chinese porcelain, ivory, rich fabrics, and rare paintings. We all anticipated that.

But instead, we uncovered a shallow grave lined with dozens of identical sacks of the same size and shape. Sacks of seed? Bullets? Or something much greater?

Sea of Ruin

No one moved as I slid into the hole and tore open one of the bags.

"Gold doubloons." My lungs crashed together, my heart laughing. I scrambled to the next sack. "Pieces of eight."

Priest and Ashley jumped in, helping me open bag after bag. They were all filled with coins, gems, and pearls. The value was unfathomable.

On a squeal of laughter, I turned to Priest, threw myself into his arms, and crashed our mouths together.

My father hadn't just left me enough treasure to make every man aboard *Jade* wealthy beyond retirement. He'd gone through the painstaking task of converting his spoils into a currency that was ideal for easy transport, dividing amongst the crew, and using as trade in exchange for property and goods. He'd thought of everything.

My boisterous pack of sea tars clamored over the coins, howling with glee and singing about the land they would buy in the colonies and all the rum they would pour down their gullets.

Priest kissed me enthusiastically, saturating my lips with the salty taste of sweat and sea. "Your father was a genius."

"He was so selfless and brave, and you would've adored him."

"Bennett, come here." Ashley stood amid the treasure, holding a shallow box the length of his arm. "This was beneath the sacks."

My pulse hammered as I slipped out of Priest's arms and made my way there.

"We've gone through everything." Ashley handed me the wooden object, his smile teeming with anticipation. "There's only one of these."

I set down the box, my hands trembling as I opened the lid. It appeared reasonably airtight, safe from the elements. From within, I removed a wide, flat package wrapped in leather. The edges felt like an engraved frame.

It took forever to unwrap it, my fingers tearing through layers of protective cloth and tough hides. At last, I cleared the coverings and found myself staring down at two familiar faces.

"God confound me body and soul." I fell to my knees, my hand shaking too violently to touch the canvas. "I don't believe it."

The oil portrait blurred behind a sheen of searing tears. Priest and Ashley held the painting as I wiped my face and chased the moisture from my eyes. Then I soaked in the image with my heart in my throat.

A young Lady Abigail Leighton perched upon a bench that was entirely too elaborate for its woodland surroundings. Edric Sharp leaned against a tree at her side, wearing a flowing shirt of silk, knee-high jackboots, and a cutlass that glinted in the sun. At his feet lay a sleeping hound dog.

"I'm wearing those boots." Priest crouched beside me, his hand stroking my hair.

I choked, nodded, tears overspilling.

My mother's gown possessed the lavender hues and delicate ruffles she favored. Where she was painted pale and lithe, my father bore the freckled complexion and muscled frame of a seafaring Irishman. He looked so young. So in love.

His face tilted downward, smiling upon my mother as if utterly distracted by her, the painter's presence forgotten. My mother's pose on the bench was relaxed yet stately, her eyes pointed at her lap.

"Look at that, Bennett." Ashley hovered on my other side, his finger motioning at the spot I'd just discovered.

My mother's hands surrounded a small bump on her lap, the fabric of her gown stretching over the roundness beneath. No one would notice that detail in a passing glance, but it was there, declaring the year it was painted.

"I don't know how or why this was created," I said. "But she's pregnant with me, and I recognize those trees as the same kind that surround the estate in Charleston."

Grief was the reason my chest felt too tight. But joy had a hand in that, too. My father hadn't just given me a memory that wouldn't fade. He'd gifted me with a glimpse into something that had been kept from me my entire life. Not once had I ever seen my parents together. Until now.

I wept. How could I not? The emotions I'd carried for so long had been waiting for this moment. The connection I had with my father through the compass reached its zenith. Loss and longing spread its wings, and I needed to let it out. Let it go.

Priest reached for me, the lightest touch, and I was undone. My quiet sobs rose like fists. I leaned into him, and he was there, bending around me, drawn by his need to take care of me.

Ashley stood a few feet away, directing the crew as they carried out the treasure. But his gaze stayed with me, loving me without words, without touch, seeking my eyes with a look that would readily give me anything, if I asked.

Crying within view of my crew wasn't ideal, but no one stared or whispered. They continued about their work in uncharacteristic silence. A sign of respect. They understood.

Sea of Ruin

With Ashley's gaze reaching out to me and Priest's breath upon my cheek, my tears faded as quickly as they'd surfaced. Sadness gave way to tranquility, for I had no regrets, no misgivings. For the first time in my life, I felt complete.

I dusted myself off, packed up the precious painting, and followed my men home, to *Jade* and whatever adventure awaited us.

One week later, I sat behind the desk in my cabin, talking with Ashley and Jobah. They bent over a spread of charts, plotting our course. Priest and Reynolds sat at the table, sprawled and relaxed, drinking more than their share of rum.

We were headed south, back to the West Indies. Then what? We were trying to work that out.

Ashley had been straightforward about his disapproval in pirating the king's ships. Yes, there were other vessels worthy of marauding, but he raised some thoughtful questions. Every man on my crew was now rich beyond his means. Why plunder at all? If we didn't raid, then what? Where would we go? What did we want?

The answer to the last question was easy.

"We want adventure." I picked up a brass spyglass and absently spun it on the desk. "We need the prize."

"What prize?" Ashley crossed his arms over his chest.

"Any prize. The harder the raid and greater the danger, the better the reward."

Reynolds shouted a huzzah from the table and hoisted his bottle of rum.

"You want a challenge? Very well." Ashley exchanged a look with Jobah.

Then he presented a proposal that made my blood at once sizzle and chill.

Priest and Reynolds straightened, their expressions as uncertain and piqued as my thoughts.

What Ashley proposed would change our purpose, our business. But not our hearts. No, our hearts were already in this fight, and mine thundered to dive in.

I peeked at Priest and caught the smile curving behind the rim of his rum glass.

"All right." I grinned. "Put it to the crew for a vote."

Fifty-six

March 1722
St. Christopher, Leeward Islands Colony

St. Christopher. To anyone settling here, it was a dazzling island of beauty and opportunity. To anyone except the African slaves who were barbarously shipped in and forced to work in the sugar cane fields.

Then there was me, the bastard daughter of noble blood, willing to lead a band of seafaring ruffians into a war against those more evil than I was.

"Starboard batteries, target the mainsail!" My breaths cleaved as I jumped onto the gunwale and held the spyglass to my eye.

Fifty feet away, iron guns protruded from the slave ship's bows, belching smoke and hauling in for reloading.

"Aim high and true, gunners!" My hand clenched around the glass, my heart pounding. "If you hit her belly, I shall seize you up by your pissers and dangle you from the yard-arm!"

We were here for the precious cargo in her hold. If we lost those innocent lives, I wouldn't be able to forgive myself.

A crack of cannon fire erupted from *Jade's* starboard. The volley of shot hissed across the turbulent waves, and the slave ship's mainsail erupted in flame.

Yes! The metallic scent of gunpowder burned the air. A few yards away, Priest caught my eye from behind the smoking bronze snout of a gun. He held a lit wick and flung me one of his roguish smiles, flirting with the rhythm of my heart. Viciously handsome man.

I grinned into the choking smoke. "Jobah, bring her about! Hard to starboard! Keep her as tight as you can."

My helmsman grunted and strained against the tiller, driving all his strength into turning the arm.

"D'Arcy and Saunders!" I spun, scanning the fray of whooping and hollering pirates as they flew to the sheets. "Haul your arses to the helm and help Jobah with the rudder. Lively now, lads! Throw your weight into it. We can't board that ship from here!"

I raced across the upper deck and leaped onto the larboard gunwale, shouting orders as *Jade* tacked hard and cut toward the enemy. The change in direction didn't just bring us closer to board the enemy ship. It also swung our heaviest, double-shotted guns around to bear down on the slave traders.

"Gun crews to larboard! Prepare those batteries!" I pivoted on the gunwale and sprinted aft.

And stopped, caught by an iron fist around my ankle.

Ashley stared up at me, both hands clamping down like shackles on my boot. Capable hands. Strong and manly. I loved the commanding way he touched me, the way he looked at me.

The calculation behind those glowing blue eyes held my fate and that of every man on this ship.

This had been his idea, after all.

His proposal to besiege slave trade routes had been met with a unanimous roar of *Aye's* from *Jade's* crew. The men had been attached to this cause since the day we'd accidentally raided the ship that had enslaved Jobah.

But we were just one crew. To fight an entire island and the vessels that surrounded it was an impossible undertaking.

Until Ashley.

With his wartime naval experience as a commodore, he knew how to wound the enemy without getting ourselves killed in the process. We wouldn't be able to stop the importation of slaves, but with his depth of knowledge, we could save more than just a few.

We'd spent the past six months preparing for this, gathering more guns, *bigger* guns, recruiting fierce sailors, scouting the courses of slave ships, and planning tactics and maneuvers against St. Christopher's slave traders. I commanded the crew, but Ashley had led the entire effort.

"Get down from there," he ordered in his imperious tone and tightened his hold on my ankle. "My heart can't take another second of your balancing act."

"But you're so good at saving drowning women, my lord." I hooked an elbow around a shroud, kicked my free leg beyond the gunwale, and leaned far out over the waves. "Will you put that fine-mannered mouth on mine and give me air?"

"With pleasure. *After* you come down from there."

My blood purred, but a kiss would have to wait. Jade was finishing her sharp turn.

"Ready about, Chops!" I jumped to the deck and sprinted toward the gun crew at the bow, pausing behind Priest. "Load those guns and run out!"

On the lower gun decks, Chops roared back, "Gun crews at the ready!"

Priest darted along the lethal armament on the upper deck. His shirtless back flexed and glistened with sweat as he heaved eighteen-pounders into long bronzed noses.

The slave ship was directly on *Jade's* larboard, neatly in the sights of our heaviest guns. But we were also in the range of theirs. Through the glass, I spied enemy gunners holding wicks soaked in saltpeter, the fuses glowing red hot. Others waited with wadding, shot, and powder, ready to reload once the guns were discharged.

My stomach hardened as I filled my lungs with air and bellowed, "Fire!"

Both ships fired at the same time. Shot from cannonades blackened the sky with smoke and tore through *Jade's* forward sails.

"We're hit!" Reynolds screamed from somewhere behind me. "Damnation, Captain! We lost the fore topsail—"

"Jobah!" My pulse slammed through my veins. "Put her a point more to larboard. Priest, lay a shot across her mizzenmast."

If the slave ship didn't strike her colors by the time the smoke cleared, we would load up with chain shot and take out her rigging. The difficulty lay in not injuring the cargo hold or the enslaved men shackled within it. Had the ship been empty, we would have sunk her an hour ago.

"May I make a suggestion?" The velvety steel voice caressed up my spine.

I turned and stared up into glimmering blue eyes. "By all means,

Lord Cutler."

"Maneuver into a windward position and hold the weather gage. If you approach aggressively with the wind, you'll blind them with smoke as you take out the rigging."

He quickly explained the advantages and risks of a tactic he'd used in his battles against the Spanish.

My mind reeled at the sheer perfection of it. "You have an exalted natural mental ability, my lord."

"Thank you, Captain."

"Pass along the details of the maneuver to Jobah, if you please. And remind me to properly thank you later. With my mouth. While on my knees."

"Gladly." His gaze smoldered, dipping to the sharp rise of my breasts in the corset.

We pivoted, parting ways to prepare the crew for our attack.

The fight passed swiftly and flawlessly. The slave ship was caught in the thick billowing draft of smoke, her canvas afire, and her gunners far too blinded to thwart *Jade's* approach.

By the time I hoisted our red flag with the intention to board, my crew was already flinging grappling hooks and storming onto the enemy ship. I threw myself into the throng, flanked by Priest and Ashley with our cutlasses raised.

The slave traders resisted with swords, coming at us in a clash of steel. The deck shuddered beneath the stomp of boots, and the scent of battle encompassed me. Gunpowder, blood, sweat, death. It infused me with a sense of purpose.

With every stab of my cutlass, I lay my heart naked. With every vile life that I took, I felt replete.

I was a pirate captain, a rebel queen of the sea, fighting against the conformities of society and the oppressive laws of man.

Slashing and thrusting, I hacked down every slave trader in my path. In my periphery, Priest and Ashley maintained a protective circle around me. I couldn't fault them for that. I was protecting them, too.

At last, the pained cries of our enemies fell quiet. My crew stood amid the dead bodies, chests heaving, and blades dripping with blood. I searched the corpses and found no familiar faces.

"We're all accounted for?" I bent at the waist, trying to catch my breath.

"Aye, Captain." Jobah wiped his dagger on his trousers.

"To the hold, then! Get those men out of irons! Make haste!"

Sea of Ruin

As if I could magically sense them, my gaze shifted to the starboard bow. Priest and Ashley leaned against the gunwale, watching me. Both had traded their shirts for cuts and bruises. Muscles layered upon muscles, flawlessly honed, beneath soot and sweat.

The battle looked good on them. More than good.

I strolled toward them, picking my way through the bodies and dodging the low-burning fire of a fallen sail. Reaching Priest first, I dragged his whiskered face to mine and kissed him hungrily, needing his closeness. I needed them both, needed to taste their breaths, their proof of life, upon my tongue.

My hand found Ashley's beside me, and he drew us to him. With a grip in my hair and his other on Priest's neck, he kissed us, one after the other, deeply, openly, without shame or quarter.

I loved them *more* because they loved each other. What we had was rare. We were magic. No one understood it, and nothing could touch it. I would protect it with my life.

At length, the kiss melted into peaceful smiles, and we turned toward the bow, facing the shoreline of St. Christopher in the distance.

Sugar cane stretched inland beyond the sand, and amid those fields were enslaved men and women, working their bodies to the bone.

"We're going to free them." Ashley pulled me close and kissed my head.

"I believe you."

"The three of us together cannot be stopped." A savage glint lit in Priest's eyes. "We're an exquisite force of destruction."

I couldn't agree more.

Love prevailed, not in the windless calm of life, but in the ruin.

Other Books

LOVE TRIANGLE ROMANCE
TANGLED LIES TRILOGY
One is a Promise
Two is a Lie
Three is a War

DARK COWBOY ROMANCE
TRAILS OF SIN
Knotted #1
Buckled #2
Booted #3

DARK PARANORMAL ROMANCE
TRILOGY OF EVE
Heart of Eve
Dead of Eve #1
Blood of Eve #2
Dawn of Eve #3

DARK ROMANCE
DELIVER SERIES
Deliver #1
Vanquish #2
Disclaim #3
Devastate #4
Take #5
Manipulate #6
Unshackle #7
Dominate #8
Complicate #9

STUDENT-TEACHER ROMANCE
Dark Notes

ROCK-STAR DARK ROMANCE
Beneath the Burn

ROMANTIC SUSPENSE
Dirty Ties

EROTIC ROMANCE
Incentive

About the Author

New York Times and USA Today Bestselling author, Pam Godwin, lives in the Midwest with her husband, their two children, and a foulmouthed parrot. When she ran away, she traveled fourteen countries across five continents, attended three universities, and married the vocalist of her favorite rock band.

Java, tobacco, and dark romance novels are her favorite indulgences, and might be considered more unhealthy than her aversion to sleeping, eating meat, and dolls with blinking eyes.

EMAIL: pamgodwinauthor@gmail.com

Printed in Great Britain
by Amazon